FIRST PRINT EDITION

979-8-9910961-2-6

OTHER TALES OF
FORBIDDEN KNOWLEDGE

Shadow of the Past

Summer of Sins (Winston & Churchill #1)

Fall of Shadows (Winston & Churchill #2)

Dead of Winter (Winston & Churchill #3)

The Shadow of Victory

Coming Soon

A Disease of the Will

SEE ALSO:

ForbiddenKnowledgeComic.com

SHADOW OF THE PAST

For Allie

CHAPTER ONE

Darren sat on the edge of his bed and he could feel the house across the street, staring back at him through the darkness.

He was 10, and things like a house weren't supposed to scare him, but that house was different. It was the oldest house in the neighborhood, and no one, at least none of the kids he knew, ever saw the man that lived there. The closest he had ever come was a couple of months ago when he was getting ready for bed and noticed a man in a black overcoat and hat pass through the mass of hedges in the front. All he could see from his window was the peak of the roof and the two second story windows, shuttered tight like black eyes. Everything else was blocked from view by the hedges and twin oak trees that twisted in front of everything like wooden sentinels. The entire scene made for a house that no one in the neighborhood talked about, looked at, and certainly did not go near.

Until today

Darren and the rest of his friends from Briarcliff Avenue had been playing stickball in the street all summer in a subway series against the kids from Munson Drive. The Briarcliff kids were the Brooklyn Dodgers and the Munsies were the Yankees. Ralphie DiMartino, the Munsies answer to Yogi Berra, hit a beautiful pop fly that arched back towards Darren, who was playing left field. Darren raced along the street to catch it, but out of the corner of his eye he saw he had passed the outfield boundary and was coming upon that house's sinister wall of brown-green foliage. His foot caught the curb and he sprawled out on the lane of grass between the street and the sidewalk.

Flat on his stomach, he watched as the ball hit the sidewalk, bounced, and then rolled under the hedge and out of sight.

There were hoots and hollers from behind him, and he glanced over his shoulder to see Ralphie rounding second base already. Only Kenny Mitchell turned to yell at Darren. "Get the ball! Hurry!"

Darren scrambled to his feet, all fear vanishing at the prospect of Ralphie the Fink gloating all summer about his miraculous home run. Darren dashed through the thin gap in the branches and into the yard. The ball had rolled through the hedges and was visible in the dense, unmowed lawn. Darren raced over, scooped it up and hurled it over the hedge with a grunt. "Comin' at ya!" he yelled, praying to God that they caught it and tagged Kenny out.

Once the ball left his hand, he realized that he was standing in the Forbidden Zone. The grass was at least ankle deep and tinged with brown from the heat and it didn't look like anyone had set foot in it at all this summer. He was standing on what passed for the walk, right between the twin guardian oaks that loomed over him. He saw a couple of other balls laying in the yard that other kids obviously hadn't bothered to go in after, but he had just waltzed in without a second thought.

He turned and there it was.

The house was smaller than he'd imagined; it had dirty white paint and each of its dozen windows were shuttered tight just like the two he could see from his bedroom. The green trim had faded and cracked into a cancerous black. Even the door had faded that way, except for a small patch of dark green high in the center, where the door-knocker should have been. A screen porch snaked around the left side of the house, although most of the screen was shredded to bits. The only thing sitting on the porch was a rusted patio chair, tipped over like a turtle.

Everything was still. Darren realized he had been holding his breath for so long that his heartbeat was pounding at his temples. He let it out as slowly as he could, careful not to make a sound. He was drawing in his next breath just as slowly when he saw it, lying on the front porch, just past the top step.

It was a brown shoe, just a little smaller than his.

He took a step forward, making sure his eyes weren't fooling him. It was a girl's shoe, and the only thing in the entire yard that was new and not rotten, faded or broken.

He shuffled his feet, desperately trying to get them to work, when something else got his attention.

Down at the corner of the house, almost hidden by the tall grass, was a small basement window. In the corner of that window was a tiny white speck.

It was a cloudy blue eye narrowing at him under a thick blonde eyebrow.

That was all Darren's feet needed to start running.

He raced between the hedges, coming out to find the entire game had stopped and everyone staring at him. He couldn't tell if they were so slack-jawed over the fact that he had been in that yard or that he had made it back.

Ralphie broke the silence. "What. . .the. . .frick?"

"I was gettin' your hit, pansy," Darren said.

Some of the other kids let out low whistles, others just shook their heads. "Balls," DiMartino said, tipping his cap. "Big frickin' balls."

That night at dinner, things were quiet. At first he thought his parents had been fighting, but then he realized that they were glancing over at him every few seconds. Had someone ratted him out? Did they know where he had been? There had been something in the air for weeks, it seemed. They were always asking him where he was, where he had been, if he had seen anything strange. He hadn't thought anything of it before, but now he knew.

They were afraid.

"Darren," his father began, and Darren felt his rear-end clench at the thought of how many swats they would give him for trespassing.

"Yeah, Pop?"

"Have you seen Suzie Morris around lately?"

"What?"

"Doesn't she go to your school?" his mother piped in, tapping at her plate with the tip of her fork.

"Yeah, she's a grade behind me."

"Have you seen her?" his father asked again.

"No, I haven't. Why?"

"Well…" his father started, but then gazed across the table. His mother stopped tapping her fork. "She was supposed to spend the weekend with her aunt on Maple Street while her folks were out of town. She didn't make it, and no one noticed until yesterday. Her aunt thought the parents had taken her with them, but her folks had sent Suzie to walk to Maple Street herself. So you're sure you haven't seen her?"

"I'm sure." Darren replied, putting his silverware down.

They sat in silence for a few minutes, and then Darren pushed his plate forward. "I'm not hungry. Can I be excused?"

His parents looked at each other, and then his Mother nodded. "Sure thing. Do you want to watch Sullivan? Rosemary Clooney is going to be on."

Darren made a face and shook his head, carrying his plate into the kitchen. "I'm gonna go upstairs."

He stayed up there, door closed, watching the house across the street for the rest of the night. He could hear his parents arguing over Rosemary Clooney's warbling. His Mom blamed his Dad for upsetting him and his Dad saying this was serious and that they needed to know. Later, his Mother poked her head in and told him it was time for bed so he went through the motions of getting ready and saying goodnight.

Instead of sleeping, Darren just sat in bed watching the house across the street as dusk turned into night. After a few hours, the streetlight out front clicked on and began its night-long hum. His eyelids began to droop, and he realized that trying to maintain a vigil through the night was pointless.

With a giant yawn, he got out of bed and went over to the window. It was hot and muggy, like most New Jersey summers, but there was no way he was going sleep with the window open tonight. He shut it as quietly as he could, not wanting his parents to hear and wonder what he was still doing up.

Just as he turned to head back into bed, the streetlight flickered. He turned, pressing up against the glass, scanning the entire street. For a second there was something dark moving out of the circle of light and heading towards the driveway. He stood there for at least five minutes, mashing his face against the glass, trying to see down into the driveway. There was nothing but darkness.

It was stupid, he realized. If there was anything out there, Mom and Dad would have seen or heard it. Darren turned and crawled back into bed, but once there, he found that sleep had left him. He tossed and turned, and after a couple of minutes he realized he'd been humming that stupid Rosemary Clooney song from the show.

Irritated, he kicked the sheet off and rolled over, still trying to get comfortable.

"Come on-a my house, my house-a come on . . ."

Darren snapped up in bed, eyes scouring the room. The voice had been faint, but he had definitely heard the deep rumble of a voice that wasn't his father's. He couldn't see a thing, the lamp from the outside not even making a dent into the oppressive darkness of his room. Not even the light from the hallway was coming under his bedroom door.

He trained to listen but the only noise was the faint whisper of the curtains as they brushed together in the breeze. His eyes passed over them at first, but then darted back.

The window was open.

He should have screamed then, he realized, but his eyes still darted from side to side, trying to make out anything in the darkness.

"Come on-a my house, my house, I'm gonna give you ca-andy . . ."

It was so faint that he almost thought he was imagining, but he knew that even in his darkest dreams he wouldn't have been able to imagine the rumbling, cracked voice that was whispering to him in the dark.

He drew in a breath to scream, knowing that getting his parents attention was his only chance. Before he could even make a sound, the darkness on the far side of the room exploded towards him. There was a rustle of fabric and then a gloved hand clamped down on his throat.

"Shhhhh," the harsh whisper came from all around him.

"You wanted to see, didn't you? You came and you wanted to see, isn't that right?"

Darren tried to shake his head but the grip on his throat was too tight. His chest burned with the trapped air in his lungs and he could barely make out the face in front of him.

"Don't you lie to me, boy!" The face was wrapped in a black scarf with a black, wide-brimmed hat pulled down as far as it could go. Between them, he could make out the blue eyes that had stared at him from the basement window. "You want to see Him? I can make you see."

Darren's chest thought his swollen lungs were going to crush his heart. Before that could happen there was a flash of silver that slammed into his temple.

Around the blue eyes everything fell into a haze.

He felt himself being effortlessly hauled over the man's shoulder, and the last he heard before the darkness completely overtook him was his whispered singing.

"Come on-a my house, my house, I'm gonna give you everything. . ."

CHAPTER TWO

Mark Watson liked to watch people, but watching a couple of senior girls in short-skirted field hockey uniforms instead of where he was going was what almost got his face smashed in.

His foot stopped the stairwell door just before he completely collided with it, but when he tried to twist out of the way his feet went haywire and he toppled to the ground.

"Oh, God," a girl's voice said. "I'm so sorry!"

Whatever mumbled, irritated remark he was going to make was swallowed when he looked up and saw her in the doorway. She had long red hair loosely tied back and her pale skin was lightly dotted with freckles. It was the kind of relaxed, "oh, this old thing?" beauty that you were born with or spent your whole life trying to emulate.

"Here, let me help you," she said, offering her hand. After a second he took it and pulled himself up.

"Thanks," he said, clearing his throat and failing to shake the sad and unpopular off of his clothes.

"Sorry," she said. "I'm new and--" she was interrupted by the sudden shrill ringing of the late bell. "And now I'm late."

"Well," Mark said, running a hand through his shoulder length hair. "If you, ah, let me know where you're going, I might be able to help you get there."

"Well," she said. "If I remember my schedule right, I've got Chemistry in 213. I'm just trying to figure out which way the numbers go."

"With Reynolds?" *Be careful, jackass. This could be using up whatever small quota of luck you've been allotted.*

"Yeah."

Well now you don't have to worry about playing the lottery. Way to go.

"Well, I was heading that way myself. Would you care to, ah . . . walk with me?"

She smiled, and he realized he was too. "Don't worry," he said, "Renny rarely cares if you're late."

"Okay," she said. "I'm Christine."

"Mark." His hand twitched at his side. Handshake? Wave? Salute? *For fuck's sake stop fidgeting!* "This way," he finally waved down the hallway. *Maybe you can pretend you have epilepsy.*

Mark found himself falling behind as they walked, taking in how she confidently moved down the hall, a total opposite to his hunched, drawn-in shuffle. He was drawn to everything about her. This was the kind of instant crush he'd have every once and a while; a magnetic snap that would grab him by the senses and lead him around like a dog. It'd be great if it didn't make him feel like a pathetic loser who never did anything about it.

His junior year at Cedar Ridge High had started a month ago and until now it looked like it was going to be the same as every year. He'd spend time in his room, Steve and Clara would try to get him out of his shell, and he'd do just enough homework to keep up his straight C average. He'd thought that after getting some wheels this summer he'd be able to turn over a new leaf, but it'd dawned on him this morning that he was simply incapable of changing and that clung to him like a lead shroud.

And then he realized the field hockey team had a game today, and they'd be in uniform all day. That made things a little better.

The dream last night didn't help any either. He'd been having it or one like it for the past few weeks. They just jumbled images of a 50s neighborhood, a swirling darkness that filled him with dread and the sound of metal scraping against metal. There was a low, whistling tune that was irritatingly familiar and then it was shattered by an explosion of pain in his head, and he'd find himself rolling or falling out of bed with the smell of ashes so strong he'd be gagging.

"Is it over here?" she said, glancing over her shoulder at him.

"Yeah," he said, widening his strides to walk at her side. "Last door on the left." *Easy, Casanova. This is directions, not progress. You're still the boy who broke down in elementary school when his aunt died; who Mr. Wallace humiliated at the blackboard in seventh grade for not understanding fraction addition; the kid who got hit in the face with a basketball and cried as the whole class watched in disapproving silence.*

Talking to a new girl meant none of that stuff had to have happened. It could just be dead and buried, never to be reanimated in an awkward moment of lulled conversation. Last year when he was about to ask his lab partner Stephanie Murphy out she filled the awkward moment of silence by asking if he'd been that "boy who cried that time."

Christine pointed at the door on the left, and he nodded. Mark sat in his usual seat near the back and stifled an incredulous laugh when she took the seat next to him. She gave him another little smile as she got a crisp new notebook out. He smiled back, now fumbling with his bag, putting every fiber of his being into doing it without dropping something.

"So," he said as they were packing things up after class, "where are you heading now?" Forty minutes of not studying chemistry had gone into coming up with that. It beat out "You're a goddess" and "I want to have your babies," but not by much.

"Lunch."

"Really," he said. "Me too." This was torture.

"Great," she smiled.

"Would you like to . . ." Mark started, and then seized. Asking her to eat lunch with him caught in his throat, the very notion of doing so contrary to everything inside him. He had to say something, he realized, not just stand there gaping like a fish.

"Do you think you could show me where the cafeteria is?"

"Yeah, sure," he said. "That's . . . well, it's something."

Cedar Ridge High might have a fancy brick and glass exterior that showed the quiet dignity of age with the fresh breath of the modern, but beneath its comforting exterior lay a place that dignity and freshness had mutually agreed was beneath them. There'd been places like this before. Sodom, Dresden, Fallujah, and now, CRH cafeteria. Jocks, goths, thugs, emo kids; all mixed together in a horrific mash-up of cliquish teen disharmony.

"Well," he said, having to raise his voice a little to be heard over the crowd. "Here it is, in all its glory."

She took a step forward, scanning the room for anything familiar. She looked back at him. "Aren't you coming?"

"No, I usually eat lunch outside."

"Thanks for warning me," she smiled. "What, you were just going to abandon me here?"

"What? No! God, no! I just . . . well, Juniors and Seniors get to eat lunch off campus, so I usually eat outside. You just, well, you said you wanted the cafeteria, so I was trying to help."

"I know, I'm just messing with you. Want some company?"

"Yeah," he said. "That'd be great." *If by great you mean "A great opportunity for you to continue looking like a fucking fool," then yes, by all means, let's go have ourselves a sammich with a side of crippling shame.*

There was a small park behind the school dotted with some other kids in various clique-sized groups. Climate change, plus New Jersey being New Jersey, made the weather warm and mild. He led her over to his usual spot for lunch a secluded bench under a tree.

"Wow," she said when they sat down. "That was something alright."

"Yeah," Mark said. "They've been trying to get a tighter grip on stuff for years."

"Still, I'm just glad I talked my Dad into not sending me to private school," she said, getting a lunch bag out.

"Around here? Your family must be pretty loaded."

"Yeah, well, my dad thinks we're not rich enough. He's getting a pretty big raise with this new job."

Better and better. Beautiful and rich. If only she'd quit giving him false hope, then she'd be perfect.

"Hello?" she called, waving her hand in front of him with a slight smile. "Are you still in there?"

"Yeah," he said, blushing. "Just thinking. Sorry 'bout that."

She shrugged. "Nothing wrong with that. What about?"

"Oh, just . . . stupid crap. The usual."

She looked at him for a moment and he thought that she was going to call his bluff, but she just ate her sandwich in the sudden, uneasy silence.

"So, ah, where're you from?" Mark asked, trying not to sound as lame and desperate as he felt. Coolness. Deep, inner, once in a lifetime coolness was what he needed, and he could feel it just within his grasp.

"Well, I was born in upstate New York and then we moved to Cincinnati for four years, Cleveland for five, Pittsburgh for three, and most recently Boston for four. This, however, is the first time I was able to get my dad to let me attend public school. The great schools are supposedly why we picked this town."

Mark smiled. "That's what a lot of people say. I think the schools were really good in the 70's or something, but this place has pretty much gone to hell. In the past couple of years we've had more fights and stabbings than ever before. A lot of people blame it on an 'increased gang presence' or something like that, but that's just crap."

She rolled her eyes. "Great. My dad hears 'stabbings' and his head's going to explode and the leftover bits are going to move me to boarding school"

"Well," Mark shrugged, "there hasn't been one since last spring so I think you're stuck with us for now."

"Believe me, I hope so. Every other private school, no matter where you go, is full of these prima donna rich kids who think they're the shit."

Mark smiled a little bit. "Aren't you a 'rich kid'?"

She shrugged. "Well, you've got me there, but at least I still try to be a human being."

"Well, you're way better than the others," he said. "When most of the people here run me over they don't say a thing. You at least talk to me."

"It hasn't seemed like they've been able to stand to talk to me either, so I guess we're stuck together." She smiled and Mark could feel his five-minute lifetime allotment of coolness slipping away.

"Well, I hope you don't feel too 'stuck.' I'm kind of a social pariah, so hanging with me may not be wise. Y'know, if you want to keep your options open."

"I so don't care about that anymore. I tried so hard to do the whole popular girl thing in Boston but I just morphed into an uber-bitch. I think I just need some time to chill."

"Well, I know how that goes," he said, replacing coolness with outright lies. "I've had some things that I've had to work out too, and, y'know, it's just something everyone goes through."

"Really? Like what?"

"Oh, it was . . . ," Mark brushed some stray hairs from his face, finding something interesting across the way to look at. "It was just some . . . family stuff. Nothing too major, I guess."

"I'm sorry," she said. "I'm so just prying away, like you'd wanna discuss your crisis of faith or whatever with a stranger."

Mark chuckled. "No, can't have a crisis with something you don't have." He opened his mouth to say more, and then stopped. "You're not, like, religious or anything are you?"

"My mom kinda is but my dad's too much of a workaholic for church. Personally . . . I think that's one of the things I'm trying to figure out." She paused. "So you don't believe in God or anything?"

Mark studied the ground, trying to pick his words before he blurted out more nonsense.

"It's not that big a deal or anything," she said. "If you don't wanna talk about it--"

"No, I've had this conversation before, kinda, but my friends are . . . well, they're a little divided on the issue." He looked up at her. "But hey, I don't want to be weird or anything. I mean, we just met and we're already delving into the big questions and all."

"Well, I've had my fill of stupid conversations about clothes and TV and all that shit. But if you're not comfortable talking to me-"

"No, no, I'm comfortable!" Mark blurted out.

"I hope so," she laughed. "I'd hate to see you when you're uncomfortable."

"Well, y'know, it's just that I'm enjoying talking to you, and I don't want you to flee in terror or anything."

"I won't flee in terror, Mark. You're far too nice."

"Well, I can't think of anyone who wouldn't be nice to you," he said, trying not to grin like an idiot. "But the whole God thing . . . no, I don't believe. I don't believe there's some big old white guy with a beard sitting in the cloud that's got Pat Robertson's back and making sure the teams that pray the most make it to the Superbowl." She laughed, and he paused to enjoy it. "I just can't accept the fact there's something out there guiding our lives for some master plan. There's too much wrong with the world for me to accept that."

He leaned back and took a bite out of his sandwich before he said anything else. She stared at him intently and Mark inwardly cringed. *This is it. She's going to get up and walk away and every time I see her I'll replay this conversation in my head and want to die.*

"Is this a private party or can anyone jump in?" a voice called from behind the tree.

Mark jumped with so much surprise that he crushed his sandwich in his fist. "Jesus, dude. Relax, it's just me," said the lean boy with the long, black leather coat who stepped from behind the tree.

"Steve, Christ! You scared the crap out of me!" Mark said, throwing the remnants of his sandwich at him.

"Sorry, man. I thought I was expected, but clearly you found some better company." Steve grinned wide, not taking his eyes off Christine. "I've gotta say, you definitely traded up."

"Yeah, this is Christine," Mark said, his face growing red as he wiped the mayo and mustard off of his hand.

"Nice to meet you," she said, extending a hand which Steve took with an even bigger smile.

"Charmed," he said, clasping it firmly. "Steve Rhodes, pleased to meetcha." Steve plopped down between the two of them. "So," he said, looking from one to the other, "what are we talking about?"

"Oh, nothing much," Mark said, before Christine could answer. "Just giving her the lowdown on the whole Cedar Ridge High thing."

"Ah, you're a new kid, huh?" Steve said, grinning even wider. "Well, there's just one thing you need to know."

"What's that?"

"Don't hang out with us, we're losers."

She chuckled a little, and Mark felt his whole body cringe. "Seriously," Steve said, "It's not that bad. You're young and pretty and the world is your oyster. You'll do fabulously."

She rolled her eyes a little. "Yeah, well, I'll settle for normal."

"Better than normal from what I can tell, but that's just me being forward," Steve said.

The three sat in silence for a few moments, and Mark's mind raced for some way to regain control of the situation.

"So, Christine, uh, what class do you have next?" was all he could come up with.

Christine rummaged through her bag and pulled out her schedule. "Well, let's see . . . I've got English, French and Study Hall. And then, it's the weekend."

"Any big plans for it?" Steve asked, looking at her but elbowing Mark at his side.

"Just unpacking," she shrugged. "Haven't been here long enough to find something interesting to do."

Steve looked over at Mark and grinned widely. If he says anything I'll kill him, Mark thought. I swear to God I'll kill him right in the fucking face.

"How about that?" Steve said.

The three made more small talk the rest of the period, Mark only throwing in a few comments here and there to make sure he wasn't forgotten among Steve's ADD-charm. When the bell rang and the three got up to leave, he drew in a deep breath, turned to Christine and said, "Can I walk you to your next class?" If he didn't know any better, he'd say he was calming down. She had been getting to her feet and putting her backpack back on. She turned, hair flipping over her shoulder.

"Sure," she said, "I'd like that."

So much for calming down.

CHAPTER THREE

"Well, here you go," Mark said.

"Thanks for the walk," she said. "You've been really sweet."

"Oh, well, that's . . . It's my pleasure," Mark said. "Really."

They stood for a few moments, Mark trying so hard not to stare at her that he ended up admiring the tile work.

"Well, I should see you later, okay?" Christine said, and Mark snapped his head back around.

"Yeah!" He said, and then took a breath, trying to reel in the enthusiasm. "I guess I will see you in class and stuff." *They still have that most days, and she'll be in at least one of them, genius.*

"Yeah," Christine said, smiling over her shoulder as she walked into class. "See you then."

Mark stepped backwards, keeping an eye on the door until Steve crept up behind him and clapped him hard on the shoulder.

"Man! You are smitten!"

"Shut up!" Mark said, elbowing him in the ribs and walking away.

"Relax! It happens!" Steve said, falling in alongside him.

"I know!" Mark said, feeling the eyes of everyone in the hallway on him. "I just don't need you advertising it everywhere, alright?"

"Yeah, fine." Steve said.

As they entered the gym, Steve turned to Mark and grinned wickedly. "Hey, didya hear? She's free this weekend!"

"Would you shut up?" Of course he heard and knew exactly why Steve had brought it up.

"Think about it, man," Steve said as they headed down to the locker room. "She's a pretty hot chick, and if you don't make your move now, pffftt!" threw his hands apart in a dramatic gesture. "She be snatched up by some other guy and she'll forget you even existed."

"I wish we could forget you existed," called a voice from the other end of the row of lockers. Mark closed his eyes and prayed for the thousandth time for a world where Steve knew when to keep his damn mouth shut.

"Hey," Steve called over his shoulder. "Not talking to you, Jack."

"Fuck you," Jack said. His eyes focused squarely on Mark, who stared back in impotent silence. Ever since the sixth grade Jackson Cole went out of his way to make sure that Mark was miserable. If he wasn't throwing paperclips at the back of Mark's head, he was bumping into him in the halls or finding some other way to embarrass him. Jack was Mark's anti-matter; clean-cut, athletic, social, well-liked, wealthy, and whenever they crossed paths Jack tried to destroy him.

Towards the end of sophomore year Jack had been pushing each confrontation with Mark further and further. The last time Jack and his friends had found Mark heading for the South Exit after school. It had become typical fare by this point, especially after school without anyone else around. Before Mark could get away Jack bounced him off a couple of lockers to the delight of his minions. Mark just closed his eyes and rode each shove like a humiliating wave, keeping his eyes shut so he wouldn't have to see Jack's twisted grin every time Mark made contact with metal.

The ride ended when he grabbed Mark by the lapels, drawing him close to his face and snarling, "Look at me!" Mark cracked his eyes open a little, wincing at the fury raging in front of him. "You're a loser, Watson," Jack hissed. "A failure. A nobody. You could just disappear right now and no one would ever care."

Mark felt tears of shame and rage welling up and he knew that Jack could see them too. Jack let go and Mark slumped to the floor, stripped of his will to exist, let alone stand. He didn't open his eyes until he heard Jack and of his friends leaving.

Mark had hoped that the summer had given Jack a chance to cool down but Mark could tell that things were just as bad as before when Jack chose a gym locker in the same row as Steve and Mark.

Jack strode forward and Mark couldn't keep himself from stepping back a bit. "No, fuck you," Steve said, his voice wavering. Steve was bigger than Mark but it was all height and not muscle. Jack didn't even acknowledge Steve's existence, keeping his gaze locked on Mark. The corners of Jack's mouth turned up a little and it took every ounce of Mark's willpower to not look away.

"You shouldn't even bother looking for a girlfriend, Watson. No girl would go out with a pathetic waste like you." He snickered and started to turn away. "Besides," he said over his shoulder, "I've probably already fucked her." He said it loud enough for the rest of the people in their row to hear, and there was a wave of chuckles and smirks.

Mark could tell Steve wanted to say something to him, but Mark ignored it. It was just going to be his usual, "Stand up for yourself," "Don't let him push you around," and "You're ten times better than he is."

It's hard to fight back and stand up for yourself when you know he's right, isn't it?

When everyone was changed they headed up stairs and sat in their assigned spots on the gym floor as Coach Roberts checked off their names. The nets were already set up, dashing Mark's hopes that they were doing anything else but volleyball. The gym had been divided into two separate courts and the class had been split up into four teams, which they went to after attendance was taken.

Mark absolutely hated volleyball. Despite whatever hand-eye coordination he'd gotten from video games he couldn't hit the ball to save his life, much less get it over the net. Accepting his own ball-and-net shortcomings was one thing but playing out his sports inadequacies for everyone to see was just cruel.

Jack and his friends being on his team made it unbearable.

"There," Jack said, motioning for Mark to take a spot in the middle of the court after. Mark opened his mouth to protest but remembered it wouldn't do a damn bit of good. He shuffled to his spot, trying not to look as nervous and mortified as he felt. Mark soon found himself flanked by two of Jack's friends, Victor Barnes and Kyle Ferris. It was going to be bad today, he realized.

The game got underway, and Mark watched the ball dreading it coming toward him. It came down towards Vic, who moved out of its path and called, "Get it!" Mark stepped over, gritted his teeth and swung at the ball. It caromed off his fist and arced up behind him.

Kyle tapped it straight up in the air and said, "Send it over." Mark scrambled to get under the ball and managed to get it over with a healthy dose of luck.

The pattern soon became obvious. The ball would come down and Jack's friends would either move out of the way, ordering Mark to get it, or send it over towards him deliberately. Mark found himself racing back and forth, arms flailing at the ball and sending it off in random directions.

Finally Mark was rotated back into the serving position. The ball was dropped at Mark's feet, somewhere near his pounding heart and self-esteem. Kids on the other team rolled their eyes and some took the opportunity to sit and stretch out. Mark closed his eyes, trying to keep his face from flaring to red with embarrassment. "Any day, Watson," Vic snickered next to him.

Mark opened his eyes and picked up the ball. It rested in his palm and after a few seconds he pictured Jack's head in its place. Hitting it hard no longer was a problem. He tossed it up and swung as hard as he could. It flew high, narrowly missing the maze of ducts and pipes on the ceiling. Mark thought for a second that he'd actually score a point, but it headed towards one of the few people on the opposite team that was actually paying attention. The ball went back and forth, and thankfully Mark's team lost the point so he didn't have to serve again.

When he moved Kyle took his place at Mark's right again, and it seemed that the game had changed. Instead of running him ragged all around the court they went out of their way to bump, jostle and ram into him. They'd dart to the sides when a ball was coming near Mark and slam him to the ground while trying to get at it. Soon exhaustion at running around became the least of his worries and he found himself too tired to even move out of the way. As they headed back down to the locker room towards the end of the period, Steve jogged up alongside Mark. "Hey, it looks like they were knocking you around pretty bad out there, huh?" Mark just looked away, not wanting to confirm the obvious.

"I'm fine," Mark said, fumbling with the combination to his locker.

"Look, Mark," Steve said, finally soft enough for only Mark to hear. "I know you don't want to hear this, but it's only gonna get worse. You have to--"

Mark slammed his locker door open, cutting Steve off. "I'm fine," he said, still not looking Steve in the eye and feeling the eyes of everyone in the room on his back.

"Watson that was a great game!" Jack called from his locker.

"Look," Steve said, "why don't you leave him the hell alone, huh? What the hell did he ever do to you?"

Jack shook his head and looked down at his feet. "What did he ever do to me? Y'know, I didn't realize I needed a reason. I just figured losers like him deserved it."

Steve walked up to Jack stepping between him and his locker. "Let me tell you something you spoiled little bastard--" he began, but Jack didn't give him a chance to finish. Steve didn't even know what was happening until he was doubled over and gasping for breath, his hands at his stomach where Jack punched him.

Mark rested his head on his locker for a second and then walked over to Jack, who was staring down at Steve's crumpled form with murderous intent in his eyes. "Hey," Mark called, his voice squeaking out of his rapidly tightening throat. Jack looked up and actually smiled.

Jack stepped over Steve and leaned against the locker next to Mark. "I can't believe you've got to get some theater geek to fight your battles for you," Jack said. "Fucking sad, man." Mark looked away from Jack's gaze, his fists clenching and unclenching. Jack leaned in close enough so only Mark could hear. "But if you did, I'd fucking *destroy* you." Moving before Mark could register it Jack shoved him hard to the ground and then pinned him there with a foot on his chest.

The spectators that appeared around them let out gasps and murmurs and Jack's face contorted into an evil grin. He pressed his foot down harder, and Mark's breath hissed past his teeth. Jack leaned down. "Don't bother to fight me, Watson. I'll bury you."

With that, Jack lifted his foot up and walked back to his locker to continue changing, not even looking in their direction. Mark just lay there, listening to everyone change and head upstairs to wait for the bell. His breath came back but not his will to stand.

"Hey," Steve said. Mark looked up and saw him sitting on the bench next to him. He was dressed and just stared down at Mark.

"What?"

"What?" Steve repeated. "We got our asses kicked, that's what. That and we're late for class."

"Yeah," Mark said, sitting up and wincing. Mark avoided Steve's gaze and got changed as quickly as his aching muscles would allow. *If you'd stood up for yourself,* his little voice sneered, *this never would have happened and your friend wouldn't have put himself in danger. But what do you care? You're a coward. A worthless coward.* He slammed his locker drowning it out.

***

All in all, Christine thought, it hadn't been a bad day. Sure she'd started a couple of weeks behind but it looked like catching up wasn't going to be that big of a problem. The only confusing thing was how spread out the campus was, making it almost impossible to figure where you're going unless you literally run into someone who is more than happy to show you around. She smiled thinking of Mark's wide-eyed and eager to please face that showed up once he lightened up a little. He certainly wasn't the type of guy she was usually interested in. In fact, she wasn't even really sure if she was *interested* in him or just found him interesting. Either way there was just something about him that made her want to know more.

She stopped just outside the school's main entrance, trying to remember which way her house was, when she saw Mark over by the bike rack unchaining what looked to be a small scooter. Spotted with rust and dirt, it suited his sloppy charm. She headed over, hoping to catch him before he took off.

"Hey stranger," she said, and he whirled around so fast it made her jump. When he recognized her, his eyes opened wide and he nearly dropped the helmet he was holding. "Oh! Hi!" he squeaked.

"Remind me never to sneak up on you," she laughed.

"Sorry, it's been a rough day."

"That's alright. This is a really cool. Is it a moped?"

He smiled a little. "No, it's a scooter. A Vespa 180 Super Sport, actually, from 1965. Total classic. I finally got it fixed up this summer. Steve and I call it the V."

"That's totally kick-ass," she smiled. "Your parents don't worry about you on a bike like this? Mine would freak."

Mark shifted, gaze drifting away. "Ah, well, they don't really worry about much. I take care of it myself and I wear my helmet. I've only crashed once, but I was screwing around and doing something stupid."

"You? Stupid? I find that hard to believe," she grinned, making him blush and getting his attention again.

"Well, it was Steve's fault really," he said. "He's always trying to get me to ramp stuff or race cars or something moronic like that. That time I think he was chasing me around my backyard. I swerved to avoid running him over and crashed into the garage. So yeah, no playing tag with the V, that's what we learned."

"Good to know," she smiled. "Well, I've got to go, I've got quite a walk." she said.

Mark paused and then said, "Y'know, I could give you a lift. I don't have my spare helmet with me, but I'll go slow."

"Thanks, that'd be great. And don't worry about me, I don't mind going fast."

***

Mark pulled up in front of Christine's house and was more convinced than ever that he was way out of his depth. As Christine yelled and pointed directions from the back of the V he realized that they were moving further up the Hill, towards Cedar Ridge's big homes with huge yards and fantastic views of Manhattan. Sure enough, she directed him into one of the secluded little cul-de-sacs near the top. She motioned him to one of the houses at the end. It had a wide front lawn and a driveway that curved around the back.

"Thanks a lot for the ride," she said, standing up and pulling her hair back.

"Yeah, no problem," he said, still transfixed. "That's a pretty nice house."

"Oh," she said, glancing at it over her shoulder. "Yeah, it's alright. My dad wanted another one on the other side of town that was bigger but the deal fell through so we got this one instead. He says this'll do for now."

"Gee, I hope so," Mark said before he could stop himself. He felt his face get red, but Christine just smiled. "I know what you mean," she said. "I told him I was sick of moving and this place was more than enough, but he says he only wants 'The Best.' He's a little crazy like that."

Mark smiled, mostly from relief. "Hey, I was, ah, wondering," he started, and then clamped his jaw shut. *What are you doing? Are you insane?*

"What?" Christine said, smiling, and suddenly all hesitation was lost.

"I was wondering if you'd like to come to a little party at a friend of mine's this weekend," he said, getting it out before it was too late.

"I'd love to."

"Oh, wow, okay," Mark said. "I've just gotta check and make sure it's okay. I mean, it was gonna just be me and Steve but I don't think it'll be problem. It should be great, though. Really, really great."

"Sounds like fun then," Christine said. "What kind of party is it?"

"Well, it's actually my birthday next Tuesday, so it's like a pre-birthday thing. Nothing fancy. Like I said just me, Steve and Clara, hanging out, watching movies that kind of stuff."

"Oh," Christine said. "Who's Clara?"

"She's just a friend of mine. An older lady who owns a store downtown. She's pretty cool."

"Great," she said, smiling. "Let me give you my number so you can call me later with the details."

"Yeah, sure," he said, each one reaching into their bags for pen and paper. As Mark took hers, their fingers touched, he could swear that she let her fingers linger for a second before drawing away.

"Well," Mark said, now even more flustered than before, "I'll call Clara and make sure we've got room for another person and then I'll give you a call. Is later tonight okay?"

"Yeah, that'd be great."

"Okay, yeah. Great." Mark fumbled to get his helmet on. He rode off, watching Christine in his little rear view mirror until he turned the corner and she vanished from view. Oh wow, he thought. I think she really likes me. Hot damn.

CHAPTER FOUR

Not even coming home could dampen his spirits.

Ever since he was seven home was the same dirty beige duplex located in scenic Wrong Side of the Tracks Cedar Ridge. He'd moved in with his mom's older sister Martha and her husband Joe when his parents died in a car accident. The childless couple, faced with familial obligation, did their best to turn the house into a home. Martha did the tucking in, the comforting and the "there, there, it'll be alright," while Joe specialized in "Don't touch that" and "Keep it down, I'm trying to watch the game." Mark had begun to adjust when the world got re-scripted again shortly after he turned eleven.

That day Aunt Martha wasn't there to meet him when he came home after school. At first he just chalked it up to some errand that she had to run and he went on with business as normal. Hours passed and Mark realized that not only was Martha late but Joe should've been back from work. Food, TV and even homework couldn't keep things from blowing past "weird" and heading deep into "scary."

The car pulled in well after dark. Mark waited in the hallway, watching the backdoor but not wanting to get his hopes up. After what could have been a dozen trips from the garage to the back porch the door opened and Joe walked in. He shuffled straight ahead, right up to the refrigerator and opened the freezer. He took out a bottle and took a long drink from it. He closed the door, bottle still in hand, and slumped forward, leaning his head against the door.

"Uncle Joe," Mark said, as soft as he possibly could as he stepped into the kitchen. Startled by the noise, Joe's head jerked up and the bottle of Vodka slipped from his fingers and shattered on the tile. Mark jumped but Joe didn't even flinch. He turned towards Mark and his eyes were red and blurry, and the face that had once been merely gruff had collapsed into one etched with age and wear.

"Damn you."

"What did I do?" Mark whispered.

"You wore her out." His voice was a harsh, ragged croak. "She did everything for you, and you just took all she had and didn't give a damn thing back. You just took and took."

"Uncle Joe--"

"Don't you dare!" Joe yelled, dropping down on one knee, barely missing bits of glass. He grabbed Mark by the shoulders and shook him. "Don't you cry, dammit! She was my wife, you don't get to cry!" Mark sniffed in deeply only to get a nose full of Vodka fumes. "Stop it!" Joe snarled, shaking him even harder, and then pushing him back into the hallway with a disgusted shove. Mark flopped back, not even trying to break his fall. Against orders, Mark began to sob as he watched the still kneeling Joe lean against the doorjamb, head down and body shaking.

When the shaking stopped Joe mumbled something Mark could barely hear.

"Wh . . . what?" Mark said, catching his breath from his own sobs.

"Get out!" Joe snapped, glaring up at him wet, hate filled eyes.

Mark just sat there, stunned. Was he throwing him out on the street? Joe slammed his palm down on the floor with a thunderous crack. "I said get out of my sight, goddamnit!"

Mark scrambled backwards, arms and legs working frantically until he got himself rolled over and heading up the steps, taking them three at a time. His foot caught on the top step and he stumbled forward, crashing into the door to the attic. Breathless and terrified, Mark made it into his room, pausing only to lock the door behind him. Mark pushed his bed across the room and wedged it against the door. He snatched the blankets off and threw them into the closet, arranging them into a makeshift nest. *If he wants me out he'll have to come and drag me out.*

Mark slept in the closet for two weeks after Martha's fatal stroke, wedging the door closed with his bed every night. When he was thirteen Joe let him move into the attic space that had been Martha's sewing room. It was small and cramped, the ceiling slanting down so much that he could only fully stand up in half of it. It was sweltering in the summer and freezing in the winter, but it had a lock on the door and Joe never went near it. For Mark, it was a safe haven in the dark, narrow, not-quite-a-house.

They didn't ever talk about what had happened the night Martha died. They lived almost as they had when she was alive; the two barely acknowledging each other. When they did it was usually some fight about money, chores, or schoolwork. Their last ten rounds had been about the last of the money that was left from his parents. It wasn't much, but it was just enough to buy and fix up the V. "Fine," Joe snarled in defeat. "But that's the last of it. If you want anything else, you're going to have to actually earn it."

Like most days, the house was empty when Mark walked in. Joe worked at the post office and after work he usually headed to a bar to hang out with his friends. Mark suspected Joe didn't like spending time in the house any more than he did. The house had become a rusty bear-trap of grief and loss, barely cleaned and unchanged since that night.

Once upstairs, Mark dropped his stuff as fast as he could, flipped on the TV and grabbed the phone to call Clara. Martha had been acquainted with Clara through their church and Mark had been to Clara's store a couple of times before Martha died. Mark found himself in her store a couple of months and Clara asked him how he was holding up. Without warning everything poured out of Mark in a spasm of tears. She closed up and they went up to her apartment upstairs where she eventually got everything out of him. After that she made a concerted effort to be a part of his life and be as good a friend to him as middle-aged black woman could to a teen-aged white kid.

"Mystic Books," Clara answered.

"Hey, it's me."

"Hey kiddo," she said. "You sound pretty excited. What's up?"

"Well, I was wondering if you wouldn't mind if I brought another person to the party this weekend."

"Sweetie, it's your party! Bring whoever you want!"

"Well," he said. "I just wanted to check and see, in case, y'know, there were problems or something."

"No, Mark, no problems. I'll just bring out another chair. So, is it anyone I know?"

"Well, no," he said. "She's new in town, and I just met her today."

"A her?" Mark knew this was coming and knew he could only ride it out. "Don't tell me you've got a girlfriend now? And on the first day that you met her? That's impressive!"

"Clarrrrrrre," Mark groaned, "She's not my girlfriend. She's just a girl that I met and well . . . I asked her and she said yes."

"Well she'd have been a fool to say otherwise," Clara said. "I've got customers, so I've gotta run, but I'll see you tomorrow okay?"

"Sure," Mark said, hanging up and flopping back on the bed. He dialed through the few TV stations he could pick up with the rabbit ears and after a half hour of boring reruns he got stuff out of his bag so he could begin to think about doing some homework. The piece of paper with Christine's number sat on the table near his phone. It stared at him, daring him to be the guy that actually called when they got a number and not just "the guy who finally got a phone number." *She probably wrote the number of some pizza place on it. That's no trophy, that's a seven digit path to mortification.*

He dove and snatched it up. "Christine Baker" it said and underneath the number she'd written: "Call me!" a looping, cheerful challenge to what passed for his manhood.

He looked over at the phone, lying on the bed next to him. He reached it over, picked it up and then dropped it right back down.

He reached out again. Phone up, phone down.

"This is stupid," he muttered grabbing the phone up again, his other hand quickly stabbing at numbers before he could chicken out a third time. The phone rang for what seemed like an eternity, and he almost dropped the phone back down when she picked up.

"Is that you Mark?" Christine answered.

"Yeah," he said. Oh God, she was there! "There's no surprising you, is there?"

"Well, you're the only person I've given my new number to so far and I don't think the telemarketers could get me that fast. Sorry that took so long, I was stuck behind a pile of boxes. So what's going on this weekend?"

"Everything is good to go, so I can give you the address of Clara's store or I can swing by and pick you up. Whichever is cool with you."

"I'd definitely take another ride if you're offering. I think you were holding back on me today."

"Hey, I told you, I'm a terribly responsible driver. You get no fast rides out of me." He paused. "Wait, I think that came out wrong." The phone was good, he realized. She couldn't hear wincing and foot twitching.

"Really?" she laughed. "I hope so."

"Yeah, definitely came out wrong."

"So," she said, "aside from the fact that you're disaffected with your home town, a bitter atheist, good with directions and drive a snazzy little scooter, what else do I need to know about you?"

"Oh, not much," he said, "But then again, me just telling you would just spoil the mystery, wouldn't it?"

"Well, I'll just have to see how much of this mystery I can uncover before I get called back to unpacking."

He smiled. "Ask away. My life's an open book, pretty much."

CHAPTER FIVE

Mark was rooted to the V, holding his helmet in a death grip. With the lights of Manhattan shimmering to life behind it Christine's house managed to look even more elegant and formidable than it did almost 24 hours ago. Tiny lights lit the crooked walk up to the front door and then twinkled off the panoramic windows that curved around the side of the house.

He knew nerves were stupid, as the conversation with Christine was amazing last night. While they didn't have much in common interest-wise (he wrangled out the secret of her young love affairs with various boy-bands of mediocre talent), he laid back and listened with wonder as she regaled him with tales of the various places she had lived. Almost every story began with "We were hanging out" or "We were at this party." Mark had spent almost a decade in Cedar Ridge and had yet to see a single party. The closest he came to hanging out was when Steve dragged him to one of his Theater Club things, where Mark just ended up practicing for a spot on the Olympic Wallflowering Team.

When they finally had to get off the phone she said that she "was really looking forward to the party." Mark found himself playing that, and the rest of their conversation over and over again when he went to bed.

It was easy to say over breakfast that nerves were stupid, but walking up the path to the world's prettiest house of horrors he remembered all the things he'd left out and avoided on the phone last night - like his lack of wealth and parents. Nerves were the only things that existed in his body. As he walked up the path he could see the driveway curve around the back of the house and down, nestling under the porch and providing the perfect resting place for the pair of nearly matching sports cars.

He jabbed the doorbell quickly, expecting it to shock him with some kind of poor kid detector. The chime was as perfect and inviting as the rest of the house had led him to believe it would be and it did nothing to put him at ease.

The door opened and an older, shorter-haired Christine smiled at him. "Well hello," she said. "You must be Christine's date."

Date? She called this a date? Maybe someone else is coming by when you're done. "Ah, yes ma'am. I'm Mark Watson. Pleased to meet you." He wiped a hand on his jeans and offered it to her, and she shook it warmly.

"Won't you come in, Mark? I've got a roast in the oven, but Christine will be right down," she said, heading back into the house and gesturing at the stairway in the front hall that curved up the wall and up to a second floor balcony.

"Sure thing," he called after her, walking into the living room wondering if "roast in the oven" was a euphemism or if people actually did that. The living room was a fancy "not for watching TV" one like Steve's, and the windows he'd seen from outside swept along the back wall and offered a breathtaking view of Manhattan in the distance.

If Mark hadn't known better he'd have thought the Bakers had lived here for years. The furniture, all sleek, modern and stylish, was meticulously placed. The only hint of the nasty act of unpacking was the couple of boxes tucked away in a corner. There was an array of pictures hanging on the wall above a black leather sofa that looked like it cost more than Joe's car. Mark leaned in to take a look at them, mindful not to touch anything.

The pictures looked like they had been beamed in from some distant universe where everyone was cheery and visited exotic places like lighthouses, mountains, and what may or may not be Japan. There was an older boy in the pictures with Christine and her parents; a perfect, handsome clean-cut male specimen to go with their fantastic daughter.

"Hey," Christine said, tapping Mark on the shoulder. "Ready to go?"

He turned and his bitter envy melted away. She was at least twice as lovely as she'd been yesterday, hair down and face slightly more made up. Everything about her look pushed his jeans and t-shirt down from "casual" to "sketchy hobo."

"Yeah, totally," he said. "I was just looking at some pictures of you and your family. They're all . . . man, you guys get around."

Christine shrugged. "Yeah. My mom loves taking pictures and stuff, so it's always posing and smiling." She glanced over her shoulder. "Speaking of which, we should roll out before the inquisition starts."

"Yeah, sure," Mark said as they headed for the door. "I've got the spare helmet, and it should fit you just fine."

"Excuse me," Christine's mother said, stepping into the foyer. "Did you say 'helmet?'"

"Um, yeah," Mark said, stopped dead in his tracks by Mrs. Baker's almost magical appearance.

"You didn't tell me he was picking you up in a motorcycle, Chrissy," Mrs. Baker said.

"Mom," Christine moaned. "It's not a motorcycle, it's just a scooter. Totally harmless. Helmets and everything!"

"I don't know Chrissy maybe I should drive the two of you."

"Please!" Christine said, with a wave of her hand. "Mark's a safe driver, and we're going to be late. It's perfectly fine, okay?" Christine opened the door, waving for Mark to take the lead out but he just stood there, eyes going from Christine to her mom and back again.

"Fine," Mrs. Baker said with a sigh, "As long as you're safe. And remember, you're supposed to be home by midnight. No later."

"Yeah, sure, thanks Mom," Christine said, grabbing Mark's hand and almost dragging him out the door.

"I hope I didn't get you in trouble," Mark said, handing her a helmet.

"No, it's just been 24 hours and she hasn't found something to bitch about so she had to latch on to something. With my Dad settling in at the new office and my brother away at college, it's gonna be me."

"Well," he grinned, "I'm sure she's just worried about her little Chrissy."

She punched him on the shoulder with a smile. "Please! They've been calling me that since I was a little girl and it's so fucking Nick at Night. Don't you start!"

"Yes ma'am," he said, starting up the V.

"A beverage for madam?" Steve asked Christine, laying a bottle of soda across his forearm for her like a maitre d'.

"Thanks," she smiled.

"Raging party, huh?"

"Very . . . intimate." This was an apt description of the guest list and the store itself. Nestled between an appliance store and a Chinese take-out place on one of the main drags through town, it was lined floor to ceiling with bookshelves. The books themselves ranged from science fiction and horror to books on mysticism and the occult and there was a small case next to the register with crystals and tarot cards. Towards the back of the store there was a small sitting area, where Clara had set up a card table and wheeled out a TV with a DVD player.

"This place is cool," Steve said, "but there's always something here that I can't figure out. A couple of months ago she had coffin nails, and I *so* didn't want to know what that was about."

"I think she said they were for protection spells or something," Mark said, wandering over from the new releases.

"All I know is that I don't wanna meet who she gets 'em from, y'know?" Steve smirked.

The three stood there, sodas in hand, the only noise drifting in from the street. After a few seconds, Steve cocked a thumb towards the back of the store and said, "Hey, speaking of, I'm gonna go upstairs and see what's up with that cake." With that, he strolled to the back and vanished behind the curtain labeled "Employees Only."

The two stood there in the near silence, Mark rocking back and forth on his heels. "This is nice," Christine said a couple seconds later.

"Yeah," Mark nodded. "I mean, I know you've done way cooler stuff in Boston and wherever, but I'm glad you like it."

"Mark," she said, stepping closer and putting a hand on his shoulder before he wore a hole in the carpet. "That stuff's not important. You helping me out at school and being, maybe, the best conversationalist in the past decade is way more impressive."

"Really?" he said, eyes focusing on the hand on his shoulder. Talking on the phone had been one thing, but being in front of her put him right back in the hallway, flat on his ass and staring up in stupid, mute awe.

"Totally," she smiled. "I just don't want you to be all stressed out and nervous or anything just because I'm here, okay? There's nowhere else I'd rather be right now."

He opened his mouth to say something, but was cut off as Steve brushed back the curtain and Clara came in with a candle topped cake. Clara began to sing, and Steve and Christine joined in. Christine linked arms with Mark, who was flushed with embarrassment, to drag him towards the table in the back.

"You didn't have to go to any trouble," he said when they were finished.

"Trouble?" Clara said, waving her hands and rolling her eyes. "It's your birthday and we love you! Of course we have to make a fuss."

"Yeah," Steve said with a wide grin, throwing an arm around Mark and squeezing him close and pulling him away from Christine. "Happy sweet sixteen, baby. Now let's get at that cake!"

When they finished the cake and the Chinese food, Steve and Clara gave Mark their presents. Steve gave Mark a copy of an imported Kung Fu movie and Clara gave him a large hardback collection of Lovecraft stories. "Thanks, you guys," he said, grinning from ear to ear at the two of them. "You knew I wanted this, didn't you?" he asked Clara.

"Well you've only picked it up and put it down a dozen times, kiddo. How could I not?"

"I'm sorry I didn't bring anything," Christine said, "But I'm sure Clara can point something out to me later."

"Oh, hey," Mark said, pushing the book aside. "Don't worry about it. I mean, we just met and all, it's no big deal."

"Yeah," Steve said, rapping out a beat on the table with his knuckles. "You're like the little drummer girl, but, y'know, without the drumming."

"Exactly," Mark smiled, but then stopped. "You don't drum, do you?"

"Not a musical bone in my body," she laughed.

"Annnnnnyway," Steve said. "We were gonna watch *The Thing*, but now I vote kung fu kick-ass action, what say you?"

"Totally," Mark grinned, and then looking back over to Christine, the smile again giving way to concern. "Unless you hate kung fu. But this looks really good."

"No," she smiled, patting him on the arm. "I'm really not down with the scary movies. I saw 'The Ring' with my brother nearly had a panic attack. Kung fu is fine."

The movie was just as good as Mark had hoped it would be, but most importantly in the dark he was able to steal glances at Christine. He loved watching her watch the movie, her eyes lighting up when she laughed or growing wide during some outrageous fight.

During a slow point, Mark excused himself and stepped behind the curtain marked "Employees Only". Behind it was a small hallway with stairs along the far right wall that led up to Clara's apartment and a narrow hallway to the left that led to the bathroom.

When he finished in the bathroom he was about to turn and head back into the store when he heard a creak from the upstairs door. He paused, cocking his head to see if he heard it again. After a few seconds he did, and it sounded like a footstep. Mark walked up to the foot of the steps and squinted up at the darkness above.

He could barely see the top, but it looked like the door was closed, which was unusual. There shouldn't be anyone up there, but there were fire stairs leading down from the small patio at the back of Clara's apartment and into the lot below where Mark had parked the V. They weren't in a bad neighborhood per se, but it was as close to urban as Cedar Ridge got.

Mark took a couple of steps backwards, trying to keep the door in sight. When he reached the curtain he turned to ask someone if they heard something as well, but he realized that another massive kung fu fight broke out. Christine laughed out-loud, and the light from the TV sparkled in her eyes.

This is stupid, go sit with her.

Mark was about to go back in when he heard a definite creak above him. He looked from Christine to back up the door, and then turned and crept up the steps.

The stairway was dark and Mark tread softly as he could. He hadn't turned on the light downstairs, and if the door upstairs wasn't closed, Clara hadn't left a single light on upstairs.

What are you going to do? Sneak up on a burglar, wrestle him to the ground and be a hero for your new "girlfriend?"

Mark stopped at the second to last step, one hand on the wall to his left, the other reaching out to feel for the door. He looked back down the steps behind him. The muted light through the curtain of the TV was still flickering, but everything else was as black as pitch.

He turned back and reached out for the door. His fingertips brushed against wood, and he realized that the door had been closed. He listened for anything out of the ordinary, which was easier further away from the kicks and chops, but this time there was nothing. He felt around until he found the doorknob, and gently pushed the door open.

"Hello?" he called, and then winced at his own stupidity. *Oh, that's a great way to sneak up on a burglar. Why don't you take up yodeling?*

The door opened into the living room. To the left was a wide archway that led to the kitchen and through there, the patio. The apartment was dark, the only light coming from the narrow windows that faced the buildings next door. Everything looked normal, although it was odd that Clara hadn't left a single light on.

He took a few cautious steps around the living room, straining his eyes to peer into the inky depths of the shadows around him. He stopped, trying to hear whatever it was that had been moving around up here but there was nothing. Not even the kung fu mayhem was making its way up the steps.

"Hello?" he called again, his voice bouncing around him.

There was a flutter out of the corner of his eye, near the kitchen. As he turned to look a breath of air washed over him, carrying a thick odor of smoke as if it had just blown out a thousand candles. He wrinkled his nose as he peered around in the dark, not wanting to leave the little island of light from downstairs.

There it was again, a flutter of something in the deep blackness of the kitchen. He stepped forward, and then the dark exploded towards him like black smoke. He stepped back, trying to get into the light, but the shape was on him in a second, enveloping him and filling his nostrils with the scent of ash and fire. His stumbled back, waving one arm behind him to find the wall and the other in front of his face. The darkness was so absolute that he couldn't even see his own flailing limb in front of him.

All he could see were two lights flickering in the distance. They bobbed slightly, getting bigger, and then he realized they were eyes.

He turned to run but then realized he was inches away from the top of the stairs. He pinwheeled his arms, frantically trying keep from toppling forward. Stretched out, trying to keep his balance, he realized the stairway had changed, become old and wooden. This wasn't Clara's anymore, and the light from downstairs didn't come from a kung fu movie, but flickered like an open flame. Smoke wafted up at him, carrying with it a heavier smell of something burning like a rancid barbecue.

Mark heard the low whistle of a familiar tune and when he turned the flaming pair of eyes towered over him.

"Come on-a my house, my house . . ." a voice whispered through the darkness.

There was a flash of silver, a brilliant contrast to the darkness, and then he was tumbling backwards down the stairs.

CHAPTER SIX

"What the hell was that?" Christine said, jumping to her feet. Steve and Clara raced behind the curtain where the racket had come from and when she squeezed past them she could see Mark sprawled out at the base of the stairs, staring up at them in bewildered panic.

"What, are you taking up stair-sledding?" Steve asked.

"Are you okay?" Clara said, elbowing Steve out of the way.

"Yeah, I just remember--" Mark scrambled to his feet. "Upstairs! There was . . . something. Someone, I think."

"What?" Clara said, reaching over and turning on the stairwell light.

"But . . ." Mark said, taking a hesitant step up the empty, well-lit, non-life threatening stairway. "I heard something. I went up there and it was totally dark, and then--" Mark eyes met Christine's, and he could see the "He is strange and not one of us" look everyone eventually caught around him. *Now she's getting a taste of the real Mark Watson.*

"It was nothing," he said, giving the stairs a second glance. "I must have . . . I dunno, slipped. No big deal."

"And here I thought we *weren't* gonna watch *The Thing*," Steve said.

"Are you sure?" Clara said, elbowing Steve.

"Yeah," Mark said, his color coming back. "Sure. It was probably the wind or a curtain or something, and I just lost my footing coming down the steps. I'm fine, really."

"We should check, just to be sure."

"Clara, it's nothing," Mark said.

"If it's nothing then nothing is what we'll see," Clara said, heading up the steps. Mark darted after her as fast as he could, Steve and Christine trailing behind them.

The upstairs door was open and all four of them crowded into the doorway, peering into the living room. "Mark?" Clara asked, but he just opened his mouth and then closed it.

One of the small lamps on the sofa end-table was lit, and down the hall there was a dim light coming from the back of the apartment. The kitchen was dim but not impenetrably black, lit by streetlight coming through the windows and back patio door.

"Where was it?" Clara asked.

"The kitchen," he said, feeling his old friend humiliation creeping up on him. "I guess I thought I saw someone on the patio."

Clara walked over and pressed her face against the glass of the back door. "I don't see anything." She gave the door a tug and the doorknob a rattle. "Still locked. Are you sure that's all?"

"Yeah. Must've been my overactive imagination or something." Mark said, forcing a smile.

"Well, if we're done with the homeland security portion of the evening, can we finish the movie?" Steve said, waving everyone back down the stairs.

"That was fun," Christine said, handing Mark back the spare helmet. "We should really do that again sometime."

"Yeah, totally. Hanging out is good," Mark said, fumbling the helmet as he tried to strap it back on the V.

"Why don't you give me a call tomorrow or something? We could hang out some more."

"Yeah, okay," Mark said. He couldn't take his eyes off the helmet and kept fiddling with the strap even though he knew it was secure. He'd avoided eye contact ever since seeing that look on her face after he'd taken his tumble down the steps. It was only going to get worse, he realized. The whole evening would be beyond a waste if he wasn't able to look her in the eye ever again. He glanced up and she was just standing there, hands still in her pockets and head tilted down as she tried to catch his eye.

Oh God, do something. Do something, you silly spineless bastard.

"I hope you had fun tonight," he said, standing up and smoothing out his jacket. "My life's kinda boring, and that about summed up the highlights. Well, there's usually less falling down. I think."

"I don't know, you've been doing it an awful lot since we met," she smiled.

"Yeah, I guess so," he said, looking away again.

"Mark," she stepped closer, "I'm sorry, that was kind of mean. I'm just glad there wasn't someone up there or something."

Yeah, it's better that I'm crazy. "I know, and I know you're not being mean. It was just weird. And, well, humiliating."

"You shouldn't be humiliated. It was kind of cute."

He finally looked up, and she was right there, less than a foot away. Her hair had fallen over her face a little but he could still see the green of her eyes reflecting the tiny lights of the walkway.

"Really?"

"Yes, really."

He reached out, every micron of his willpower keeping his hand steady, to brush the hair away from her face.

"It was in the way," he said, his hand lingering in the air next to shoulder.

"It was," she said, and then they were kissing. Every single one of his senses seemed to shut down so he could focus on this terrifying and wonderful new experience.

"So I was wondering if you wanted to go out on a date sometime. Would that be okay?" he said when their lips finally parted.

"I thought I just asked you out on a date! How much clearer do you need it to be?"

"Well, I'm slow, what can I say?"

"Well, to clarify," she said, wrapping her arms around his neck and pulling him closer. "Yes, I would very much like to go out with you. Tomorrow even."

"I just wanted to make sure," he said, and they were kissing again.

"Still need convincing?" she whispered, drawing back but still holding him.

"Yeah, I think so."

"Well, that's going to have to wait until tomorrow."

"Really?"

"Yes really, unless you want to deal with the parental Gestapo."

"Gesundheit."

"And good night," she said with a final kiss before she pulled away.

"Night," he said, letting his arms fall to his sides and not moving an inch as he watched her back up the walkway.

"I'll call you," he said.

"You better," she said with a wink, and the disappeared inside.

He didn't yell in triumph until he was a block away, racing the V home as fast as it would carry him.

Mark crept quietly through the back door and into the kitchen. He wasn't sure if Uncle Joe was awake or even home, but he didn't want to ruin a near-perfect evening by finding out the hard way.

Yeah, near-perfect except for the psychotic hallucinations. Other than that, picture perfect.

It had been easy to forget it all with friends and laughter and kissing (my god, the kissing), but sneaking through the dark he couldn't help but conjure up the image of those flaming eyes and that sickening, sing-song voice. Not only that, the dream he'd had the night before about the boy watching the house across the street and getting attacked in his room was crystal clear.

Just like the song he'd heard in Clara's apartment. The same one from the dream.

He stopped, closed his eyes, took a deep breath and then exhaled slowly, opening his eyes as he did.

Nothing strange. Nothing unusual. Nothing black and smoky and on fire. Just a kitchen with a sink full of dirty dishes and a pile of pizza boxes by the trash. The only scary thing here was that this was his life.

Mark tip-toed his way through the hallway and then heard a low, faint whisper coming from the living room. He took another step forward and peered into the living room. The room was dark except for a soft light and a large figure on the couch and Mark reached out for the wall to keep from falling down.

He's here he's here he's--

Joe, he realized. Joe, in his usual seat in front of the television.

"Jesus," Mark said. "You scared the . . ."

He should've realized what was going on, but the sudden rush of panic had taken him by surprise. Not only was Joe in his normal seat in front of the TV, he was also passed out drunk. Mark just shook his head, spying the glass with the mostly melted ice.

Mark started upstairs, stealth completely abandoned. He paused at the third step, looking over at Joe. With a pained sigh, Mark turned around and headed back for the living room.

"Joe," Mark shook his shoulder. "Joe, you need to go to bed."

Joe's head lolled back and forth, eyelids fluttering. "Vah . . . whu . . ."

"Joe, you need to go upstairs."

"I don't gotta do nothin'," Joe said, finally lifting his head and peering around the dark room. After several clumsy pans around the room his eyes landed on Mark.

"What are you doin' here?"

"I live here. You fell asleep watching TV and I thought you'd be more comfortable upstairs."

"Th' hell do you know?" Joe pulled himself to his feet, wobbling like human Jenga.

"Just thought I'd help." Mark rolled his eyes and headed for the stairs before this got even more pointless.

"Hey!" Joe barked. "It's almost midnight. What the hell'er you doin out so late?"

"I was at a party," Mark said, not stopping.

"Dammit stay still when I talk to you! What damn party?"

Mark stopped, gripping the banister as hard as he could. "A birthday party. For me. Y'know, since my birthday is coming up?"

Joe's face scrunched together as he tried to get as much power as he could to his remaining brain cells. "Your birthday? When?"

"It's on Tuesday," Mark said. "Three days from now? Same as last year."

The Big Wheel of Drunken Emotions spun around and then settled on anger. "You fuckin' smartass. You can go fuck yourself and your snotty at'tude. You're not too old to get kicked the fuck out, y'hear me?"

"Yeah, I hear you," Mark turned and headed up the stairs. The threat of getting kicked out had lost most of its weight by now.

"Hey! Dammit, come back here!" Joe yelled, shuffling to the bottom of the steps. Mark kept going, pausing only to slam and lock the attic door behind him. He took the steps up to the attic room two at a time and then threw himself onto his bed.

At least last year he had gotten a card, a stern nod, and a "Happy Birthday." He should've known to expect less as the years went on, but every year he strolled forward whistling like an idiot going "This time it'll be different!" The only thing that was different was how hard he got shoved back on his ass.

Clara loved talking about the future and how full of possibilities it was. "This is High School," she'd say. "When your life really begins you'll look back and see how strong all of this has made you." He didn't have the heart to tell her that the only thing it was making him was more and more certain that the future was a joke. His grades were mediocre and that meant no scholarships, and if Joe wasn't putting up money for birthday cards he sure as shit wasn't going to put anything up for college. By the time graduation rolled around he'd be lucky if he was working minimum wage at a burger joint with Joe charging him rent.

All of the red-headed, green eyed, angel-lipped girls in the world couldn't change any of that. Damned if they still didn't put a smile on his face though. Maybe, just maybe, she could give him a glimmer of something to hope for until then.

It was that glimmer that let him fall asleep with a smile on his face.

CHAPTER SEVEN

While Mark Watson dreamt a figure made his way around the tiny islands of street-light on Briarcliff Avenue, hat pulled low and coat collar turned up. The only sound on the suburban street was the scuff of sneakers on pavement as he hurried towards his destination. He stopped between the two giant oaks and peered through the overgrown tangle of dead and dying bushes.

"Home," he said in a soft, dreamy voice.

He pushed his way between the overgrown hedges and into the yard. The grass was almost knee high and the only gaps in it were from the cracked cement tiles of the path leading to the door. The entire yard was filled with the thick, damp smell of fall and at the center of everything was the house.

His house.

Time and neglect had savaged the place. The paint was all but gone, and the house itself sagged as if it were in the midst of a deep inhale that would end in a death rattle. He walked through past the rusted sign that proclaimed that "Yes, this wonderful castle could be yours! Just ask Dave Keener (Northern New Jersey's realtor of the year, 1981, 1983)!"

He'd visited Dave Keener in a dream once. After that, Dave left the house alone, losing it in a shuffle of paperwork.

Not to mention sleeping with the light on for a couple of years.

The figure took a cautious step onto the porch, avoiding the hidden patches of rotted out wood that could break underfoot with the slightest bit of weight. Like the big hole on the top step that Tommy Reardon's leg plunged into when he ran into the yard and up the steps on a dare twenty years ago. He could still smell the blood on the ragged edges on the hole where the step had bitten into his leg all the way up to his middle thigh.

Tommy woke from a dream shortly after, screaming and tearing at his bandages to make sure that there weren't really any maggots making their way through his cuts.

The doorknob was stained almost black, and the door itself still had slightly lighter patch of wood in the center where the knocker once hung. He touched it there and the locks released their hold and the door slowly swept open, cutting a swath in the years of untouched dust. He hesitated for a moment, savoring the musk of rot and age that washed over him that he'd waited decades to experience again. It was happening. Finally, he was in this wondrous place again, and this time it was no dream.

Before him a wide staircase headed up to the second floor, and next to it a hallway led into the back of the house. On either side of him was two wide archways; right to the living room, left to the dining room. Each room was spotted with furniture hidden under dusty, molding shrouds.

He walked down the hallway and into the kitchen. Nestled into the wall to his right was a thick wooden door. He walked forward and placed a trembling hand on the cool, dusty wood. He moved his fingertips down to the doorknob. It twisted, but would not open. He concentrated for a few moments and there was a faint metal scraping sound as the bar on the other side unlatched itself and the door swung open. Before him were spindly wooden-stairs leading down into darkness.

He let his fingertips linger on the handrail as he walked, pausing at the small landing at the bend in the steps and then continuing down to the right. Once at the bottom, he was in total darkness.

He didn't need to see where he was going. He walked forward, between the twin support columns and then tilting his head to avoid the piece of chain hanging from one of the pipes in the ceiling.

It was right in front of him now. He stopped and put his hand out, feeling the warm metal. All the years of neglect weren't enough to put the fire out. He dropped to his knees, running his hand down the metal until it reached the glass window in the front of the furnace.

"I'm sorry I've been gone so long, Lord. It's been difficult to be away, but it was necessary."

His hand moved to the handle. He twisted it and the door opened with a shriek of rusted metal. He brushed the hat off his head and leaned forward, resting his head on the edge of the chamber. He took a deep breath of the stale, ash filled air until his lungs were full and he thought he was going to burst.

He could feel Him in there, just below the surface. An ember waiting to catch flame.

He reached inside, his hands moving through the ash until his fingers found the long bundle of cloth. He drew it out, shaking the ash from it before unraveling it. The long, thin black cane topped with silver was as lovely as he remembered it. He turned it slowly over in his hands, moving up to the dragon's head that served as the cane's handle. He flicked the switch at the dragon's neck and drew the long, thin blade out of the shaft. The sound of the instrument being freed was as glorious as remembered. He swung it through the air, spinning and slicing through the darkness. With a flick of his wrist, he snapped the blade smoothly back into its sheath.

He dropped back down on his knees in front of the great steel furnace. He closed his eyes, both hands squeezing the cane in front of him. "Thank you for bringing me back, Lord. I will feed you and make you strong again."

There was a slight stir in the chamber of the furnace. A tiny breeze shifted the dirt and ashes.

"Yes. Yes, yes," he said.

A warm and smoky breeze passed over him. He drew it deep into his lungs and it filled him completely. He held it inside, concentrating, bearing down on it until he could feel the fire explode in his lungs.

It spread through his insides, burning everything. He screamed in ecstatic agony as the fire took him over, sizzling in his ears and then bursting through his eyes like tiny, volcanoes. Fire burned up his throat and the smoke and embers that burst forth pooled around him, clinging to his body. He shaped it whimsically around his body as the coat, hat and gloves he remembered so well.

"I will nourish You," he said, kneeling with reverence before his steel god. "I will bring you the blood that You require, and I will make him ours once again."

***

Clara Washington woke with a scream. The dream that startled her awake racing from her as she realized she was safe in her own bed. The only sound was her own gasping breath, and she closed her eyes and forced herself to breathe steady and even, willing her heart to calm down.

Mark.

There had been dreams like this before; when her husband died, when her daughter had her car accident. Sometimes all she could remember were small details that would pop up in the moment and she'd find out that she'd been seeing something as it happened. Others times it was what was about to happen. It didn't happen often, but she'd learned to trust it and be on the lookout for signs of what was about to come.

This one had been a doozy. The specifics were fading fast, but she could see Mark in the center of it. Just focusing on the details made her shiver, but if she had to make a guess she figured she'd been shown something that was coming, not what had happened.

She got out of bed, put on her robe and headed for the kitchen. She noticed the time and knew that it'd be too late to call to make sure he was okay. The last thing she wanted to do was deal with that ogre of an Uncle that he lived with. Even when Martha was alive she'd only talked to him a few times, but it was enough to know that they wouldn't ever like each other beyond strained small talk.

What she needed to do was get something to drink, take some deep cleansing breaths and get some sleep. After some focused meditation in the morning she could tell Mark whatever she could remember about her dream and what she thought was going to happen.

The smell of something burning stopped her in her tracks, hand on the refrigerator door. She wondered for a second if she'd left the stove on when something peeled itself from the darkness and grabbed hold of her wrist, crushing it. The sound of breaking bones echoed through the room and electric piranhas ran riot up her arm.

Her wrist twisted upwards, raising her arm and dropping her to her knees in pain. She looked at the hand covered in swirling black smoke clamped to her wrist, watching it swirl and writhe like a living thing. Two points of fire began to blaze in front of her. She forgot about the pain in her wrist, but she suddenly remembered her dream and why she had been screaming.

***

"I'm here," he said, kneeling back in front of the furnace. The fire in his eyes blazed brighter than before. "I've brought it for You."

He drew the blade from its sheath. Drops of blood pooled on its edges, ready to spill to the floor, but he held them there with sheer force of will. He took the blade and stuck it gently in the pile of ashes in the furnace's chamber. The blood ran down the blade, congealing in the ash.

After several seconds there was a rustle in the ashes. The warm breeze was back, joined by the sizzle and pop of fire trying to spark to life. The flames in him pulled back, healing his body as fire and smoke rolled down the blade and into the furnace, feeding and nurturing the newborn flame.

There was a rush of warm air and the fire caught, lighting the basement and filling it with the acrid smell of burning blood.

He pulled the blade from the chamber and slid it back home in the sheath, placing it in front of the furnace and leaning forward as close as the heat would allow. He drew a deep breath, taking the aroma into his lungs and savoring it. He peered into the flames, eyes wide and tears running down his cheeks from the stinging heat.

"I see You. And I will make him see you too, and remember your glory."

CHAPTER EIGHT

Mark sprang out of bed like it was Super Christmas New Years Vacation Field Hockey Skirts for Forever Day. Better than that, it was Date Day. Not "Gee Whiz Do You Like Me if So Check This Box" Date Day, but "We Totally Made Out Last Night and It Was Awesome Let's Never Stop Doing That" Date Day.

He showered and dressed, actually looking at clothes before putting them on. It seemed like some of them went better with other ones. He brushed and combed his hair, debating the placement of each strand as if he were some sort of hairologist.

There was a moment, looking in the mirror, when he felt something turn in his stomach. It shook him more than the nerves he'd felt last night and he had to grab the edge of the sink to steady himself. The joy the promise of this day brought was faltering under the intensity of what he'd remembered and seen yesterday and now he could feel something else in there, half remembered and gnawing away at him.

"Not today," he said, forcing it back down in his mind. "Any other day, fine. But not today."

He ate his cereal over the sink like it was some sort of bomb ready to explode all over his well thought out clothing choices. When he finished and headed back upstairs he realized that it was only 10:00. Was it too early? Did she even expect him to call right away? Was this too desperate?

Of course it's too desperate. You kissed a girl that wants to kiss you again and it's turned you into a fucking madman who eats cereal over the sink like a crazy person. You left desperate five miles back.

Mark flopped back down on the bed, watching the world's slowest second hand spin. The only other time a girl had showed interest in him was a drama club party Steve dragged him to their freshman year. Sarah Bingham had found him hiding out in a corner watching everyone else have a good time and started talking to him. After some awkward conversation, the two ended up kissing in the hall closet. Badly, he now realized, although he decided to attribute that to the fact that he'd been balanced on one leg so he wasn't stepping in a mop bucket. He tried talking to her at school later that week, but she ducked him like she owed him money. He had tried calling her a couple (dozen) times, and it wasn't until he watched her duck behind a friend as she snuck through the cafeteria that he realized she probably didn't want anything to do with him.

It took talent to make a young woman attempt a marine crawl through a chaotic and crowded high school cafeteria, and until now he thought that might be his only gift to women.

Settle. She said you were nice, and sweet, and that she wanted to see you again. As long as you don't hump her leg or drool, you should be come off as normal. For you.

He reached over for the phone. Normal was a stretch, but he thought he might be able to pull it off.

It rang forever, each chime daring him to hang up and chicken out, but then a breathless young female voice answered.

"Hey you," she said.

"I hope I didn't call to early. I just . . . wanted to see what was going on."

"Nothing important. My mom's been dragging me out of bed way too early to help unpack and all this crap. What're you up to?"

"Same thing. Well, I don't have any crap. How much stuff do you guys have, anyway?"

"Too much! I can't wait until we're done and they can leave me alone. It's such a pain!"

"Yeah, I bet," Boxes upon boxes full of fancy brand new stuff. Total pain, what a hassle.

"So how about you swing over and arrange a jailbreak?"

"Yeah, that sounds . . . arrangeable."

"Great! Get here fast before they wall me in with more boxes."

Does this get any easier? Mark fantasized that standing at her door waiting for someone to answer would become second nature, but for now it still filled him with the same dread it did yesterday. It was just well-lit so there was nowhere to hide.

Before fleeing became an option, the door opened and a tall, almost painfully thin man beckoned him in.

"You must be Mark," he said. "Come in, come in."

"Thanks," Mark said, hands clenching to fists in his jacket.

"Can I take your coat?" Mr. Baker said, placing a hand on Mark's shoulder.

"No, I'm good," Mark said. Mr. Baker smiled and nodded, giving his shoulder a little squeeze. The man's short, crinkly hair was gray at the temples, and he wore tiny silver spectacles that seemed designed to add menace to his glare.

"So Mark," Mr. Baker said, "Chrissy tells me that you have some sort of scooter you ride around on, is that correct?"

"Yes. Yes, sir," Mark said. *Here it comes.*

"Well," Mr. Baker said, beginning to circle around Mark with slow, deliberate strides. "I'm sure it's fine for you to get around and all, but I think you can understand that her mother and I may be a little cautious about her safety."

"Yeah, I guess I can understand that," Mark said, trying not to obviously look like he was trying to keep Mr. Baker from getting behind him. *I am not at all afraid of him latching onto my neck with some sort of crazy parent death grip.* "But I do have a spare helmet and I've never been in an accident."

"Well, that's all well and good, but--"

"Daddy!" Christine said, bounding down the stairs, and coming to a stop between the two. "What did I say about cross-examining my dates?"

"Now Chrissy," Mr. Baker started, but Mark quickly interjected.

"It's okay," he said. Over time he'd learned to do the opposite of what Joe would do, and Clara had told him these were called 'manners.' "My friend Steve's mom feels the same way about the scooter, but I've always brought him back safe. I can promise to do the same with your daughter."

"Well . . . ," Mr. Baker said, rubbing his chin as if confused by these 'manners' and what they meant for the viability of scooters.

"Daddy, please! It's not really a big deal, okay?" she said, taking a hold of his arm with both hands and looking up at him with fluttering eyes.

With the heavy sigh of one performing an act of unspeakable kindness, Mr. Baker nodded. "I suppose you're right, Chrissy. But don't be too late. We still have some work to do."

"Best Daddy ever! Thank you!" she darted up on her tiptoes and kissed him on the check. She slipped away and pushed Mark towards the door.

As they headed down the walk, Christine tossed her hair back and gave Mark a pained look, "God, they're such a pain in the ass. But you," she grinned. "That was amazing. And they say Jersey's filled with bad boys."

"Hey, fuhgedaboutit," said Mark, shrugging his shoulders and tossing his hands in the air.

She tossed him his helmet and winked at him. "Cute, tough guy. Let's get out here so I can greet you properly."

She wanted to know where all the "cool stuff" was so they drove around for a bit. Mark pointed out his favorite places to eat, the good movie theater up on the Hill and Ridgemont Park near his old middle school, hoping it could pass for cool.

"I think this is it," he finally said over the metal wasp-buzz of the engine.

"This is fine," she said, squeezing him just enough to make him almost run them off the road. "Let's stop here."

They pulled over near a secluded end of Ridgemont, at one end of the big pond near the group of large trees. They picked a seat under one that had a nice cushion of leaves and a pair of big roots that forced them to squeeze close together.

"So this place is nice," she said, nuzzling up next to him.

"The park? Yeah, I used to hang out here all the time, pretending I was fighting ninjas or army guys or whatever." She chuckled. "Or something cooler. Smoking the drugs, or something like that."

"I meant the town. It's kind of charming."

"Oh yeah, real charming. Designed for smug yuppie assholes to feel better about themselves and built on a geographical sliding scale so you can be sure where you fit in on the economic food chain. And if you do live down with the rest of the Morlocks, you better be a tough guy or you're going to eat shit for the rest of your life."

"Well, speaking as one of those yuppie assholes, not every guy from Morlock village has to be a tough guy."

He could feel his face flushing. It was tough remembering the only difference between her and the people he hated was the fact that she was here with him and apparently didn't hate him.

"I'm sorry. It's just that I never wanted live here, but my folks . . ." he stopped, realizing that he was in forbidden territory. There was no way he was going to go into all of that now, if ever.

"Yeah," she said, rolling her eyes. "Folks never give you much choice in anything. You just get dragged around like a rag doll. My brother is older and it was way harder on him. If he hadn't gone to college when he did I think he and Dad would've come to blows by now."

"Really?" Mark said. "In those pictures everyone looks so happy and, well, normal."

"Oh Jesus! My folks are *not* normal. My folks wouldn't know normal if it jumped up and bit them on the ass. My dad's a total workaholic freak and my mom is just obsessed with making sure everything looks okay and in its right place. They're the anti-normal."

"Well, I guess it beats the alternative."

"I dunno. Ever since Ryan moved out my folks have just been all over me, but with the move and everything done it'll be nice to just slow down and just let everything settle."

"That's cool," he said. "Slow is good."

"Well," she grinned, shifting up to kiss him. "Not that good."

After exhausting themselves with an hour of kissing and over-the-clothes groping they just leaned back against the tree, arms and legs intertwined and enjoying the crisp fall air.

"I should be getting back soon," she said. "The last thing I want is my dad getting on your case again."

Mark grinned. "For this, he can get on my case all he wants."

She reached up and took a leaf out of his hair. "You're sweet."

"Really?"

Her fingers left his hair and softly traced a line from his cheek to his chin. "Yes, Mark. You're very sweet. I can't remember if I've met a guy who's been sweeter. You're kind, you're caring, you're considerate. . ."

He chuckled. "What am I, a Cub Scout? Next you'll say I'm loyal and honest."

"Oh, you're those too, I'm sure, but I don't think you realize how rare that is."

"Are we going to get disgusting boyfriend/girlfriend names now?" he asked, kissing her fingertip.

"Well, we'll have to play it by ear. Have to give it some time to find the really disgusting ones."

Mark dropped her off after she made sure neither of them had too many dirt or grass stains on their backs. "Trust me," she'd said, "they're a dead giveaway." At the head of the driveway she gave him a quick kiss on the cheek and a whispered promise to call later.

He spent the ride home trying not to think of the small mound of homework that had piled up over the weekend as he'd lost himself to the sheer awesomeness that was teenage make-outs. He was so into reliving his PG sex-life that he didn't notice the car parked in front of the house as he pulled into the driveway. He locked the V up in the garage and happily dashed to the back door, taking all three steps in one big jump.

He was two strides into the kitchen before he saw Joe sitting at the kitchen table, clutching a coffee mug in both hands and glaring at a man in a suit sitting across the table from him. The smart remark Mark was going to make about them never having company was cut off when he noticed the badge hanging from the man's lapel pocket.

"Mark," Joe said, very evenly, putting down his cup of coffee, "This is David Prescott. With the cops. I think you should have a seat."

Mark sat and listened, but it became more difficult the more that Detective Prescott talked. Mark's gaze dropped to his suddenly lifeless hands on the table as the Detective used words like "fire" and "death." The Detective asked Mark about the party that night and if that was the last time he'd spoken to Clara.

"Party?" Mark mumbled. Everything was quicksand, words and thoughts sinking into the nothingness in his chest. Why would there be a party?

"The delivery guy from the Chinese place next door said he dropped some food off at the shop after hours and that there were a couple of other people in there. Alvin, the delivery guy, said he recognized you, that you were at Clara's a lot."

"Yeah, he hung out there," Joe said, wringing his hands on the coffee mug.

Mark nodded in agreement. Everything was graying back out again. Yes, he hung out there. He was supposed to keep hanging out there. It was his place. Mark's vision was blurring and his pulse was roaring in his ears. He knew the Detective was saying something else but he was concentrating on blinking away his tears.

"Excuse me?" he said softly, hoping his voice did have too much strain in it.

"This wasn't an accident, Mark. This is being treated as a homicide."

"What?"

"Mark," David said, "Can you think of anyone that may have had a reason to hurt Clara, or if there was anything unusual about that night? Did she say or do anything out of the ordinary?"

Well, there was this phantom guy that tried to throw you down the stairs, but he probably wasn't real or even human, so that doesn't mean much aside from the fact that you're batshit crazy.

They stared at each other for a second, Mark's eyes still misting and he realized he was taking too long to answer. The longer he didn't say anything the more obvious it was that he could be saying something and wasn't.

But there was no man, and if you say anything you'll look so crazy they'll probably take you downtown to talk about it more. And I bet they don't need the phone books or rubber hoses to crack your shell, sissy.

"No," Mark said softly. "Nothing at all. She was the greatest person in the world. She . . ." Mark tried to think of a way to convey to these men that would never know her how important she'd been to him, but realized that it was futile. Nothing he could say would show how much she meant and how impossible someone wanting to murder her was.

"She had a daughter," Mark said, trying to stay away from total blinding despair and focusing on being helpful.

"Yeah," the Detective said. "We found her information in an address book and we've already notified her. We're going to have to talk with the other people that were with you that night. Just a formality, but we have to be thorough."

Mark's heart sank. Steve's mom would freak, and Christine's dad would now have something better than the V to worry about. He recited their names and address for the Detective to jot down in his little notebook, so he could go forth and make an even bigger wreck of his life.

Before he left, the Detective turned back to Mark, handing him a business card. "If you can think of anything, and I do mean anything, feel free to call me."

Mark nodded and watched him go. Joe walked him to the front door and Mark made it as far as the hallway before he stopped and leaned on the wall. When the door closed behind the cops, Joe turned and said "I know this must be hard but . . . I just want you to know--"

That was all he needed to get him off the wall. "Save it," he shook his head and pushed himself back onto his feet, storming past Joe and heading for the stairs. "You hated her. You couldn't stand that someone gave a shit about me and I don't need your pity. Not now." He took the stairs two at a time, pausing only to throw open the attic door before bounding up the rest of the stairs. Before he made it to the top of the steps, everything was blurry and wet and shaking. His foot didn't clear the top step and he sprawled forward onto his knees and hands, crashing into the side of his bed.

He shoved it as hard as he could, and then swung at it over and over again, not seeing anything but indistinct shapes. Whatever it was in front of him, he wanted it gone. Destroyed. Burned.

He screamed until all he had left were silent, chest heaving sobs and sore hands that lashed out in weak futility.

CHAPTER NINE

Mark wasn't sure when he'd pulled himself into bed but it hadn't made him any more comfortable. He woke up with a wet pillow and limbs tangled in sheets. Something had startled him awake and he wasn't sure what it was until there was another yell of his name from downstairs and getting closer.

"Mark! Telephone!" Joe yelled through his door.

"I got it!" Mark screamed back, picking up. "Hello?"

"Mark, it's me," Christine said. Mark dropped himself back on the bed.

"Hey."

"Mark, I'm so, so sorry. How're you doing?"

He sighed, rubbing his forehead. "I . . . I don't even know. It doesn't seem real."

"Yeah, I know. The detective guy just left, and . . . god, my parents are so freaked."

"I'm sorry," Mark said.

"Don't be, they're just being dicks. I just hope yours are handling this better."

Now this too. "Christine," he said, "I don't have any folks."

"What do you mean?"

"I mean," he said with a deep sigh, "I don't have parents anymore. I live with my Uncle Joe, that's the guy who picked up when you called. I've lived with him since I was little, and Clara . . . Clara was like a mom to me, and now . . ." he stopped, trying to keep the crack in his voice from exploding into tears.

"Oh, Mark," Christine said, and he could feel the pity in her voice. He wasn't sure what made him feel worse: her thinking he was a weirdo or her pitying him. "I'm sorry. This has got to be so hard for you."

"Yeah, it's . . . well, there aren't really any words. I'm just sorry I got you involved in all of this. I knew you were going to find out about my folks sooner or later, but I didn't want it to be like this. It was stupid to hide it and I'm sorry. I know I must seem like a freak and you probably don't want anything to do with me after all this."

"Mark, as fucked up as all of this is, I'm not going to abandon you or anything. I really like you and I want to help you get through this, okay?"

"Yeah?"

"Yeah. Look, I should probably go try to settle my folks down or something, but I'll see you tomorrow. Try to take it easy, alright?"

"I will. Christine?"

"Yeah?"

"Thanks. I mean it."

"No problem. Bye."

After hanging up he staggered downstairs and got some food while dodging Joe's questions of "Who was that?" and "What did she want?" He mumbled his way through an explanation and as soon as he was finished he went back upstairs to try to make a dent in his homework.

Despite his nap earlier, he felt his mind sagging under the weight of exhaustion. His eyes fluttered and he let the pencil fall from his hand. He rolled over, pushing the books off the edge of the bed. That would fix it, he realized. He'd just sleep for years and it would all just be a distant memory by the time he woke up.

It was supposed to be a good day, right? The best day? Well, I guess we all get what we deserve.

He was waking up, but he felt lost again. He was dizzy, and when he went to rub some sleep from his face he realized there was nothing there. No hands and no face. He was just floating and formless in near total darkness. He thought for a second that something had ended and he'd be snuffed out just like Clara had been. Before he could decide if that would be a relief or a tragedy someone turned on a light.

It was Clara, still alive and in her apartment, walking towards him. She was coming from her bedroom and wearing a nightgown, wiping sleep from her eyes. He was standing (or floating) in her kitchen. He called out to her, but there was nothing. No hands, no face and apparently, no voice.

She stopped in front of him and reached out for the refrigerator. She paused for a second, her nose twitching, and then she turned to look right at him. Before he could tell if she could tell he was there a hand launched out of the darkness next to him and crushed her wrist, forcing her down on one knee.

Mark was screaming and thrashing in his own mind, but nothing he thought could affect anything around him. From the darkness stepped the figure he'd seen in the apartment before, covered in swirling smoke and where eyes would be under the hat shaped smoke two tiny flames burst to life.

The cane with the silver head swung out from the smoke, and just as Mark recognized it from his dream it smashed into Clara's head. Once, twice and then a third time. He let go of her wrist and she tumbled to the ground, finally letting out a low moan as she pulled her injured wrist close to her chest.

He circled her as she rolled over, swinging the cane down on her back. She doubled up in pain, trying to cover as much of herself as she could as he swung down on her again and again.

The man stopped, turning his fiery eyes to Mark, and he could see the swirling smoke and blackness of his face twist into a smile.

"Oh yes," he said, his voice a rumbling echo of the one Darren had heard in Mark's dream.

There was a long metallic scrape and Clara, who'd been doubled over and whimpering, looked up. The man drew the blade from the cane-sheath slowly, moving to stand directly over her, his legs straddling her.

"Don't! Don't! Whatever you want, just don't do this! Not her," Mark tried to yell, but there was still nothing.

Clara turned, and Mark realized she was looking towards him. The flames in the man's eyes followed her gaze and then the blade swung down on the back of her neck.

With no eyelids or hands, there was no way for him to look away as her head did a little hop and then rolled about a foot to the left of her body.

The man stood there watching as the blood drained onto the tile. He dabbed the tip of the blade into the growing puddle and the blood began to creep upward, coating it with red. When the blade was fully covered, he slipped it back into its sheath.

He turned and headed for the door, rubbing the fingers of his free hand together. A ball of smoke collected in his hand, and then with a snap of his fingers a tiny flame burst to life in his palm. As the man walked past Mark's disembodied dream-self and out the back patio door Mark found himself pulled along with him. As he reached the edge of the patio the man tossed the ball of flame over his shoulder. It landed in the center of the kitchen, a few feet in front of Clara's headless body. The flames spread quickly, burning along the floor fast but curving around Clara's body and head as they made their way towards the living room.

The man stepped off the edge of the patio and Mark found himself plunging into darkness again.

CHAPTER TEN

Mark never got around to finishing his homework. The next day in class he mumbled an excuse to Mr. Bucco, who stared at him with his beady, rodent eyes and told Mark that he expected it tomorrow, no excuses. Mark wasn't surprised that threats from a balding algebra teacher didn't have the same weight as they had on Friday.

Steve met him at his locker after class, and after a moment of the two just staring at each other, Steve reached out and put his arm around Mark's shoulders.

"Dude. I don't know what to say."

"It's okay," Mark said, shrugging Steve's arm off his shoulders before anyone saw.

Steve shook his head. "Light years away from okay. This has got to be . . . well, I can't imagine it. I mean, when my Grams died, it was weird, but this--"

"It's a little different," Mark said, walking off. By the time Steve caught up with him Mark was relieved that the hallway was a little less crowded.

"I know, totally different, you're right." Steve said. "I have to tell you my mom was wicked pissed when that cop showed up. I mean, you know how much of a hard-ass she can be, but this? Whoa, baby."

"I'm sorry it's such an inconvenience to her," Mark said, making a quick left into a stairwell.

"Dude, tell me about it. I mean, this is the fucking *cops!*" Steve said. Mark glanced sideways as one of the field hockey girls walked past, her eyes actually shifting over a bit to look at Steve and Mark.

Mark let out a sigh and drew up short on the steps when they were finally alone. "Look," Mark said, stopping Steve with a hand on his shoulder, "I know you're trying to help and all, but please don't talk about this at school. I don't want people knowing this kind of shit about me, okay?"

"Oh," Steve said. "Of course. Yeah, you're right, that was dumb of me."

"Steve . . ."

"What?"

"Did you--" Mark didn't even have to finish the question before he knew they answer. So much for acting.

"I'm sorry," Steve pleaded. "I just mentioned it to Shannon in first period. I mean, she asked me what I did this weekend, and, y'know, this is kind of a big deal."

Mark balled his hand into a fist and pressed it into the throbbing pain growing between his eyes. Shannon Brown wasn't the biggest gossip in the whole world, just the biggest one in the drama club. And no one in drama club ever spoke out of turn, or gave much thought to rumor. No, not someone in the theater.

"I'm sorry," Steve said, but Mark couldn't see past the knot of rage that was spreading in his brain. By the end of the day it'd be over half the school, by tomorrow, it'd be everywhere. "She's in my next class and I'll tell her not to say anything to anyone."

Oh yeah, that'll work. He can totally put that gossip outbreak monkey back in her cage.

"Just . . . don't tell anybody else, okay?"

"Yeah. Of course. Man that was so stupid, I just can't believe that I didn't think--"

"Can we just drop it please?" Mark brushed past him and tried to leave the knot on the stairwell behind him.

"So, how's your girl? How's she handling all this?"

Mark let out a sigh. "She's fine. She called me last night and we talked, but I think her parents are going to give yours a run for their money in the 'freaked' department. Not to mention the fact that I had to level with her about Joe and the whole 'I'm an orphan' problem."

"Ouch. But she's cool, right? I mean, you don't want to let a chick like that slip away."

First smart thing he's said all morning.

"Yeah, she's cool."

"Very cool," Steve said with a wink and a nudge. "Look, I'm sorry for the screw up, but I'll try to think of some way to make it up to you, okay? Or I'll think of a way and tell Christine to do it to you from me."

"Get out of here," Mark said, rolling his eyes. "I gotta get to class, and you do too."

"Right on, man." Steve turned to go, but then stopped and looked over his shoulder. "I really am sorry, Mark. About everything."

"I know, man. I know."

It didn't come up again the rest of the day, and lunch was spent with Steve and Christine talking about happier things, although Mark could swear that more people glanced their way than had the other day. *You're being paranoid. Not like you don't have a right to be, but still.*

Even though the conversation didn't turn back to what happened to Clara it never left Mark's mind. It was as clear in his head now as when he woken up with a yell last night. What little sleep he'd gotten the rest of the night was punctuated with wondering if what he'd dreamt was just a mélange of his crazy visions and dreams or something that had really happened.

It crazier than anything else that had happened this weekend (and what an accomplishment that was), but when he remembered the dream he could feel the heat from the fire and smell the smoke and burning blood. No dream had ever felt so real, and he knew that there was only one way he could be sure if he going crazy or if this was something far worse.

***

"Detective Prescott? You've got a Mark Watson here to see you," the desk sergeant said.

"Okay, I'll be right down," David said, hanging up the phone.

David welcomed the distraction from staring at the paperwork and various reports on his desk. Maybe Mark could tell him something that would help him make sense of all this. He'd been planning to go see him again anyway, so this saved him some time.

Mark was sitting downstairs on one of the benches near the desk sergeant, drumming his fingers on the backpack on his lap. He knew Ms. Washington's death had disturbed Mark a lot, but today grief had been replaced with a nervous energy that was usually reserved for the guilty or the scared.

"Mark, how're you doing?" Dave said as he came up to the bench.

"Well, I'm okay. Better, I guess."

"That's good. What can I do for you?"

"Yeah . . . is there was some place we could talk?"

David nodded. "Sure, I think I can arrange that. Follow me."

He led Mark down a hallway and into one of the small interview rooms. He sat behind the table and motioned for Mark to do likewise. The kid hesitated, taking the room in before sitting, setting his backpack on the table between them.

"So what's up?"

"I . . . I just wanted to talk about Clara," he said, still glancing around the room.

"Don't worry, all the recording stuff is off. This is just between you and me. What about her?"

"I just wanted to know, to really know, what happened to her."

"Mark, I don't want go in too much detail because this is still an ongoing investigation and well . . . it's a little gruesome and I don't want to upset you. Obviously you and Clara were very close."

"I'm not . . . Yeah, okay, I'm upset." He started rubbing his forehead, eyes down on the table. "Clara was like a mom to me. When my aunt died, she was one of the only people that was able to be my friend without coddling me or making me feel like I was being pitied. She was one of the greatest people I ever knew and now she's gone, and I'm just trying to figure out what happened."

David waited as Mark's hand wiped at his eyes. "Mark, this is a real terrible tragedy, but--"

"That's what I'm saying!" Mark said, throwing his hands in the air. "Yeah, it's terrible that she's dead and now I'm all alone, but what if it was just an accident? How do you know someone did this?"

"Mark, we're pretty sure about this kind of stuff."

"How? If there was a fire how can you be so sure?" Mark was leaning forward, gripping the edges of the table. "If her body--"

"Mark, her body wasn't burned. Yes, there was a fire, but she wasn't in it. She was assaulted. That's how we know it wasn't just the fire."

Mark trembled, dropping his arms to the table so suddenly that it echoed around them.

"No. It can't be . . . that can't be right." Mark's trembling hands came up to his face as he tried to hide his tears. "Not like that. Not like that."

"Mark," David said, getting up and moving his chair next to Mark's. "We're going to figure this out. We're going to find who did this."

Mark wiped his eyes, quickly and then he gave a manic chuckle. "Oh god I hope so. I hope he fucking fries."

"I can get you a tissue, if you--"

"No, no." Mark said, shaking his head violently. "I'm sorry. I shouldn't have come down here, I just . . . I just needed to know. I just can't believe she . . ." His hand drifted down to his neck, squeezing it for a second. "I just was hoping she didn't die like that. I just wanted it to be an accident."

"I know, Mark." Dave said, getting to his feet. "Are you going to be okay?"

"Yeah, I think so, thanks. I'm sorry, I didn't I mean to get all . . . y'know."

"Don't worry about it."

Mark picked his backpack up from the table, and was just out of the door when David called him back.

"Mark, can I ask you something?"

"Yeah, sure."

"Why didn't you tell me about hearing something upstairs that night?"

Everything that had drained out of Mark came rushing back, his body tensing and his face flushing with color. It was a cheap ploy but David knew it was his best chance at getting an honest reaction out of him. Sudden panic seemed pretty genuine.

"What do you mean?" Mark said.

"Well, both Christine and Steve said that you thought you heard someone upstairs that night, but you didn't say anything to me about it."

Mark swallowed, and David just stared, hands in his pockets.

"I was a little embarrassed. I fell down the stairs because I thought I saw someone but it turned out that it was nothing. I was trying to forget about it, and with Clara's death and all I didn't think it was a big deal."

"You forgot about it or you didn't think it was a big deal?"

Mark's eyes narrowed for a second, but he relaxed and shrugged his shoulders. "I dunno. I guess I forgot about it when you first came to see me, but later, when I did remember, I didn't think it was important enough to mention. We didn't see anyone up there."

"Yeah, that's what they said, but I was just curious. If there's anything else like that, you let me know. Even if you don't think it's important, it might mean something to us."

"Yeah, of course."

David nodded and walked Mark back to the front entrance where they parted ways. Back at his desk, David pushed the various photos and scene reports around, as if they could make sense in different piles. His favorite was the note from the fire investigators that said "Fire doesn't burn like this," noting the perfect circle around Clara Washington's body and head that had been left untouched as the rest of the apartment burned.

The fire hadn't burned for long before the neighbor in the next building saw the smoke coming out of the back, and David wondered if that patch of floor would've been left in the rubble of the building still untouched and proudly displaying its decapitated passenger if the fire had been allowed to burn.

Now, instead of that mystery preying on his mind on his mind he had something else bothering him. It was Mark, clutching his throat protectively, muttering "Not like that."

CHAPTER ELEVEN

"I really don't want to do this," Mark said, tugging at his collar.

"Oh relax, it's clean. Now stop doing that or I'll never get this damn thing tied," Steve said, slapping away Mark's hand and going back to work the tie. "I'm used to doing this on myself and everything looks backwards."

They were in Steve's luxury suite sized room getting ready for Clara's funeral. Mark had realized that the suit that he had worn to his Aunt's funeral was now painfully small and called Steve in a panic. Of course, Steve had an abundance of clothes that could pass as funeral wear. Unfortunately Steve was an inch taller and wider than Mark, so he felt like he was getting ready for clown college instead of a funeral. It was just one more thing to feel uncomfortable and awkward about.

"No," Mark said, "this whole thing. I shouldn't go to the funeral, no one even invited me."

Steve rolled his eyes. "Mark, funerals aren't invitation only. There's a reason why they put them in the newspaper, y'know, with the date and time and all that shit. Besides, we're getting the day off from school. There," he said, wiggling the knot around. "You're gorgeous. Go check your fine ass out."

"I could give a crap about school," Mark said, pushing his hair around, not really sure what else he should be doing with it. The enthusiasm he'd had for grooming had left him when Clara did. "I still feel . . ."

You feel like if you actually saw the person get killed you shouldn't go to the funeral.

"Mark, she was one of your closest friends. Not going is something that you'd regret for the rest of your life."

"I know, I know," Mark said, turning away from the mirror. "I'm just really nervous."

"What do you have to be nervous about?" Steve said, still looking in the mirror and fixing his hair.

"I just feel like everyone will be watching me. That I won't . . . I dunno. I just don't want people to freak out because I'm there."

"Mark," Steve said, turning to glare at him out of the corner of his eye. "I'm not trying to be a dick here, but I think people are going to have other things on their mind than you."

Mark sighed. "You're right. Let's just get this over with, okay?"

Steve had gotten his parents' permission to miss school for the funeral and to borrow his mother's car for the day so they wouldn't have to drive around in formal clothes on the back of a scooter. Joe had just shrugged his shoulders and told Mark that if he needed to go he could go. Clara's daughter, Persephone, who had flown in over the weekend, arranged the funeral. Mark had never met her and Clara had told him that the two hadn't been in touch much since Clara's husband passed away.

The funeral home was irritatingly cheerful and in the same middle-class DMZ that Steve lived in and helped Cedar Ridge put a happy face on class warfare. They walked in and headed towards the archway marked "Washington Funeral," and were handed tiny prayer cards by the funeral directors.

There were at least forty people milling about the room, standing together in small groups. There were a couple of glances towards them when they entered, and that was enough to make Mark stop in his tracks and take a seat at the closest chair.

"Yeah, here is good," Steve said, taking the chair next to him. "Why walk around when there's a chair right here?"

"Knock it off," Mark said with his mouth clenched, looking around the room.

"Do you see anyone you recognize?"

"There's the guy that has the Chinese food place next to hers. A couple of the regular customers, but that's it. I never really met her family."

"Do you want to go say Hi or something?"

"I'm fine right here."

Steve sighed. "Okay, fair enough."

There was a large photo of Clara on a stand next to a podium at the front of the room. The photo had been taken outdoors and she looked years younger. She was looking over her shoulder and smiling, the sunlight behind her giving her a divine luminescence. Next to the photo was a small pedestal with an urn on top.

He didn't want her burned, so they did it anyway. Way to have the last word, family members.

After several minutes, a woman in her early thirties came to the podium, and everyone in the room who was still milling around found a seat. Next to her mother's picture, the resemblance between the two was striking.

Persephone began talking but Mark tuned her out, staring only at Clara's picture. When Aunt Martha died, Clara had told him that she never believed death was an ending, just another step in a never-ending journey. Whenever Clara talked like that he'd just roll his eyes behind her back and nod and smile. She'd also told him that everything "worked out for the best," but Mark knew that was crap too.

There wasn't anything about this that worked out for the best.

Persephone stopped talking and there was a smattering of applause and "Amen's."

Only a few more people spoke, and then the service began to disperse. Mark and Steve got up, and as Mark turned to leave the room, he found himself face to face with Detective Prescott.

"Mark. Steve. How's it going?" he said.

"Good. Y'know, all things considered," Steve said. The detective turned to look at Mark, who just nodded his head in agreement.

Hey, maybe he wants more lame, half-assed answers for your erratic and sketchy behavior. Or maybe he's a crying enthusiast like you.

"Well, if you guys will excuse me, I'm going to go pay my respects," Detective Prescott said.

Steve continued towards the door, but Mark stayed where he was. Once Steve realized Mark wasn't with him, he turned back to him. "Hey, what's up?"

"I . . ." Mark started, but trailed off as he watched the detective go over to Persephone, who was standing next to a wide, stocky Asian man with a crew cut. The detective held out his hand, and after a moment, Persephone and her companion took a turn shaking it.

"Mark?" Steve repeated, coming back up along side of him. "What's wrong?"

"Nothing." Mark said, still not looking at him. The detective and Persephone were talking, and he could tell that whatever he was saying wasn't what she wanted to hear. Her voice was rising but not loud enough for Mark to hear from across the room. The Asian man put his arm around Persephone and she leaned into him.

Then she turned and meet Mark's gaze.

Everything froze as she squinted at him, trying to place where they may have met before. Mark's first instinct was to turn and look away, but he realized that if he did it too quickly he'd look strange. Stranger than staring someone down at their mother's funeral at least.

Detective Prescott looked over as well and Mark suddenly felt the weight of his lie pressing down on him like a giant, bloody stamp saying "GUILTY!"

"C'mon, let's go," Mark said. Breaking the stare took every ounce of willpower he had.

"Mark do you want to go over there, pay your respects?" Steve said, trailing after Mark as he headed for the door.

"No," Mark said, pushing open the door and taking a deep lungful of air. "Clara knew she had my respects."

"I think you're being paranoid," Christine said the next day after school as they headed for the bike rack where the V was parked.

"Why?" Mark said, trying to keep his voice down to an inconspicuous level. "Why else do you think he was there? Why do you think she was looking at me like that? They think that I'm involved! They--" he lowered his voice as someone passed by. "They probably have me as a suspect."

"Mark, c'mon," she said. "There's no way he thinks any of us are involved. He was probably just there to be nice."

"No," Mark said. "When I went to see him last week he asked me why I didn't say anything to him about the whole falling down the stairs thing."

"You didn't? Why not?"

"I don't know," Mark said, fumbling with his keys. "I just didn't think it was important. I mean, I thought it was just me falling down the steps, not some huge deal."

"It wasn't," she said, putting a hand on his shoulder. "It just came out when he asked if anything unusual happened. I wasn't trying to say anything about you or--"

"I know, I know. I just hate how it makes me look. Like I was trying to hide something."

She reached out and placed her hand on his cheek. "You don't have anything to hide, do you?"

Yes.

"No."

"Then relax. There's nothing you can do about what they think."

He knelt down, placing his helmet on the ground as he unlocked the chain around the bike. He just had the chain unlocked when he heard Christine say "Mark," in a warning tone. He glanced up and the keys slipped through his fingers.

Jack was strolling towards them with three of his friends in tow: Victor and Kyle from gym class and Eric Simmons, Jack's co-captain on the lacrosse team. There was nothing like a quartet of assholes to really drive home a bad day.

"Hey Mark," Jack said. "How's it going, buddy?" As they got closer Vic, Kyle and Eric spread out in a semi-circle around Mark, trapping him with his back to the bike rack.

"What do you want, Jack?" Mark said, picking up his helmet and getting to his feet, straightening up as tall as his limited self-confidence would allow. Christine drifted behind him, apparently laboring under the delusion that he'd be able to protect her.

Fuck that. You better do something about this you coward, before she sees you for what you really are.

"Nothing, man. This has got to be a tough time for you," Jack said with a lazy grin. "I mean, I know blacks liked barbecue, but damn!"

Everything slowed down. He could hear Christine gasp as Jack and his friends snickered in satisfaction. His hand was damp and sweaty from clutching his helmet in a death-grip.

"That's fucking sick," Christine said, moving out from behind him.

*Oh look. *She's* going to protect *you!**

"Oh, don't get your cunt in a twist, sweetie, I'm just having fun with him."

"Go fuck yourself," she said, taking another step towards Jack.

Jack rolled his head around from right to left, letting out a deep, sorrowful sigh. "Mark, control your bitch before I put her in her place."

"Like you could, asshole," she said, crossing her arms over her chest.

Jack turned and glared at her. "Mark, I'm going to seriously hurt this bitch if you don't tell her to keep her fucking mouth shut. Now, why don't we--"

"Leave her alone," Mark growled.

"Well," Jack said, turning his head to look at Mark. "Look who grew a pai--"

And then the helmet smashed into Jack's mouth.

He stumbled backwards, blood spilling from his already swelling lips. Jack raised a hand to his mouth, wiped it, and looked at the red in his hand. Mark looked down at his own hand, still rattling slightly from the impact, and the bike helmet he hadn't even realized he'd swung. The shiver in his arm was replaced by his heart pounding in his chest. It felt good.

Really, really good.

The good feeling lasted only until he looked back at Jack. Jack's surprise had been converted to anger, his cheeks blooming with red that nearly matched the blood dripping from his mouth. Jack spat a bloody wad of it on the ground and raised his fists, shuffling to one side and then springing forward.

Jack swung wildly, and Mark barely stepped out of the way. His dodge carried him inside the swing and he brought the helmet up, catching Jack on the point of his chin. His head snapped back, and Mark kicked him in the stomach, pushing him down on his back.

"Motherfucker," Eric said, stepping in from Mark's right. Mark turned and snarled. That flash of anger was enough to make Eric's drawn back fist waver, and Mark rewarded his indecision by clasping the helmet in both hands and driving it forward with all of his strength, smashing the top into Eric's nose. He toppled backwards, hands going to stem the sudden eruption of blood. Eric's foot caught on the edge of the bike rack and he lost his balance, falling ass over elbow to the ground.

There was a high-pitched yell that gave Mark just enough time to dodge out of the way of Jack's berserk charge. He crashed into the bike rack and whirled around. His blood smeared mouth twisted in rage, eyes bulging and face purple. He pushed off from the rack and sprung forward. Mark retreated, backing towards the crowd of kids that had begun to form.

Mark planted his feet, cocked back his helmet-hand and held his other hand palm-out, fingers spread. Jack stopped short and raised his fists again. Around them, Mark could see more kids running to join the expanding crowd.

There had been times where Mark had fantasized of this moment. He was usually wielding a sword or flame thrower or a high powered rifle, but revenge was revenge.

Destroy him. Put him down now, once and for all.

Jack lunged forward with a jab, and Mark stepped to the side, swatting the fist away with his free hand. Jack swung again, and Mark ducked under it and swung the helmet up, hitting him across the jaw. Jack staggered, and Mark swung again, smashing him on one cheek, and then swinging backhanded and hitting the other. Jack wobbled on his feet, hands dropping down to his waist. With a triumphant scream, Mark swung again, hitting Jack in the temple and driving him down on one knee.

Mark tossed aside the helmet with another yell and moved in for the kill.

***

Fist-fights and male teenage bullshit were nothing new to Christine. The boys she knew in Boston were practically choking themselves on it to prove whose balls were bigger. Even "messing with the nerds" was standard fare, and although she'd never admit it she'd done her share of laughing at boys like Mark when they got put on the spot and started tripping over their own social inadequacies.

She'd never seen anything like the gleeful venom that spewed forth from Jack or the rage on his face when Mark hit him. What erupted before her was wholly new, and as Mark screamed in triumph after battering Jack with his helmet she wasn't sure which if the two was more dangerous.

Mark tossed the helmet aside ("I had to save up for months to get it," he'd said with earnest pride just a couple days earlier) and it skidded to stop at her feet. Along the top there was a jagged crack forming, dotted with blood.

Mark had crawled atop Jack, grabbing a handful of t-shirt with his left hand and slamming his right down into Jack's face.

"Leave . . . me . . . alone!" Mark snarled, accentuating each word with a punch. Jack flailed his arms, desperately and pitifully slapping at the punches as they rained down on him.

"Mark!" she shouted, stepping forward, but one of the boys that had surrounded them grabbed her wrist and pulled her back.

"I don't think so, bitch," he said, putting a hand on her shoulder and pulling her out of the way as he walked past her. Jack's other friend, who'd watched the whole thing in gape-mouthed silence was shaken to action by his friend's sudden movement. Mark didn't notice either of them, concentrating instead on Jack's bloody face.

Christine grabbed the boys hand before he pulled away, and when he turned to look she swung her knee up into his balls. His surprise turned into gasping pain and the shocked look that boys got when every urban legend and health film about exploded testicles flashed before their eyes.

She ran forward and got to the other boy just before he grabbed Mark, slamming into him with all her weight, and sending him skidding on his face across the gravel of the parking lot.

"Mark!" Christine screamed, grabbing the back of his jacket and trying to pull him to his feet.

Mark turned and his eyes were blurry with tears and squinted with concentrated hatred. For a second it didn't seem like he recognized her, but she grabbed his clenched fist (it was sticky and hard to get a hold of) and pulled Mark away from Jack's stunned and moaning figure.

"We have to go!"

The fist in her hand began to tremble, and she realized Mark was coming back from whatever ugly sinkhole he'd lost himself in.

The kid Christine pushed had rolled over and was glaring at them. Mark took a couple of steps back, and then grinned, letting out a coughing, tear-choked laugh. He stumbled towards the scooter, reaching down and scooping up his helmet.

After a couple of false starts the scooter lunged forward. Mark held the bloody helmet in his lap and once she knew her grip on him was solid, she looked back to make sure they weren't being chased. Jack was sitting up and watching them drive off, face spattered with blood and eyes burning with impotent rage.

***

"Mark! Mark, slow down! Please!"

A blurry car-esque shape sped in front of him with a horn blaring and Mark realized he couldn't see clearly. He swerved out of the way, the V listing perilously. Christine's hold on him tightened and he could feel her face press into his back.

For a way to go this wouldn't be half bad. Go out on a high note, right?

Once the scooter had righted itself he slowed down and risked using a hand to wipe at his eyes. Once he could see clearly he rounded a corner to a quiet side street, pulled over to the curb and shut the engine off. He was panting, wheezing in and out through a phlegm-packed nose, and his entire body was shaking.

Well, it's what you get for acting like a rabid animal. Was it everything you hoped for, killer? Better than the fantasy with the axe, or the one where you're strangling him in front of all of his smug fucking friends?

She was tugging at him, trying to get him to turn around and look at her. Whatever sudden adrenaline-fueled strength he had was now gone, leaving only a panic stricken mess. It was the last thing he wanted her to see.

"Oh god, oh god," he sobbed, pulling away and putting his head on the handlebars.

"It's okay," she said, getting off the V and kneeling in the street next to him. She pulled him to her again and he didn't have the strength to resist this time, letting the sobs come in full force as he leaned into her shoulder.

Again with the crying? Jesus, it's a wonder you're not dehydrated all the time. Pick one: crybaby or lunatic. We can't do both, you don't have that much depth.

He thought he could smell blood on her but he realized it was him, on his hands and probably on his face from when he wiped his eyes. He tried to pull away but she held him in place. "It's okay," she whispered. "It's all over now."

He rested his head on her shoulder looking down at his stinging, wet hands in his lap.

No it's not, tough guy. Now it'll never be over. You know that, right? Jack will never let this go and he's going to turn your temporary victory into the first shot in an all-out war.

CHAPTER TWELVE

What Mark hated the most after subjecting someone to one of his hysterical crying breakdowns was how they looked at him afterward. First it's with sincere looks of concern, as if he'd break down again at any moment over something ridiculous, like "I asked for Coke not Pepsi! Bawwww!" Over time, when it became obvious that pathetic weeping wasn't going to be an all the time thing, the reaction became a kind of offhand teasing as if the whole thing was a joke or magic trick that he'd maybe whip out if given enough encouragement. "Hey, I made sure I brought you a Coke so you wouldn't freak out like you did last time."

Why couldn't they just let it go? Did they think he enjoyed reminiscing about it? Last year in Biology Ken Shenkman randomly turned to him and said "Hey, remember that time in 7th grade when Mr. Hollman made you cry at the black board? That was pretty wild, huh?"

No, it wasn't "wild," Mark thought, it was something I was trying to forget but thanks for bringing it up fucknozzle.

It was even in Steve's eyes, sometimes with concern, like the other day at the funeral, and sometimes with that mischievous "I take things too far" glint. The only person that never had it was Clara and she'd seen him plenty of times at his blubbering, snot-caked worst.

Now it was in Christine's eyes.

He saw it when he dropped her off at home and she waved at him when he looked back at her. He realized there was more to it when he kissed her cheek and she pulled back ever-so-slightly. This wasn't just about crybaby Mark Watson, this was about the "New and Improved Holy Shit He Beat That Guy with a Helmet" Mark Watson. He wanted to say the perfect something to make her realize that today was just the final straw in a long line of horrid, humiliating straws that he never thought he'd get rid of, but there was no way.

The girl he was going to have the fresh start with and who he wanted to be perfect for just saw him at the worst he'd ever been. So much for that plan.

Mark wasn't surprised when he got to homeroom the next day and there was a referral to go directly to the office. He'd spent the night wondering when Detective Prescott would show up at his door, helmet retrieved from the garage and held aloft in a plastic bag. Finally, the piece of evidence he needed to bring Mark Watson down to the station and sweat him out under the lights.

There was no helmet or lights, and thankfully no dreams that night either (although he wasn't sure if he'd slept long enough to have any). A couple of the kids he knew nodded at him when he passed them on the office, one of them even putting up his dukes and bobbing and weaving around until he passed. Mark wasn't sure if he was being congratulated or mocked.

Are you Mark Watson? What do you think?

The office for Mark's end of the alphabet was in the basement and when he got there he showed his pass to the secretary. She waved him to a seat while she buzzed the inner office to let them know he was here and probably to bring out the Lecter-style restraints. He hadn't said a thing to Joe about what happened, and it finally sank in that he wasn't going to be able to keep it from him. And Joe would not just talk about it he'd yell and take things away because that was the way things were done.

"Mr. Watson, right in here," a voice rumbled at him. Standing in the doorway of one of the offices was Mr. Lafayette, the assistant principal assigned to this office. Mr. Lafayette was tall and built with the semi-loose muscles of an athlete who had left his prime far behind him. His skin was deep brown, his head was clean shaven and he wore a pair of glasses that were almost comically small for his stern, imposing face.

Mark squeezed past Mr. Lafayette and was directed to take a seat in front of the desk next to Ms. Kennedy, Mark's guidance counselor. She was in her mid twenties and as small as Mr. Lafayette was large, with shoulder length, tightly curled black hair and an olive complexion. The only times he'd talked to her was when he was picking out classes for the next year.

He'd never been in Mr. Lafayette's office before, but realized that if it had the two-way glass it'd be a dead ringer for the "interview room" he'd talked to Detective Prescott in.

"So," Mr. Lafayette said, taking a seat across from Mark "would you care to explain to us the events of yesterday afternoon?"

I think they speak for themselves.

"Well," Mark said, sitting on his hands to keep them from shaking. "I, ah, got into a fight with some guys, and, uh, then I went home."

"You just 'got into a fight?'" Mr. Lafayette said, leaning back and crossing his arms. "A fight that landed one student in the hospital because you hit him repeatedly with a," he paused to look down through his glasses to consult the folder that lay open in front of him, "helmet of some sort. It just sort of happened, right? Just like that?" Mark took a breath and held it, trying to make everything perfectly still.

"Not just, I . . . I was minding my own business and they came up and started it. I didn't do anything!"

"You don't put another student in the hospital by not doing anything, Mr. Watson. Do you know that Jack's father was talking about suing? Not just you, Mr. Watson, but the entire school district."

"I . . . I didn't know that."

"Now you do," Mr. Lafayette said. "So what do you have to say for yourself, Mr. Watson?"

"They . . . " Mark said, his voice a tiny squeak, looking from Mr. Lafayette to Ms. Kennedy, who sat with her fingertips at her chin like she was carved from marble. He swallowed and tried again. "They started it, sir. They just came up, and they, they just started messing with us! I was just defending myself and they just kept pushing at me!"

Mr. Lafayette's eyes narrowed and Mark hoped that he hadn't made things worse for himself. "So 'they started it'," he said, no trace of question in his voice. "That's your story."

"It's no story! That's the way it happened! Jack and his friends have been pushing me and pushing me for years and this time I pushed back! I was defending myself, and my, uh, girlfriend."

"If these boys have been bothering you so much, why didn't you report it to a teacher or Ms. Kennedy?"

Do you seriously work at a school? Really? Are you sure you don't just hunker down in here and wait for the lights to go out?

Mark closed his eyes and tried to keep from letting his breath out in an exasperated sigh. "Well--" Mark started, trying to find a way to explain it that wasn't like how you'd talk to a child.

"Actually," Ms. Kennedy interrupted, "this happens quite frequently. Students don't feel comfortable reporting bullying or intimidation to other authority figures. I thought I had given you that article about it I found over the summer to read. Fascinating stuff, really."

"I must have missed that one," Mr. Lafayette said, turning his glare to her.

"I'll be sure to put a copy in inter-office mail for you." Mr. Lafayette opened his mouth to say something, but she turned to Mark. "As I said to Mr. Lafayette, Mark, when we talked to the other three boys that were there yesterday none of them gave me very convincing explanations as to what led up to the incident in question, but they were more than willing to point fingers your way. I guess that makes a little bit more sense now."

"However," Mr. Lafayette said, "that doesn't excuse what happened. This was an assault, with a weapon, and that's not acceptable no matter how justified you think you may be. We have to suspend you for a week and then evaluate the situation from there."

Mark let out a sigh, and Mr. Lafayette's scowl deepened. "Let me be very clear on this, Mr. Watson: if anything like this happens again, and I do mean anything, you are gone. Cut class, have excessive absences, *anything*, and I will have you removed from this institution. This is not a license to create mayhem. Am I clear?"

"Yes, sir. Crystal clear." *Licenseless mayhem WILL NOT BE TOLERATED.*

Mr. Lafayette collected his papers and files into a neat stack. "Ms. Kennedy will sign you out and give you some forms to give to your parents. See that they get and sign them."

"Yes sir. They won't miss them."

Mark got up, gripping his backpack with white knuckles as he darted out the door.

"Mark," Ms. Kennedy said, following him and placing a hand on his shoulder to keep him from going any further. "I'm sorry about that. He must not have read about your parents in your file."

"He's not a big reader, apparently."

He could see that she was fighting a smile, but before he could go out on a high note she stopped him.

"Mark, this was a really big deal. I made sure nothing more serious happened to you because I know these boys. I've dealt with them on a couple of other incidents and I know they are definitely capable of pushing someone to this."

"Well, it's nice to know that I'm not just crazy."

"Mark," she said, giving him a warning look. "What happened wasn't your fault, but you messed up, big time. Aside from the possible legal trouble and school punishments, you're going to have to deal with those boys again. They aren't going to let something like this go. I've seen things like this escalate very quickly, and I want to be your advocate if anything else happens. You have to be straight with me and I need to know that you can keep your temper in check and talk to me, really talk to me, if there's trouble. Believe it or not, I'm on your side."

"Really?"

"Yes, really. And for the favor I did you by keeping you in school, I want you to do me a favor."

"What's that?"

"Talk to me. Twice a week, before school or after, it doesn't matter, but I want to know what's going on up here," she tapped her temple, and then a tap to the chest, "and in here."

Oh, supervomit.

"And I take it there's no way to politely decline?"

"Not and stay in school."

"Well," he said, shrugging his shoulders. "Checkmate, I guess. I'll come see you the morning that I get back, okay? Does that get me off the hook?"

"All except the paperwork," she smiled.

***

"Please, please, please tell me it's true!" The blur running up alongside Christine said. For a brief second she thought it was one of those boys Mark had beaten up, but finally Steve stopped in front of her.

"God, you scared the crap out of me! What the hell are you talking about?"

"It's running all around school already," Steve said, hands clasped and eyes wide with excitement. "I just have to know if it's true. Please, God, let it be true that Mark kicked the shit out of Jack!"

"Yeah, it's true," she said, trying to keep the grin from her face. "He--" she didn't even get a chance to finish before Steve dropped to his knees, threw both hands into the air, leaned back and screamed "THANK YOU, JESUS!" A couple of girls walking by rolled their eyes, and Christine reached down and dragged him to his feet with a smile. "Get up, you spaz!"

"Yes, you're right. Total spaz," he said with a crazed grin. "Damn, I wish I'd been there! I mean, I heard it was the best fight ever! Was it? You were there, right? They say there was a beautiful redhead chick, and that had to be you."

She rolled her eyes. "Well, I was there, but that's not the most accurate description."

"Oh, don't be bashful," he said, wagging a finger in front of her face. "You're a looker, don't deny it!"

She swatted away the finger with a laugh, and he smiled back at her. "There's that smile, I knew I could get it out of you."

She opened her mouth to say something back, but he just carried on. "This is just too good. I mean, that asshole has been fucking with Mark since the day before forever, and now, finally, revenge!" He finished with a grandiose yell, waving a fist in the air.

"Yeah, that's one word for it."

"Speaking of," Steve said, lowering his voice, "I heard it was more than the usual fare, if you catch my meaning."

"You can say that."

"That bad?"

"I've never seen anything like it. He just . . . exploded. I guess with Clara and everything they were saying it was just too much, but that was something else."

"Wow," Steve said, shaking his head. "I mean, don't get me wrong, I can't blame Mark for going all Columbine on him, but I don't think Jack is going to take the hint, y'know?"

"Awesome. Just what he needs."

The late bell rang, and Steve gave a long drawn out sigh. "God, how do they expect me to work like this?" He turned to go, and then stopped and spun around on his heels. "Hey, did I forget to tell you that it sounds like Mark was sent home today?"

"Oh my God, really?"

"Oh yeah," Steve smirked. "The students aren't the only ones using the grapevine. Do you still want to get together at lunch?"

"Well, my options are kind of limited, so sure."

Steve rolled his eyes. "Oh geez, don't sound so excited about it. Would it kill you to say 'Steve, I would love to have lunch with you today, you big handsome stud.'"

"Steve, I would love to have lunch with you today."

He cocked a hand by his ear, but she just smiled and turned and walked away.

"Okay then, no problem," he called after her. "We'll get to the last part later."

She waved over her shoulder at him without looking back, and he stayed where he was, watching her disappear around the corner.

CHAPTER THIRTEEN

In the darkness, every muscle in Darren's body hurt.

He rolled, and the ground crunched and shifted under him.

He tried to get up but a sudden wave of dizzying sickness shoved him right back to the ground. He was lying on a thin layer of sand and tiny rocks, and after a deep breath he tried sitting up again. It worked, although the nausea stayed with him. He put a hand to his head and there was a sudden flare of pain. The side of his face was covered in a tight, almost dry-almost sticky film.

"What happened?" he mumbled, but when he actually saw the almost-dried blood on his fingertips it all came back to him. His room, the house and those eyes coming towards him in the darkness. He scooted backwards, thinking they were going to come for him again. He didn't move very far at all before his back ran into a wall.

He was in a corner he realized, cold stone walls on either side of him. He felt along the wall to his right, looking everywhere as his eyes slowly picked out more features in the blackness. A few feet ahead of him the ceiling dropped down so low he wouldn't be able to get up off his hands and knees.

He crawled forward, one arm outstretched to hopefully touch anything before he ran into it. The ceiling was cold, rusted metal and firmly in place he realized after as many shoves as his still weak arms would allow. He looked back at where he'd be lying, and saw that the ceiling there was wooden and slanting downward in an odd up and down pattern.

He kept crawling forward until he came to another wall, made of the same rusted metal as the ceiling. He followed it along, seeing a tiny flicker of light up ahead. After a couple more feet he came to a makeshift door, cut unevenly from the metal, with several small holes poked in it and a slit big enough to see through.

He pushed as hard as he could on it but realized the door was barred from the outside and it wouldn't budge. Looking out the slot in the door he could see the bottom of a staircase to the left, and he realized that the wooden part of the ceiling of his little cell was the underside of that staircase, leading upward. He was in a basement, he realized.

HIS basement.

"Oh God." His voice was a tiny croak, and it echoed pitifully in the darkness around him. He slammed into the metal door as hard as he could but it still didn't budge. He pushed again, slamming his palms painfully into it.

"Hey! Hey!"

"Shhhhh! He'll hear you!"

Darren whirled around, looking into the darkness for whoever spoke. In the far corner there was a girl, hunched over in a dirty ball, holding her knees to her chest and peering at him.

It was Suzie Morris, and she shrunk away when he moved close to her. He could see the skin on her wrists was rubbed raw and there were dark spatters over what had once been a nice dress.

"What's going on?"

"He'll hear you," she said, shaking her head. "He doesn't like it when we talk."

"Who?" he asked, lowering his voice to match her ragged whisper.

"The Shadow Man."

She was staring straight ahead, not at him but through him. "He saw you. He took you and brought you here. And he's going to make you witness."

"Witness? Witness what?"

Before she could answer, there was a pounding on the ceiling. Once. Then again. And again.

Someone was coming down the steps. Darren watched the boards above them bend and creak, sending tiny rivers of dust down on them. Darren crawled to the cell window to get a glimpse of his jailer. The footsteps were steady and calm, pausing at the landing above Darren's head. The boards creaked, as if he was testing them under the weight of his foot.

When he came down the next half-flight of stairs his back was to Darren, and all he could see were tall, gangly limbs and the silhouette of shaggy, unkempt hair. In his hand was the cane and he let it tap along the stone floor. Watching the man (the Shadow Man) walk away from him, limping slightly, Darren was able to take in the rest of basement for the first time.

About twenty feet from the cell door was the basement's only source of the light: a large coal furnace, its door open and the flames inside flickering bright reds and oranges. Hanging directly in front of the open furnace door, maybe three feet from the opening, was a black boy who could be no older than he was. He was chained at the wrists, his hands stretched over his head and feet barely touching the floor.

"Hey!" Darren yelled, shaking the door as much as he could, succeeding only in making the chain rattle.

The man stopped right behind the chained up boy, towering over him. The man turned slightly, looking back at Darren, but then returned his attention to the child in front of him. The boy, who had been hanging limply, stirred slightly as the man knelt down next to him. The man reached under the boys' chin and lifted his head. The boy's eyes flickered open, and when he saw the man in front of him he began to twist and writhe in his chains.

The man made calming, shushing noises and clamped a large hand around the boy's neck to keep him still.

"You see Him, don't you?" The man's voice echoed in the cavernous room.

The boy was still writhing and struggling, making whimpering, panicked noises. With a snarl, the man slammed the silver top of the cane into the boy's bare chest. The chains rattled with the impact and the boy doubled over as much as he could, legs swaying wildly.

"Stop struggling. I know He's there, I know you can see Him! Tell me that you see Him!"

The boy was just sobbing, shaking his head back and forth. As the boy writhed around in his chains, Darren could see numerous cuts and bruises all over the boy's body. Who knew how long he had been hanging there.

"Stop it! Stop it!" the man roared. He let go of the boy's neck with a disgusted shove and swung the cane up into the boy's stomach. The boy's legs actually left the ground, the impact causing him to swing back and forth.

"He's in there!" the man said, pointing with the cane at the gaping mouth of the furnace. "Don't lie to me! Don't tell me that you can't see!"

Darren looked, expecting to see something, but all he saw were flames staring back at him.

The boy just hung there, sobbing, his toes barely touching the ground.

"You liar," the man hissed, bringing the cane up. "I'll make you see Him."

Darren tried to close his eyes, but he couldn't. All he could do was hold his hands in front of his face and try not to see the torture played out between his dirty fingers. The sound of it echoed all around him: screaming, grunts of exertion, the rattle of chain on metal. Above it all the flames of the furnace roared in approval. Darren screamed as loud as he could. He couldn't stop the sight of the beating, of the blood flying through the air and silver flashing up and down, but he could drown out the noise. At the end, all he could hear were his screams and the flame.

***

Mark sprung out of bed, arms thrashing in the air, ducking low to avoid ceiling. When he stopped, out of breath and covered in panicked sweat, he realized he wasn't a little kid, or in a basement, or in any real danger.

He got back into bed, reminding himself that it was a dream, like the one he'd had about Darren before but far more powerful. The sensations were fading but he could feel the stinging in his palms from hitting that tiny metal door, and his throat felt raw from screaming. These were not normal dream feelings. Seeing a man beat a little kid with a cane is not a normal dream experience.

Yeah, how about that cane, huh? Kind of looked familiar didn't it? If you're having trouble remembering, I'm sure Clara could help.

He rolled over, trying to drown out the nagging voice with the rustle of sheets. It was right, though. If Clara's death happened the way he saw (*and it did!*) and the cane was in his dream both before and after, then what he was dreaming could be real.

Could be? Kiddo, you're really dreaming if you think there's any doubt here.

He rolled over again, grabbing his sheets with balled up fists. It wasn't true. Clara died and it was horrible, but these were just dreams. He squeezed his eyes shut, but in the blackness he could still see the fire-eyes of the Shadow Man staring back at him.

***

"I fucking hate grapefruit juice." Jack snarled at the viscous pink concoction in the carton before taking a long drink. It was all they had to drink and his late night thirst left him with little choice. The cuts on his lips had healed some in the days since the fight but the pink menace's tangy "goodness" still burned. So did his pride every time he looked in a mirror. Or touched his face. Or breathed.

Every useless part of every stupid fucking thing in the world reminded him of that goddamn fight.

"Fight." It was a beating, handed out by a weak, crybaby little faggot that sucker punched him, with a helmet of all things.

What burned worse than all the citrus in the world was that he could've turned it around, even after the cheap helmet shots. He'd had his chance, two of them even, and he fucked it up. He fucked it up so bad Watson left him bloody and on the verge of tears in the middle of the parking lot.

And for that, he was going to do everything in his power to kill him.

"I mean it. I am going to kill him for this. If he thought losing that bitch was something, wait until I get done with him," he'd told Eric when they were waiting in the emergency room, Jack waiting to get a couple of stitches in his chin and Eric's nose wrapped and stuffed with gauze.

It hadn't been the smartest thing in the world, but then again, Dad always said he had a "propensity to think with his fists and not with his brain." If there was one thing his dad loved it was doling out nuggets of wisdom like that. *This is why we don't behave like savages. This is why we try to keep our emotions in check. This is why your mother couldn't see reason and left. This is why grapefruit juice is healthy and nutritious.*

With a deep rumble, Jack called forth a giant ball of spit and phlegm and then spat it into the remaining cup's worth of juice in the carton. *This is why I spit in your food, you cold, arrogant piece of shit.*

"You want to kill him, don't you?" a deep rumbling voice said, from just behind his right ear.

Everything in Jack's body skidded to a halt, and when it restarted it added up to: run. As soon as he tried something swept his feet out from under him. He toppled over, arms flailing and managing to turn so that he didn't land on his still stitched up chin. As soon as he hit the ground he started crawling, knowing he needed to get away as fast as possible.

"Stop it."

He obeyed, freezing in place with one arm still outstretched. Something hard pushed under his armpit and flipped him onto his back. He tried to get up, but a thin black stick planted itself just below his throat with enough pressure to pin him to the floor like an insect.

He looked up, tracing the stick to the silver at its top and the swirling black hand that held it. That same swirling darkness covered the entire body of the man pinning him to the floor with his cane, billowing out to give the illusion that he was wearing a long trench coat and wide-brimmed hat.

Jack's gaze stopped just below the hat's brim, at the two burning embers where the man's eyes should be.

"You didn't answer my question."

Jack opened his mouth to ask, but then he knew who he meant. Mark.

"Yes," Jack said, when he voice returned to him. He kept staring into the Shadow Man's eyes, and they seemed to widen and flare with more intensity the longer he stared into them. There was something deep beyond those flames, and he could feel it drawing him in.

"I can help with that," the Shadow Man said, breaking the spell for a second.

"How?"

"All you need to know is that I'll send you a sign when it's time. Wait for my call, and then you can have your revenge. *Not* before." The cane pressed into him harder at the last.

"I understand," Jack said. The pressure was close to cutting off his breath.

"Excellent," the Shadow Man said, and then the pressure on Jack's chest was gone, and with just a ripple in the darkness around him, so was he.

CHAPTER FOURTEEN

Steve had taken up post by the school entrance nearest to the bike rack. It wasn't his usual point of entry, but with this being Mark's first day back after suspension he figured he should make the effort and give him the grand welcome back. He clambered to the top of the once-impressive decorative concrete barriers and sat with legs dangling over the edge.

He nodded at a couple of girls as they passed his perch and when he got his usual eye-rolls and disgusted looks he called after them. "You don't want to miss it, ladies! The conquering hero of Cedar Ridge High is coming back today, and I know you want to feel those hands of steel!" Hair flips and the annoyed sucking of teeth were his only response.

The V's distinctive whine turned him away from watching the rest of their retreat. Mark jumped the curb faster than his usual safety-first mindset allowed and he skidded to a stop in front of the rack, just in time for the second bell to ring. Steve watched while Mark frantically chained up the scooter and then made it four steps towards the entrance before realizing he still had his helmet on.

"Mark Watson, you're my hero," Steve said, dropping down next to him as he passed, tugging the slightly worse for wear but much cleaner looking helmet.

Mark scowled and brushed past him. "I know you're running late, but don't worry dude. You're a fucking rock-star! If I were you I'd drop that thing in your locker before people want to start touching and signing it and shit."

Mark glared at him and Steve finally got a good look at him. Mark's eyes were dark and sunken and his face was paler than his usual "I don't go outside without a helmet" pale. Everything about him was more ragged, mismatched and frantic than normal. If Steve hadn't seen it with his own eyes, he'd have sworn the scooter rode Mark to school today.

"I'm glad to see you've had time to relax, take care of yourself. Y'know, have some me time."

"It wasn't a vacation," Mark growled, fast walking towards his locker. "Joe wouldn't even let me leave the house, and he had me cleaning and doing all kinds of other bullshit chores. I had to make sure the garage was spotless before he'd let me ride to school today."

"Well, you wear captivity well. At least as well as can be expected."

"Gee, thanks." Mark said. He tossed the helmet in his locker and slammed the door shut. "I had to wait for him to inspect things before I could even leave for--Fuck!"

"Well, I'd inspect things before then, too. Who knows what you'll find."

"No, I was supposed to see Ms. Kennedy before homeroom."

Above them, the bell rang.

"Dum dum DUM!"

"It's not funny," Mark snarled, turning on his heel and heading for the stairs. "I could get kicked out of school."

"Think of all the time you'll have for chores, though!" Steve called into the stairwell. When he didn't get a response, he rolled his eyes and headed towards his own homeroom.

***

Mark vaulted down the last four steps and spun around the group of kids who came through the doors. One of them called after him, and it took

Mark a second to realize it wasn't the usual smart remarks but something about the fight and how he was the man.

It was hard to feel like the man when everything in your body was tired and sore, with a side of terrified and possibly insane.

He was either awake and hauling garbage or asleep and watching torture. His dreams continued with the same intensity and theme, each night bringing a new variation to horrors he'd seen the first night. Mark would've tried swearing off sleep if all the physical labor wasn't making him want to pass out before 10.

"This is what happens," Joe growled the first time Mark complained. "If you're going to screw up so bad you have to stay home, I'm going to make damn sure this isn't a good time." He'd made sure to take the power cords to both TVs with him to work. He was able to convince him to leave the phone in his room hooked up so he could still talk to Christine when she got home from school, so long as everything on the list for the day was taken care of. He managed, barely, and every day brought a new list of chores and the implicit threat that if all the work wasn't done his punishment would continue past his suspension, not to mention the loss of his "phone privileges."

Of course, since he'd screwed up getting to school on time, it looked like his suspension would probably continue anyway.

He ran into the office and was about to ask the secretary about Ms. Kennedy when she walked up beside him.

"You're late," she said with a smile.

"I know," Mark said, his breath mostly gone from his run across the building.

"Well, at least you made the effort. Since we're out of time now, what period do you have lunch?"

"Fifth. Why?"

"Well, we can just do it then. That's when I usually take my lunch anyway." He tried to keep himself from gritting his teeth in frustration. "What's wrong?"

"I have plans."

"With Christine?"

"Yeah."

"Well, I'm sure she'll understand. After all, it's not like I'm giving you a choice."

She understood, of course.

After a long kiss in a deserted stairwell and her fussing over how tired and worn out he looked, he explained the situation and she nodded with perfect understanding. "Anything that keeps you from getting into trouble is fine with me."

He, of course, was filled with disappointment. Frustration, exhaustion and now disappointment, but she just batted her eyelashes and told him everything was going to be fine and she was okay with it.

He watched her walk off to class. She looked back at him just before she turned the corner and gave him a wave and smile brimming with understanding and not a molecule of disappointment.

"So," Ms. Kennedy said after clearing a space at the small table next to her desk so they could eat, "let's talk about anger."

"Why? I'm not angry," Mark said.

"Mark," she said, picking at her Chinese food with chopsticks, "you don't go beating someone with a bike helmet if you're not at least a little angry. And yes," she said, holding up a hand to cut off his protest, "I understand it was self-defense. But still, you can't tell me you weren't angry at these boys when, by your own admission, they had been bullying you for quite some time."

He failed to hold back a heaving sigh and took his sandwich out of his bag.

"Okay. So, I'm angry. What am I supposed to do about it?"

"But why are you angry?"

"Well, you just said, they were messing with me. That tends to make people angry. Unless I missed a memo or something."

"No, getting upset about that is normal. Reacting the way you did is extreme. I'm just worried about where that comes from."

"I don't know. I guess it's just who I am."

"Mark, I've talked to some of your teachers and they all tell me the same thing. That you're a good kid who gets okay grades and doesn't say much. They were all genuinely shocked when I told them about what happened."

His derisive snort was both unexpected and uncontrollable.

"Are they wrong?"

"Well, my grades are okay and I'm not a hand raiser."

"But?"

"But nothing. They all knew what was going on and they either don't care or think it's funny."

"I doubt that."

"Oh really?" he said, leaning up against her desk. "In the 8th grade we went to the shore for our end of the year class trip. We were all just goofing around, playing and whatever, but when Jack and his friends found out I couldn't swim they all grabbed me and carried me towards the water to throw me in. I was kicking and yelling, and they carried me right by Mr. Eccelstein, our Math teacher. Right by him, like three feet away, and he was just chuckling, hands in his pockets, watching them drop me in the water. He actually nodded at them as they walked by. Forgive me if I'm not exactly trusting of what your colleagues are and aren't shocked about."

She put her chopsticks down, folded her hands on top of each other and leaned forward as well. "I'm sorry that happened to you. It wasn't fair, and that's really awful. But there are things you can do about that and ways that you can react so that you don't keep stuff like that bottled up inside you."

Mark leaned back into his chair. "Yeah, I doubt that."

"Sure there is. You could talk to someone, and we could've figured out a plan for you to take control of the situation. Without violence. Jack and his friends still have to follow the rules like everyone else, and there are plenty of things that we can do to combat their behavior effectively. Like conflict resolution or mediation."

"Mediation? What the hell am I supposed to say in mediation? 'I'm sorry that I make you so mad you have to shove me to the ground and mock me. I pledge to work on that issue with you.'"

She just stared at him. "Are you done?"

"No. Yes. See, now I'm mad. Seriously, where did you come from? How do you work in a high school and not understand how they work?"

"My high school career isn't really up for discussion, Mark," she smiled. "And all I can work with is what I know about. Now that I know about this, here we are talking about it."

"I don't like talking about things."

"Yeah, it really sucks sometimes, but sometimes it's the only thing that helps. What about your Uncle? You two talk don't you?"

"Oh god no! I mean, things like 'Pass the salt' or 'Where are you going to be.' This week there was a lot of 'These are your chores' too, so thanks for that."

"So you don't talk about your parents, or your aunt?"

"No, we don't. He's an old-school guy who doesn't talk about his feelings and tells me my hair is too long."

"That's really unfortunate. What about your friends? Christine?"

"My one friend? Well, he knows and he's cool but he just doesn't take anything seriously. And Christine . . . well, she doesn't need to worry about me and my weird and embarrassing past."

"Well, if you want to have a relationship with her, you're going to have to try to be honest with her. But that's it? There's no one else?"

If there was anything the chores and the dreams had done it was take focus off Clara's death and the emotional sucking chest wound it had caused. For the first time in almost a week he thought of Clara again, and he was stricken by her loss and how he'd been able to forget about her. Ms. Kennedy could see it on his face, and she leaned forward again.

"What is it, Mark?"

She's like an emotional vulture. She can't wait to explain to you how this is "natural" and what you're feeling is "normal." How much horseshit is that, huh?

"I . . . well, there was someone. A friend, a real good friend who . . . she died."

"I'm so sorry. When?"

"A couple of weeks ago."

She straightened up, and for a second her sympathy was over-shadowed by a look of triumph. *Fucking hell, she loves this. It's like she found the trauma prize in the emotional cracker-jack.*

"Just before the fight." She nodded, all of her pieces put together. "This is important, Mark. Loss, especially loss of a good friend, is so traumatic and hurtful. If you don't have time to grieve and accept the loss, then things like this can happen. All of your emotions get all jumbled up and you can't process anything in a real way."

"If you say so," Mark grimaced, tossing his sandwich back into the bag. Chicken salad wasn't going to soothe his hunger any more, or his irritation.

"Who was it?"

Don't do it. Don't do it, man. Don't let her play emotional whack-a-mole with you.

"Her name was Clara. She was an older lady, a friend who was there for me when my Aunt died and she helped me and now . . ."

It was too much. It was buzzing and burning in his head and settling in his eyes. He was tearing up and his voice was cracking.

Not this crap again. C'mon, this is what she wants. Mark the crybaby. Mark the damaged. Mark the vulnerable. This is a one way ticket to a lifetime of therapy.

She reached into a desk drawer and handed him a small stack of tissues.

"I'm fine," he said, wiping his eyes with the back of his hand.

"It's okay, Mark."

"Like hell it is. She's dead and gone and I'm still here."

"Tell me about it, Mark. You can't keep this ins--"

"Yes I can! I don't need to tell you a damn thing! It's done, okay? No amount of talking is going to bring her back, or change what I've seen! She's dead, okay? Killed, gone, murdered before my eyes and she is never, ever coming back."

Oh yeah, that told her. That'll make her back off, genius.

The look on her face was enough to confirm that he'd fucked up royally. Her cracker jack prize had turned into an angry scorpion called "Holy shit did he say murder?"

"Mark," she said, back stiff and palms flat on her desk. "What do you mean by that? Exactly."

They stared at each other for a second. "It's just an expression."

"Really? I've never heard it before." Her face twitched, and Mark realized she was trying to smile it off.

"Look . . . My friend, Clara, she was killed, okay? They were talking about it in the papers and stuff and on TV so it's like . . . I can't really get away from it, y'know?"

She stayed still for a moment, and then nodded. She picked her hands off the desk and rubbed them together. "Okay, I guess I can see that. But Mark, this is serious business. You can't just go off and drop a bomb like that and expect me not to react."

"Oh, I'm sorry. I should've realized my friend's murder would be such a bother for you."

"Mark," she said, her voice almost reaching 'I'm a serious disciplinarian' levels. "That's not fair. I'm just trying to process this."

Stop. Think. Don't say something stupid.

"I'm sorry. I'm just really tired and stressed and worn out."

"I can imagine. This must be a terrible time for you, Mark. I had no idea that your friend was the one they'd been talking about on the news. These things are never easy when they're this sudden, but I want you to know that there's nothing you can't talk to me about, okay?"

"Well, thanks, but I should be fine."

She stopped and stared at him intently. "Mark, you're not fine. That's why you're here. Now . . . Is there anything else I need to know about Clara's death?"

"No, I told you. It's just an expression, that's all."

"Mark, I think we both know--"

"You don't know, okay? Just drop it! I'm sorry I said anything."

"Mark, it's just that you said . . . what you said and I think it's important that we be honest with each other. If you know something about what happened then you need to tell me about it."

"I don't need to do anything."

She paused. "That's different than there not being anything to tell."

"Look, it's just . . . I'm fine, okay? It's nothing."

Oh yeah, that'll shake her.

"Mark, I think we should--"

"No, we shouldn't," he said, leaping to his feet and grabbing his bag. "This is pointless, okay? I was upset because my friend died and Jack thought it was funny, that's why I got all crazy. That's all, there's nothing else. I'm not going to sit here and have you grill me because you think I maybe saw or did whatever." He darted for the door.

"Mark," she said, and he paused with his hand on the knob. "You can go, but this is serious and I still want us to talk about this tomorrow, okay?"

He didn't look back, and slammed the door behind him.

***

"Oh, c'mon, never?"

"No," Christine said with a laugh. "I've never seen the *Sopranos*. Is that horrible?"

Steve threw up his arms and fell backwards in the grass with a great sigh. "Yeah no, it's fine. I mean you're a Jersey Girl now and you don't know the gospel of the *Sopranos*. That's fine. I'm just going to lie here quietly and die from the shame you should be feeling."

"Oh quit it," she said, kicking his foot. "I just hate that kind of stuff. Plus, it's old."

Steve propped himself up on his elbows. "They have this thing called the Internet, and you can get stuff from it. Like, shows and music and all kinds of magic stuff."

"Ugh, whatever. There's plenty of good new stuff on."

"What, like Gossip Girl?"

"Well . . ." she said, tapping her chin in mock thoughtfulness.

"Oh my god, you trash TV slut. Wait, here comes lunch," he said, rolling over and retching with an exaggerated heave.

Lunches with Steve had almost always contained some kind of heaving on his part, especially after she had told him that she hated that sound. In the week of Mark's suspension they'd had lunch together every day, a couple of times with some of the other kids that Steve knew from Drama club, but most of the time was spent together under the tree where she and Mark first had lunch.

She'd been looking forward to Mark joining them but if there was anything that the counselor could do to help him out, she was all for it. He was so flipped out over them not being able to eat together, so she'd done her best to make sure that he knew that she was fine with it and he didn't have to stress.

"I'm going to miss our vomit filled lunches together," Steve said, straightening up.

"We'll still be having lunch together, and it'll be even more fun with Mark around."

"Oh yeah, since he's such a barrel of laughs nowadays."

"Steve!"

"I know, I know. I don't want to be a dick or anything, but I just wish he wouldn't make such a big deal out of everything."

"Well you're kind of a dick, because this is a big deal."

"Yeah, I know. When things like this happen he just tenses up and everything becomes the end of the world. It all works out, no matter how much things suck. If he just relaxed, he would realize that he'll be fine, but he'd rather punish himself."

"He's not punishing himself," she said. "He just feels things, probably a lot more than you or I do. Under all that shyness is a lot of passion, and I like that. It's better than feeling nothing."

Steve leaned closer. "Oh so you're an emotional passion-junkie, is that what it's all about? I don't really know what's going on with you two, since Mark was never really one to kiss and tell. Or kiss at all, for that matter."

She pushed him away with a smile. "Well, he does just fine and I'm not one to kiss and tell either, wise guy."

"Nuts."

"Seriously. You think Mark's going to be okay, don't you?"

Steve rolled his eyes. "A thousand times yes. I mean, he's kind of a 'getting shit on' magnet and he can be painfully emo about it but he always manages. It was the same thing when his aunt died and it was like his whole world was ending. But he realized it wasn't and he got over it."

"This is a little different though."

"Yeah, I know, but Mark's a lot of things. Sure, he's weepy, he's sensitive, he's melodramatic, and he may have the fashion sense of a homeless guy, but he's still a great guy once you make it past all of those things. . ." Steve looked up and saw Christine's gaze focused just over his shoulder. "And I'm saying these things only because I know he's standing right behind me."

"Oh really?" Mark said, standing right behind him.

"Of course, and just so that we're clear, exactly how long have you been standing there?"

"I'm a lot of things," Mark said, taking a seat in the small space between Christine and Steve. Mark placed his hand on Christine's knee, and she felt it trembling. She put her hand on his and gave it a squeeze.

"Are you okay? I thought you were going to be there all period."

"Yeah, just fine." He didn't look over at her, his gaze still locked on Steve. Steve just stared back, tugging at the grass with a playful smile.

"Good, it'd suck to have you in guidance counselor jail all lunch. And look, I was just fooling around, man. You know I love you.

Mark's hand trembled again.

"Mark," Christine said, putting a hand on his shoulder and trying to turn him towards her. "We're just worried about you, that's all. We just want to help."

"Of course you do," he said, giving her a sideways glance, but still focusing on Steve.

"I've just got your best interests at heart," Steve said.

"Oh really?"

Steve's facade faltered a second when he glanced down to see their intertwined hands, but he looked up, cocked his fingers like a pistol and gave Mark and wink and grin.

"You know it, buddy."

CHAPTER FIFTEEN

"You'll be okay, right?" Christine said in the stairwell before they parted ways after lunch.

"Yeah, it's no big deal. Nothing is going to happen."

She knew that gym with Jack and his friends was next because Steve couldn't shut up about it. It was as if he was trying to give Mark something else to worry about because the half dozen other things weren't enough. Gym was the only class that he had with Jack and his friends, so this was the first opportunity they'd have for payback.

"Just be careful," she said, kissing him before heading up the steps.

"It'll be fine," Steve said, meeting up with Mark at the bottom of the stairs.

"Sure."

Neither Jack nor his friends were there when they got into the locker room, and Mark thought the inevitable was going to be postponed a day until Kyle and Victor walked in. They didn't even look at him, just headed to their lockers and got ready. Other than the scrape on Vic's forehead, everything was completely normal.

Until they pull a pair of shotguns from their lockers and blow you away.

Steve didn't even notice. Steve, of course, was too engrossed in his own changing. Apparently it was just Mark who was the weepy melodramatic homeless guy.

When they got to the gym floor, Mark saw why Jack hadn't been in the locker room. He was seated on the bleachers, still in his street clothes. He was reading a book when Mark first saw him, and when he looked up Mark finally got a look at his handiwork. Jack's face was still bruised, one of his eyes still blackened and he had a small line of stitches on his chin. His face was blank and if he saw Mark he made no sign of it before turning back to reading.

Mark sat on his spot on the gym floor, and for a moment all the worry was washed away by a sudden swell of pride. I did that, he thought. I did that to him, and he has to look like that for how much longer? A week? Two weeks? There's no hiding it.

It felt good. He hated it, but aside from Christine it was the only thing that had managed to make him feel good all day.

The games went fine, better than they had all year. Mark couldn't tell if he was playing better because of his sudden surge of manly confidence or because no one was gunning to make his life miserable. At the end of the period changing happened without incident. When he got upstairs and waited for the bell, he let out a breath he'd been holding for forty minutes. Leaning against the wall he looked up and found himself staring across the gym directly into Jack's gaze.

His expression was still as blank as it had been before, but a smile began to spread across Jack's face and he gave a lazy wave. Mark turned, too quickly and obviously, squeezing his eyes shut.

Yeah, things are going to be just fine. You think he doesn't know he has to walk around with your beating all over his face? Of course he knows, and he's not going to take revenge in a gym class. But you go ahead and keep thinking about how you did better at volleyball today, champ.

"Hey you," Christine said, sitting on the V with a smile. "Still giving rides?"

"For you, always" he said, stopping in front of her and letting his helmet and backpack fall to the ground. He wrapped his arms around her and kissed her.

"Wow," she said when she finally pulled away. "What brought that on?"

"You. And the fact that this piece of shit day is over."

"Well, let's get out of here so you can get some more of me."

"I don't have the spare with me, but you can wear it," he said, handing her the helmet.

"Is that the same one from . . . the other day?"

"Yeah," Mark said, wiping nothing in particular off the top of it. "It's takes a licking and all that."

"I'll go without if that's okay," she said.

They rode to the park by Christine's house, and the whole way there the feel of her arms around him and her body pressing up against him was almost more than he could bear. When they pulled up near their tree he turned and kissed her again, and they barely let go of each other on the way to lie down.

"I missed this," he said, pulling her close to him.

"I can tell," she said, stroking his cheek. "I missed it too. One of these days we're going to have to go out someplace and just tear ass on that thing, see how fast we can get it up to."

"And just get away," Mark murmured, eyes closed and leaning back. "Just drive off and never, ever have to look back."

"Rough day?"

"The roughest."

"I could tell when you got to lunch. And don't worry about what Steve was saying. He was just trying to help. In a weird way, but still. He cares about you."

"I'm sure he does." He opened his eyes and saw her propped up on one elbow, staring down at him.

"So nothing else happened today?"

"Well . . ."

"Tell me about it. I want to help."

How the hell is she going to help? Flutter her pretty eyelashes and make Jack and Ms. Kennedy fly away to magical fairy land?

"It's complicated."

"I know it is. I mean, this has got to be a really shitty time right now, but if I can do anything, anything at all to help you, I want to do it."

"I know you do," he said, leaning up and kissing her. "And you do, you really, really do. There's just some stuff that's just hard to talk about."

"Well, what did Ms. Kennedy say? What was that all about?"

He let out a deep sigh. "That's part of the problem right there. When she found about what happened to Clara she acted like it was this huge deal and she was going to try to help and then got all weird."

"Well, Mark, it is a big deal. I mean what happened was awful, and I'm not surprised she was worried about it."

"It's not just that. I . . . well I don't really want to bother you with it."

"Mark," she said, taking his hand. "Tell me, please."

"Okay, okay." He took a deep breath. With all of the sudden build up he'd given it, he'd rather drop his pants and do a couple laps around the park but it was clear that she wasn't going to let it go.

"I've been having these dreams. Weird, messed up dreams, about what happened to Clara and this other stuff, and when she found out about Clara I kind of lost my shit. I think she thought I was talking about knowing about her murder instead of just the fact that I'm dreaming about it and thinking about it all the time."

"Mark, she can't possibly think that. I mean, what would you know?"

Not what her head looks like three feet from her body. No ma'am, not me.

"Exactly. Nuts, right?"

"Yeah. But what about these dreams? That sounds really messed up."

He shifted, trying to turn away from her so she couldn't read the lies on his face as easily as Mrs. Kennedy did. "It's nothing. Just messed up stuff."

"About Clara?"

"Yeah."

"It's okay. I mean, I can't imagine something like this happening and what it would do to me, but you can talk to me about anything, you know that right?"

"I know," he said, but his voice felt empty and hollow.

She leaned down and kissed him again. "Mark, we're going to be okay. I promise."

"Are you sure?"

She kissed him again. "Very sure."

"I'm still not convinced. You're going to have to try harder than that."

They stayed under the tree for at least an hour, until Christine finally had to pull herself away from him and remind him that she still had tons of homework to do, and her parents were bound to start getting worried if she stayed out too late.

"I don't want to do anything to jeopardize us being able to do this every day."

"Okay, okay," he said, letting her go. "I'm doing this just because you're promising more later."

"Count on it."

When he dropped her off in front of her house, she leaned in and quickly kissed him on the cheek. "I'll call you tonight, okay?"

"Okay," he said, heading out of the driveway with a look back over his shoulder.

He didn't want to go right home, having had enough of that blue collar dungeon to last several lifetimes. Just before his grounding he'd gotten himself a full tank of gas and now was the perfect time to use it.

He rode aimlessly for a while, doing a circuit of the town and trying not to think about anything but the road in front of him. He was just about to head home when he caught sight of the street sign he was about to pass. He weaved over to the side of the road, trying not to squeeze the brake so hard that he'd lose control.

When he came to a full stop he craned his head around, pulling off his helmet to be sure.

Munson Drive.

He turned around and headed down it, knowing that all he was going to do was confirm his suspicions and probably give himself a heart attack.

At least that would solve a lot of your problems. Solve some other people's problems too.

He'd gone down a couple of blocks on Munson, just enough to make him begin to doubt himself, but there it was.

Briarcliff Avenue. He didn't even have to look too hard to see its star attraction.

He turned slowly, taking his time getting down there, and as he did he could feel his dream coming to life all around him. He could see the little kids running around, playing baseball and trying to ignore the big shadowy pimple on this perfect neighborhood's face.

He stopped across the street from the house, which had gotten worse over the years since he'd seen it in his dream. Of course no one had moved in there. Of course it hadn't burned down in some freak lightning strike or flash fire. Of course it was a real thing right in the town he lived in.

This place, withered and sunken and shrouded by crooked trees was too nasty to have just gone away.

The neighborhood was quiet except for the stuttering cough of his engine. He wanted someone to walk by just so he could make sure he wasn't just making the place up.

If it was still here, still empty and ugly, then what did that mean? Did people know about what happened in there? Was everyone getting a sweet break on their property take being "homicide adjacent?" Did any of what he'd been dreaming happen at all?

If it was real then there had to be a connection between it and Clara's death, something more than just his crazy visions. If there was then it was probably in that house. His hand hovered over the scooters key. It'd be a simple matter to see, right? Just turn the V off, head through the hedge and find out, once and for all.

His hand closed on the key and then there was a shriek of a horn behind him.

"Hey, out of the road!"

Behind him was a lovely new car with an exasperated housewife behind the wheel. Mark waved a weak apology and pulled the scooter up and over to the side of the road. She drove past him, glaring at him with a lecture on the tip of her tongue. She looked past him and saw the house behind him and drove off without a word.

Yeah, Mystery Machine, you go in there and solve the case. Maybe you won't fall through the floor and break your legs, or just get caught and hauled off the jail for trespassing. Joe would love that, wouldn't he?

His hand was over the key again. Just turn it. Turn it and go look.

He revved the engine and sped away, the little engine whining a high-pitched laugh at his cowardice.

CHAPTER SIXTEEN

Mark woke staring down at concrete. He'd been trying to catch up on all the work he'd missed over the course of his suspension but he ended up sleeping face down in a pile of it after just sorting it. He braced himself for whatever horrors his dreams of the basement on Briarcliff Avenue held for him, but realized that this wasn't the cell under the stairs, it was a parking lot.

Not just any parking lot, he realized, but the one tucked away behind the administration wing at his school. It was empty and sparsely lit, and the only car in the lot was a compact with various politically active bumper stickers on it. There was a metallic whine that echoed through the empty lot, followed by a slam. He tried calling out but realized he was formless, just as he was when he'd seen Clara murdered.

"No, that was just the door. I know, right? They keep saying they're going to fix it but they never will."

It was a familiar voice, and Mark felt his stomach turn. Not this, not again.

Ms. Kennedy came around the corner of the building, walking under the security light and up the driveway that ran along the building and out the street. It was perfect, Mark realized. Isolated and dark, just the way he would like it.

She was talking on her phone and trying to put her coat on, not doing either one particularly well. "Yeah, I know. I know. Look, I'm gonna get off now, but I'll call you when I get home okay? Yes, I'm just leaving now, but I was getting some good stuff down for my book and I wanted to look over some stuff. For one of my students. He just . . . look, it's complicated. Can I tell you about it later? Okay, call you soon."

She'd gotten her coat on, dropped the phone in her purse and started digging in it for her keys. The security light on the building behind her flickered and then went out. She didn't notice at first, still walking towards her car and looking down in her purse for the keys. She pulled them out just as the light she was passing under went out.

"Seriously?" she said, looking up in irritation. There were two more lights between her and her car, the last positioned directly above it.

Her stride remained steady until she got under the next light and it went out as well. She stopped for a second, turning and looking around, keys dangling from her hand. They began to jingle as her hand began to twitch.

She started walking faster, humming to herself. Her shoes clicking on the pavement echoed off the sides of the darkened building, she kept looking around to every very dark corner of the lot. "Amazing grace . . . how sweet the sound . . ." Her voice was trembling.

She made it around the car to the driver's side and was looking all over the lot and not down at the lock the she tried to find with her key. "That saved a wretch like me . . . was blind but now I se--" The note jumped up to an ear piercing shriek as a spear of silver flew from the trees and pinned her hand into the car door.

He came out from the trees, sprinting towards her noiselessly and surrounded by a fog of complete darkness. When he reached her, she was thrashing about and frantically slapping at the long blade protruding from her hand. He grabbed a handful of her hair and slammed the side of her head into the car window.

Her head bounced off the splintered glass and she stopped moving. She stood still for a moment as he placed a boot on her wrist and yanked the blade from car and hand with a swift tug. Her arm fell limply to her side and she staggered backwards, eyes glassy from the sudden blow and shock running riot through her brain.

Her eyes went from the blood-pouring hole in her trembling hand to the man covered in swirling smoke and flame-filled eyes. She drew in a breath to scream, but he smashed the cane sheath into her jaw.

She fell backwards, turning just enough so that she didn't land on her wounded hand. She rolled over and pushed herself feebly along the pavement. She didn't make it more than a foot before he plunged the blade down into her shoulder, pinning her to the ground. She screamed, and the Shadow Man clamped a hand over her mouth to silence her. Her body twitched and flailed and her eyes grew wide as he twisted the blade ever so slightly in her shoulder.

"Shhhhh," he said in the same rumbling voice Mark had heard under the staircase in his dreams.

She kept trying to pull away, but the blade in her shoulder and the hand clamped tight on her jaw held her still. He pulled her closer to his face, dragging her shoulder further up the blade.

"Who did you tell?"

Her eyes grew wide, and Mark couldn't tell if it was from the panic of staring into a face made of swirling smoke or confusion at the question.

"The boy. Watson. Who did you tell about him? What have you said?"

She shook her head again and he let her go, pulling the sword from her shoulder with a practiced flourish. She shrieked in pain and rolled onto her side.

"I . . . I don't know what you're talking about! Please! Someone help me!"

She tried to push herself away from him, but with a hand run through on one side and a shoulder similarly impaled on the other all she could do was inch herself along the ground.

"I want to know who you talked to about him. What you said. Who you told it to. What . . . suspicions you shared with some other nosy little maggot."

She just shook her head wildly, inching along the ground. "Help me! Someone help me!" Her feet finally found purchase on the ground and she began to push herself up to stand. The Shadow Man rolled his head in annoyed impatience and drove the blade into the back of her knee, forcing her back to the ground.

"Who did you tell? What did you say?"

He swung blade again, cutting her across the small of her back. He swung again, catching her ear and sending it flying in Mark's direction.

She flailed again and he stepped around to stand in front of her. He pressed a foot down on her wounded hand, focusing her attention back on him.

"I just want to know, and then I'll disappear into the night like a bad dream. Just tell me what I want to know."

She tugged at her trapped hand, but Mark could see she was fading. Shock and blood loss may well kill her before the Shadow Man did. "I don't . . . I don't know what you mean."

He squatted down, and she winced as he put more pressure on her hand. "You talked to the boy. You watched him squirm and lie and you knew he was lying. You suspected and maybe you said something to someone. Maybe you said 'That Mark Watson boy is trouble, and we should take care of that trouble.'"

She shook her head. "No. No, I don't know what you're talking about."

He slammed his fist down onto the earless side of her head, causing her head to bounce sickeningly off the pavement. "Yes you do. I can see it, see right through you and I know when you're lying to me. You knew that there was a problem with him, and you were going to tell someone about it. About your *concerns*. Who?"

She stopped shaking her head. From the looks of her she had stopped most things altogether. "No . . . no one. I was . . . but there was a meet. A meeting. I was going to, but . . . I won't. I think I was miss. Miss .. . taken. Good kid. Good boy."

The Shadow Man threw his head back and howled. It took Mark a moment but he realized the Shadow Man was laughing. He stood up and swung his blade across her trapped wrist and severed it.

She didn't even react this time. She just lay there and watched more of her blood pump weakly onto the already soaked pavement.

"Oh, he's a good boy. Yes, a very good boy, right you are. Hopefully now he's a boy that knows when to keep his mouth shut." The Shadow Man turned and was looking right at him. Or right where Mark would be if he was real.

He was bigger than he was when Mark had seen him at Clara's. The flames of his eyes were brighter and the curls of smoke on his body darker and stronger than they were before. He placed the blade down into the pool of blood forming at her severed wrist. Just like at Clara's, the blood made its way up the blade until it was completely covered.

The Shadow Man turned and walked around to her car. He smashed the driver's side window with his cane, and then slid the blade back into place. There was a rumbling, retching sound, and then he spat a small glob of fire onto the seat. It sizzled and hissed before catching the seat on fire.

The Shadow Man turned and walked back into the clutch of trees, leaving Mark to watch as Carrie Kennedy bled to death by the light of her burning car.

CHAPTER SEVENTEEN

"Mr. Watson?" Ms. Olivio called

Mark turned away from the window, but before he could respond he saw past her and out the doorway of the classroom. It was Detective Prescott, standing in the hallway and doing a poor job of nonchalance. Mark had been waiting for this since showing up at school, trembling with the pitiful hope that what he'd seen last night hadn't been real.

Of course it was, and even though it looked like most of the emergency vehicles had moved along before school had started, the back parking lot was still closed off and there were plenty of teachers and staff with red-ringed eyes and far-off stares. The most that anyone else knew was that there had been an accident and Ms. Kennedy had died. Few people thought it had anything to do with what was going on in the back lot, and no one had said anything about murder.

Remember that, stupid. Nobody here knows anything about murder. Let's keep it between us, the cops, and the shadow demons.

"They need to see you down in the office," Ms. Olivio said.

"Sure," Mark said, picking up his backpack and jacket as he headed towards the door. There were a few low "oohs" and "ahhs," but probably less than there would've been since the now classic Bike Helmet Episode.

"Hey," Mark said when Ms. Olivio closed the classroom door behind him. "What're you doing here?"

"I need to talk to you, is that okay?" He took his badge out from the chest pocket of his jacket and let it hang from there.

"I guess. What's going on?"

"I think it'd be best if we did this downstairs in the office. I don't think we want to talk about this out in the hallway."

"What's going on?" Mark asked again, his voice trembling.

"Let's talk about it downstairs, okay?"

"Sure," Mark said, and they were silent until they got down to the basement office. A couple of the secretaries looked away when he made eye contact and Mr. Lafayette glared at Mark intently as they walked into his office. Detective Prescott nodded at him and then closed the door behind them.

"Have a seat," the detective said, taking one of the ones in front of Mr. Lafayette's desk.

"Mark, I'm sure you've heard that something happened here last night. Do you know what that was?"

"No. I mean, I heard some kids talking in homeroom. They said there was some sort of accident and something happened to Ms. Kennedy?"

The detective sighed and reached into his pocket, bringing out a small notebook. "Well, something happened to Ms. Kennedy, but it was no accident. She was murdered."

"Oh my God," Mark said, struggling with the balance of sounding surprised and not sounding too surprised. "How?"

"The details aren't important, except for the fact that there are some similarities between her death and Clara's. I wanted to talk to you about it, not just because of that, but because they said that the two of you had a pretty loud confrontation in here yesterday and then you ran off. Is that true?"

"Well, I met with her and everything like she asked me too but I don't think it was a confrontation. And I didn't run off, I just left." Unlike last time they spoke, Detective Prescott seemed totally closed off. The nice "I'm your buddy McGruff the crime dog, here are some tissues" cop was gone.

"Mark, I'm going to level with you. I'd like to think this is just a coincidence, but there are two things that connect this killing and Clara's. One of them is you, and you're my only lead here. If you're in some kind of trouble, or if you're scared of something or someone, I want you to tell me about it. Before someone else gets hurt."

"Shouldn't I have a lawyer or something? I mean, I don't even know what's going on here." He was getting hot, and the stupid chair was making him slide everywhere.

"Mark, if I you want to I can take you down to the station and we can wait for a lawyer there, but I don't think we have to do that. I just want to talk. I can tell you're real scared, and--"

"Of course I'm scared!" Mark yelled, perhaps a little too loudly. He flinched, but the detective was stoic. "I mean, one minute I'm in English and the next minute I'm down here in the Assistant Principal's office talking about murder! I mean, this is pretty crazy! What you want me to say?"

The detective just looked at him, and before he could say anything, there was a bellow from out in the office. A very familiar bellow.

"Where is he?"

The detective turned to look out the window, and Mark answered the unasked question. "My Uncle Joe. I think he's here to pick me up. Or kill me."

Detective Prescott sighed and opened the door, just in time to see Joe practically steamroll over Mr. Lafayette, who'd been trying to keep him out. Joe wasn't having any of it and was in mid finger-wagging bellow as the two of them got out of the office. As soon as Joe saw Mark he dodged around Mr. Lafayette with surprising agility.

"Will someone tell me what the fuck is going on here?" Mark had to resist the urge to crawl under a table, no matter how lucky his arrival had been.

"Mr. Nelson," the detective said, getting Joe's attention. "I'm Detective David Prescott from the Cedar Ridge Police Department. We met when I came to talk to Mark about his friend's death. I just wanted a moment to talk to your nephew about an incident that happened here last night."

"Just because you've been in my house doesn't mean you can just talk to my nephew whenever you want. I'm still responsible for him."

"I know," David said, "but if you could just calm down, we can talk about this rationally."

"Rationally my ass," Joe said. "I get a call down at work," he tugged on the postal jacket for effect, "to say that the police are going to talk to my nephew and you wanna talk 'rational' to me? Like hell, buddy! If you want to talk to him," he jabbed a thick finger in Mark's direction, "then you talk to me, and my lawyer, understood?"

"Mr. Nelson," David started again, but Joe waved him off.

"Don't fucking 'Mr. Nelson' me, alright? Save that shit for someone else, 'cause I ain't buyin'. Last I checked we had rights."

David's eyes narrowed, and then he said. "Fine, if you want to do this the hard way, we will. I'll take Mark down to the police station and we'll wait there for *Mark's* lawyer. I just wanted to ask him a few questions, but if you want a lawyer present that's your right. Agreed?"

"Good." Joe said, crossing his arms and puffing out his chest like he'd won something. He looked at Mark and said, "You go with him. Don't say *anything*, get me?"

Mark just nodded.

Joe looked back at the Detective and then turned on his heel and left, not even looking at anyone else.

"C'mon, Mark," Detective Prescott said. "I'm parked on the street."

They left the building and Mark's heart sank. David had come in an unmarked car but it was flanked by two squad cars. There weren't any cuffs and Mark knew that you couldn't see David's badge, but it was obvious to anyone looking out the window where Mark was going. If Mark knew anything about high school kids, he knew they were all looking out the window.

His guidance counselor gets killed and then he's taken away by the cops! Holy shit he's as crazy as they always said he was.

Thanks Joe, he thought. I really needed a lawyer to lie and tell them that I don't know anything.

The questioning took a pathetically short amount of time. Mark told David he'd had an appointment with the guidance counselor during lunch that day. They talked about a fight he had been in the week previous. He hadn't had any interaction with her before then. That night he'd been home, upstairs in his room all night. All in all, it was a terrific waste of thirty minutes.

Mark had been more emotional in his last visit and been close to that in the Vice Principal's office, but the car ride to the station and the wait for his Uncle and lawyer to join them did exactly what David hoped it wouldn't: calm him down and make him less like to give something away. The lawyer that Joe Nelson showed up with looked like he'd been picked randomly from the phone book and had barely been told what was going on. Mark, Joe and the lawyer spoke for only a couple of minutes before they told David they were ready for his questions.

"Do you know anyone that might want to hurt her?" David asked.

It was the one time that Mark hesitated. "No, I don't. I didn't really see her much."

"Until the fight."

"Yeah."

"And you two argued because why?"

Hesitation again. "It was stupid. She was trying to help and I didn't want her to bother me. She thought I should do mediation or something because of the fight and I just wanted to be left alone." There was a genuine crack in his resolve then. "She was just trying to help. I wish I'd been better."

"Better?"

"Nicer. I mean nicer."

He hadn't meant nicer, David was sure about that, and it left him with more pieces of the Mark Watson puzzle than he'd had before. A puzzle that was as easy to see as a polar bear in a snow storm.

CHAPTER EIGHTEEN

"I do not need this," Joe shook his head from side to side like a mule. "*We* do not need this. First the fight and now this? You are really fucking lucky that Morty was able to come down and help you out. You'd be in deep shit if I didn't know a lawyer, you know that?"

"I thought Morty was a tax attorney," Mark said, head leaning against the passenger window.

"Yeah, but he's all you've got so I wouldn't be throwing around that lip of yours."

Life would've been so much easier on them both if Joe didn't insist on setting Mark up like that. When he was a kid, Joe would tell him to watch his mouth and Mark would run around the house with his jaw and lips jutting out, trying to stare down at them. Clean up your act? Get me a broom. It was the only thing Mark could think of to combat the comical pointlessness of Joe's tirade. As if that were the biggest thing Mark had to worry about.

"I'm just saying if I *am* in any trouble, which I'm not," Mark said, "he wouldn't be able to help anyway. He'd just sit there and not say anything."

"Oh, he'd say something! Believe me, young man he most certainly would say something. You think you're so smart don't you? If he hadn't been there they would have twisted things around and before you knew it you'd be sitting in some cell! Do you even understand that?"

"Yeah, sure." Now that he was too old for childish mockery this was his only way of dealing with Joe. Yes, you're right. I'm wrong. I'm mistaken. I'm worthless. I never will amount to anything. You're right. You've always been right. They pulled into the driveway and Mark got out as soon as the car stopped moving.

"Hey! Hey!" Joe yelled, rolling down his window. Mark stopped and turned to listen. "I'm going back to work. *Someone* has to pay the bills around here. I want you up in that room of yours till tomorrow. I don't want to see your ass till then, you get me?"

"Yeah," Mark said, "and you can kiss it then too."

See, you were almost free and then you had to go and do something like that.

Joe's eyes narrowed and he was out of the car before Mark even realized that he'd spoken. "You think you're so goddamn *smart*, don't you?" He shoved Mark hard, almost knocking him off his feet. "You ain't too smart or too big for a beatin', I'll tell you that right now!" There was another shove and this time Mark landed on his back.

"I will not tolerate that kind of shit from some dumb punk who gets his dumb ass taken down to the goddamn police, you hear me? I promised your Aunt I wouldn't take my hand to you, but I swear to GOD I will if you keep that kind of shit up, do you get me?"

Mark nodded furiously. Joe was practically on top of him now, finger pointing, face reddening, and saliva flying. "Now, *Mr. Smart*, get your worthless ass in that house so I can get back to work. And don't make any fucking plans, because you are going to be in that house for a long time, do you get me?"

Mark nodded again, and Joe turned back to the car. Mark just sat there, and when Joe got behind the wheel and saw Mark still sitting there, he yelled "Go!" so loud Mark was sure the force of it was what pushed him to his feet.

The ceiling above his bed was fascinating, Mark realized. He'd been staring at it for hours since he'd gotten home, hoping that he'd drift into some sort of dreamless sleep he'd never wake up from before anything else epically shitty happened to him.

Instead, the phone rang. The chances were slim that whoever was on the other end wanted to kill him, so he figured he'd pick it up.

"Mark, are you okay?" Christine asked.

"Yeah, I'm alright. It was no big deal."

"Really? Steve said that he heard from someone that you were taken to the police station. Is that true, 'cause that sounds like a big deal."

"It got around that fast, huh? Why am I not surprised?"

"Mark, please! Are you okay? They're saying on the news that Ms. Kennedy was killed at the school last night!"

"Yeah, that's what they told me. They just wanted to ask me some question because of Clara but it was no big deal."

"Mark," she said, letting out a deep sigh. "These are the police, okay? They don't just haul you down to the station and put you in a room for nothing. And . . ."

"And what?"

"What about those dreams? You said you told Ms. Kennedy about dreams you were having and that she thought that it was serious, but--"

"But nothing! I don't know what she thought! She got all weird and was making a way bigger deal about the whole thing than it really was."

Nice way to speak of the dead. Well, the murdered. The murdered because of . . . well, let's not make a big deal about it.

She was quiet for a long time, and then said "But why would she think it was such a big deal? What did you say?"

"It was nothing."

"Mark, how could it be nothing if she thought this and now--"

"Now what? Now she's dead, and that means what?"

"I don't know what it means, Mark! It's just weird and fucked up that this happened, again, and I just--"

"Oh, 'again?' That's great. Don't worry I can assure you that I don't make a habit of this."

There was a long pause.

"I'm just trying to help Mark," she said. "You don't have to be so fucking defensive about it. This is a big deal."

"I know it's a big deal! I know because it's happening to *me*, okay? *I'm* the one whose friend was killed. *I'm* the one who got taken into the Police station in front of fucking *everyone*, okay? So don't you tell me that this is a *big deal*, okay? I kinda fucking got that already."

The pause was longer this time. "I know you've had a really bad day so I'm not going to tell you to fuck yourself, which is what I'm *dying* to do, by the way. I'm just trying to be supportive and help you out because you've laid some pretty heavy shit on me and I'm just trying to figure out how to deal with it, okay?"

He was chewing back the next wave of bile and anger when he remembered Ms. Kennedy, bleeding to death in the fire light. He remembered Clara, and her head rolling across the floor towards him. If he didn't watch his mouth then she could be next.

"I'm sorry. I know you're trying to help and this whole thing has just been so fucked up."

"I know," she said. "I just don't know why this is happening. Why would someone do this?"

"I don't know. But Christine, they were just dreams. I promise. I don't know why Ms. Kennedy got so excited about them, but they weren't any big deal. I promise."

"Okay. Okay, that's fine. I just . . . it's scary, y'know? And I just want to know what's going on."

"Believe me, I know the feeling. I'm so sorry that this is something you have to deal with and I hate the fact that you have to put up with me being a basket case about it on top of everything else. I'd totally understand if you want to just jump ship right now and never talk to me again."

He held his breath though the silence on her end of the line, and then she let out a long sigh. "Don't say that, Mark. I mean, this is pretty fucked up but I want to be able to help. I just remembered you said she got all weird and I hoped that she didn't say something to anyone else about it and for the cops to take it the wrong way. God knows how touchy everyone is with that kind of stuff now."

"Yeah, I know. It was just questions, okay? Nothing major, no intense grilling. Or any of that Law and Order shit."

"Thank god. So . . . your dreams are okay?"

"Not great, but nothing serious."

"Okay. Look, I better go. I think my Mom would freak if she knew I was talking to you."

"Good news travels fast, huh?"

"Something like that. I'll see you tomorrow, okay? Take care of yourself."

"I'm trying."

He was pulled awake from a shallow and dreamless sleep by the door to his room slamming open.

"Hey!" Joe yelled up the stairs.

"Yeah?" Mark said, looking over to check the time. It was after midnight, which meant the Drunk Uncle Index was about as high as it was going to get.

"Hey! Get down here when I'm talking to you, dammit!"

Mark sighed and walked to the top of the steps. "Yeah?"

"I'm not gonna put up with that bullshit like from before, y'hear?" Joe bellowed, leaning on the door frame.

"Yeah, I know. I'm sorry," Mark said. He didn't mean it and it probably didn't look like he did. Joe wasn't so drunk that he didn't notice.

"Yeah, yeah, you're real fucking sorry. I bet. Get'cher phone and TV down here. You're not gonna have any luxuries after talking that shit to me."

Mark opened his mouth to protest, but realized it was pointless. He unplugged the small TV first and brought it down the stairs, trying to think of anything he could say that could keep his lifeline to the outside world intact. Joe just motioned for Mark to drop the TV by the door, clear he didn't even want Mark to see where it was going.

"Do I really have to give you the phone, too?" he said, desperate.

"Yes, goddamnit!" Joe barked, giving Mark a light shove back towards the stairs. "And I don't want to hear any more of your shit, alright?"

"Yeah," Mark said, turning and heading back up the steps. Grabbing the cord, he had to resist the urge to yank the thing right out of the socket. He stood at the top of the steps and in his mind's eye he could see the phone flying down the steps and smashing into Joe's thick, drunken skull.

Go ahead, give it a shot. You better fucking pray it knocks him out and gives him amnesia, because you can bet what the next thing to go flying down the stairs will be.

Mark marched back down the steps and thrust the handset out, Joe grabbing it from him after a couple of tries. Mark turned to go, but Joe pushed him into the door frame with a swipe of his arm.

"Hey, look at me. *Look at me!*" Joe snarled. "You listen to me real good. I'm in charge here, okay Mr. Smart Guy? I'm the boss. You, my little smart friend, are nothing. The sooner you get that through your head, the better things are going to go for you. You're grounded. For two weeks. You're going to come right home after school and you're not going to do a damn thing but chores and homework. Got it?"

"Oh, come on! You just got done grounding me!"

"And I wouldn't have to keep doing it if you stopped fucking up! You keep this up and I'm going to take an axe to that faggy little scooter of yours! Do you get me?"

"Yeah," Mark said. "I get you."

"So I'm grounded. Again."

"Are you serious?" Steve said, flopping down onto the grass. Mark hated bringing up the bad news but he knew it was better sooner rather than later.

"What happened?" Christine asked.

"Turns out he wasn't too happy with the whole 'going down to the police station' thing. So yeah, grounded. For two weeks."

"Christ," Steve said sitting up with a great sigh. "Cops, groundings. It's like you're turning into the bad seed or something."

Mark wished he could prove him wrong but from the looks he'd gotten from not just students but other teachers it was clear that word of his questioning at the police station had spread as far as he'd feared. He never thought he'd wish for his painful anonymity or his crybaby reputation to return but they were so much better than "possible murder suspect." The only thing he could be thankful for was the fact that the news crews that had been camped out that morning when students had arrived were gone by the time he'd been taken down to the station. Without much more to go on they'd been fairly stymied in their "Breaking News!" coverage, with the exception of talking heads from concerned citizens that "didn't think something like that could happen in a nice town like this."

"So what are you going to do?" Christine asked.

"I dunno. I've got to be home 15 minutes after school is over to get a call from my Uncle and if I'm not there then he adds another week to my grounding."

"Wow, that's way harsh," she said.

"Oh you have no idea," Steve chimed in. "That dude is Mister Order and Discipline. He makes the guy from Full Metal Jacket look like Ryan Seacrest. There was this one time--"

"Look," Mark said, not knowing which embarrassing Joe story he would trot out but knowing none of them were suitable for Christine's consumption. "It's not that bad. I just have to do some stuff around the house and that's it. We still have lunch and class and we will be able to talk on the phone again soon."

"He took your phone?"

"Yeah. Totally lame."

"One of these days you've got to get yourself a cell phone," Steve said. "This 'handset' thing is just so . . . primitive."

"Any time you want to pay for it let me know. Plus he can keep track of who I'm calling with a land line."

"No chance to try calling before he gets home from work, huh?" She asked.

"I don't want to risk it. He catches me and he's going to make these next two weeks look like a vacation."

"It'll be okay," Christine said, giving him a quick kiss. Mark couldn't help but catch Steve's eye-roll in the background. "Steve and I are here for you. Right?"

"Oh, yeah," Steve said, nodding. "I mean, I'm not sure what I could do but I'm here for you, 100 perfect. Go Team Grounded."

"Maybe you could loan him your phone or something one night?" Christine said.

"No way, man. I've got dick picks on there."

"What? Do you mean--"

"Yes, it's what it sounds like," Mark said. "One of the reasons why I'm actually glad I *don't* have my own phone."

She looked back to Steve, who just shrugged and smiled.

"You are so weird," she said, leaning against Mark. "It's only two weeks, right?"

"Yeah," Mark said, kissing the top of her head. He was thankful that he'd been able to catch her before she made it to homeroom that morning so she could accept a nearly tearful apology. Now thanks to this stupid grounding that kind of early morning meeting and a quick one at the end of the day were going to be the only times the two of them were going to have by themselves.

He looked over at Steve, who tossed a potato chip into his mouth with a smile. He wanted to find a way to ask Steve if he'd be able to get the lunch period alone with his girlfriend but he didn't really want to hear whatever excuse he'd come up with as to why he couldn't.

CHAPTER NINETEEN

The door swung open with a loud shriek or rusted metal, waking Darren. He'd fallen asleep, curled up on the concrete floor in the front corner of the cell next to the doorway, and when he looked up he saw the Shadow Man's form silhouetted by the furnace light.

They'd taken to sleeping during the day, but it was hard to tell exactly what time it was since it was so hard to see one of the small windows from their dark little cell and they were too dirty to let much light in. The Shadow Man spent most of the night in front of the furnace, staring into it and muttering to himself. It was during these fits that he would leap to his feet, storm to their cell in the back of the basement and drag someone out to be forced to "witness."

After several days he'd brought another boy down to the basement. Like Darren had been, he was unconscious when the Shadow Man dropped him off in the little cell. When he woke he screamed and yelled and nothing Darren or Suzie could do would quiet him down. Eric, the boy Darren had seen beaten after he first woke up, was too weak to do much of anything. After hours of screaming the Shadow Man came back downstairs and made the new boy, Oscar, "witness" for the first time. It gave him something else to scream about.

It took Darren a moment to realize that the Shadow Man had another boy with him, unconscious and being held up by one limp arm. Darren scooted out of his way as the man ducked down and pushed his new captive into the cell with the other children.

Darren could see the Shadow Man more clearly now. His face was narrow and his eyes were wide with dark circles under them. He scanned the crowded cell as if he was taking it in for the first time. His nose wrinkled at the smell of bodies confined in close quarters mixed with the lingering smell of the bucket he'd left for them to "do their business" in. He took away the plate he'd been piling food for them on and the canteen that he filled with water, placing them just outside of the cell's door.

The new arrival was lying next to Eric, who hadn't moved at all since the Shadow Man had arrived. He'd been listless when Oscar first arrived but had barely moved or woken up since his last session in front of the furnace and his breathing had settled in a slow, uneven wheeze.

The Shadow Man reached in, his arm going right by Darren, and shook the unconscious boy's foot. At the far end of the cell next to Eric's outstretched arms Suzie and Oscar pressed themselves up against the wall.

"Wake him," he said to them

Oscar reached down and shook Eric's arm, but Suzie didn't move, just muttered "Wake up, wake up," so softly Darren could barely hear it. Eric did nothing but twitch at the boys' touch.

"Useless."

The Shadow Man leaned into the cell and grabbed Eric by the foot, dragging his limp body out. Darren watched as Eric's head lolled slightly to the side, the rough concrete opening one of the many cuts on his cheek and starting a bright red trail towards the door. Eric still didn't move, but the new boy stirred as Eric brushed past him.

"Leave him alone!" Darren yelled, grabbing one of Eric's limp arms before they cleared the cell's doorway and tugging as hard as he could. Eric finally stirred, moaning in pain as the jagged chain-abrasions on his wrists began to crack and bleed. Darren could feel his fingers begin to lose their grip.

The Shadow Man reached into the cell, shoving Darren and pinning him down on the floor. Darren flailed and tried to get up, but he was lifted and then slammed down onto the concrete.

"No!" The Shadow Man snarled. "He can't see any more, and if he can't see then he's useless. Then he's fuel."

Darren tried to sit up and say something, but his head flopped back onto the ground with a painful thud as the rusted metal ceiling swam above him.

The door slammed shut and the bar clanged back into place, echoing in Darren's shaken brain. He rolled over on his side, pulling himself up to his perch by the window so he could see what he'd failed to stop.

Instead of hanging Eric from the chain, he'd been left on the floor in front of the furnace. The Shadow Man picked up the cane from its resting place and pulled a long, thin sword blade from it. He placed the cane sheath on the floor and then picked up one of Eric's legs, holding it up off the ground by the boy's heel.

The blade wavered for a second before it came down in a great big sweep, right where Eric's leg met his body. "No, no, no, no," Darren muttered over and over, but he could barely hear himself over the screams of the other children in the cell as they realized what the wet, tearing sounds were.

Eric never woke up. It was the only thing Darren had been thankful for in a long time.

When it was finished, he picked up the various pieces that had been Eric and threw them into the open furnace mouth. When each piece hit the flames the furnace roared. Darren watched the entire gruesome spectacle, until all that was left of Eric was stains on the concrete and the roar of flames.

The Shadow Man dropped to his knees in front of the roaring furnace, lowering his head to the ground and resuming whatever strange prayers he made to his god of iron and fire.

Throughout the entire ordeal Darren didn't budge. The buzz in his head was gone, replaced with the roar of the flames whispering in his ear as the fire raged in front of him.

"I've missed this," Christine said, stretching and repositioning herself on Mark's lap.

"Me too," he said, absently stroking her hair. After two weeks of home incarceration and lunches hampered by a third wheel being alone together was heavenly.

"What's up?" she asked.

"Nothing," he said, faking a smile. "I'm just thinking."

"Anything good?"

Go ahead, tell her: Well, my nightmares have progressed from beatings to dismemberments and I've been trapped in my house unable to look into what I think might be the answer. Same old, same old.

"Just stuff."

"Mark," she said, sitting up, "is there something going on? I thought you'd be a little bit more excited to be here."

"I am, really. I've just been stuck at my place without much to do but think about all this stuff that's happened. It hasn't exactly been thrilling."

"Well, if you need to talk about this--"

"Why?" he blurted out. "Why is the answer always talking about it? Why can't we just let it lie and maybe it'll just go away?"

"Because life doesn't work like that," she said, sitting up. "You can't just ignore the problem and hope it'll go away."

"I'm not ignoring, I'm just . . ."

"Just what?"

"It's nothing."

"Mark, just tell me. Please."

"I . . . I can't, okay. You just have to trust me, but I'm trying to take care of things."

"What things? Will you stop with the cryptic shit and just say something?"

"I'm just . . . I'm just trying to figure out who could've killed them. I've been wracking my brain, trying to figure it out, but I can't."

"Mark," she smiled, no doubt relaxed and comforted by the realization that this was just him being a gigantic fucking spaz. "You can't do this to yourself. This whole thing is probably just some kind of coincidence, and there's nothing that you can do that the police can't do. They even said on the news that they had some leads that they were investigating."

"I know, but it's just not right. They deserved better, and I wish I could do something about it."

"There's nothing you can do, Mark." She leaned in and kissed him, and after a few seconds she pulled away. "You really don't know anything about it, right? What's going on, I mean."

You better lie, kiddo. Make her believe it.

"No, there's nothing to know. I'm just kind of freaked out."

"I can only imagine," she said, leaning back into him. "Are you still having those dreams that Ms. Kennedy asked about?"

He paused again, and figured he'd better try to sprinkle some truth in to make his lies come out a little easier. "Bad dreams, but I think it's just stress and being freaked out."

"Well," she said, kissing him. "That's what we're here for. Getting rid of stress."

***

"Lookit 'em go," Eric whistled.

"Shut up," Jack snarled.

"Hey, I'm not the one who thought it'd be fun to play peeping tom, okay?" Eric shifted uncomfortably in the driver's seat. "Y'know, I can understand you being pissed at this little cocksucker, but this is just kinda . . ." he trailed off when he felt Jack's gaze on him. He cleared his throat and tried again.

"I'm just trying to say that, as much I want to kick this loser's ass, why do we have to follow him around? I mean, can't we just wait for a day when all of us have some free time, follow him and just jump the shit out of him then?"

Jack just kept staring at him.

"Right. Stupid of me to ask," he murmured. Jack turned back to watching the couple, and Eric started tapping the steering wheel impatiently.

A few more minutes passed, and finally Eric tried again. "Look, I told Becky I'd help her with her math homework, and if we get that done fast enough she might even blow me before her parents get home, so really, unless you think they're gonna fuck right here in the park I gotta pull rank as the driver and say we're leaving, okay?"

Jack just kept staring at him. "Man, will you quit that crazy eyes shit? I mean, that little fucker almost broke my nose, okay? Trust me, I will be holding him down when you go ape-shit on him, but right now, for me, it's dick sucking time. We're leaving."

Not waiting for an answer, Eric started the car.

"I knew it," Jack said, his voice flat.

"What?"

"That you're a fucking queer."

"What?" Eric said, finally looking over at him. Jack's face had lost the blank stare that had become more and more common place over the past few weeks, and there was a glimmer of the Jack that he actually wanted to be around.

"It's dick sucking time?" Jack said. "I knew you were a fucking queer."

Eric broke out into a grin of his own, more from relief than anything else. "You are so goddamn juvenile, you know that?"

"Just drive the car, pussy," Jack said.

***

"I have to get going," she said.

"Really?" Mark said, not letting go.

"I know the timing is lousy, but I'm totally swamped with work and crap." She kissed his cheek and disengaged with practiced ease.

He got to his feet with her. "I just was hoping we'd be able to get some more time together."

"I did too. It's just that I'm still on something resembling probation, and I want to be on my best behavior so my parents forget about all this negative shit that been going on."

"Your folks still freaked out about the thing, huh?" Mark asked, picking his backpack with a resigned sigh.

"Oh yeah. But don't worry I've been working my charms on them. You're not the first guy I've had to work to get them to like."

"Really? Don't I feel special."

Oh, don't be surprised. This chick is a pro. Just be happy you have her while you do, until she gets bored of your handholding and moves on to a guy that actually knows what he's doing.

"Don't worry," she said, linking her arm in his as they walked towards the edge of the park. "Once my parents are done with their overprotective freakout, I'm sure they'll be more than happy that we're together. They really seemed to like you at first."

"You think?"

"Oh yeah," she said. "If it wasn't for all this stuff I'm sure my mother would have had you over for Sunday dinner by now. She loves it. I think it gives her a chance to show off the nice china or something."

"Oh. Well, I'll keep my fingers crossed."

"Hey," she said, tugging on his jacket. "It's gonna work out. I'll see what I can do, okay?"

"Okay," he said, faking a smile.

After dropping Christine off with a kiss and a promise to call him that night, he drove back towards Briarcliff Avenue. He didn't go up the seemingly harmless street, but from where he stopped the scooter he could see the top of the house peeking up to remind him that it was still there waiting for him.

When he wasn't trying to catch up on homework or trying to sleep he'd spent his time trying to figure what he was going to do next. It was only a matter of time before the Shadow Man came for him. Or Steve. Or Christine.

All that he could put together was that if what he'd been dreaming about had actually happened, there'd be a record of it. If he could find out how it all ended then maybe he'd be able to point Detective Prescott at someone that had a connection to it, or at least give him a place to start looking.

Mark turned the V back on and drove away. The computer that Clara had handed down to him could theoretically have helped him but Joe was too cheap to actually get any kind of Internet service. Any web surfing Mark did was at Steve's house, and he wasn't about to look this stuff up there, which meant his only choice was to go to the library.

He parked and locked the V in front of the vaguely Communist Bloc looking building and headed inside. He picked a computer relatively out of the way so there wouldn't be much of a chance of someone walking by and seeing what he was looking up.

"Okay internet," he muttered. "You're supposed to have all the answers. Let's see what we can find out."

A half hour later Mark realized he'd have had better luck talking into the mouse and telling it what he was looking for. Every search item he could think of brought up thousands of pages about current crimes and kidnappings, or ridiculous nonsense like the Jersey Devil. Not that a goat-legged jumping demon was any less plausible than what was happening in his life.

He resigned himself to the fact that not only was he a shitty Internet detective but that this was not going to be the magic bullet that cracked the case. He closed the browser and stared at the bland institutional wallpaper they had put on the desktop. It was depressing, but it looked like if he was going to have any success he'd have to try real books.

He brought up the library's computerized card catalog and tried to remember how the damn thing worked. After a few false starts, he managed to figure out that there was a local history section down in the basement.

He wandered the stacks for a while until he found the right section, a single narrow bookcase conveniently located next to Ancient Indo-China studies and the restrooms. Three great tastes that tasted great together, apparently. He leafed through some books that seemed promising but were about bootleggers and the Revolutionary War until he spotted one, jammed sideways behind a couple of others.

He pulled it out, and the gold leaf on the plain brown cover stated "Bizarre Crimes of Northern New Jersey." If anything was going to have it, it was going to be this. He flipped back to the index, scanning for "Cedar Ridge" and "Briarcliff." He didn't realize that he was holding his breath until he let out a deep exhale upon seeing "Cedar Ridge Slayings, pgs 78-99."

There you go, junior detective. This is the book for us. You still think 21 pages are going to be all the ammo you need?

"It better be," he muttered. He looked up and realized that it was almost 5. While Joe's speedy return home wasn't guaranteed, Mark figured it was best to at least appear as if he wasn't trying to get into any more trouble.

He snapped the book shut and went upstairs to check it out. All he had to do was read the book, solve the case and put the whole thing behind him. Simple, easy.

"Bizarre Crimes" dedicated a whole chapter to what had taken place on that street in the summer of 1951, and the title of the chapter gave the Shadow Man a name: "Justin Corwin and the Cedar Ridge Slayings."

Justin Corwin had returned home from the Second World War and lived with his parents, working various odd jobs around town. He had apparently been through quite a bit of trauma during the war and that, coupled with an injury to his knee that had cut short his military service had made it difficult for him to hold down a steady job and move out of his parent's house. After a couple years, Justin rarely left the house.

The first picture of him in the book showed a tall, lanky blond boy (probably only a couple of years older than Mark) in an army uniform, smiling and waving like he was heading off to camp and not war. The next was after his return, leaning against porch steps of that house, staring at the camera as if he were trying to will the photographer to hurry up and be done with it. Corwin was slumped over, hair disheveled and sporting what at the time must have been an unacceptable level of stubble.

The book detailed the disappearances of the various children from Cedar Ridge and its surrounding towns, and Mark could easily recognize them from the tiny photos they reprinted. There'd been no leads in the three weeks since the first child, Eric Campbell, was taken, and it wasn't until a group of the neighborhood children came forward and said that one of the kidnapped children had been in Corwin's yard the day of his disappearance. One of the detectives on the case had been at the house, trying to ask the Corwins about it when he heard a disturbance from an old coal chute leading down to the basement. Once down there, he made the gruesome discovery that Justin Corwin had not only kidnapped the missing children but murdered his parents as well.

"Justin Corwin," the book had said, "must have experienced a psychotic break after his experiences in the War, and after killing his own parents, he began to stalk and kidnap children from the surrounding neighborhoods. His parents' remains, as well as those of four of the children that he killed, were found dismembered and burned in the basement furnace of his home. Corwin's mental break was so deep and complete that it led him to believe that there was a presence in the furnace that was directing him to kill. The extent of his breakdown was never fully explored, as Corwin took his own life in a prison cell two weeks after his capture."

In the final picture, Corwin was being led out of the police station downtown by a pair of officers. There was a crowd around them, frozen in their rage, being held back unenthusiastically by several other policemen. Corwin's slump was gone as he pulled away from the crowd. He face was bruised and cut, and his confusion was as clear as the rage on the crowd's faces.

Of the five children taken, only one survived. They named all four victims (Eric Campbell, Suzie Morris, Oscar Lukacs and Randal Sims), but there was no mention of Darren. He was simply "the surviving child." The book had been written in 1969, and Mark wondered if they had decided against using it or had been asked not to.

Given that the book seemed to be the only public record of what had happened in that house Mark was probably one of the only people alive who knew that Darren Cox had been the one who'd survived.

Some magic bullet, huh? At least now you know how it all ends. Don't you feel better?

CHAPTER TWENTY

"Hello?" Christine called into the house after Mark had dropped her off. She hadn't really expected her parents to be home but given their lack of regard for her privacy it was better to be sure of their whereabouts.

There was no response, and Christine started up the stairs. A noise stopped her halfway up the steps. She cocked her head to see if she could hear it again. When there wasn't anything to be heard, she shook her head and chalked it up to the anxiety coming off of Mark making her a little paranoid.

When she made it to the top she heard it again.

It could have been a foot creaking on one paf the loose boards on the second floor near her room but it could just been the house settling. She stopped and listened again, but this time there was just silence.

"Hello?" she called again, wishing her voice wasn't wavering. There still wasn't any response.

"Fine," she murmured, and with a sudden dash of speed she pulled her bag from her shoulder and swung it in front of her as she rounded the corner to her room. If there wasn't anyone there she was going to have a great time explaining to her Mom the scratches on the just repainted wall.

Instead of wall, the bag found a set of ribs and the man attached to them.

When she realized that there was someone there she let out one of the loudest screams she could muster while still swinging her purse at the doubled over intruder.

"Ahhhh, Jesus!" he yelled in a familiar voice. "I give up! I give up!"

"Oh my god," she said, dropping everything. "Ryan?"

"Yeah, it's me." her brother groaned, lowering his hands and straightening up. "Oh my god," he said. "Did you join a fucking gang or something? I haven't been hit that hard since the lacrosse finals."

"I am so sorry, Ry, are you . . ." she trailed off, and then punched him as hard as she could in the stomach. He gasped and sprung up, waving a hand to bat her away.

"Fuck!" he yelled. "Enough with the fucking hitting! What is the matter with you, are you on your period or something?"

"Fuck you!" she snapped. "You were going to jump out and scare me weren't you? You freaked me the hell out!"

"Good! What did you think I was going to be?"

"Oh, fuck off," she said, picking her stuff off the floor and then following him into the guest room across the hall from hers. It was going to be where Ryan would stay while he was home from college, but he was supposed to be there for at least another two weeks.

"Why the hell are you here early, anyway?"

"Well," he said, kicking one of his bags towards the dresser. "I finished one of my mid-term projects early, so I got a head start."

"Like what? You've never finished anything early, although now that I think about it I did hear some girls complaining about that in Boston."

"God, you are so classy. I'll tell you, but if you say anything to Mom and Dad before I do, I'll tell them you got home an hour later than you were supposed to."

"Fine," she said. "Hey! I'm only twenty minutes late you fucking liar!"

"They don't know that," Ryan grinned evilly. "My God, have they got you on that short a leash already? I was just guessing."

She rolled her eyes and dropped down onto the bed next to him. "Fine, whatever. What have you screwed up this time?"

"Jeez, you sleep through one midterm and all of the sudden it's a big screw-up."

"You didn't!" she said, but wasn't the least bit surprised. Ryan's athletics and Dad's money had gotten him into college, not his grades or his willingness to actually work.

"Yeah, I did," he said with a resigned sigh. "The prof's a real prick too, and there is no way he's gonna let me retake it, and there's no way I can pass the class with a zero on it, so I figure that's just one less research paper I've got to work on."

"Well, that is a spectacular screw up," she said.

"Mmm-hmmm," he said, getting up and looking around his new room. There had been two other bedrooms, but Mom and commandeered the other room for doing "craft projects," and that left Ryan with the smallest room in the house. "Anyway," he said, tossing another bag in the direction of the closet, "what the hell kept you at school so long?"

"I was at the park. With my boyfriend."

"Boyfriend?" he asked. "Oh my god, you've been here for like five minutes! Are you incapable of not latching on to some guy to make yourself feel better?"

"It's not like that. He's not like those other guys I used to go out with. He's actually nice and doesn't act like a giant prick all the time."

"Oh, he's gay! Okay, well, do go on."

She just flipped him off and continued. "I'm sick of dating those sports car driving, immature jock assholes. Mark's really sweet and seems to like me for who I am and not just something to try to have sex with."

"So he's a loser. A gay loser, apparently."

"He is not a loser!" she snapped. "He may be different, but he's not a loser. He's sweet. And cute."

"Cute and sweet. But different. Huh. So have Mom and Dad met this spastic gay loser yet?"

"Yes, they have," she said, hitting him on the arm. "They have some issues. They don't seem to want to give him a chance."

"No, not Mom and Dad! They wouldn't possibly be close minded about something!" he said, sitting down next to her.

"Yeah," she said, hoping he wouldn't press her for details. "They've known we've been going out for almost a month and a half and Mom hasn't even mentioned having him over for dinner."

"Shit," Ryan murmured. She had tried to downplay the importance her mother placed on "Sunday Dinner" to Mark, but once she or her brother even mentioned the fact that they were seeing someone, her mother was all over them every waking second to have that person over.

"Look," Ryan finally said, "if you keep my academic screw-ups on the down-low, I bet I can get Mom and Dad to have this totally straight, normal boy over this Sunday."

"Really?" she said, sitting up quickly. "You'd actually do that?" While Ryan had a spectacular track record of irritation and disappointment as a brother, he did have a way of negotiating their parents into doing what he wanted.

"Yup. Besides," he grinned, "you'll owe me one, and I have got to meet this 'super-different guy' for myself. I haven't had a good laugh in ages."

***

Deep breaths. Just take deep breaths and you'll be fine.

It was easy to think that, but as soon as Christine's door opened on Sunday, deep breaths went right out the window.

"You must be Mark," the brother from the pictures said with a wide, gleaming white smile. "I'm Ryan, Christine's brother. C'mon in, big guy."

"Yeah, that's me. I . . . well, it's nice to meet you."

"Don't worry about it," Ryan said, waving Mark further into the house. Mark had tried to be as excited as Christine had been when she told them her brother had talked their parents into asking him over that weekend. As the day got closer, Mark realized spending time in the Baker's palatial estate was far, far down on his list of things he wanted to do.

"Take it easy, buddy," Ryan said, clapping a hand onto Mark's shoulder and leaning in to whisper. "This'll be over in about an hour, tops, and then you guys can take off. Have a little, y'know." He shot out his fist with a little whistle, giving Mark's shoulder a hard slap. "You know what I'm talking about, stud."

"Right," Mark said. Ryan's pictures hadn't done him justice. He was at least a foot taller than Mark and with every slap and squeeze Mark could feel himself getting smaller and Ryan's smile getting wider.

Boy, we've got to get him and Jack together. They would have a field day with you. Literally. I think this guy could throw you 50-yards, easy.

"Hey," Christine called when they walked into the dining room, looking up from the silverware she was arranging on the table. "You're sitting next to me. I hope that's okay," she winked.

"Uh, yeah, fine," Mark said, taking the rest of the room in. In addition to the gigantic conference table they were apparently going to eat at, the room was lined with glass-faced hutches all filled with various plates and silverware that looked like they belonged in a museum rather than somewhere Mark could knock into and send them and his future spilling to the floor.

"Hey," Ryan said, clapping Mark on the back so unexpectedly that it almost knocked him over. "Let me get your jacket. Don't want to get it all messed up, do we?"

"Yeah. I mean, I guess not," Mark said, fumbling with the ratty denim he wore almost year round. Getting dressed had been funeral-level nerve wracking. What he'd managed to put together was a button-down shirt that was trying to squeeze him to death and pants that screamed 'Hey, check out these crappy socks!'

"Nice jacket," Ryan muttered, probably too low for Christine to hear in her time-zone on the other side of the table. "You don't see a lot of these anymore." Mark sighed and made his way over to Christine.

"You'll do fine," Christine said, kissing Mark on the cheek while they were still alone.

"You sure? I think Ryan might be hiding my coat. I hate when that happens."

"Mark, just relax," she said, patting him on the arm.

"I'll try," he said, looking around some more. "Do you eat in here every night?"

"Yeah," she said, going over to a cabinet and getting a set of cloth napkins and napkin rings. "It's a little weird with just the three of us, but Dad hates to eat in front of the TV."

"Right. That would be weird."

Ryan came back in with his parents in to greet Mark with almost warm smiles and loose handshakes. They sat while Mrs. Baker and Christine went back into the kitchen to retrieve the food. After several trips, the two managed to fill the table as Mark took turns nodding and smiling at all the members of Baker family.

When they finally sat down and he was served, Mark realized that he had too many forks. Like, twice the normal amount of forks. He almost opened his mouth to say something, but caught himself when he realized he hadn't just been given everyone's forks but there was an equally excessive amount of forks for everyone at the table.

There was salad, soup, bread, cheese for the bread, and some kind of steak and mushroom dish he wouldn't have been able to spell, much less pronounce on his own. Ryan and Christine's parents had white wine, and he and Christine had soda.

"We wouldn't want you riding your moped under the influence," her father said, smiling and getting a laugh that was a little too big from Ryan. Mark would've corrected him, but realized that it was about as pointless as his assortment of many-sized forks.

The only thing that made Mark feel better was the fact that Christine's parents (Harold and Cynthia, they offered, but Mark stuck to Mr. and Mrs. Baker) seemed as uncomfortable as he was.

"So what do your parents do, Mark?" her mother asked during the soup course, Mark heard the quick gulp from Christine, who had been taking a drink.

"Actually, Mrs. Baker," he said, "my parents passed away when I was young. I live with my Uncle Joe." He paused, and then said. "He works at the post office."

"Oh." Cynthia said. "I'm so sorry. Christine didn't say anything about your parents."

"Why would I?" Christine said, an edge creeping into her voice.

Mark wondered if he dropped one of his forks, how long he could stay under the table "looking" for it before he was missed. Long enough to tunnel to freedom? Worth pondering. He glanced across the table at Ryan, who smiled at him from around his third glass of wine.

Harold simply cleared his throat, and Mark watched as the Baker women stifled the rest of their argument. Ryan gave Mark another nod and smile.

Well, someone's having fun, so that's good. Chin up, kiddo, only two more courses to go.

Ryan's estimate was right, and about an hour after he had given up his coat he got it right back. Mark tried not to look like he was running for his life as he and Christine left, and he was sure he saw a fair share of relief in her parent's eyes. "You kids take care of yourselves," her father called after them as they headed down the walk.

"Dad!" Christine called over her shoulder.

"Right. Just . . . be careful out there."

"Oh, that was a blast," murmured Mark, reaching into the storage compartment to get the spare helmet.

"It wasn't that bad, Mark," Christine said, lightly slapping him on the back. "I've seen much worse, and I am so sorry about the whole 'parents' thing. I *know* I told my mom about your whole family situation."

"Great," Mark muttered, passing her the spare helmet.

"What was I supposed to say?" she said. "I mean, lying to them wasn't going to do any good, and they'd find out sooner or later."

"I would have preferred later," he said, staring the V up and just barely avoiding peeling out of the driveway.

"Hey!" she yelled, grabbing a hold of his jacket. "I wasn't even ready back here!"

"Sorry, sorry," he said, stopping at the intersection and waiting for her to get situated.

"They saw that, y'know. You're not exactly endearing yourself to them if you keep up shit like that!"

Mark let out a deep breath, and was very glad that his helmet covered his whole face so he could keep her from seeing his clenched jaw and flushed cheeks. He blew out a large, lungful of air and then finally said, "I'm sorry. You're right I just . . . fuck! I can't even breathe in this get-up! I look fucking ridiculous! And your brother? Oh my god, are you kidding me?"

"Hey," she said, reaching around and stroking his chest. "You look fine, okay? And yes, he is a giant ass, but this will really help you out with them, okay? Trust me."

"I do, I just--" he was interrupted by the impatient beeping of a car that had crept up behind them. "Fucking A," he muttered, taking off down the street.

"What do you want to do?" she asked when they next came to a stop. "Do you want to go home and change or something?"

He thought about it for a moment, and then realized that Joe was probably out at the bar with his crew, and the house was just sitting there empty. It was also a giant mess, as it always was, but the thought of an empty house was far too tempting.

"Well," he said. "Joe has left for the night, and won't be back until late. We *could* skip the movie and hang out at my place for a while. If you wanted too."

"That," she said, giving him a squeeze, "definitely sounds doable. Besides, I've been very curious to see your place anyway."

"Don't get your hopes up."

In his rush to get her over there, Mark had forgotten *how* messy and disorganized he and Joe had left the place. The living room was filled with empty beer cans, and as Mark was showing her around trying to act cool about the whole thing, he suddenly remembered the half-eaten bowl of cereal in his room that was quickly spawning life.

"Well," Mark finally said, waving an arm around the small, cluttered living room, "this is it."

"It's nice," she said, looking around and taking it all in. Mark couldn't help but wonder if he looked as out of place in her house as she did in his. "What's upstairs?"

"Just the bedrooms," Mark said.

"Oh really?" Christine said, wagging her eyebrows, and then with a sudden burst of speed she took off.

"Hey!" Mark cried, racing after her.

By the time he got to the top of the stairs, she was already down the hallway. "Hmmm!" she called in a loud, sing-song voice, "which one is Mark's room?" She was heading towards the door at the far end of the hall, and before Mark could call out to her, she flung open the door to Joe's room.

"Whoa," she said with a grimace. "Please tell me that's not it." As messy as he left the rest of the house, Joe saved his special messes for his boudoir.

"No," Mark said, coming up behind her. "That's my Uncle's room."

"Thank God," she said, backing away and closing the door. She spun around, and before she could dart around him, Mark grabbed her.

"Is this part of the tour?" she said.

"No, the rest is upstairs."

"The roof?" she said with a wry smile.

"No, the attic. That's my place."

"Oh really?"

She kept stepping closer, and Mark found himself backing up with each step until he stumbled back into the doorknob.

"So am I the first girl that's gotten to see your attic hideaway?"

"Maybe," he said, reaching behind him to open the door. She stepped back just enough for him to open it, and when he did she squirmed past and raced up the stairs.

"It's messy!" was all Mark could bring himself to say as he darted after her. As delightfully forbidden as the idea of having her in his room was, faced with the reality of it, he found his mind racing to see if he could remember if he had left anything embarrassing out that she shouldn't see. He was pretty sure all his dirty underwear was in the laundry basket, and the Playboys he liberated from the garage were safely under the mattress.

"I've wondered what this would look like," Christine said, as he came up the steps. She was standing on the far side of the room, where the ceiling was the highest, turning slowly in place.

"I hope it's not too disappointing."

"No, this is cool," she said. "The house we had before the last one had a big attic for storage, but my folks wouldn't let us even play up there."

"Well," he said, "it's not much, but it's mine."

"You make it sound like your own sovereign nation," she said, turning back to face him and putting her arms around his neck.

"In a way, it works like that. My uncle and I don't do a lot of family time."

"Really?" she said with mock surprise. "I never would have guessed. I mean, given the positively *glowing* way you've mentioned him in the past--"

He cut her off with a kiss, and within a couple of seconds Mark had found they had drifted over to the edge of the bed. "Whoops," he muttered, and then the two of them toppled sideways down onto it.

"Whoops indeed," she said, rolling over on top of him, and before Mark could warn her, she sat up and bumped her head on the low, sloping ceiling. The head of the bed was right up against the wall where the ceiling was at its lowest, giving only about two feet of head room.

"Ow," she whined, rubbing her head. "I bet that happens a lot."

"No, I don't get a lot of girls bumping their heads in my bed," he said.

"I find that hard to believe," she said, leaning down closer to him.

"No, it's true, I . . . well, this is really embarrassing, but I've never really done anything like this before."

"Don't worry," she said. "It's no different than being in the park. Just more comfortable. Okay?"

"Okay," he said, leaning up to kiss her.

CHAPTER TWENTY-ONE

"I love you," he said, kissing her hair.

She kissed his bare chest, but she knew she wasn't going to get off the hook that easily. As the seconds stretched on she could feel the arms around her tense up and she knew she was going to have to say something.

"Mark," she said, lifting her head, "I really, really care about you, and," she paused, seeing the sudden flash of hurt in his eyes, "I could definitely love you too."

"But you don't." He looked away.

"Hey," she said, using her finger to turn his face back towards her. "Maybe not yet, but I just need a little bit more time before I say that, okay?"

"I understand," he said, the glum slowly creeping away.

"I hope so, Mr. 'I've-never-done-this-before.' What kind of line was that?"

That did the trick, and he looked away, blushing this time. "What's that supposed to mean?"

"It means," she said, leaning down to nibble at his ear (which she had discovered made him squirm and make the cutest little "squeaking" noises), "that either you were just messing with me or you're just naturally gifted."

"Now you're just teasing me," he said, pushing her away with a smile.

It was more exaggeration than teasing, but frankly it was a relief to be with a boy who wasn't pushing her head down or strategically guiding her hand every ten seconds. He'd gotten her down to her underwear, but he hadn't pressed the issue any further.

"Did you mean that?" Mark said, pulling back from her.

"About what?"

"About me being . . . well, 'loveable,' I guess."

"Mark," she said, trying to keep her rising exasperation out of her voice, "I mean everything I say to you. You're special to me, and I could see myself getting only closer to you. I don't want to just say, 'I love you' back just because, y'know?"

"I know. I just--" Mark started, and she placed her finger over his lips again.

"If it makes you feel any better," she said, "you're the best thing in my life right now, and you make me very, very happy."

He smiled and kissed her finger. "That does help."

"Good," she said, and then glanced over at the alarm clock, "because if I don't get home in fifteen minutes this'll be the last time we get to do this before the end of the year. Where did you throw my pants?"

"I didn't throw them. They're right over there." She got up and picked them up, and as she did she made the small pile of books they were resting on fall over.

"Sorry. I'll get it," she said. She started picking up books and setting them all together in a pile when one of them caught her eye.

"What was that?" Mark said, pulling his shirt over his head. "Oh, hey! That's okay, I can get that later!"

The book was old and brown, and the gold leaf on the book read "Bizarre Crimes of Northern New Jersey." There was a pen stuck in the middle of it, and she opened it to the pages it marked. "What's the big deal?" She playfully pulled the book from him. "This looks wild!"

"Hey, wait! Wait!" Mark said, scrambling over her shoulder to grab the book from her. Before he grabbed it from her, she could see the chapter heading. "Cedar Ridge Slayings" leapt out at her as the pages whizzed past her face.

"Whoa," she said. "What's the big deal?"

"Nothing," he said, backing away and flushing deeper than he had in the entire time they'd been in the attic. "It's nothing, I just . . . it's just something stupid. For school. I didn't want it to get, uh, damaged."

"Oh really," she said, putting her pants on. "You didn't want it to get damaged so you snatched it from my hands? That said 'Cedar Ridge Slayings,' didn't it? And who's Corwin?"

"It's nothing," he said, tossing the book under the bed. "It's just something I was reading, okay? It's not a big deal!"

"Mark," she said, taking a deep breath. "I'm not making it a big deal. You are. If you don't want to talk about it for some reason that's fine, but don't go ape-shit on me okay?"

He took a deep breath, and after a couple of seconds walked over and put his hands on her shoulders. "You're right. I just thought with everything that's happened you'd be weirded out."

"So it doesn't have anything to do with Clara, or Ms. Kennedy?"

"No, of course not," he lied to her.

"Okay," she said kissing him quickly and then walking over to get her shirt. "That's fine, because I didn't even think that it might be, but since it's not then there's no big deal." If Mark wanted to look in to old crimes in the area for some reason that was his business, especially if it helped him deal with Clara and Ms. Kennedy's deaths.

"Oh," he said. He could feel the flush coming back. "Good. I'm sorry, really."

"I know. Now c'mon. We don't want to be late."

Their kiss in her driveway was too brief, but Mark was desperate to make sure that she forgave his panic over the book. She pulled away quickly, inclining her head slightly towards the lighted window on the second floor. "I don't think you want them to notice your wardrobe change."

"Okay. Tonight was great, and I'm sorry. I didn't want to ruin it by being such a spaz."

"It's okay," she kissed him again. "It's no big deal. I'll see you in school tomorrow."

He drove off, not wanting to go home at all. He knew that if he wasn't there when Joe got home, nights like this were never going to happen again. He'd had no idea that they were going to end up nearly naked and making out in his bed and he didn't want to do anything that was going to jeopardize the chances of that happening again.

Yeah, if only you hadn't freaked out on her over a library book. You had a nearly naked girl in your bed for the first, and now probably last, time and what do you do? You get pissed that she touches your library book! Too bad that was all she wanted to touch.

His own internal berating distracted him so much that he didn't hear the sudden rev of a car engine or see the glare of headlights reflecting back at him in his mirrors until the impact threw him forward, hurtling the scooter towards the curb.

He desperately tried to get control back while slowing and pulling over to the side but he was hit again, harder this time. The front tire of the V slammed into the curb and Mark flew over the handlebars, rolling across asphalt and grass and into the park he and Christine had spent so much time in.

He propped himself up onto his knees, pain flaring in his wrist. He tried to figure out what had happened. Were his lights off? Had he slowed down suddenly? He could only imagine Joe freaking out on him for getting into an accident, not to mention getting sued by some yuppie bastard who hadn't even noticed he was in the road.

He reached up with his uninjured wrist to take off his helmet when there was a rustle of movement from behind him. Before he could turn to see what it was, something crashed into the back of his helmet, knocking him forward and onto his injured wrist. He rolled over, trying to get to his feet when he was kicked in the side, knocking out his breath and rolling him over onto his back.

Through the dirt on the helmet's plastic faceplate he saw Jack standing over him, a baseball bat in hand and sanity or restraint nowhere to be found.

Mark scrambled backwards, moving out of the way just in time to watch the bat swing past so close he could see the pattern of the wood grain on its tip. He tried to move faster, but his feet were losing traction on the wet leaves and grass. When the next swing came he had just enough time to roll with the impact. It flipped him back over onto his stomach and impact on the helmet echoed through his skull.

Mark couldn't see anything and for a second he thought he'd been struck blind, but realized the blow had been so hard that the plastic in the visor and cracked almost completely, reducing everything to out of focus spider webs. There was wetness all over the side of his face and he couldn't tell if what was rattling around in the helmet was shattered plastic or skull.

He crawled forward with one hand, holding the injured one up to his chest. He couldn't see where he was going, but before he could make any long-term plans another blow from the bat fell straight across his back, driving him into to the ground.

All his air was gone, and he was gasping for breath so hard it felt like he was going to vomit up dinner in order to make more breathing room. *It'll choke you to death. You'll die re-tasting some steak and mushroom thing you didn't like the first time and couldn't even pronounce.*

Jack kicked him again, rolling him onto his back. Standing over him, Jack was a cracked, blurry phantom and for a second he was Justin Corwin's smoke covered form, eyes on fire and darkness around him writhing with life.

But then the second was gone, and Jack swung the bat down again, smashed squarely down on top of the helmet. Mark's entire body jerked uncontrollably for a moment, as he felt shards of plastic dig down into his skull. The wetness on the side of his face spread over his whole head. Mark flopped flat onto his back, unable and unwilling to move. It was over, and if Jack was going to keep swinging there wasn't much helmet left for him to beat his way through.

Over the ringing in his ears, Mark thought he heard voices yelling, but he couldn't be sure. A glob of spit landed on the shattered visor, and then Jack backed away. There was a squeal of tires and an engine revved away into the night. After three ragged breaths, Mark convinced himself that Jack was gone. After a dozen more he actually believed it.

This was fine, though. Mark resigned himself to never moving again. He knew he should try, that he needed to get the helmet off and see what kind of damage Jack had done, but the shame and pain and fear were coiled around his body like weights, tighter and heavier than they had ever had been before.

All he wanted to do was lie there and wait for someone to finish the job Jack had started.

"That looks like it hurts."

The bored resident stitching up Mark's scalp didn't even glance over at Detective Prescott, who had poked his head around the ER's totally misnamed privacy curtain. "My patient will be ready in a few minutes, Detective."

"Of course," the Detective said, waving an apology but holding his ground.

At the park, when Mark had finally gotten to his feet and managed to get the helmet-remains off his head, he staggered towards the stalled out V, having decided if he was going to bleed to death he was going to do it in his own bed. He made it about five feet before he toppled back to the ground. Thankfully, it was just in time for a college girl coming home from a date to see him. She pulled over, and after a sudden freak out at Mark's blood covered face, she insisted that she was going to take him to the hospital.

The hospital wait was minimal, but Mark had time enough to call the house and leave a message for Joe about what happened. Clearly, he realized later, he had sustained massive amounts of head trauma.

They were cleaning Mark up when Joe arrived, not nearly drunk as Mark had feared but drunk enough for him to be a raging dick to the girl that picked him up. Mark could only sit in the exam room listening in embarrassment as they checked him over. Despite what Mark thought was a spot-on diagnosis, his skull was not crushed and he was far from bleeding to death. In fact, all he had was a mild concussion, a sprained wrist and a single cut that would require stitches.

Four of them even.

Way to go, drama queen. "Oh, oh, I'm dying! I give up, the bad men win!"

When the resident finished his stitching, he droned a lecture to Mark about not exerting himself, keeping the stitches clean and how they would dissolve out when the healing was done. For once, Mark hoped Joe had been there but he'd disappeared from earshot after his shouting match with Mark's good Samaritan, probably to arrange the pickup of Mark's abandoned scooter.

"So what's the deal?" the Detective asked as the resident passed him on the way out of the faux-cubicle.

"I got into an accident. What's the deal with you? You like hanging out in hospitals?"

"One of the uniforms settled down your Uncle earlier, and he knew I had an interest in what's going on with you so he gave me a buzz."

"That's good to know. I've got some papers due soon, my teachers going to send you my grades?"

"C'mon, Mark," Detective Prescott said. "You're a smart kid. You know I've got to keep an eye on what's happening with you. Plus, I actually detect things for a living, and that tells me this was more than just some accident. Unless you've got some nitrous stowed away in that scooter of yours."

"No, I don't. I just got unlucky. Spoiler alert: It's kind of my specialty."

"Let me help you, Mark. I think you're not telling me something. Nothing really bad, but something that you might know that can help me find out who hurt Clara and Ms. Kennedy. Maybe even stop who's trying to hurt you."

"Jesus, will you let it go!" Mark got up and stuck his head out the curtain, desperate for Joe's bellowing interference. "Can I go? The guy didn't say if I can go. Do I stay here or what?"

"Mark, c'mon," David said, putting a hand n his shoulder. "Let me help, before something else happens to you. Or someone else."

Mark shrugged the hand off, forcefully enough that it made him dizzy for a second. "No! Fuck, this was nothing, okay? I got unlucky, I made a mistake, and then WHAM! It has nothing to do with Clara or Ms. Kennedy or Cor--"

"What the hell is this?"

Drunken aggression to the rescue!

"Mr. Nelson, I just wanted to ask your nephew a questions about his accident, and--"

"What the hell for? He was screwing around and he got into an accident. End of story. I don't know why he has to have you pestering him over it."

"I just want to make sure he's safe."

"Oh, and I don't? C'mon, Mark. Let's get out of here."

Mark tried leaning his head against the glass of the window on the way home, but every bump of the road rattled his brain so much it made him want to throw up. After the sexual high, the savage beating that came after and interminable hospital wait and exam, he was thoroughly spent.

Hey, maybe if we're lucky you'll turn into one of those weird sex perverts that can only get sexual satisfaction if he gets the shit kicked out of him after fooling around. That'd make life pretty interesting, at least.

When the car stopped in the driveway, Joe just sat staring out at the garage. Mark waited a few moments, but when no explanation came, he went to leave. Joe's hand clamped down on his arm, holding him in place.

"I know I give you a hard time," Joe said still looking straight ahead. His voice was something Mark had never heard from him before: calm. "I do it because I have to look out for you. Because no one else will. But I'm also not dumb enough to think that this was from some accident."

Mark opened his mouth to say something, but Joe gave his arm a squeeze that let Mark know that he wasn't interested in what he had to say.

"I know you never wanted to be here, especially after your Aunt died, but we're all each other has. It's a pain in the ass, but that's the way it is. And right now, whatever is going on with you, you just need to settle it down, okay? I'm at the end of my rope with you."

"I didn't do anything wrong," Mark said. "I was just driving, and there was a--"

Joe slammed a fist down on the steering wheel. "Goddamnit! I am trying my damnedest not to think about the fact that that is a hospital bill we *cannot* afford, or the fact you're going to be bugging me for money to fix the damage to your little scooter, or even the fact that you could have been killed, so don't fucking lie to me! You give me this attitude all the time, you start spending time with this girl, you start getting into fights, I have to talk to the police, and now this? I don't expect you to tell me what's going on, but I want it to stop! You better just stop it, because the one way I know how to make you I promised your Aunt I wouldn't use. I swear to God, Mark, she'd be begging me to smack you around by now if she were still with us."

Joe's hand was still on his arm, but all Mark wanted to do was shake it off and run as fast as he could. Finally Joe spoke, his voice going back down to normal.

"You need to fix it, get rid of it, and get it done, because I am tired of this shit. You wanna act like Mr. Tough Guy? Fine, you solve your own messes, okay? I'm telling you right now, I'm not bailing you out of jail and I'm sure as hell not going to let you throw your life away. You're going to graduate, get a job, and start acting like a responsible fucking adult. Anything else is just unacceptable, okay? I'm not going to deal with it anymore."

"Like you've dealt with it at all," Mark muttered, slipping out of his grasp and heading for the back door. Mark made it halfway before Joe grabbed him and spun him around.

"I mean it," Joe hissed at him. "I am not going to go through some crazy rebellious teen bullshit. You fix this. You make it through, or there are going to be some broken promises in this house. Clear?"

Mark did his best to screw up a mask of defiance, but all it did was make his face throb even more. "Clear?" Joe said again, louder, and giving Mark a shake.

"Clear," Mark said, just letting go.

"Good," Joe said, letting Mark's arms go. "Now go to bed. It's fuckin' late."

CHAPTER TWENTY-TWO

Mark didn't go to school for the next couple of days. He and Joe only spoke of it that Monday morning when Joe poked his head in the door to the attic room and yelled, "You going to school?"

"No," Mark called down. He'd been sleeping off and on as the emergency room doctors directed him too, although he was more exhausted than he was tired. "Fair enough," Joe called up closing the door.

His head still throbbed, but did with less intensity when he was lying down, so he had stayed that way for most of the day. He flipped channels for some of the time but mostly just stared up at the ceiling, the TV just droning background noise. He thought about getting up and getting something to eat, but decided against it. He drifted off to sleep a couple of times, but thankfully, he didn't dream.

Exactly when he thought it would, the phone rang. Mark thought about letting the machine downstairs get it, but then decided against it.

"Hello?" His voice was dry and cracked.

"Mark? Is that you?" Christine said.

"Yeah, it's me. What's up?"

"Nothing," she said, obviously confused. "I was wondering what was up with you. I missed you today."

"Yeah," Mark said, turning his attention to the far window.

"So . . ." she said a few moments passed. "Were you just ditching or what?"

"No, I . . . I got into an accident."

"Oh my god! Are you okay?"

"Yeah, I just didn't feel like being in school, and my Uncle was cool with it, so . . . y'know."

"Mark, what happened?" she said.

"I had an accident on the V on the way home last night. Nothing major. I just sprained my wrist, and got a little bit of a concussion. I'm okay, just not really school material right now."

"Oh my God, why didn't you call me last night? Or this morning?"

"I didn't want to bother you," he said, twisting the phone cord around his fingers. This was going exactly as he thought it would, but it still made him nauseous.

"Bother me?" she said incredulously. "Mark, stop it. Why would you think telling me about an accident would be a bother?" Her voice lowered, became more serious. "Were you embarrassed? I mean, I'm not going to think less of you because you had some accident."

"It's not like that," he snapped. "It's not like I was hot-rodding or anything like that. I was hit by a fucking car!"

"Oh my god!" she gasped. "And you're okay? Thank god you weren't hurt worse."

He heaved a long sigh, annoyed that he had been still prideful enough to blurt that out. "I didn't get this hurt by getting hit by the car."

"Then how--" she started, but he cut her off.

"Look, I'm only telling you this because I want you to be careful, okay? I don't want to make a big deal about this or anything. I just want to make sure that you're okay." He paused again, and thankfully, she didn't interrupt.

"This car that hit me ran me off the road, and then someone got out and beat the crap out of me with a bat or something. That's what fucked me up."

He couldn't even hear her breathing on the other end of the line.

"Are you serious?" she whispered.

"I couldn't kid about this if I tried," he said closing his eyes.

"Mark . . . oh God, I thought this was over. How could--"

"You thought what was over?" he said, taken completely by surprise.

"There hasn't been anything about the killings or anything in so long, I just thought that finally it was safe."

"Look," Mark snapped, cutting her off, "this and that other thing have nothing to do with one another. This was just some stupid, macho bullshit, okay? That other thing, you don't have to worry about it, okay? That's my problem, not yours."

"Mark!" she shot back, "You don't get the monopoly on being worried about people getting killed, okay? I mean, how do you even know that this doesn't have anything to do with it. I mean, you . . ."

"I? I what?"

"It's like you said before, how you're the only link between the two, and then this happens."

He could feel it boiling up in him, and as much as he tried to keep it down it exploded out of him.

"It was Jack, okay! God damn! It was Jack, I saw him, but I'm not going to say anything because that's just . . . I'm just not going to do anything, okay? He beat me. He won. He's the alpha-fucking-male. I was stupid to think he would just let shit go, and I was stupid to get involved in that macho shit when I knew, I fucking *knew* that he'd just take it further. So yeah, I get that the only thing to think if I get attacked is that some crazy killer is after me, but I told you that wasn't the case, alright?"

She was quiet again, and it gave Mark time to reflect on what a totally stupid ass he was.

"God, you stupid boys and your macho horseshit. I'm so sorry that it bugged you so much that I was worried for you, but I was, okay? I don't think it's so fucking unreasonable. Especially with that's happened. People getting killed is actually kind of scary, y'know?"

"Christine," he said, trying to find a way to squirm into his bed. "I'm sorry, okay? I'm scared too, okay?"

"Fine," she said, sniffling, and then she hung up.

***

She sat and looked at the phone for a long time. Anger at him for being a dick wrestled with concern about his accident, and it looked like they were going to stay locked in battle for a while. It was bad enough some teenage head case wanted to hurt Mark so badly he'd run him off the road and attack him, but having to worry about some murderer on the loose was getting to hard to ignore. As much as she hated to admit it, she'd been waiting for either some report on the news to tell her that the killer was caught or for someone that wasn't a friend of Mark's to get killed.

She was wondering if she could call back and apologize or wait to see if he would when her phone rang. He hopes that he'd snapped out of his self-pitying funk were dashed when she saw the name on the ID.

"So what's the verdict?" Steve said on the other end of the line before she could even say hello.

"What?" she said. "Oh, you mean with Mark?"

"Yeah, I figured you'd have called him already, and your number is easier to dial."

"Really?" she smirked.

"Well, it sounded good on paper," he chuckled. "So is it the flu, the kissing disease, what?"

"Actually, it's a lot worse than that. He told me he got into an accident on the way back from my house on Sunday night."

"You're kidding," Steve said, sounding less concerned than she'd have thought. "He drives like an old lady on that thing."

"Well, it wasn't his fault," she said, her temper rising. "He was run off the road and attacked with like, a bat or something."

Steve made a low whistle. "Jesus, this doesn't have anything to do with the whole specter of death thing lurking about, does it?"

"No, he told me that it was Jack that did it, and he definitely seems crazy enough for something like this."

"Most definitely. In fact, one of his goony little friends was giving me the stink eye in class today. I thought he was just going to ask me out or something." He paused, and then added, "Mark's okay, right? He's not in the hospital or anything, is he?"

"No," she said. "He just has a sprained wrist and some stitches, he said. Of course, knowing him, he could be paralyzed from the waist down and he wouldn't tell me because he wouldn't want to be a bother. Why does he do this? I just want to . . . I dunno. It's very frustrating."

"Mark can be a very frustrating guy. I mean, he's real sweet and all, and I love him to death, but he's so closed off, y'know? We were friends for *years* before he told me about his parents, and I remember when his aunt died, he just shut down. He didn't say a thing to me about it."

"That's so sad," she murmured.

"Don't let it get you down. You're really the best thing that's ever happened to him, it's just that your timing sucks."

"I feel bad," she said. "We kinda had this fight about it when I called him, cause I was all freaked out he was hurt and I think he got pissed off that I jumped to the whole 'people getting killed' thing."

"Oh, I doubt he could stay mad at you. Just give him a little space and he'll calm down. Trust me, guys *love* space. Why do you think guys like science fiction so much? Space."

"Okay, okay," she chuckled. "I'll give him his space. It just goes against my grain, that's all."

"Well, you can go against my grain any day, okay?"

"Riiiiight," she said. "I'll keep that in mind. But anyway, what about that history paper? Did you find your notes for it? I'm kind of in a bad way here." Thanks to the late start of the school year and covering a completely different time period at her old school she had found herself almost completely lost in the history class she was in. Steve had the same class last year and had volunteered some of his notes to help her out.

"Really? How bad a way?"

"Steve."

"Right. No, I think I've got them. Do you want to come over sometime and I can go over them with you? My handwriting's really bad but I'm sure I can make up some kind of Rosetta Stone for you."

"Sounds good. How about Friday? I don't think Mark is going to be up for doing anything."

"Sounds like a plan. How about you come over here, we get some pizza and get our learn on."

She opened her mouth to say yes, but paused. "Steve, do you think Mark would be okay with this?"

There was a pause from Steve as well, and when he spoke again, he actually sounded like he wasn't just joking around.

"I understand what you're saying, and yeah, Mark may find this to be a little . . . I dunno, a little something. I mean, you and I have had lunch a couple of times by ourselves without anything weird happening, so I think we're okay."

"Yeah. Should we tell Mark? I mean, it's no big deal, and if I was seeing anyone else, I wouldn't even think to mention it, but . . ."

"It's Mark, I know what you mean." After a moment, he said "Look, I'm not going to go out of my way to tell him. With all of this other stuff going on, he doesn't need anything else to stress and obsess about. If you want to tell him, though, that's fine with me."

"Okay. I didn't even ask if he was going to be in school tomorrow but maybe I'll bring it up."

"That's cool. And besides," he said, switching into some weird, European accent, "I promise it won't get weird, baby."

"What was that?" she laughed.

"That was my Austin Powers!" he indignantly. "What, no good?"

"I think you need to workshop it, that's all."

"So that's the way it's going to be, huh?"

"Looks like," she said with a smile.

CHAPTER TWENTY-THREE

It was Friday when Joe put his foot down and made Mark go to school. Mark tried to get him to hold off until the next Monday, but it was clear Joe's charitable streak had been worn thin. Mark stared at his face in the mirror in his room for ten minutes before Joe began leaning on the car horn as he waited in the driveway. He tried to tell himself that he didn't look so bad, but he wasn't that self-delusional. Between getting the shit kicked out of him, the laying in bed for days straight, and his newfound aversion to food and sleep, he was a wreck. One of the bruises on his check was an odd mix of yellow and purple, and his eyes were baggy and bloodshot. If it weren't for cede bandage on his wrist, he'd probably have been able to pass for just being tired or sick, but as it was, he was sure everyone would be wondering what kind of trouble he had gotten himself into this time.

Joe grumbled at him when Mark finally got into the car, but he didn't care. If his back didn't still feel tight and compressed, he'd have walked the mile and a half, but Joe had actually offered (if "I'm driving you to school" can be considered "offering"). On the drive, Mark tried to convince himself not to be so self-conscious. It was ridiculous to assume that people wouldn't have anything better than him to talk about, but at the same time he was sure that Jack and his cronies had done their share of gloating to select people, most likely about "what they heard" or some other thin lie to cover their involvement.

His stomach clenched at the thought of seeing them again. Any joy he may have had about handing Jack a beating was long gone. They'd reasserted themselves, and now it was just a matter of time before they let that be known in a more public forum.

Or they could just try to kill you again.

"Keep out of trouble," was all Joe said before he drove off, and Mark couldn't even come up with a smart remark before he sped off. It was probably for the best.

When he finally found Christine, he wasn't sure how she was going to react, but she kissed him and gave him a hug. "I'm sorry," he whispered in her ear.

"It's okay," she said. She pulled away from him to examine the damage. "How're you feeling?" she asked.

"I'm fine," he said, as they walked down the hall towards class. "My back hurts a little, but I'm okay." He'd been hoping that his disappearance would have made folks forget about his little jaunt to the police station but apparently disappearing for almost a week and showing back up bruised and beaten up just added fuel to the fire of speculation.

"It doesn't look too bad," she lied with a smile, and Mark tried to smile back.

"How's the scooter?" she asked.

"Not totaled, but I think the wheels might have gotten bent. Not to mention the body damage."

"That sucks."

"Yeah. I have no idea how I'm going to afford to pay for it."

"I'm sure you'll figure something out," she said with a less than convincing smile.

Oh yeah, because if there's anything that Mark Watson knows it's figuring things out, right?

"Oh geez," Steve said, when he met them outside for lunch. "The way she made it sound I thought you were in a wheelchair or something. I got worse than this when *I* fell off that thing of yours."

When lunch was over, Mark felt the panic from earlier in the morning begin to rise. He had been dreading gym all day, even though he was going to get out of it for the next few weeks or so.

Oh Jesus, can you be more of a girl? Why don't you just cry and run and hide? You won't even have to be in the locker room with him, and it's not like he's going to grab a piece of gym equipment and try to finish the job.

It's true, he was being ridiculous, but all he could see is those eyes, and it made his back twinge in pain.

Mark slinked into the gym, gave his note to Coach DiMarco, and sat high up on the bleachers. He tried to do some Algebra but couldn't keep his mind focused on the book. When everyone started lining up in squads, Mark found himself staring at Jack as he casually sauntered to his spot and sat down, his back to him. There were no threatening glances or wicked smiles his way, just casual indifference.

Mark was about to turn back to his homework when he noticed Victor staring at him. When he saw that Mark noticed him, he turned away quickly, shuffling his feet and missing a step before falling into place.

Aside from Vic's glance at the beginning of class, no one, not even the Coach or any of the other classmates (including Steve) paid Mark any attention. When the class was over, Mark took up a spot by the door as the other kids got changed.

Mark couldn't help but freeze with panic when Jack and Victor came up the stairs before everyone else. He looked away, trying to see if the Coach was anywhere nearby, but he was nowhere to be found. Jack just leaned casually on the wall across from Mark, looking down at the floor. Eric, however, was fiddling with the straps on his backpack and pacing back and forth.

Steve was the next person up the steps, and judging from how out of breath he was, he had taken the steps at least two at a time.

"Hey," Steve said to Mark, and then turning to stare at Jack and Vic.

"What?" Vic finally snapped at Steve. Other kids had come up the steps by now, including Jack's other two friends.

"You know what. You fucking thugs," Steve snarled.

"Go fuck yourself, fairy," Vic sniped with a dismissive wave of his hand.

"Whatever. Why don't you guys try to kick my ass, huh? Oh wait, it's not the middle of the night and you don't have a bat or anything."

"Steve!" Mark hissed. "Knock it off."

"You should listen to your girlfriend," Jack said, not even looking up.

"You are such scum, you know that?" Steve said, walking over and getting right in Jack's face. Jack didn't move a muscle.

"All I know," Jack said, very softly, "is that if you don't settle the fuck down, your little friend over there will have more than just bats to worry about."

"Leave him alone," Steve snarled, his entire body trembling. "I mean it. If you want to fuck with someone then step to me, okay?"

Finally, Jack looked up and locked eyes with Steve. With Jack rising to Steve's challenge, the rest of his friends found themselves preoccupied with the scenic view of the rest of the gym. Kyle had come up from the locker room during the exchange, but he managed to stay back from all four of them.

The bell rang, but Jack and Steve didn't move at all. The small crowd of kids that had been waiting by the door watching the exchange decided that nothing was going to happen and began to file out the door.

Finally, Jack just smiled and patted Steve on the shoulder, and Mark was actually surprised that Steve didn't just explode and start swinging. "That's good," Jack said. "'Step to me.' Very street." Jack just turned and left, with Steve's eyes burning a hole in his back.

Victor followed after Jack, glaring at Steve. Mark wasn't sure if it was for standing up to them or outing them for running him off the road. Kyle still hung back, blending in with the rest of the crowd as they left for class. Mark just stood there, staring in disbelief at the whole exchange.

"C'mon, let's go," Steve said, waving Mark towards the door.

Mark just stood there as the last of the kids from the locker room filed past them.

"Hey," Steve said when they were all gone. "Let's go man, we're going to be late." Righteous Fury Steve, with Public Humiliation Action was gone, apparently replaced with Punctual Steve, complete with "What Did I Do Now?" look.

"Mark?"

"What the fuck is your problem?"

"What?"

"What?" Mark echoed, his voice wavering. "That! What the hell were you thinking? What was all that 'step to me' bullshit?"

"Boys!" Coach said, poking his head out of his office door. "Watch the language and get to class!"

Mark turned and stormed out the double doors, not caring if Steve was behind him or not. "Hey," Steve said, jogging up alongside Mark. "What is your problem?"

"Oh Jesus," Mark snarled. "Take your fucking pick why don't you."

"What's that supposed to mean?" Steve said, and then he waved his arms dismissively. "Look," he continued, "what is the big deal? I wanted to let Jack know he couldn't keep fucking with you like this and--"

"Of course he can keep fucking with me!" Mark whirled around. "Look at my face! I was minding my own goddamn business when they followed me, and who knows how long they were doing that, by the way, and he just . . . " Mark could only wave his bandaged wrist at this point as his words piled on top of each other.

"I don't have any idea what you're talking about," Steve said, sounding like an impatient mother. Mark clenched his jaw as tight as he could, hoping it would keep him from bellowing obscenities up and down the hallway.

"Look," Mark finally said through clenched teeth. "If Jack wants to fuck with me he's going to do it. He made that *painfully* obvious. I do *not* need you to finally try and stand up for me and to get your big brother merit badge or whatever the fuck you were trying to over-compensate for back there."

"I was trying to be your friend," Steve said, an edge creeping into his voice.

"Because you've been doing such a bang up job of that lately. Thanks for checking up on me this week, by the way."

"What? I didn't have to! I called Christine and she told me you were fine so I didn't think I had to bug you."

"What do you mean you called her?"

"Like . . . on the phone?" Steve said. "Is that a problem?"

"How long have you been talking on the phone with her?"

"I don't know, man. I got her number when you were suspended because she asked about some school stuff, but it's no big deal."

Mark just stared at him.

"C'mon, man," Steve said. "We just talk about what's going on with you because we're worried, okay?"

"I know," Mark said flatly. "Because you're such a good friend."

"Mark," Steve started, but Mark turned a corner and headed for the stairwell. Steve's class was down the hallway the other way.

"Just leave me alone," Mark called over his shoulder as the door closed behind him.

Everything else in Mark's last two classes was just a blur. At the end of the day he had wandered to the bike rack lost in turning his conversation with Steve over and over in his head. He rolled his eyes at his own foolishness, and turned and started the walk home. "Hey," a voice called after him. He sighed, turned around, trying to feign excitement.

"I was hoping I'd run into you," Christine said, throwing her arms around his neck with a big smile.

"Well, consider me run into," he said, trying to grin.

Hey, maybe Steve texted her between classes and she's trying to be extra sweet to you.

"How're you feeling?" she said.

"Okay," he lied. "Tired, but I'm not that sore anymore."

"Well, aside from that. You seemed so distant at lunch."

"Oh," Mark said, breaking their embrace and taking her by the hand. "I dunno. I just felt kinda out of the loop."

"Well," she said, giving his hand a squeeze, "it's not like you missed anything this week. Just basic stuff."

"Yeah, I know," he said. "I just . . . Steve and I got into it after Gym, because he had to try to stand up for me or some shit to Jack and his buddies, and really he just made himself look like an ass."

"Oh," she said, supportive demeanor beginning to crumble. "I'm sure he was just trying to help."

"I know, I know. Everyone is just trying to help. I just wish I wasn't so fucking sad that I needed everyone's help. It's just . . . what'd you call it? Stupid macho horseshit? I guess I'm just really pissed off at him right now."

She laughed a little and then gave his hand another squeeze. "Look, I forgot to mention it at lunch but he and I were going to get together tonight and study. He has some history notes that would be really helpful for that big paper I'm so lost on."

"Really? He didn't mention anything to me about it."

"Oh," she said. "That's weird."

"That's Steve for you."

"Look, if you'd rather me not go over there until you two have had a chance to work this out that's fine. I understand."

Mark rubbed his forehead, trying to buy himself some time before he had to answer.

"I," he started with every intention of finishing that with *don't think you've got to worry about it. You do what you need to do.* Instead, it came out, "think that would be a good idea. Just until things cool off, y'know?"

"Oh," she said, seeming even more confused by what he said than he did.

No. Not confused. Disappointed.

He wanted it to be ridiculous but he could see it flash across her eyes. "That's cool," she said looking away. "I don't want to cause problems between you guys. It sucks, because even if I don't go over there, I still have to get cracking on this thing or I'm going to totally bomb this class."

"That's fine," Mark said, alternately wanting to take it back so she wasn't so hurt and eager to get away from her so her disappointment didn't hurt him so damn much. "I have a shitload I've got to get done too."

"Okay," she said, forcing a smile. "Do you want to do something tomorrow?"

"Sure," he said. "I'll call you, okay?"

"Okay," she said. She leaned in a kissed him quickly and then turned and walked towards home.

As he watched he go regret began to seep into him. What if what he thought was disappointment about not going to Steve's was really just disappointment in Mark being such a goddamn baby about the whole thing?

Then again, he knew exactly how most of Steve's "study dates" went.

Even if everything was perfectly innocent it was probably for the best, he thought. With everything in his life flying in every which direction the last thing he needed was to have some kind of panic attack laying in bed at home worrying what his girlfriend and his best friend were up to.

CHAPTER TWENTY-FOUR

Christine had gotten used to the walk home in the absence of Mark's scooter. She had tried not to take it for granted given how irregular it had become with his suspension, the grounding and now the sick days. A free ride home from school wasn't something she could count on all the time.

Of course, nowadays, neither was Mark.

She'd wanted to shriek at him when he asked her not to go to Steve's. It was so stupid and pointless. He might as well have started pounding his chest and tried to drag her back to his house by her hair.

Then again, she thought, maybe I'm just angry because I was disappointed that I'm not going to go. Or that I even asked "permission" in the first place.

She'd ask to be polite, thinking he wouldn't be bothered by it, but then she remembered that this was Mark she was dealing with. She never would've asked any other guy she'd been seeing if she could hang out with another boy, especially one of his friends. She'd had "study dates" with plenty of boys before, ones she was far more attracted to than Steve, and nothing had happened. In Mark's case it was just a matter of making sure he didn't freak out about something that wasn't a big deal, no matter how much Steve playfully flirted with her. He had enough on his plate without worrying about something like this, no matter how much of a pain it was.

When she got home, she deftly avoided her brother, who was in the living room watching reruns of Magnum P.I. in his bathrobe. He'd settled into a weird, summer-vacation like schedule of staying up really late, sleeping in until at least noon, and then hanging around the house for the rest of the afternoon to make himself a pest to everyone, especially Christine. She was well barricaded in her room before he could throw anything or bait her into a tedious exchange of insults.

She ended up staring at the phone for almost ten minutes before she picked it up and dialed Steve's number. She had to do this quickly, like pulling off a band-aid.

"Yellow," he answered cheerfully.

"Hey Steve," she said.

"Hey yourself." He was positively beaming over the phone, and she knew why. "What's going on?"

"Well, this is kind of awkward . . ." she started, and she could feel Steve's mood crash on the other end of the line.

"Oh geez," he mumbled. "Did he say something to you? I was just trying to stick up for him, that's all!"

"I know, but . . . can you blame him?"

"What's that supposed to mean?"

"Steve, c'mon, you know what Mark's like, don't you? You've been his friend longer than I have, and I know how something like that would get under his skin. He's so, y'know, insecure about stuff like this, and if you try to stand up for him or be so overt in helping him out, he's just going to resent it."

There was a long pause, and then "Really?"

There was no way she could stifle her laugh. "Of course!" she smirked. "God, how long have you known him? Since like, the third grade or something, right? And you haven't figured that out yet?"

"Well, I'm a teenager, not a therapist."

"Clearly," she said, still chuckling.

"Well, I'll just have to make it up to him by making sure that you get a kick-ass grade on that paper, huh?"

"Yeah, about that . . ."

"Oh you didn't, did you?"

"Yeah, I did. I'm sorry, but I couldn't just look him in the face and lie. Even if it was by omission."

"Was this before or after he and I had our own lovers spat? If it was before, that'd explain a lot."

"What're you talking about?"

"Well, during our little quarrel, I mentioned how we'd been talking about what's going on with him, and--"

"Oh, and you're mad at *me* for mentioning stuff to him?"

"Yeah, I know. Let's just say he didn't take our little heart-to-hearts well."

She grinded her teeth together as the anger rose in her. She wasn't even allowed to *talk* to someone else? Who the else did she have around here to talk to? Mark hadn't been lying when he said that dating him wasn't the best move for her social life.

"Super," was all she could bring herself to say.

"I know it sucks, but look, you still need these notes, right?"

"Yeah," she murmured.

"So why don't you just swing over and pick them up. He doesn't want you to fail, right?"

She closed her eyes and sighed. The fact that she even had to think about just going over and get notes made her even angrier. "Sure," she said.

"So you were just trying to get away?"

"Yes," Christine said, tapping her fingers impatiently on the dashboard.

"So you don't want to see the movie?" he brother asked, furrowing his brow in confusion.

"No," she said, forcing the words out through gritted teeth. "I just want you to drive me somewhere, that's all, and not have Mom and Dad ask me a bunch of stupid questions, okay?"

Ryan just grunted and kept driving. "Where are we going again? I thought you said Puppy boy was poor."

"I'm not going to see Mark. I'm going to pick up some notes from a friend of his. After I do that, you can drop me off at the mall while you see whatever testosterone fest movie you're going to see, okay?"

"Yes, Miss Daisy," he snickered.

"What?"

"Nothing. I didn't say anything."

"Keep it that way."

She had scribbled down the directions to Steve's place, which turned out to be fairly close to her house. Not as big, but still very nice and well looked after. There was only an old station wagon in the driveway, and Ryan parked as she headed for the back door. Steve opened the door with a grin before she even had a chance to knock.

"Hey, study buddy."

"Hey," she smiled. "So you've got the notes, right?"

His smile faltered a little bit, but he backed up and waved her inside. "I'll run upstairs and get them."

She tapped her foot impatiently, looking around the immaculate kitchen. Mark had said a couple of times that Steve's Mom was kind of a clean freak, and it was clear that he wasn't exaggerating. She could hear Steve's footsteps going up stairs, and a TV playing softly somewhere in the house, but other than that the place was deathly quiet.

Steve came down a couple of minutes later, a three-ring binder under his arm. "I think these are it."

"You think?" she said, taking the binder from him and beginning to leaf through it. He hadn't been kidding when he said his handwriting was bad. "How am I supposed to read this?" she said, desperation creeping into her voice.

"Well, it's not that bad, is it?" he said, leaning over her shoulder to take a look. "Well, I think that's . . . that's 'Lincoln.' I can tell because of the little stick figure with the hat. I think that says 'Gettysburg.' And I think--" but Christine snapped the binder shut before he could finish.

"Steve," she said, "I thought you said they weren't that bad."

"Well, I was probably just having on off day that day. The rest can't be that bad," He smiled at her crookedly.

"Steve!"

"Hey, look," he said, raising his hands defensively. "I'm just trying to help, that's all. I know you don't want to hang out here or anything, and I don't blame you, really, but that's all I've got."

She let out a sigh and opened the binder again to take a closer look. From cover to cover, it was indecipherable. She looked back up at Steve, who just shrugged his shoulders. "Can you help me figure this out?"

"I'm sure I can," he smiled sweetly. "I mean, it's not like we'd have to pull an all nighter or anything."

"Yeah," she smirked. "It's not like you took tons and tons of notes. It won't take too long, right?"

"An hour, probably no more than that."

"And your folks will be cool with that?"

"Oh, they're in the city for some party my Mom's office is throwing. They'll crawl in near dawn, I'm sure."

She heaved another sigh. Of course they were. "Okay, let me go tell my brother to take off." She dropped the binder on the table and headed back out to the car.

"Took you long enough," he said before she could even say anything.

"Look, I have to stay here and figure this out, okay?"

Ryan just raised an eyebrow.

"Stop it."

"Stop what? This is one of his friends, right?"

"Yes," she said, "His best friend."

He raised the eyebrow further.

"Quit it, Ry."

"I'm not doing anything," he said, smirking. "So you'll be in good hands?"

"Just fucking leave, okay?" she said, turning around and storming back to the house.

"Well, you know what they say," he muttered to himself as he backed out of the driveway. "Nice guys finish last."

"Slow down," she said, breaking the kiss.

"Sorry," Steve mumbled, moving his hand north of her waist.

"No," Christine smiled, guiding his hand back downward, "You were just doing it too fast."

"Oh," he said, smiling back at her. The notes, half-organized, were strewn over Steve's bedroom floor and rustled under her naked body. She gasped, squeezing her thighs on his hand as he continued fingering her. She was kissing his neck and bare chest, and soon her hand began to work its way into his pants.

Everything had started innocently enough. They moved from the den to his bedroom so they'd have more room to spread out. They laughed when both their hands went for the same sheet of paper and they touched by accident.

She'd felt it coming almost an hour before when they inched closer to each other and when there was a lull in the conversation Steve leaned forward to kiss her. She'd had plenty of time to think it over and make a decision as he drew near.

When he leaned in to kiss her, she moved forward to kiss him with no hesitation.

She knew it was wrong, but there was a small, angry part of her that didn't care about that. This was familiar ground for her. No matter how sweet it was with Mark this didn't have any of the reassuring, consoling or comforting he seemed to require. It was simple, and that was something she didn't even realize that she'd been missing.

"Do you . . ." Steve asked, pausing, and then simply arching his eyebrows.

"What?" she started, but realized what he was talking about before the whole word got out of her mouth. "Oh. God no."

"Ouch. You don't have to sound so grossed out by it," he said, raising himself up on an elbow to peer down at her.

"Well I'm a virgin, and I'm not going to just give it up that easily, okay?" she snapped, scooting away from him. Her nakedness quickly went from turn-on to handicap.

"Oh." He had a quizzical expression on his face. "I didn't realize that you hadn't done it before."

"Is that surprising?" she said, sitting up and trying to remember where they had thrown her clothes.

"Well," he said with a slight smirk, "I guess it was a little presumptuous, but hey, that's fine, we don't have to if you don't want to."

"Gee, thanks," she snapped, wrapping her arms around her chest. It was kind of chilly without him on top of her and all of the excitement and passion she'd unconsciously stored up was leaving as quickly as it came.

"Hey," he said, sitting up and moving next to her. "You don't have to get defensive. I mean, I know it was kind of a stupid thing to think about, this being our first, y'know, and--"

"Our first what?" she said. "Affair? Fling? Fuck? What exactly is this to you?"

"Hey, ease up, okay? I'm not the one who's . . ." he cut himself short, but she could clearly see where he was going.

"Oh that's nice," she said, getting to her feet. Modesty had suddenly taken a back seat to wanting to get the hell out of there as soon as possible. "You're not the one who's fucking around on her boyfriend, right? I'll clearly throw over someone I care about for a cheap lay, right? You're just surprised that I haven't screwed the best friend of all my boyfriends, right?"

"Methinks the lady doth protest too much."

"Congratulations, you've got me figured out. I'm just some cheap slut who was looking for a good time, and you were the only big stud who could give it to me. Does that make you feel better about this now? Why don't we just say I threw myself at you so you can be completely innocent in all of this, okay? Let's just say that I seduced you and make me more of the bad guy?"

"Like you didn't?" he yelled, his voice rising to match hers. "Like you weren't giving me the eye since the first day that we met? Like you haven't wanted to be right where we are now since then?"

"Jesus, listen to yourself," she said, snatching her bra up off the floor and trying to get it back on as quick as possible. "All your helpful advice, setting yourself up to be the good guy, the best friend, all so you could fuck me quicker, is that it? Some prize you are."

"Don't start," he snapped, wagging a finger at her.

"What, are you going to start threatening me now, is that it? Smack me around and tell me that I better not say anything about this to anyone? Please," she said, waving a hand at him dismissively and gathering up the rest of her clothes from around the room. "I've been intimidated by bigger assholes than you, Steve. You're not even in their league."

"Wow," he said, sitting down on his bed. "And here I was admiring Mark's taste in girls."

"That's funny," she said, buttoning and zippering as fast as she could. "I was going to say the same thing about his taste in friends." Finally finished, she turned and stormed out, the notebook paper crumpling underfoot.

She almost made it out of the house without getting her purse from the den, which would have been a real disaster. Of course, it's not like anything else about this night was going very well anyway. She glanced at the VCR clock as she left, and saw that it was almost 1:30. She and Steve had been occupied far longer than she had thought. The only thing to be thankful for was that Steve hadn't been exaggerating about his parents being out all night. She didn't want to top the evening off by running into his parents as she burst out the door, hair mussed, clothes a shambles, smelling like pencil lead and sex.

On top of everything else there was Mark. It had been so easy to push him to the side during, and even right before. She was still angry at him for asking her not to come here, and clearly, Mark knew what Steve was capable of more than she did.

What she'd said to Steve wasn't a lie. She'd been in that situation before but this was the first time that she had actively cheated on a guy that she still wanted to stay with. All of the others she'd just used it as an easy way to get out of something she didn't want anything to do with anymore.

Despite everything that had freaked her out so much with Mark the last thing she wanted was an easy out. Things with him were scary, insane and incredibly difficult but at least he was genuine. Even if it was genuinely screwed up.

And now she'd completely betrayed him.

She could either try to pretend that the whole thing hadn't happened, but there'd be no way for her and Steve to try to get along without Mark sensing that something had happened. Of course, she could tell him everything, but that would probably just destroy him.

It was a long, cold walk back to her place and she couldn't tell if she was chilled from the outside or inside. She was able to remember the way home clearly enough. Of course, she'd have to explain this to her folks, and since Ryan was surely home by now he'd probably come up with some wildly lame and believable excuse for where she was, which they would ask her about and she'd have no way to follow through on. She was glad she'd left her phone at home, doing so to give her an excuse for when her parents (or Mark) asked where she was and why she hadn't answered any calls.

She was walking fast, her mind leaping from one thing to the other so she didn't even see the flashing lights when she walked around the corner. It was only when a car flew past her that she looked up and noticed them. Lots of flashing lights. All different colors, all clearly coming from the same place. Police, ambulance, and maybe even a fire truck or two. At first her only thought was that maybe she should go around that block so that she didn't have to answer any questions about why she was out so late, but then she realized that wouldn't be possible.

This was her cul-de-sac. She was walking faster before she even realized it, and then she was running as fast she could. As she got closer she could see there were at least four police cars and two ambulances in the driveway, and a fire truck pulled up on her lawn. When she got closer she could hear the occasional chirp of a siren, radios crackling with static, and her mother screaming.

After that, everything became a blur.

CHAPTER TWENTY-FIVE

It **took** a couple of tries for Ryan to get his key into the lock, but he finally got it to work. With an agonizing slowness, he pushed the door open, straining his ears for any noise coming from the house. He nodded to himself several times, very enthusiastically. His entrance was a flawless masterstroke of almost-sober coordination, and it confirmed his status as a God among men. He stepped very slowly and deliberately into the house. He tried to shut the door with the same amount of quiet he had opened it with, but he slipped and the door slammed closed much louder than he had intended it to.

Leaning against the wall for support, he checked his watch and realized that it was only almost 1. He'd decided to call off the movie, and instead found himself looking for a decent bar in this god-forsaken suburban hell-hole. He'd found one in the next town over, a blue collar dive bar with the right combination of cheap beer and an atmosphere that assured you that you'd be left alone.

He nursed beers until the few sober bits in his head reminded him that he'd have to drive back home. He'd waited until he could stand without wobbling over and then drove very carefully back home. He thought it'd have taken him longer, but apparently he was a better drunk driver than he gave himself credit for.

He pushed off from the wall and headed for the steps and his "guest room." He'd taken everything he could with him to college, knowing that his folks were going to move again, but he'd expected that they'd at least put his stuff in a room for him when he showed up. Oh no, not his folks. His stuff was still in boxes in the basement. Behind a giant wall of other boxes.

It was so nice to feel welcome in your own home.

He started up the stairs, listing against the rail as he tried his best to keep the noise to a minimum. He'd made it a couple of steps up when he realized he couldn't see anything. He stopped, waving his hand in front of his face and watching his arm disappear at the elbow in a blackness that stretched everywhere in front of him. He looked over his shoulder to make sure he'd hadn't just gone blind, but everything back there was how it should be.

He could feel his brain screeching to a halt as panic drove the drunkenness from his mind and tried to comprehend what he was seeing. He turned back to look up the stairs when the fog of blackness completely enveloped him, not just shutting off his vision completely, but filling his senses with the stinging of burning ash.

He coughed but he could barely hear it, like the black fog was sealing off his ears as well. He took an unsteady step back, trying to find a way to negotiate the stairs, blind, backwards and with limited sobriety. Just as he put an exploratory foot back to find the next step, something touched his chest and pushed him backwards with surprising force.

He tumbled back, one arm catching the railing and slowing his fall some, but he still felt his ass crash down on a step and then slide down two more before he tumbled out of the senses-sapping darkness. Before him, the smoke fog had made its way down the stairs, coalescing into a vaguely human shape.

Ryan stumbled to his feet, his lower back suddenly flaring in pain and his elbow buzzing likewise. There was a long, drawn out scraping sound, and a thin line of brilliant silver appeared in the midst of the fog. When the shrill, grinding scrape finished, the man-shaped fog stopped at the bottom of the steps and the line of silver was held aloft above it.

Ryan stared up at it, and then it disappeared. There was a rush of wind past his face, and then a flash of burning pain.

He cried out, putting a hand to his suddenly wet cheek. It was blood, he realized, feeling it begin to run down the side of his face.

The shape of the smoke-fog had solidified more, with full arms and legs, and even a hat and long cloak that stretched out curling smoky tendrils all across the staircase. Under the brim of the hat, where eyes were supposed to be, two pools of flame erupted with a silent explosion.

Ryan jerked back in surprise, and then the blade reappeared, the tip not an inch from his nose and still wet with his blood.

"So. You're the brother."

"Wha . . . what?" There was no mouth, just the merest suggestion of one dimpled in the swirling blackness.

"The girl. Where is she?"

"What?"

He didn't even see the point of the blade move. There was a blur and then a sting in his other cheek. When it returned, the tip was wetter and redder.

"Where did she go?"

The tip of the blade was drawing closer, and Ryan took a step back, hypnotized by the sight of his own blood dripping onto the floor of his parents prized new home.

"Are you in there, or am I just talking to myself?"

It wasn't until that moment that he realized who this thing had been talking about, and the pain his cheeks was forgotten. He opened his mouth to make a threat of his own, but he was interrupted by a call from the top of the steps.

"Ryan? Chrissy? Is that you two?"

His father was in his pajamas and bathrobe, hair askew on his head, and had taken a few steps down the stairs until he realized what he was seeing was most certainly not the kids sneaking in after curfew that he expected.

"What is going on here?" Harold Baker said, his voice trembling with terrified indignation.

"Oh, be quiet," the figure snarled. "I'll be with you in a moment." It spun around, launching the blade at Harold Baker and impaling him in the leg. With a yell of surprise and pain, the elder Baker tumbled down the stairs, landing in a pile at the feet of the Shadow Man.

"The girl," he asked Ryan again. "Where is she?"

Ryan darted forward, the pain in his face and back forgotten at the sight of his father lying in a heap with a sword sticking out from his leg. He didn't make it a step before something smashed into his face and then again on the other side, sending him down to his knees.

"I'm not screwing around," the Shadow Man said. "Tell me where the girl is and I *might* let you and your father live. Keep being a moron and I'll kill you, your father, your mother, and when I'm done I'll *really* hurt the girl."

"I don't know! She was supposed to be here, I don't know where she is, I swear!" Ryan said, head now swimming from pain instead of liquor.

The Shadow Man stared at him with his flaming eyes for a moment, the only noise his father's moaning behind him.

"I'm not convinced. Maybe watching Daddy suffer will jog your memory." He turned, pulling his father upright and leaning him against the wall next to the stairs. He reached down and pulled the blade from his leg, drawing a fresh yell of pain out of him.

"Motherfucker!" Ryan charged at the figure's back. There was a rustle like cloth and the darkness swirled around him as the figure sidestepped him, and then there was a sharp, piercing pain right above his heel. The leg seemed to go dead underneath him, dropping him down to his knee. He looked up, now at eye level with his father, and suddenly there was an incredible pressure on the back of his neck, and it felt like every sensation in his body left him. He opened his mouth to say something, but he wasn't getting any air.

And then he was gone.

***

"Isn't that touching," the Shadow Man said, pulling the blade from the back of Ryan's neck. The body dropped down at his father's feet. Blood sprayed onto the floor, but flowed around the Shadow Man's feet, leaving him untouched.

"Still awake?" he said, leaning down and snapping his fingers impatiently in front of Harold Baker's face. The eyes focused, and then widened in horror as he saw his son laying prone in front of him, his blood flowing all over the floor. Harold looked up, his face ashen and mouth gaping open and shut.

"Good," the Shadow man said, placing the tip of his blade just below Harold's breastbone and using just enough pressure to keep him in place, but more than enough to make a small stain of blood appear in the center of his expensive pajamas. "I didn't hit any of the major arteries in your leg, so you won't bleed to death for a while. All I want to know is where your girl is? Do you know, or as you as clueless as your other offspring?"

The father was just gaping at him, his eyes blank, stunned and filling with tears. "You're utterly useless, aren't you?" the Shadow Man said, and then pushed the blade through muscle until it hit drywall. Baker gaped even more, and the tears (and blood) flowed freely now. The Shadow Man withdrew the blade with a flourish, snapping it back home in its sheath, covered with fresh tribute for his Lord.

"I've called the police," came a strangled cry from up stairs.

"Good for you," he said, watching the elder Baker slump down to one side, his breath coming faster and more shallow. He turned on his heel and headed for the kitchen. "I'll let myself out," he said.

As he passed through the kitchen towards the back door, he drew in a deep breath and exhaled a long strand of fire, covering the counter and fancy technological doo-dads. They hissed and melted, the fire quickly spreading up the fancy window curtains and wall

The porch door opened for him and he strode through as the fire roared behind him. His power was growing, and he could feel more of his Lord's righteous fury boiling through him with every drop of blood he brought back to Him. He jumped from the balcony just as the electric widgets and kitchen appliances exploded behind him, shattering the fancy, opulent windows behind him.

But before he could deliver his latest tribute, even if it wasn't what he had intended, he had one more stop to make.

***

Jack was cold. He tried to roll over and wrap more blankets around himself, but his body was pinned to the bed. He tried again, and felt his breath being slowly squeezed out of his chest. Panicking, his eyes fluttered open, and he met the gaze of the two pools of flame peering down at him.

"Hush now, we don't want to wake Daddy," the Shadow Man said, his voice low and rumbling. Jack didn't think he could make any noise if he tried. The Shadow Man was straddled on top of him, his weight pressing down on Jack. One of his hands was right next to his head, and the other held a long, silver blade pressed against Jack's throat. Behind him, darkness swirled angrily, almost completely blotting out the rest of the room.

"We had an agreement," the Shadow Man said, pressing the blade closer to Jack's neck. "You're useful, but only if you can follow instructions. If you can't, that makes you a problem. Maybe I should just end you right now."

Jack wanted to shake his head in furious disagreement, but realized that if he did he'd more likely slice his own throat open.

"I have so many things to show you," he continued, the pressure easing slightly on his chest, allowing Jack to take in a giant lungful of air. "Marvels and wonders. A whole new world and the potential for power as great as what I've been granted. But I can't show you them to you if you don't listen."

"I'll listen. I swear," Jack squeaked.

"I hope so," he said, drawing the blade slowly over Jack's neck. "Because I'm only going to say this one . . . more . . . time. Leave the boy alone. I need him for what's ahead. I need him to understand what's happened and to understand the error of his ways. He can't very well see what I want to show him if he's got his brain all scrambled up with a baseball bat, can he?"

Jack nodded as much as he dared. "I understand. Leave him alone. I will, I swear."

"Good, good." The Shadow Man said, and then with a sudden flick of his hand, the blade snapped back into its sheath. The pressure on Jack's chest began to ease again, and the Shadow Man rose up, drawing himself up to his full height.

"Pleasant dreams," he said, and the blackness swirled around him, blocking out Jack's vision completely. For a several horrible seconds, he thought he would suffocate from the sudden, oppressive darkness and the almost overwhelming smell of burning flesh, but just as quickly as it passed over him it was gone, and all that was left were the fluttering curtains in the chill autumn breeze.

He rolled over, but was shocked by sudden moisture on his throat and chest. He wiped at it with one of his blankets, desperate to get it off him. He stared at the new stain, its origins dawning on him. He put his hand back to his throat where the blade had rested, and could feel the sticky remains of the blood that had been on the blade.

He stared at it on his fingertips, so dark it was almost black. He leaned in close, smelling its metallic odor with a hint of flame. Tentatively, he touched his tongue to it, savoring the texture.

He pulled his stained blanket up close to his face, and inhaled deeply again, closing his eyes with a smile on his face.

CHAPTER TWENTY-SIX

"Where is she?" David asked one of the nurses, who pointed him down to the next waiting area. He nodded his thanks and walked down the hallway. Even though things had been quiet for almost a month he'd known that whoever had killed Clara Washington and Carrie Kennedy wasn't done. Even worse this third killing left no doubt about who the focus of these killings was.

David paused where the hallway first widened into a waiting area. Christine Baker was sitting in a chair, alone, at the far end of the room. She was staring blankly out of red, puffy, heavy lidded eyes, and while he was sure that she could see him, he didn't think she realized he was there. It was almost 5am, and from the looks of her she hadn't gotten any sleep. Mrs. Baker, David had been told, had been sedated and given a room to try to calm down in.

The first responders had told him that while they were getting the kitchen fire under control, Mrs. Baker had to be forcibly pulled from the house, screaming about finding her daughter. Christine had been nowhere to be found, and they were about to put out an alert for her when she came running up to the house.

David crossed the room and sat down opposite Christine, waiting to see if there was any reaction. After several moments, she glanced his way, and he smiled weakly at her. "Hi Christine. Do you remember me? I'm Detective Prescott."

"I guess so," she said, looking past him.

"I need to ask you a few questions. Is that okay?"

She let out a long, ragged sigh, and focused her eyes on him again. "Have they told you if my Dad is going to die?"

Dave looked down at the little notepad he had fished out of his jacket pocket, consulting his notes. "Well, he's still in critical condition, but the doctors are pretty optimistic. This is one of the best trauma hospitals in the area." He left out how they were uncertain as to the extent of the nerve damage to his leg and spine, and what that would mean for his mobility post-recovery.

"And my brother is really dead? They won't let me see him."

"Yes, he is. I'm sorry they haven't let you see him, but he's not ready for that yet. I'm sure we can arrange something for you and your mother sometime soon."

"She is such a wreck," she said, eyes drifting down to the floor. "She gave me Aunt Helen's number, and she's flying down from Hartford, but . . . I don't know when she's going to get here."

"I'll see what I can do about that if you want to give me whatever info you have on her. First, though, I do need to ask you just a few questions, okay? This is real important."

She actually smiled a little at that last part, but did not look back up at him. "I guess this is how he felt."

"Who felt?"

"Mark. He told me I didn't know what it was like to lose someone, and here I am."

"You two are dating, right?"

He thought it would be a simple question for her to answer, but instead her face seemed to spasm with pain and she let out a choked mix of a sob and laugh.

"Yeah," she said. "We're 'dating.' I wouldn't be sitting here right now if we weren't dating."

It wasn't exactly what he wanted to hear.

"What do you mean by that?" he said neutrally, and she just rolled her eyes at him.

"What do you think I mean? Clara, Ms. Kennedy, and now this!" her voice was getting louder now. "And before you even ask, no, I don't know why! He said something to me after Clara died, about dreams he was having, but after Ms. Kennedy he said it was nothing, and that I shouldn't worry about it. I knew he was full of shit, but . . ." the volume dropped off, and her eyes fluttered wildly. One of the nurses poked her head out of one of the rooms down the hall, but he just flashed his badge at her and she retreated.

"What do you mean he dreamt about these things? Did he fantasize about them? Write them down?"

"No," she said, losing patience. "He said they were about these things happening, about seeing what happened to Clara. At least, that's what he told me, but you've met Mark, he's not much of a liar."

He just nodded in acknowledgement. "Did he give you any details?"

"No, I wasn't too interested in the finer points."

"Is there anything else you can remember about what he said about this?"

"He had a book," she said. "He's gotten it from the library, and he was real mad when I picked it up. It was about other crimes in the past, something about Corning or something like that. There was a whole chapter about it he had it open to."

"He didn't tell you why he had it?"

"No, he lied about it, said it was for school. I just let it go because I thought it made him feel better, like he was actual doing something other than worrying."

"Christine, do you think Mark is involved in this? Do you think he knows who's doing this?"

She waited, staring off into space for several moments until turning back to him. "I don't think so."

Her eyes drifted away from him again, and this time it looked like they would be away for a while. He waited to see if she was going to refocus on him, but after about a minute he cleared his throat.

"Christine, I'm going to see if they can spare a bed for you here, okay? You may feel a little better if you got some sleep before the sun comes up. When you wake up, I'll have an officer take you and your mother back to the house so you can get some things together. Do you have your Aunt's information? I can try to get in touch with her and help her arrange a hotel for you three."

She made a slight head movement that may have been a nod, and then dug into her pants pocket and fished out small sheet of paper which had been torn out of an address book. On it was an address, phone number and cell phone number for a Helen Greene.

He went off in search for the nurse from earlier as he dug the cell phone out of his pocket. He'd make some calls to be sure that Christine and her family was taken care of, and then he'd make some that would probably ruin Mark's life.

***

Mark woke up with a throbbing headache, the worst he'd had since the day or two before the accident. He wasn't sure if it was from the stress of dealing with Steve and his bullshit, worrying about Christine or staying up late failing to make a dent in his homework.

Keep this up sport and you'll be able repeat a grade of high school, since you love it so much.

Joe came in late last night, so it didn't seem likely that he'd see this side of noon. Mark figured it was best to not to be in the immediate area when that happened. He grabbed some cold leftovers from the fridge and headed out back to the garage to get a look at the damage that had been done to the V.

Steve had let him use his computer so he could find a manual on the Internet and print it out. Mark had been fascinated by the tiny engine and studied every aspect of it, eager to get his hands on it and see how it worked but terrified of breaking it and having to sink more money into his prized freedom.

He'd changed the oil regularly, washed it with care, and done everything he could think of to be safe on it. Apparently, he shouldn't have bothered.

Joe had rolled it into the garage to let it lean against the wall, but in the week since it had fallen over. From the way it had been laying, it looked like the fall had caused one of the side mirrors to bend, so much so that if Mark tried to bend it back into place he'd probably just snap the thin piece of metal in half.

"How hard is it to put down the fucking kickstand?" He squatted down to fully assess the damage. He'd hoped what he'd seen of it and what he told Christine had been pessimism brought on by trauma but if anything it looked worse than what he remembered.

The back end was dented so deeply that the back panel was mashed into the wheel and had dug into the tire so much that it was punctured. The rear taillight was completely wrecked, dangling from the chassis by a set of frayed wires, and the back end of the seat was crushed and wobbled to the touch. He wasn't sure, but it looked like the wheel frame on the front tire had been bent as well, but there was no way to tell without taking the tire off.

It may have been fairly used when Mark had found it last year, but now it looked like a giant had tried to kick a field goal with it.

Joe had bought Mark a set of tools after he'd gotten it, informing Mark that he wouldn't be responsible for any repairs on it. "If you want to ride something you should be able to fix it if it breaks." Tucked into the tools was the print out of the manual.

He sat down, surrounded by tools and little bits of Vespa that had fallen off and tried to find a place to start. His head throbbed and he felt his body sink into the ground at the enormity of the task

After fifteen minutes, he realized he'd been reading the same page about removing the front wheel and not getting any closer to understanding it. His head was throbbing more and more, and with an irritated snarl he threw the stapled sheets of paper against the garage wall, hoping the whole thing would just burst into flame and he wouldn't have to deal with it anymore.

Flame. It took him a second, but then the memory of it began breaking into his brain. Bits of it at first: Corwin wrapped in shadows, eyes on fire . . . a house, stairs, watching someone get shoved down the stairs, the silver blade being thrown.

It took a couple of moments but he remembered everything, dropping to the ground and rolling over on his side. Corwin had been looking for her. He'd been there, in her house, and he killed her brother and father when he couldn't find her. Had she been hiding? Did they run into him before he could get to her? Was she okay?

It was the last thought that propelled him from the garage floor and up across the yard and into the kitchen as fast as he could. His head no longer hurt, unclogged from the psychic log-jam that the vision had caused, and he dialed her number so fast that it took about three tries for him to get it right.

It went right to voicemail, and before he blurted out every detail of what he'd seen, he stopped and tried to compose himself. No matter what he had seen, there was no way he could explain it without sounding like a homicidal maniac.

"Hey you, it's Mark and I just . . . I just wanted to see what you were up to and how you're doing. Call me as soon as you get this, so we can . . . I dunno, do something today. I miss you. Call me."

He hung up the phone and stared at it. *That was way smooth. Really. I think your voice only moved through a dozen or so octaves during that little performance. There's no way that she'll know that you know something is up.*

The police showed up about four hours and three phone calls to Christine later. Joe was up by then, and when Detective Prescott, another detective and a pair of uniformed officers showed up on their doorstep with a search warrant, Mark could see Joe's head almost cave in under the weight of not being able to strangle Mark right then and there.

While Mark and Joe waited in the kitchen, David explained to them what had happened at Christine's house, and how she was fine, although exhausted and probably sleeping in a hotel room somewhere.

It wasn't lost on Mark that he didn't tell him where she was staying. Mark didn't ask.

They brought down the "Bizarre Crimes of Northern New Jersey," and the other Detective pulled David into the living room. Mark watched the two argue quietly as he avoided Joe's glare from across the table.

After a few minutes, he and David come back into the kitchen. David hung back in the archway while the other Detective took a seat across from him.

"Mark, I'm Detective Sergeant Lobrazzo. I think we should talk about some stuff down at the station, don't you?"

"If we have to."

"Yeah, I kind of think we do."

"Um, okay. Do I need a lawyer?"

"I don't know," Lobrazzo said, shrugging. "Do you think you need a lawyer?" Over Lobrazzo's shoulder, Mark saw David nod his head.

"Yeah, I kind of think so."

***

David liked Ron Lobrazzo. He had to remind himself of this as Ron chewed into Mark in the interview room, leaving David stewing in the corner.

David had been given a fair amount of leeway with the investigation, which was easy given that most of the evidence they had didn't make any sense and the rest just pointed to a teenager with no motive and little opportunity.

But when the Baker's house was attacked and the shitstorm up at the top worked its way down and got Ron, the senior Detective in the Investigation Unit. When he read David's report of Christine's interview, the first thing he wanted to do was bring Mark in and grill him until he broke.

David couldn't bring himself to admit to him that he thought Mark was hiding something, but Ron knew enough to read between the lines.

"Three murders, all only linked by him, and you're acting like it's a coincidence. Why the hell are you protecting him?" He'd asked him in the car on the way from the judge's house with the signed warrant the Chief had insisted they get and serve immediately.

"Probably because I think he needs protecting."

"Cute. I felt that way about that girl back at the hospital."

They hadn't said much after they argued at Mark's, David telling him that going at the kid hard was going to be pointless, and Ron insisting that the problem was that the kid wasn't taking this seriously. "For all we know he's one of those crazy Columbine kids. I'm telling you we're going to find a gun, or plans for a bomb, or something like that and you're going to see this kid for the unstable, desensitized monster he probably is. Hell, he could have some accomplice bumping these people off, and you're letting him off the hook because he was what, asleep? Wake up, Dave. I expect better."

So he sat there, keeping watch over Mark as they waited for his lawyer to show up. Joe parked himself in the lobby stone-faced and silent, and when Mark's lawyer showed up David was relieved that the kid's Uncle had actually spent some money and gotten a real lawyer and not the glorified accountant he'd brought last time.

"I just don't understand this. You get run off the road and beaten, but you have no idea who did it or even what they looked like. Plus, you have no idea why anyone would want to kill people close to you. Do you have any ideas? Anything at all that maybe will keep other people getting killed, or are you not worried about that?"

Mark did what he'd done for most of the interview: stare at the table and shake his head. "No, I don't want anyone to get hurt."

"Really? Maybe you should tell that to Christine and her family. They'd be thrilled to hear that."

Mark's hands clenched, but he didn't look up.

"Mark, I just don't understand how you have no idea about what's going on, especially since you were hiding a book about murders that took place in this town up in your room."

"There's nothing illegal about taking a book out of the library, Sergeant," Mark's lawyer said.

"Yeah, that's true, but I have yet to hear why he did it in the first place."

"I was scared." Mark said. He stared at Ron with more intensity than he thought the terrified kid would be able to muster. "It was stupid, but I thought there might be something in the book that would help me understand what was going on. Maybe even tell me why this was happening to the people I care about but it turned out it's just a stupid book that didn't tell me anything. I didn't say why I took it out before because I was embarrassed. Is that a good enough reason?" Tears had begun to slide down the kid's face.

The lawyer lifted his palms to the sky. "Well, Sergeant? Is it?"

Ron wiped his mouth and chin, looking past Mark and at David, who just shrugged his shoulders. Ron tilted his head towards the door and David followed him out.

"Don't say it," Ron said just before they entered the observation room. The shrug was the closest thing to "I told you so" David would dare.

In the tiny room looking into the interview room was the Deputy Chief overseeing the Investigation Unit and the Essex County District Attorney. Neither of them looked particularly happy, and in a room that small it was hard to ignore.

"This is pointless," the DA said. "I'm not going to try to prosecute some kid, or open ourselves up to some sort of harassment lawsuit."

"He's the only connection to this whole thing," Ron said. "If he doesn't know anything, then whatever is happening is happening because of him and he's in danger. If he does know something, then he's eye-deep in it and after that performance only god knows what he's capable of."

"But this is getting us nowhere," the Deputy Chief said. "Prescott, you've talked to this kid a bunch already, what do you think?"

Ron glared back at him, and David took a deep breath to stall while he figured how far over the line he'd put his ass for Mark. "Honestly, I think he's telling the truth. If there's something going on, what he knows probably isn't going to help us. According to the hospital, Howard Baker should be able to answer some questions in a couple of days. As long as we keep him safe, he can give us an idea of who did this to him."

Which is what David had told Ron, but he didn't want to put too fine a point on it.

"Alright, let's try to keep an eye on this kid. Cut him loose," The Deputy Chief said.

"What're we going to do if there's another murder?" Ron said as the all walked out.

"Then we hold him," the Deputy Chief said, and the DA nodded. "Either for his own protection or until he tells us something useful. This is already turning into a fiasco, and the last thing this town needs is another Justin Corwin."

David stopped in his tracks, watching the two walk off down the hall. "Hold on," David said before Ron opened the door to the interview room. "Who's Justin Corwin?"

"C'mon, Dave," Ron said, rolling his eyes. "I know you're from Philly, but do your homework, would you? He's Cedar Ridge's very own serial killer. He's in that book the kid had. Happened in the 50's and the guy is long gone."

"This has nothing to do with Clara, Ms. Kennedy or Cor--"

He'd been cut off by his Uncle's yell at the hospital, but if that was why he'd gotten the book then perhaps there was more of a connection than they were seeing.

CHAPTER TWENTY-SEVEN

When they got home from the Police Station, Joe informed Mark that the lawyer cost $200 and that he'd like to be paid back by the end of the month.

Mark spent the rest of the evening and the next day in the garage stopping his futile repair job every couple of minutes to make sure he wasn't missing hearing the phone ring.

He didn't. She didn't call all weekend. Mark couldn't tell which was worse: not hearing from her and not knowing if she was okay, or knowing she was okay and that she wasn't calling him back anyway.

At school on Monday, Mark was relieved that no one at school seemed to put together that it was Christine's family that the news had been talking about. The police hadn't confirmed that there was a connection to Clara or Ms. Kennedy's death, but it didn't stop reporters from speculating about it. Steve asked him when they met for lunch about it and Mark reluctantly told him what details he had to share. It was the only thing he'd ever seen that completely shut him up. Well, for five whole minutes.

"Have you talked to her?"

"No," Mark said. "I left messages but I haven't heard anything."

He actually looked relieved. "Do you think she's okay?"

Mark just looked at him. "Right," Steve said. "Stupid question. Do you--"

"I don't want to talk about this. If you can't talk about anything else but this then let's not talk about anything at all. And I sure as shit hope you don't tell anybody else about it."

Steve opened his mouth, but then closed it and went back to his sandwich. They didn't say anything else the rest of the period or the next. At the end of gym, when the bell rang and Mark headed down the hallway, Steve followed him.

"Mark, hold up a second."

"I don't want to," he said, not stopping.

"We should talk about stuff. I mean, things are getting kind of fucked up and--"

"Oh, *now* they're getting fucked up? Thanks for the update since I hadn't figured that out yet."

"Mark, look--"

"Just forget it, okay?"

"I'm sorry!" Steve called down the stairwell. "For everything."

"Hey."

Mark didn't notice Christine until she'd called to him from inside the car as he walked past.

"Hey," he said, squatting down on the sidewalk to lean on the open window. "How're you doing? I tried to call you but all I got was voice mail."

"Yeah, I know. I've just been . . . well, you can imagine."

"I know, and I'm so sor--"

"Don't. I need to talk to you but I don't want to do it here. Can we drive somewhere?"

"Sure," he said, walking around to the passenger's side. "Whose car is this?"

"It's my Aunt's rental. My Mom's been staying at the hospital and my Aunt flew down from Hartford yesterday and has been making plans all day for Ryan . . . I told her I needed some air, and she's been kind of a push-over since she got here."

They drove most of the way in silence, finally pulling into one of the parking spaces at the park they used to go to. Christine turned off the car but stayed where she was. Finally, she turned to him and said, "I want you to tell me everything."

"What do you--"

"You know what I mean! Everything about what's going on with all of this! Why my brother was killed and my father may never walk again. You tell me everything you know about this right now or so help me I go to the police and I'll tell them it was you."

"Christine, stop, please--"

"Try me," she said.

He took a deep breath and told her.

"Are you serious?" she said when he was done.

"Yeah," he said. "I know it sounds crazy but it's the truth. Corwin's ghost thinks I'm this Darren kid, and he wants me because he escaped before he could finish . . . well, whatever the hell he was trying to finish."

"So you're saying it's a ghost? A ghost of some guy who died in the fifties killed my brother and tried to burn down my house?"

Mark could just nod. "I'm sorry, I wish--"

"Stop it!" she screamed, pounding her fists on the steering wheel. After a few seconds she slapped at her seatbelt until it let her free and then shoved her way out of the car.

Mark scrambled to follow her. She was standing with her back to him, a fistful of hair in each hand at her temples. When he put his hand on her shoulder, she shrugged it away without even looking back at him.

"I'm sorry," he said. "I just . . . I know that if we stick together we can work this out, we can get through this and then--"

"And then what?" She spun around to face him, throwing her arms up in the air and letting little threads of red hair sprinkle down to the ground. "I don't want to think about what happens after because I'm too terrified about what's happened right fucking now! I haven't been able to sleep! I can't close my eyes without thinking something is going to come into our hotel room and finish what it started! I can't even go back into my own house to get my things because it's a crime scene!"

"I know, I know. I'm just glad that he didn't find you and that you're safe. I mean, it's horrible about your Dad and brother but I'm just glad he didn't get to you."

She rubbed at her eyes and took in a deep breath. "I wasn't in any danger."

"What are you talking about?"

"I wasn't in my room, Mark. I wasn't even home."

"What?" *Well, this is a thrilling new development.*

He remembered the vision of that night, and how Corwin had been asking where she was and he'd thought she'd hidden from him, but if she wasn't there, then where . . .

"I wasn't there. I was out. I went to go see Steve."

Let's not lose sight of what matters here, okay? She's fine, physically, and now you guys have a lot more in common. So she went to see Steve, after you explicitly asked her not to and was at his place until, what, 1am? The important thing is that she's just unfaithful, not unfaithful and dead.

"I know you didn't want me to but I just went to pick up his notes and when I couldn't read them I told Ryan to just go, since he drove me, and I guess he went out and came back when Corwin or whatever that thing is was at the house. I'm sorry."

"Wh . . . why are you sorry? I mean, I didn't want you to but that was a mistake. You can do whatever you want. It's not like . . ."

She looked away.

"You're fucking kidding me."

I'm sorry, okay, Steve had said. *For everything.*

"I can't . . . How could you?" he said, stepping towards her.

"Mark," she said, turning around to face him. "It didn't mean anything, okay?"

"Is that supposed to make it better?" he said.

"Mark, stop it. I didn't want to lie to you but this isn't really that important now."

"I realize that," he said through gritted teeth. "But that doesn't excuse you going off and doing god knows what with my supposed best fucking friend!"

"I said stop."

"Why? Why the fuck should I? I mean, it's not every day that you realize your girlfriend is just a cheap whore who will--"

He didn't get a chance to finish as his head snapped back, propelled by the force of her fist.

"Fuck you!" she screamed as he staggered backwards. "Fuck you, fuck you, fuck you! My brother is dead and my Dad may be crippled all because of your stupid bullshit, so you can just fuck yourself!"

He ran his fingers along the inside of his lip, and they came back tinged with blood. "Right, that's fair. You screw around then get to hit me. Fine."

"Mark, don't--"

"Don't what?" he snapped. "Don't argue because this is all my fault anyway? Why don't you just say your brother is dead because of me and get it off your chest and then you and Steve can live happily ever after."

"I don't want Steve and don't you dare try to twist this around and try to martyr yourself. You kept saying that you were going to take care of it but all you did was read a book and try to keep it to yourself! If this whole thing wasn't so goddamn crazy I'd go and tell Detective Prescott myself."

"I get it. I fucked up and it's all my fault. You're right and I'm sorry. I wish there was more I could've done to keep this from happening, but the fact of the matter is that you were at Steve's fucking around before you knew all this had happened. I guess you knew even then that you were done with me." He turned and headed for the car.

"Fuck you!" she screamed at him as he stopped at the car to get his backpack. He didn't stop or turn, getting comfortable with the rage boiling inside him as he headed out of the park just short of running. He wasn't going home yet.

He had a stop to make first.

***

Steve was almost to his house when he heard running footsteps coming up behind him. He stepped over to the side to give whoever was hauling ass room to get by and glanced over his shoulder to see if it was one of the piss-ant 8 year-olds that lived up the block. It wasn't, and it gave him time to roll to the side as Mark plowed into him.

The two tumbled onto his neighbor's lawn, backpacks coming off as Steve tried to roll Mark off of him.

"You fucker!" Mark yelled, grabbing a fistful of Steve's jacket and swinging wildly at him with the other hand.

"Stop! Stop!" Steve batted away Mark's poorly aimed blows and squirmed his way out of his jacket, giving him a little bit of breathing room.

"Fuck you! Fuck you!" Mark finally landed a solid blow to Steve's chest, knocking him back onto the ground. Mark dove back down on top of him, but Steve managed to get a leg up, plant it on Mark's chest and then send him flying away with a push. Steve got back onto his feet and moved away from him.

"I'm sorry, okay! I swear I'm sorry!"

"Fuck you," Mark said, lunging at him. Steve sidestepped out of the way and knocked Mark to the ground, pinning him to the grass with a knee in his back and a forearm in the back of his head. Mark thrashed and writhed on the ground like an animal, screaming obscenities at him. Mark's uninjured arm was pinned under him, and his other was flailing at him with murderous intent until Steve grabbed it just below the bandage and twisted it behind Mark's back.

"Stop it, Mark, please! I'm sorry, okay. I am really, really, sorry."

"Fuck your sorry, you worthless backstabbing piece of shit!" Mark's cheek was pressed into the ground, and only one eye glared up at Steve, red-rimmed with tears and blazing fury.

"Just calm down, okay? Please." He looked around hoping none of the neighbors had come out to investigate what was going on.

"Why? So you can rationally explain why you stabbed me in the back during one of the worst times of my life. Is that why?"

"No, because if you don't I'll break your arm," Steve said, giving the captive arm a rough twist. Mark yelped in pain. "Just settle down, okay?"

"Go to hell!" Mark hissed in pain, but the thrashing all but stopped.

"If I let you up, will you try to hit me again?"

"Maybe."

Steve twisted again. Mark gritted his teeth, but didn't cry out.

"No."

"Good," Steve said, pushing off of Mark and quickly getting to his feet.

Mark just rolled over and propped himself up, glaring at Steve with raw hatred.

"Jesus, I haven't had to do that to you since the 5th grade," Steve said, picking up his bag without taking his eyes off Mark.

"Go to hell."

Steve sighed. "You're repeating yourself, man. Not good."

"You want something new and original?" Mark said, getting to his feet. "How about this? I despise you. I always thought that you'd be my friend no matter what, but now I find you're no better than Jack and his pack of assholes. Shit, you're worse. At least they are upfront about making my life hell."

"For fuck's sake, Mark," Steve said. "No one makes your life more hell than you do. You're always so fucking melodramatic about everything."

"Jesus Christ," Mark said, shaking his head. "You screw around with my girlfriend and I'm being melodramatic and over-reacting, is that it? You sick fuck."

"Look," Steve said, but then stopped and shook his head. "Y'know, I can't even argue with you. You're right, I'm an asshole. But I just . . . it just happened, okay? I don't think she's the girl for you, and--"

"But she's the girl for you?"

"No, she just . . ." Steve let out a sigh. "I just wanted to and I guess I didn't think it through. I'm sorry."

Mark shook his head and turned away from him. He was quiet for a moment, and then walked over and picked up his bag. "You fucking rich-kid prick. You want something, and you get it, no problem. When I want something, just one lousy thing in my entire lousy, miserable life you've got to have it too. What the fuck did I ever do to deserve a friend like you?"

Mark turned and walked away. He must have known that Steve didn't have any answer.

CHAPTER TWENTY-EIGHT

What did I ever do to deserve a friend like you?

The question haunted him all the way home and until he was lying face down on his bed, screaming with rage into his pillow.

Hey, if it makes you feel better she's right when she says it's all your fault. I mean seriously, if Corwin wasn't so obsessed with ruining your life, her dad and brother would be alive and kicking instead of . . . well, the opposite.

He screamed even louder at that, but he knew that it was true. Everything she'd said was true, and now she hated him even though he still loved her. He couldn't even be truly angry at her given what he'd brought into her life. If anything he deserved worse than being cheated on but he couldn't imagine feeling more miserable. There wasn't anything that she'd said that wasn't true, and what he'd said to her? Fuck, he deserved every bit of this and more.

Well maybe you'll get lucky and he'll go after Steve next.

But why bother? Corwin had completely destroyed the fabric of Mark's life. If there was anything else he wanted it was clear that he could just take it. It wasn't as if he could do anything to stop it.

"Just come and get me," he said, pulling a blanket over his head. "I'm done."

***

Darren had been sleeping, face resting on the cell door. He pulled away and the sweat from his face stuck the mesh to his face for a second. With the furnace blazing at full blast during the middle of summer, the heat had become unbearable. Life had devolved into a haze of sitting at the door and watching the fire in the furnace dance its magical dance.

Except for when he came in and took them. And if they stopped moving for too long, it was down from the chain, chopped into pieces and into the fire with them.

Like Suzie Morris, a week ago.

Like Oscar Lukacs, two days ago.

He looked over his shoulder at Randal, now his only cellmate. He was exhausted, lying flat on his stomach with his head turned to stare at Darren with blank eyes. The Shadow Man had been coming more and more often for them now, but Randal had taken the brunt of the beatings since Oscar fed the fire.

Darren turned and looked back at it. Some of the coal rolled and settled, but it just burned on quietly. Darren squinted, watching the patterns in the flame change in front of him and the mix of dark black coal and soot-stained bone burning in the chamber.

"Why do you do that?" Randal said.

"Do what?"

"Stare into the fire like that."

"It's something to do," Darren said, turning his attention back to it.

"It's horrible,"

"I dunno," Darren said. "I think it's kind of pretty."

The upstairs door opened. Darren could feel Randal begin to shiver from across the cage. Darren supposed he should be frightened too, but he didn't care. He couldn't stop him from coming, so all he focused on was the fire in front of him.

The cage door squeaked open, and the Shadow Man ducked his head inside. He glanced towards Randal, and just as his weight shifted to go for the boy in the corner, Darren stopped him in his tracks.

"Take me."

"What?" Randal said, but he'd had already been forgotten. The Shadow Man stared down at him, and after a moment he nodded and reached out for Darren.

"No, stop it!" Randal said, crawling across the floor of the cage. The Shadow Man kicked at Randal, knocking him back onto the ground where he lay still. He dragged Darren out by a handful of tattered shirt. He didn't struggle, but he didn't walk either. He just hung limply as he was dragged across the floor, never taking his eyes off the flames.

The Shadow Man stood Darren up with one hand and grabbed the chain hanging from the ceiling with the other. Darren raised his hands and stood on his tiptoes, letting the chain wind tightly around his wrists. Now, seeing him fully by the light of the furnace, Darren remembered seeing him around the neighborhood before. He'd been limping down the street and Darren's mother told him that it was impolite to stare.

He let go of Darren's shirt, and Darren blinked away pain and tears as the rusty chain bit into his wrists with all his weight. Corwin walked over to the furnace and knelt in front of it.

He bowed down, rolling open the bundle of cloth that lay on the floor and revealing the instrument Darren knew all too well.

The cane.

He got back to his feet and began to walk slowly around Darren. The familiar ring of the blade being drawn echoed around the room.

"You see Him, don't you?" His voice whispered in Darren's ear.

"I think so," Darren said through gritted teeth. He could feel a trickle of blood run down his forearm.

"I remember the first time I saw Him. I was down here working, staring off into space, and there he was. I didn't know what it was at first, so I got my parents to come and look, but they couldn't see it. They said I was imagining it, that it was all in my head because of all the things I'd already seen. But I knew! I knew He was real, and soon I could hear Him too. He said I had to make others see, and I tried! I tried to make my parents see, I tried so hard, but they wouldn't! So I did the next best thing. If they weren't going to worship Him, they'd feed Him. After that I knew what I had to do.

"I had to either bring him food, or bring him those that can worship him like I do. So which one are you? Are you food, like the others, or do you believe?"

Darren didn't say anything, and then he felt it against his chest. Something sharp.

"Tell me."

Darren screamed as the blade slowly dragged down his chest. It started high, just below his right armpit and was drawn down across to the opposite hip. His shirt fell to pieces, and blood trickled down his chest and pattered on the basement floor like rain.

"He needs the blood," Corwin said. With a flick of his wrist, he shook the blade towards the furnace, sending an arc of blood through the air. When the blood landed in the fuel chamber, the flames erupted in a volcanic burst.

"Oh, He likes you. He wants more."

Corwin dug his fingers into the open wound, fishing out more tasty morsels for his furnace-god. Darren screamed in pain and then something knocked into the two of them with so much force that Darren swung forward, feet leaving the ground. Corwin toppled over, the blade falling to the ground and something screaming and kicking latched onto his back.

Something named Randal.

As Darren swung back from the impact, he realized that it had pulled down the piece of pipe the chain had been wrapped around. His feet were now able to fully touch the ground. He grabbed the chain hanging above his wrists, dug in with his feet and pulled with all his might. The chain shivered and then gave way, dropping Darren to the ground with one end still wrapped around his wrists.

Randal was shrieking at the top of his lungs, hanging on Corwin's back swinging as hard as his tiny arm could muster. Corwin got to his feet, and with a shrug he flipped Randal to the ground next to Darren.

Darren tugged at the chain wrapped around his wrists, trying to get himself free. Corwin towered over the two of them, glowering down at the stunned Randal. Corwin reached for him, but the boy kicked up and into the man's groin. Corwin doubled over, dropping to one knee, and Randal scampered to his feet.

"Let's go!" Randal yelled.

Before he could break for the door, Corwin's arm snaked out, grabbing Randal's collar with one hand and pulling him back.

"Little bastard," he snarled, smashing Randal's head down onto the ground. His head lolled backwards and Corwin slammed it down again, the boy's eyes rolling back into head as he fell into unconsciousness, blood leaking from the back of his head. Corwin reached for where the blade had fallen, but there was nothing there.

Corwin turned and looked over at Darren, and then to the blade the boy had in his hands.

Corwin opened his mouth to say something, but before he could, Darren swung the blade as hard as he could.

***

Mark threw the blanket off his head and was blinded by the light. At first he thought it was the furnace flames, but then he realized it was the morning sun beaming down into his face.

So there it was. Justin Corwin's defeat at the hands of one of his victims. Now he'd come back to exact some sort of revenge and it was typical Mark Watson luck that he'd be singled out as the target.

"Mark, come on! I'm running late!" Joe yelled up the steps.

Mark stumbled to the top of the steps. "You go, I'm not ready yet."

"Mark, you better get a move on, I mean it!"

"I'm going, I'm going. I can walk."

"You sure?" Joe said, sounding skeptical. Mark knew that it was well past the time for Joe to leave and there was no way he could afford to stay and debate it with him.

"Yeah, I'm fine."

"Alright, but you better not be late." Mark listened to his thundering decent down the stairs and slam of the front door. He waited until he heard the car pull out of the driveway before he turned around and got back into bed.

***

"You've got to be shitting me," Joe said, staring down at the note that was waiting for him in his box. *Joe: School called, nephew not there, no answer at house.* He read it again to make sure that there was no mistaking it but it was pretty clear. That little shit ditched school to go out and do god knows what. Probably cause more fucking mayhem to get him taken back to the police station and cost Joe more money.

"Un-fucking-believable." Joe stalked through the break room, getting to the phone just before one of the new kids from sorting got to it.

"Hey, man, c'mon." the kid said.

"Hey yourself, numbnuts. Beat it."

"Joe, when are you gonna get a cell phone and join us in the 21st century?" Marty said from a nearby table, snickering around a mouthful of sandwich.

"When are you gonna mind your fucking business?"

Joe dialed the house number and waited. It rang a bunch of times, and then he heard himself say to leave a message at the beep. He slammed the phone down in the cradle.

"Walt," he called to one of his buddies just coming in the door, "Cover for me, I have to go home."

"Again? Jesus, Sal is going to be pissed. What is it now?"

"I have to go kick my nephew's ass," he snarled, yanking his jacket off its hook.

He drove home, hoping that kid was just holed up in his little attic space and ignoring the phone. He'd proven to be dumb enough to practically get arrested, there was no reason why he wouldn't be dumb enough to just be hanging around the house like a useless lump.

He'd lost count of the chances he'd given the little shit. He'd practically begged him not to cause any more trouble, and what happens? They spend a Saturday down at the police station shelling out more money they didn't have on a lawyer because the kid refused to not get into trouble.

Joe wasn't sure what he wanted more, for Mark to be home so he could slap some sense into him or for him to not to be so the kid could come back and find his shit strewn all over the yard and the locks changed.

He skidded to a halt in the driveway, and when he turned the car off he took a moment to close his eyes and take a deep breath. He'd promised Martha on her deathbed that he'd take care of him. It was the last thing he'd said to her. Not "I love you," not "You made me so happy," but "I'll take care of him."

Remembering that he'd wasted his last words on that ungrateful little brat was all he needed to blow past whatever small sense of calm and rationality that had begun to develop. He strode into the house and up the stairs overflowing with righteous anger. He tried the attic door, but it was locked.

"Mark! Get the hell down here!" He said, slamming his fist on the door.

There was no response, but he could hear the floorboards squeaking as something moved around up there.

"Dammit, Mark!" he said, pounding on the door. "Get the hell down here or I'm going to break this fucking door down!"

Finally, he heard slow footsteps coming down the stairs on the other side of the door. Joe took a deep breath and he could feel the calm trying to claw its way back to the surface. If he wasn't careful this could get out of hand fast, and then Mark wouldn't be the only one with a visit to the police station.

The door opened and Mark stood there, disheveled and blinking at the light. Joe stared at him, clenching and unclenching his fists.

"What?" Mark said.

"You cut school today, that's what. They had to call me at work, again. How're we supposed to live if I get fired for coming out and messing with you all the time?"

"Well, why not just stop messing with me?" Mark said, turning to leave.

"Dammit, boy!" Joe grabbed Mark by the arm and spun him back around. "This isn't a fucking joke! What the hell are you doing?"

"Ow! Fuck, let me go!" Mark said, pulling away.

"Watch your mouth!" Joe let go and Mark stumbled backwards against the attic steps.

"Just leave me alone, okay? I was tired so I decided to stay home. What do you care?"

"No you don't!" Joe stepped forward, slamming a hand against the attic door, pinning it against the wall before Mark could close it. He moved closer to Mark, pointing a finger right in the kid's face. "As much as I'd love to just get rid of you for all the trouble you've been causing lately, I can't. It fucking eats me up inside, but that's the truth. If you're not going to behave, then I'm going to make you."

"What are you going to do, hit me?" Mark said, batting away the offending finger.

With a snarl, Joe grabbed Mark's shirt with both hands, lifted him off the ground and slammed him against the wall. "Don't you fucking push me! Don't think that I won't take my hands to you!" Mark's eyes blinked open and shut, his head having taken most of the impact into the wall.

"Do you hear me?" Joe yelled again, shaking the boy.

"Fuck you," Mark said.

With a roar, Joe pulled Mark back and slammed him back into the door again. Mark's head snapped forward with the impact, and he began to squirm and claw at Joe's hands. He drew Mark back and slammed him into the wall again, and Mark's hands stopped their spastic groping and his head leaned forward, limp as the rest of his body. Joe lifted him again, read to drive him back into the door again but he stopped himself, realizing he'd knocked the boy unconscious.

"Shit," he said, shifting his grip so he was holding him up under the armpits. Without being held up, the boy would just topple forwards and down the stairs. It took him a second, but he realized that probably wouldn't be the best thing in the world.

Teach him a hell of a lesson though, Joe thought. At least now he knew what it was for his mouth to write a check his ass couldn't cash. Maybe he'd--

Mark's eyes flew open and his expression went from slack unconsciousness to twisted rage faster than Joe could process.

With a growl, Mark drove his knee right into Joe's stomach, doubling him over. He let go of Mark and backed up, trying to catch his breath. Mark stepped forward swinging both fists up into Joe's ears. Joe screamed, staggering backwards some more as his ears rang with pain. Even in through his pain he was aware for a second that he was standing at the very top of the stairs.

With another growl Mark stepped forward, and Joe reflexively took another step back and only finding empty air.

Joe toppled backwards, one arm waving his for the railing and missing, the other almost reaching Mark, who just stood there. Joe bounced down the steps, the pain from Mark's blows a happy memory. Things in him bent and twisted, and then his neck hit the wall at the bottom of the steps, the weight of his body bending it sharply with a snap that sent a numbing echo through his body.

Maybe the kid could cash that check after all, he thought, as the numbness sapped away his senses and everything drifted away from him.

CHAPTER TWENTY-NINE

After the blow up with Mark, Christine hadn't ventured out of her hotel room. Thankfully Aunt Helen brought her food without asking too many questions she couldn't give answers to. No, Aunt Helen, it's not just that my brother is dead and my dad's seriously fucked up, it's that my boyfriend is being stalked by a crazy ghost that did this to them.

If I hadn't liked him, she told herself, if I hadn't thought he was so adorably cute and harmless this wouldn't have happened.

She was almost sorry for losing it on Mark, but then she'd remember what he said to her and how good it felt to punch him in the mouth. It was at least doing something that wasn't sitting in bed and watching shitty TV while her mom sat at her dad's bedside and her aunt planned her brother's funeral.

Her phone rang, and when she saw who it was she let out a deep sigh. She hated the idea of talking to him, but knew that if anything being mad at him would take her mind off the fact that she'd never see Ryan again.

"Hey--" she started, but was cut off by the sobbing on the other end of the line. "Mark? What is it? What's wrong?"

"I . . . I . . . Something bad. Something bad happened."

She bit back a sharp retort. "Was it him?"

"No. It's . . . oh god, I did something really bad. It was an accident, though! I swear!"

"Mark, calm down and tell me what happened."

"It's my uncle. I think he's . . . I think he's dead."

"Oh shit," she said. "Mark, what did you . . . what happened?"

"He was hitting me, and I just . . . I just fought back, and I didn't realize . . ." He let out a choked sob. "Oh, god, I thought I was dreaming, it didn't even seem real, but he fell and he's not moving . . . Oh God, what am I going to do?"

"Mark, you have to call someone. Call Detective Pres--"

"No! They already think I'm a killer! They'll lock me away! I can't . . . I . . ." he trailed off, sniffling.

"It was self-defense," she said. "They'll believe you, but only if you call them right now, okay?"

"I can't!" he wailed, and Christine had to bite down on her lip to keep from screaming at him.

"You have to, Mark. It's the only way," she said through clenched teeth.

"No," he said again, his voice getting firmer. "There's another way."

"What do you mean?"

"I have to prove to them that I didn't do these things. I have to stop this whole thing, and then maybe they'll believe me."

"Mark, that's crazy! If this doesn't have anything to do with the murders--"

"Do you think the police will see it that way? Do you think that this time they won't just lock me up? If they do I'll never be able to put a stop to this thing, because I know that only I can!"

"Mark--"

"No," he said, the sobbing completely gone now. "You were right. This whole thing is my fault and I'm sorry, I really am. If I'd done something about it before then maybe I could've stopped what happened to your dad and Ryan, but maybe I can do something now before anyone else gets hurt. I have to end this thing, and I'm going to need your help."

"Mark, I can't just--"

"He killed your brother, Christine! He walked into your house and killed him, and who knows how many other people over the years. And do you really think he's going to leave you, or your mother, or your father alone? That he's not going to keep coming until we stop him? Do you?"

"Mark, we can't. We don't know the first thing about how to deal with something like that."

"It's his house, Christine. That's where his power is. If we can shut that down, we can stop him. I'm going to go there now but I need your help."

"That's crazy. I can't just leave, Mark."

"I need you Christine. I'm sorry for everything that's happened, for dragging you into this, but I need you. Please. For your brother." The sobbing was gone, replaced by a wobbling determination that sounded crazy enough to run into the gates of a possibly haunted house on a crazed ghost hunt. Crazy enough that if someone wasn't there with him he could end up doing god knows what.

"Okay," she whispered. "Give me the address again, and I'll get there as soon as I can." She got a pen from her backpack and scribbled it down, and Mark quickly hung up, saying he would meet her there.

Her aunt had gone down to the hotel restaurant to get some food, and Christine scribbled a note for her and took the car keys. On her way down to the garage, she paged through the contacts on her phone until she found his number.

If she had to go and stop Mark from causing more of a problem for himself she wasn't going to do it alone.

***

"Hey," Steve said, after taking a deep cleansing breath before answering. He'd been waiting for this call, but was surprised it had taken so long for it to come. "I was wondering how you were holding up."

"I'm fine," Christine said, "but Mark's lost it."

"Yeah, I know. He came at me yesterday and--"

"That's nothing. He just called me, rambling about how he and his Uncle got into a fight and he thinks his Uncle might be dead."

"Oh fuck, are you serious? What happened?"

"I don't know, but he thinks that by solving these murders he's going to keep the cops from arresting him."

"How the hell is he going to do that?"

"He . . . he knows stuff about this, Steve. He hasn't told you, but he told me the other day about what he's seen in his dreams and why this might be happening. Before he flipped out about the two of us getting together."

"Okay, wow. Look, I wanted to tell you I was sorry about how that worked out, but--"

"So not the point! Look, he's clearly lost it. He's going to the house that's supposed to be the center of the whole thing, and I need your help to try to calm him down and get him to talk to the cops."

"It sounds like he's not the only one who's lost it. I'm not exactly high up on the list of people he wants to see right now. Especially if he's gone off the deep end."

"Look, he's supposed to be your friend, right? How about you act like it and we try to make it up to him for what we did. For all we know we drove him nuts."

"Are you serious? Is he that bad?"

"Steve, he said he pushed his Uncle down the stairs and he might be dead. What do you think? I'm going to give you the address, and then you can decide if you're going to just sit around or if you are going to try to be Mark's friend and help him out, okay?"

"Okay, hold on, hold on . . . alright, go." He jotted down the address, which he realized wasn't too far from him.

"I have to go, I'm--" there was a sudden blaring of a horn and screech of tires. "I'm not good at this driving and talking thing. Be there, okay? We need you." She hung up before he could say anything else.

He looked at his phone for a minute, and then started dialing.

***

"What?" Jack said. He didn't recognize the number, but that just meant it gave him free license to go apeshit on some stranger.

"It's time."

"Who the fuck is this?" But soon as he asked, he knew. "Really?" he managed to get past the lump in his throat.

"Are you ready?"

"Hell yeah! I've been waiting for--"

"Then take what you hid in the secret panel in your closet and meet me at this address."

"Okay, hold on."

"Don't be late. I don't want to have to start without you," He hung up.

"Finally!" Jack threw the game controller he was holding in the air. He'd been waiting for what seemed like forever, and if he knew what was in the panel in his closet then he knew what Jack had been aching to do with it. He was going to be free. He was finally going to be free.

"Jackson, what's going on up there? I'm trying to grade papers!" His father yelled from the bottom of the stairs.

"Nothing, Dad," he called downstairs. He opened his closet door and moved the pile of clothes away from the panel he'd made to keep things from the nosy old prick. He reached in and fished out what he had been looking for. He grinned, turning it over in his hand.

"What was that?" he father called again. "Jackson, you know I hate it when you just yell across the house at me. If you have something to say, come and say it. Don't just yell like some kind of barbarian."

"Okay, Dad," he said, moving towards his bedroom door. "I've got something to show you anyway."

***

"Mark?" she called from the head of the walkway of Corwin's house. The hedges had grown almost completely over the entryway, but she could just make out a small break in the branches. One that looked like it had been made recently.

Mark hadn't been kidding when he said that the place looked evil. All it needed were a couple of well placed heads on spikes and it'd be a shoe-in to win Creepiest Place of All Time. She moved closer, peering through the break in the hedges and seeing the front door ajar.

"Mark?" she tried again. Still no answer.

She turned back towards the street, hoping she'd see or hear a car, a bike or anyone coming from either direction to confirm that she was still in the land of the living. She'd been waiting on the sidewalk for over five minutes, hoping that she'd beaten Mark to the place so she could try to talk him down from his crazy plan out where it was safe. She wouldn't be surprised if the door to the place had been left open as the last people that had been there fled for their lives.

Either that or Mark was stumbling around in there right now on his crazy ghost hunt.

She walked into the yard and up the porch steps, hoping the rickety old mess wouldn't collapse under her feet. She poked her head in as far as sanity let her and tried again.

"Mark?"

"Right here."

"Jesus, don't do that! This place is creepy enough."

"It has that effect," he said, walking deeper into the house.

"Mark, we don't have to do this now," she said. "We can come back later, with help." He was just walking slowly around the entryway, placing his hand lightly on the crumbling banister, taking in every inch of the graying, cracked and peeling wallpaper. Parts of it had come off in whole strips, showing a chalky, white, crumbling material that in some places had fallen away to show the thin strips of wood in the walls. He walked straight ahead, down the main hall towards the back of the house.

"Mark, are you even listening to me?"

"I am, but we can't wait. I have to do this while I still can."

She followed him down the hall and into kitchen, partly to keep an eye on him and partly to not be alone in this place for too long. They'd be lucky if it only had one ghost. Mark walked in a slow circle around the room and then finally came to a stop at a door on the far wall.

"Mark," she said quietly. "Have you been here before?"

"Yes. In my dreams." He was trembling, and she was thankful that he was still aware enough to be scared.

"What's down there?"

He placed his hand lightly on the doorknob. "Down here," he said, "is where he took them."

"Oh god," she whispered, her hands clenching at her sides. "We don't have to go down there Mark. Let's just talk about this, okay?"

"This is what it's all about, Christine. This is where he saw it, and what he showed me in my dreams."

"Mark, let's wait, okay? Let's just take a second and talk about what we're going to do in some crazy murder basement that could be haunted."

He looked over at one of the dirt stained windows. "It's getting close to dark, Christine. Do you want to be here when the sun goes down?"

"I don't want to be here at all! Will you just stop walking around and talk to me, please?"

He turned and walked down the stairs. "Sure. Let's just do it down here."

She waited several minutes, hoping Steve would show up. When he didn't she headed down the steps, afraid Mark would hang himself or try to set the place on fire. After half a flight, the wooden steps came to a small landing and turned to the right for another half a flight and then coming to an end on a worn and bare concrete floor. The only light was the soft orange firelight coming from the massive furnace at the far end of the room. Mark stood in front of it, his back to her and casting a long shadow on the ground. She walked up to him, eager to be closer to the light.

"Mark," she whispered, "what are we doing down here?"

"This is where he did it," he said. He turned and pointed back the way they came, and when she looked back she saw the rusted pile of metal under the steps they'd walked down.

Not a pile of metal. It was the cage, the one Mark had told her about. "That was where he kept them," Mark said. "He had them watch the furnace to make them see what he saw. That's why all of this is happening. Because of this thing and what it wants."

"What does it want?"

"Blood."

"Hello? Are you guys here?"

Mark's eyes narrowed. The voice had come from upstairs, and Christine could now hear footsteps moving above them.

"Down here!" she yelled, and Mark shot her a look. "Mark," she said, reaching out to put a hand on his arm, but he shrugged it away, taking a step back towards the furnace.

"Mark, please, we need help! We can't do this alone!"

He simply glared at her.

She turned back towards the steps and watched the pair of sneakers, and then jeans, descend down the steps.

"Hello?" She had recognized Steve's voice, but seeing him come into view as he descended the final flight of steps filled her with relief.

"You," Mark said.

"Yeah, me," Steve said, walking towards them.

Christine opened her mouth to say something, but then shut it when she heard something else from upstairs.

Another set of footsteps.

"Steve," she said, but he and Mark were too focused on each other.

"What do you want?" Mark said.

"You should know that, man," Steve said.

"Maybe you should enlighten me," Mark said. He had backed almost right up against the furnace like a trapped animal.

There was more movement upstairs and then she saw another set of sneakers begin to come down the steps.

"I see you brought company," Mark said, his voice trembling with anger.

"I couldn't exactly do this alone, could I?" Steve said.

The sneakers, and then jeans, made their decent down the steps, slow and deliberate. Christine's breath caught in her throat when the man's hands came into view and she saw one of them held a gun.

"Mark, we have to stop this," the voice from the stairs called down.

"Oh god," Christine said, recognizing it.

"This is your help?" Mark's voice was filled with scorn.

"I've always wanted to help you, Mark," Detective Prescott said as he reached this bottom step. He kept his arms spread and held his pistol loosely in his hand, trying to be as non-confrontational as he could.

"What makes you think you can help? You don't even have the faintest clue as to what's going on."

"Maybe if you told us," Steve said taking a step forward. "I know you don't believe me but I'm your friend and I called him because I didn't want to see you do something stupid. Just talk to us and tell us what's going on."

Christine turned to look at Mark but he sprang into action, bending down for something on the floor in front of the furnace. Before she could see what it was he was back to his feet and grabbed her wrist, pulling her in front of him. She tried to scream, but was stopped by sharp steel pressing at her throat.

"Mark!" Steve shouted, and Detective Prescott raised his pistol.

"You idiots couldn't help him before, what in the world makes you think you can help him now?" Mark's voice hissed in her ear.

CHAPTER THIRTY

Steve realized he must have missed the memo that said "When Detective Prescott shows up, everybody lose their fucking minds."

With speed Steve had never seen from him before Mark picked something up from the ground and grabbed Christine. He had an arm around her waist, pinning her arms at her sides, and a blade to her throat. Detective Prescott raised his gun aiming at Mark, who peered at them with one mad eye, hunched down behind Christine's shoulder.

"Drop the sword, Mark," Detective Prescott said.

"Oh, by all means Detective," Mark sneered at them. "After I slit this girl's throat and make you watch."

"Mark!" Christine struggled, but she held still when Mark pulled the blade tight enough against her throat to draw a thin line of blood.

"I would stop that if I were you. This blade, while very old, is still razor sharp. I'd hate to see you slit your own throat on it before I was through with you."

"Why are you doing this?" Prescott said, taking a cautious step forward.

"You're the detective, figure it out," Mark said. "While you do, try to figure out how many more steps I'll let you take before I kill her."

"Mark," Steve said, trying to find his voice. "Just . . . just take it easy, man! You don't need to do this. We can stop whatever is happening, just--"

"Are you really that stupid?" Mark yelled, turning his gaze to Steve. "He knew you weren't that bright, but seriously!"

"Steve," Prescott said, not taking his eyes off Mark. "Go up stairs, get out of here."

"He moves and she dies!"

"Mark--" Steve started.

"Mark's not home right now, you little idiot. I'll be dealing with him in a little while, but first I want the Detective to drop his weapon and kick it over here."

"That's not going to happen. Are you Corwin, is that it?" Prescott said.

The thing in Mark's body laughed, a long, drawn out cackle that echoed all around them. "Oh God, you are so brilliant, Detective. Honestly, you've really got me figured out. Now that you've cracked the case, be a good boy and kick your weapon over here."

"I can't do that."

"I believe he said drop the gun, cop," a voice from behind them said, followed by a metallic click just behind Steve's head. "Drop it, or this little shit dies."

Steve turned slowly, and found himself staring past the barrel of a revolver and into Jack's grinning face.

"Oh you've got to be shitting me." Steve whispered.

"No joke you little fucker. Move and die." Steve realized there were tiny spatters of red on Jack's cheek, and looking down he could see that Jack's t-shirt was splotched with even more. He was just at the foot of the steps, angled to keep Steve between him and Detective Prescott.

"About time," Mark snapped.

"Hey," Jack chuckled. "I had some family business to attend to." Jack stopped, realizing who he was talking to. "Are you serious? Are you . . . are you really him?"

"What do you think?" Mark said. And Jack just nodded, his smile growing wider.

"Detective, I'm going to count to three, and then . . . Jack, is it? Then Jack is going to put a bullet in that little fool's brain. You can avoid that by dropping your gun and kicking it over to me. Are we clear?"

"Super clear," Jack said, and Steve could see the anticipation glittering in his eyes.

"One.

"Two.

"Thre--"

"Okay! Okay!" Prescott said, lowering the hammer on his pistol and lowering it to the floor with one hand.

"Kick it over. And no games."

Keeping his hands up in the air, Prescott kicked the gun towards Mark. It skidded to a stop about a foot away from Mark's feet.

"Now," the wolf in Mark's clothing said to Christine. "I'm going to pick up that pistol, but you are going to remain perfectly still, because this blade will still be at your throat. I assure you I can slice you open with just a flick of my wrist. Ask your brother. Understand? And that goes for you as well Detective."

Christine nodded as much as the blade would allow her too.

"Good," Mark said, releasing his grip on her waist, and stepping away from her. He kept the blade steady as he bent down to retrieve the pistol, his eyes never leaving Detective Prescott. He picked the gun up on the first grasp and stood, moving himself away from Christine but keeping the point of the blade at her throat. She was up on her tiptoes, chin pointed to the ceiling to keep the blade from piercing her skin. Mark circled around, using it to position her directly in front of the small chamber at the front of the furnace. He drew back the hammer of the pistol and pointed it at Prescott.

"Open the door," Mark told Christine.

Christine reached out for the door, and then yelped with pain when she touched the handle.

"Be careful," he said, "It's hot."

It took a few tries, but after tentatively grasping at it she finally got it open. The roar of the flames, heat and a musky smell Steve didn't want to identify filled the room.

"That's more like it," Mark said with a smile. He motioned towards the furnace with the pistol. "If everyone would be so kind as to take a place in front that would be lovely."

"Just tell me what you want," Prescott said, slowly moving towards the furnace.

"What I want," he said, finally stepping away from Christine and taking the sword point from her throat, "is for the three of you to die, and by doing so give new life to something far greater and more powerful than you could possibly imagine."

When Steve didn't move, Jack gave him a shove to get him started. He took his place between Christine and Detective Prescott. "Are you okay?" Steve whispered to her, and she just shook her head.

"I'm glad I'm not the only one."

Jack and Mark stood side by side, both of their pistols trained on the group. "You're not going to be able to come back from this, you know." Prescott said. "You can fight this thing Mark, you can. This isn't you."

"Be quiet," Mark said. "I'm going to deal with that little traitor in my own time. But right now, I'm going to enjoy killing all three of you."

"Can I kill one?" Jack said, fingers twitching on the gun.

"Maybe the detective. These two," he said, pointing the pistol at Steve and the Christine. "These two are mine. That little bastard doesn't have enough blood on his hands yet."

"You killed my brother, and the others, didn't you?" Christine said.

"Yes, and I enjoyed it. I enjoyed the act of killing as much as I did knowing I was using his body to do it in."

"You're insane," Prescott said. "Just the shadow of a sick and evil man who should have stayed dead."

"No, I couldn't stay dead. There's still work to be done, and I'm going to finish what was started."

"Mark," Steve said, bringing the barrel of the gun, and the thing's attention, back to him. "You can fight this."

"He's as much a part of this as I am," he said. "Even more so. He can't--"

"Shut up, I'm talking to my friend," Steve said. "I know you can hear me in there and I want to say I'm sorry. I've been a lousy friend, but I have faith in you. You can--"

"Shut up!"

"You can fight this. You've been a fighter your whole life and you can't give up now. We need you. She needs you and this thing--"

"Stop it! Stop it or she dies!" he said, pointing the pistol at Christine.

"Whatever it said to you, it lies. It can't possibly know you as well as I do, and I know that you aren't going to let anything happen to her. He's going to kill her Mark, and you have to be strong, you have to be stronger than it--"

"Be quiet," he hissed, eyes narrowing and jaw clenching. The once steady hand that aimed the pistol began to shake. From the corner of Mark's eyes, small tendrils of black smoke began to seep out like tears.

"Mark, please. You're better than this asshole. This stupid, punk-ass undead piece of serial killing shit, you are so much better than--"

"Shut up!" he roared, swinging the gun back at Steve. He was sweating, and the smoke began to flow from between Mark's clenched teeth.

"Mark," Steve said. "Kick this thing's ass, okay?"

Mark grimaced and then squeezed his eyes shut, the gun trembling in his hand. Steve stepped forward. Mark was winning. He could see it all over his face and any second now--

Mark's eyes flew open and the sudden clap of thunder was deafening.

CHAPTER THIRTY-ONE

Mark watched the whole thing unfold, right from when Joe knocked him out and Corwin had taken the driver's seat. He was standing outside himself just as he had when he saw Clara and Ms. Kennedy killed and watched Corwin call Christine and then Jack. Talking to Christine, Corwin stared at Mark's disembodied form as he whimpered and did what was a painfully accurate imitation of Mark's emotional idiosyncrasies.

Corwin slipped out the small window in Mark's attic room, tugging Mark's consciousness along for the ride. He walked to the house on Briarcliff, and Mark wondered how many times he'd done this when Mark was asleep. He'd been toying with Mark the whole time, showing him bits and pieces of his nocturnal activities.

It's no wonder I've been so tired these past few months, he thought. I've been getting more exercise than I thought.

All he could do was watch helplessly as Corwin lured Christine to the basement and proceeded to hold her, Steve and David hostage. He swirled formlessly around his own body and Jack as they held the three of them at gunpoint.

When Steve began his impassioned pleas for Mark to do something, there was a part of him that wanted Corwin to just shoot the asshole and get it done with.

Sure, and then he can shoot Christine, the Detective, and then you'll probably spend the rest of your existence watching Corwin and Jack do god knows what in pursuit of their own brand of bat-shit crazy. Or, for kicks, you can listen to what he's saying and do more than just roll over and say there's nothing you can do.

Mark moved closer to his body, and he could see Corwin dart his eyes in Mark's direction. For the first time since the spirit taken up residence, he looked unsure of himself. Mark moved forward again, and he could feel the tug of his own body trying to drawn him back in.

Corwin's black smoke began to seep out of his eyes and mouth and the tendrils moved up, trying to block Mark's progress. Mark dodged from one side to the other, trying to get around them. He could move, he realized. He wasn't sure if it was because he was awake this time or because Corwin was more distracted, but this wasn't the same as before.

"Mark, kick this thing's ass, okay?"

Mark darted forward, forcing himself through the smoke, blinding and burning him for a moment until he felt the familiar tug of gravity and rush of oxygen into lungs that burned like they'd been filled with charcoal.

He sprung up, expecting gun-toting Jack or a shadowy Corwin to pounce on him, but they weren't there. Neither was Christine or Steve or Detective Prescott.

"You think it's that easy, don't you?"

The voice came from all around him, and Mark spun in place trying to get a read on his surroundings. The basement was darker than it was in reality, and when he turned to face the furnace he stopped in his tracks.

In Corwin's mind (or was it his?) it wasn't just a furnace. It was a mammoth atrocity of black coiled metal stretching from floor to ceiling and extending impossibly far back into the darkness, beyond what his eyes could see. The fuel chamber door wasn't a small window of bars and glass, but a crisscrossed network of bars barely containing a roaring wall of flame.

The pipes that ran along the ceiling were twice as numerous as they were in reality, and Mark could hear them straining at things moving inside them, trying to get out. The fire surged, and the bars holding it back began to yield to their power.

It wasn't a furnace, it was a prison. And whatever it held wanted out.

"You think you can just waltz back in here and kick me out, is that it?"

The voice was behind him now, and Mark turned to see Corwin's smoke form issue forth from underneath the stairs, the fire in his eyes roaring brighter than Mark had seen before.

"This is my mind," Mark said. "I'm not going to let you use me anymore."

The smoke under Corwin's eyes twisted into a sneer as he began to make a slow circuit around Mark. "Oh, like you have a choice. Like you've ever had a choice."

"Of course I do."

"You don't even know what this is. I know everything that's been in your head these past few months and what you think what I've shown you means, but you don't know anything."

"I know enough," Mark said, turning with Corwin as he paced around him.

"Oh, yes. You think I'm Justin Corwin, crazed killer of children and I think you're Darren Cox, the innocent boy that escaped Corwin's rampage. I've come back somehow to finish the job I started 50 years ago."

"That's what you've shown me, isn't it?"

"You've only seen what I've allowed you to see. Let me show you the rest."

He waved a hand and everything rippled and dissolved into smoke. It reformed around them, taking the shape of the final vision that Mark had of Darren, Corwin and Randal. Off to the side of them, Mark watched as Randal raced from the cell that Corwin had neglected to latch and the three of them struggled just as Mark had seen in his dream.

Darren, tattered shirt barely hanging on to his blood-streaked torso, picked up the blade as Randal and Corwin wrestled. Corwin smashed Randal's head into the ground, knocking the boy unconscious and blindly reached for the blade. When he couldn't find it, he turned to see it clutched in Darren's hands, drawn back as if the kid were a major league hitter.

Corwin's eyes went wide as Darren swung with all his might. The blade nicked a tiny bit of Corwin's hair before slashing through Randal's neck, sending a spray of blood across them. Randal flailed weakly, head tilted at an obscenely impossible angle.

Darren dropped the blade on the ground in front of him, eyes wide. There was no fear in the boy's eyes, just awe at the wondrous sight in front of him.

"I'm a believer," Darren said.

Corwin nodded, picking up the blade. He dragged Randal's body closer to the furnace and bent down to finish the job Darren's swing started. Corwin paused, looking over his shoulder at Darren.

"I knew I wasn't crazy. I knew there was something in there. It's why I have to do this. I just need someone to understand and see it."

Darren nodded and took a step forward, and as he did there was a commotion above them like a clumsy, drunken parade. Darren and Corwin looked at each other, and then the door at the top of the stairs burst open. Blue clad legs raced down the steps, and when they reached the landing they bent down, and a young face topped with a policeman's cap peered at them.

"Down here!" the officer yelled, face going white.

Corwin turned back to his work, taking a fistful of Randal's hair and pulling and twisting with all his might. The officer raced down the steps, followed closely by three more officers, all of them with their nightsticks drawn. Darren was almost knocked over by the group of them, and they started swinging as soon as Corwin was within arm's reach.

Randal's body fell to the ground, ignored as the four of them pummeled Corwin with all their might.

"Easy! Easy!" shouted a plain clothes detective, running down the stairs. "I want him alive! Alive, dammit!" The group grudgingly stopped, pulling the barely conscious Corwin away from the furnace and his final victim.

"Mother of God," the detective said, coming to a stop at Darren's side. He bent down and turned Darren away from Randal's nearly headless corpse. "It's all over now, son. We'll have you home to your mum and dad quick as we can."

The Detective led Darren up the steps, following the officers dragging Corwin up the steps. Darren turned and looked back, staring deeply into the furnace fire until he was completely up the stairs and out of sight.

"That wasn't real," Mark said. "You're lying."

"Why would I? You read it yourself in your little book. Only one survivor, Corwin kills himself in his cell. It was all there."

"Corwin kills . . . But you, you're . . ."

"Not him, Mark. I never was. See what you get when you assume?"

The smoke melted away from his body, revealing a young man, just barely 20, maybe a few years older.

"Wh . . . who?"

"Here," the man said. "Let me give you a hint."

He unbuttoned his shirt and held it open for Mark to see the long scar, wide and dull with age, running from hip to shoulder.

"No, that's not possible," Mark said. "It was me. I was Darren Cox."

"No, I just showed you all the things that I remembered after I was taken, when I was made to watch what happened and when I saw my Lord in the fire. When my life was given purpose."

"Why me? Why did you have to come after me? I don't have anything to do with this!"

"Because we needed you Mark. He needed you. You were the first one to see Him. You were the one that showed me the way. We had to wait for decades for his soul, your soul, to be drawn back here, but now it has and you're back where you belong.

Justin."

Mark squeezed his eyes shut, trying to block it all out, but he could feel it rising to the surface. His parents, the war, coming down to this basement, staring into the furnace . . . it all came back, filling in all the blanks the visions and the book had left behind.

His past life as Justin Corwin burned into his memory.

He remembered how, after being in his cell and away from the fire the memory of what he'd done coming to him. He knew that he had to pay, before the lawyer his relatives had hired got him sent to some mental institution for the rest of his life, claiming the war made him do those horrible things.

He had to pay, and with a bed sheet wrapped around the cell bars at one end and his neck at the other he made sure that he did.

"Why? Why would you bring me back here? Why do you need me?" Mark said when his breath finally came back.

"Because you ran away, you coward! You took the easy way out and left me there on the edge of something truly great, something divine! I had to wait for years, to pretend that what I saw was horrible and in my imagination. My family moved away, and I had to wait until I left home to come back here, and even then He still wanted you. He needed you, and I knew that the only way I could bring you back here was to sacrifice my flesh and wait until the day you were brought back here. I stayed in this house, protecting it, until you were old enough for me to use you."

Mark leaned against one of the basement poles for support. He slid down in under the weight of his former life and Darren's trembling rage.

"But why? It wasn't me . . . not really."

"Mark, Mark, Mark." Darren bent down close to him. "Don't tell me you haven't ever thought 'What have I done to deserve this? Why me, why me, why me?' And don't lie and tell me you don't, because I know you have. You'd sit in bed and you'd wonder what you did, what happened that you ended up with such a horrid, miserable life. Well, now you know. And do you really think that the universe would just let something like that go? That it wouldn't bring you back here to face what you left behind when you took the coward's way out?"

"That's not fair, it wasn't me! I'm just a kid!"

"So was I! I was just a kid but you opened my eyes! You made me watch, and right there at the end, when I had accepted it, when we were on the verge of bringing the thing we worshipped into this world, you quit! You left me after seeing those things, and now, so help me, we are going to finish what you started!"

Mark shook his head. "Never. I don't care what I may have done, or what happened to you, you can't make me!"

"Oh yes I can, Mark. Where do you have left to go? Who do you have out there to help you? No one! I walked you around this town and picked them off, using their blood to make our Lord strong again. Now we're here again and all we have to do is kill these three and He will come through and grant us power beyond our wildest dreams. We will spread his fire across this town, across the world, and nothing will be able to stop us."

"I'll never let you hurt them, or cause whatever hell on earth you think you can create."

"Oh, come on now," Darren said. The room shifted again, showing the wear and neglect of 50 years time. His body, as well as all the others, materialized where they were out in the real world, frozen in place.

"What are you going to do Mark? Tell them 'Whoops, it turns out that I'm a reincarnated serial killer and this whole thing is my fault.'" He motioned to Christine. "Are you going to tell her that her brother was killed because she showed pity to a killer?"

"It's not--" he started, but Darren cut him off again.

"Is that what you're going to tell the Detective here? 'Sorry, sir. It turns out that I *did* kill all those people, but it wasn't really me, see? I was possessed by a ghost, that's all. No harm, no foul.' Do you think he'd even hesitate before sending you to jail? Or an asylum? Or the electric chair?

All those people are dead, because you did something so awful, so evil, that it will always be with you no matter what you do. You can't control it and you can't change it. All you can do is give in to what I'm offering you."

"No, you're wrong. They'll know that it was you that did all those things, not me. They care about me, and--"

"Bullshit!" Darren said, waving at the three time-frozen hostages. "You're just a case to the Detective, something to be solved, accounted for and forgotten. Even before she knew this was your fault, the girl was sneaking around on you. She never loved you and she never will! Even your own so-called best friend betrayed you! Why on Earth would they stand by you now?"

Darren moved closer, placing a hand on Mark's shoulder. The rage was gone, and now he was wide-eyed and pleading. "There's only one way out of this, Mark. Accept me. Continue what you started all those years ago, and I promise you the rewards . . . oh Mark, we'll have whatever our heart's desire. I've seen the kind of power He has at his disposal. Their lives, their blood, will free Him, and this world will be ours."

Mark looked over at his body, frozen in place with the blade that had killed so many held down at his side with one hand, the gun in the other, pointed at Steve. He was frozen in the act of pleading with Mark to fight, and Mark's own face twisted with strain and rage.

At Mark's side was Jack, still pointing his pistol at David and as full of rage as Mark was, Jack had one thing in his eyes that Mark's body didn't: Joy.

Mark looked back at Darren.

"Go back to hell."

The pleading innocence vanished as Darren's eyes burst with a roar of fire and anger, and the smoke he'd hidden himself with rose like a tidal wave and dove towards Mark. Mark leapt for his frozen body and almost made it there before the wave of darkness crashed over him.

The blackness muffled everything. All he could feel was searing heat as what felt like dozens of tiny, burning fingers dug into him, trying to pull him back. The rest of his senses were reduced to a dull, underwater roar as he pushed forward hoping he was still going in the right direction.

The roar and pain intensified, and then there was a burst of light so bright that he couldn't make out anything. He could feel his body shaking as his mind took control again. His eyes began refocusing as the light faded away, only to be replaced by a smoky haze that hung in the air in front of him. There was a clap of thunder and then he could hear again.

Steve was in front of him, and he wasn't pleading anymore, just looking at Mark with surprise. He backed up, mouth moving, but all Mark could hear was a high-pitched shrieking. Steve bumped into the furnace behind him, and then raised his hands to cover the ragged hole in his throat that was pouring blood all down his shirt.

The shrieking was Christine, and the smoke was coming from the gun in his hand.

CHAPTER THIRTY-TWO

"Fucking sweet," Jack said.

The kid kept shifting his gaze away from David to Steve, who slid down the front of the furnace blood seeping around the hands at his throat.

Christine's scream trailed off into a choked sob as she backed away from the puddle of blood forming around the floor where Steve now sat. Jack was too absorbed to notice Mark backing away from the spreading blood, the viciousness in his face replaced with shock. He lowered David's gun and then the blade in his hand fell out of his trembling hand.

"Oh god," Mark said.

It's him, David realized.

David opened his mouth to say something, but Steve gave a deep, ragged gasp and then stopped breathing. "My turn," Jack said, turning his full attention to David now that his entertainment was over.

Before he could pull the trigger, Mark dropped to his knees and let loose a deep retching sound. Jack turned and Mark retched again, his whole body doubling up and his mouth strained as wide as possible. What came out of his mouth wasn't vomit but thick black smoke. It tumbled to the ground, piling up like fog and drifting towards the furnace and the puddle of blood. There was a burning hiss as it hit the blood, and the fire in the furnace began to roar higher.

"What the fuck?" Jack said, and David charged, ducking under the gun that had drifted away from his center mass and tackling Jack squarely in the midsection. They fell to the ground in a pile, the boy thrashing as David forced Jack's gun hand up towards the ceiling and grabbed for it. Their hands tangled together but David managed to slap the pistol out of the boy's hands and send it clattering to the floor.

Jack slipped a hand from David's grip and punched up with enough crazy teenager strength to push him just enough to bring a leg up between them. Jack scrambled out from underneath him, legs kicking frantically as he crawled away towards the pistol. David tried to grab the boy's leg, but before he could he took a kick to the temple.

David rolled backwards, trying to blink away the pain clouding his vision and hopefully crawling towards where Mark dropped his gun.

"Freeze you son of a bitch."

David stopped, vision coming back into focus. Jack was up on one knee, both hands gripping his pistol and one eye squeezed shut as he took careful aim.

There was a roar of anger and the open eye disappeared with a burst of gunfire.

The gun in Jack's hand went off and David felt the breeze of the bullet's passing as it just missed him and ricocheted off the floor. Mark let out another scream and fired again, putting another hole in Jack's face. The suddenly cyclopean teenage psycho fell backwards against the basement wall. Mark kept screaming and pulling the trigger until there was a fist sized hole where Jack's eye and nose used to be and the room echoed with the metallic clicks of the dry-firing Glock.

***

When Jack's body fell face-first onto the ground Mark realized he was still pulling the trigger on the empty gun. He dropped it and sat back, pushing himself away from it. He stopped when the gravel behind him went warm and sticky in his hands.

"Mark?" Christine said from behind him. "Is that you?"

He couldn't speak, and he couldn't bring himself to turn around to look at her. He just nodded.

"What the fuck?" she said, walking around in front of him. "What the fuck just happened? Was that . . . what the fuck was that, Mark?"

He didn't want her to see him. He knew that if she looked at him, she'd see that twisted, psychotic face that Cor . . . that Darren had given him; the face of the crazed, ghostly lunatic that killed his best friend. He raised his hands to his face to cover it, but stopped when he saw the red on his fingers.

"I'm sorry," Mark said, putting his hands on the dry ground and trying to rub the color off them. "It wasn't me. It was . . . I can't even begin to explain."

"It was the ghost, wasn't it?" Detective Prescott said.

He nodded. His hands were still wet, and all he was doing was scratching the hell out of them on the gravel and concrete. Defeated, he just let them hang limply in his lap.

"Is he . . ." Christine asked, looking behind Mark. He turned and saw David standing at the edge of the pool of blood, leaning in and checking Steve for a pulse. For a brief second of stupid optimism, Mark thought David would shout that Steve was okay, and that if they hurried he'd survive and it'd be like this whole thing never happened.

Instead, David shook his head and stepped away from the body.

"Jesus Christ," Mark said, resting his head on the top of hands.

"Are you two hurt at all?" David said.

Christine shook her head, and Mark just shrugged. David crouched down next him. "Mark, I know this is hard, but we have to get out here. I have to call this in, and then we can figure out what to tell them."

"What's to tell?" Mark said. "It was me the whole time. He used me like a fucking puppet, and I don't think there's anything that we can say that's going to make people believe that."

"We'll come up with something," David said. "Come on, we need to get out of here first, alright?"

Mark nodded, and with David's help he got to his feet. He made it a couple of steps before everything went gray and hazy. David grabbed him before he fell over, and with an arm under him to keep him upright, David walked Mark up the stairs.

Mark shook his head to clear it of its sudden heat and weight but it didn't help. Everything was fuzzy, but before they made it up the stairs he looked back down into the basement at the two bodies laying in puddles of blood and the fire in the furnace raging on.

***

David and Christine got Mark upstairs and seated in one of the old kitchen chairs. He was completely white, aside from the smears of blood on his hands and drops of it on his face. Christine knew that Mark wasn't the snarling savage that had held her hostage but it was hard to look at him and not feel the edge of the blade pressing against her throat.

Or realize that her brother's killer was sitting in front of her muttering for forgiveness.

"Mark, can you hear me?" David said, squatting down in front of Mark.

Mark nodded, and then with a deep gulp, said "Yeah . . . I just needed some air. It's so hot down there."

"I know," David said. "Can you stand?"

Mark nodded and then got halfway out of his chair before falling right back down in it.

"I guess not," he said.

"That's okay," David said. "Just take your time." He reached down to his belt, unclipped his cell phone and flipped it open. He frowned, put the phone to his ear, and then flipped it shut.

"I'm not getting any signal in here."

"Let me try," Christine said, welcoming the excuse to look away from the blood on Mark's hands. She checked her phone and shook her head. "I'm not getting anything either."

"Okay," David said. "I'm going to go and try from outside, I want the two of you to stay here, okay?"

"Sure," she said, and Mark just nodded.

David headed down the hallway for the front door and Christine tucked her phone back into her pocket. Mark leaned forward, elbows on his knees and moving to rest his head in his hands. He pulled up at the last second when he remembered what they were covered with.

"Jesus Christ," he muttered, sitting back upright.

"Let me see if there's something you can wipe your hands with," Christine said, turning away and scanning the dust laden counters for something even remotely clean.

"Don't worry about it," Mark said.

"Dammit!" Christine whirled around, expecting to see the blade and the wicked gleam in Mark's eye coming at her again. The yell hadn't come from Mark or the basement, but towards the front of the house where Detective Prescott had gone.

Mark had staggered to his feet, but Christine pushed him back into the chair as she passed on the way to the front door. "Stay here," she said. Once she was in the hallway she could see Detective Prescott gripping the door handle and pulling with all of his strength.

"What is it?" she said as she came up behind him.

"The door was open when I came in here with Steve. I don't know if that Jack kid closed it and found some way to lock it, but it's not moving now."

"Let me help," she said, coming around him and wrapping her hands over his and helping twist. All their combined might achieved was two pairs of sore hands, deep breaths and muttered curses.

"Dammit!" David said, shaking his hands. "There has to be some other way out of here. C'mon, let's check around back," he said, but before Christine could follow, he stopped. "Oh shit."

"What?"

He pointed down the hall and into the kitchen and the empty chair where Mark had been sitting.

"Where'd he go?"

***

Mark watched them struggling at the door and the guilt in his stomach turned to cold clarity.

Whatever was trapped in the fire in the basement was burning merrily along, waiting for them to exhaust themselves trying to get out before whatever remained of Darren flowed back up the steps to finish them off. If it was going to end, Mark was going to have to stop it. He got up, the uncharacteristic bravery chasing most of the light-headedness away. He would've let them know what he was doing, but they'd probably just try to argue. Once he was sure of his footing, he headed back down the stairs.

When he got to the base of the stairs he tried to focus only on the furnace and the flames in front of him. Not the hole through Jack's head that seemed to follow him as he walked. Not Steve's body, staring off into infinity in a pool of his own blood.

Mark stepped around the blood and squatted down as close as he could to his dead friend. He wanted to touch him and close his eyes, but he couldn't bring himself to do it. He'd done enough already.

"I'm so sorry, Steve."

From where he was kneeling, Mark could stare directly into the open furnace. The heat from the flames was oppressive, and he could feel it pulsing in his head. In the fire he could just make out something moving with the flames.

"I'm going to kill you," Mark said to it. "I'm going to find out how and I'm going to end you, you demonic piece of shit."

He got to his feet, breaking his gaze with more effort than he would've liked. The closest he could find to an "off" switch on the furnace was a temperature control. He hoped something as simple as turning the flame down to nothing would at least stall whatever was powering Darren long enough to . . . to what? Darren had said he'd had enough power to live on in the house for decades, presumably with the furnace turned down to non-demonic levels. If anything, snuffing the flames would be satisfying enough for now. He could come back later with a priest and a bulldozer.

As he reached out for the gauge a hand clamped down on his.

"Not so fast," a ragged voice whispered in his ear. "I'm not done with you yet." Before he could turn, Mark was hurled forward. His head hit the front of the furnace, the impact knocking him off his feet and down onto the floor.

"I'm honestly sorry it's come to this," the voice said, coming closer. "But you brought it on yourself."

He tried to push himself back up to his feet, but everything was wet and slippery and he couldn't find his balance. Over the roar of flames and throb of pain in his head he heard the familiar sound of metal scraping home and the tiny click as the blade was locked into place. Something smashed into the back of his head, causing his arms to buckle and dropping him flat onto his stomach.

"I'll be back to deal with you, but right now we have some guests trying to leave the party, and that's just not acceptable."

Mark raised his head weakly and found himself staring into the ragged mass of flesh that used to be Jack's face. The hole in his head now filled with the swirling black smoke of Darren's essence

"Sweet dreams," the Darren-driven Jack said. He swung the cane down onto the back of Mark's head again and drove him down into the floor and unconsciousness.

CHAPTER THIRTY-THREE

"This is not good," David said.

"Oh really? You could've fooled me," Christine said, turning in place in the middle of the abandoned kitchen.

"Christine, relax, okay? We're going to be fine," David said. He put his hands on her shoulders and guided her towards the seat that Mark had been in.

"What if . . . whatever the fuck was in him got back in him? What if it comes after us?"

"Nothing is going to come after us, okay? We're going to be fine. I just want you to sit here, take some deep breaths and I'm going to look around. I'm not going to go out of your sight, okay?"

She nodded, and he got up and began to walk around the kitchen. There was an archway that led into the dining room they saw from the front of the house, and a doorway that looked to lead into the back of the house. David pushed it open, sending up a large cloud of dust.

"Mark, where are you?" David called into the back of the house. There was no answer, and Christine turned to look at the only other way out of the room.

"Detective?"

"Yeah?"

"The basement."

"Dammit."

He crossed over to the basement door, leading with his pistol. "Just stay here, okay? If something happens to me, just go. Try to break a window or something. If Mark's not down there, I'm going to come right back up, okay?"

She nodded with little enthusiasm.

"It's going to be alri--" The cane swung out at him from the basement doorway, arcing downwards and knocking David's pistol out of his hands. David turned back to face the doorway just in time to catch the cane flying back up and into his face, sending him down to the ground. With a scream, Christine leapt to her feet, and had half turned to run for it when the voice stopped her in her tracks.

"Don't move, sweetheart."

In the doorway was Jack's body grinning and staring at her with its one eye. The hole where his other eye and nose used to be now swirled with the black smoke that Mark had vomited up.

Detective Prescott reached for his gun, but Smoke-Filled Jack stomped his foot down on his hand, grinning wide at the sound of bones crunching underfoot. Before David could finish yelling in pain, Jack swung the cane down into the back of his head. It took four solid hits before David stopped moving, and Jack added a fifth just for fun.

"That was invigorating," he said, turning his attention to her.

She found herself shuffling for the door and wondering why she'd stopped when he told her too. It was magic, she told herself. Smoky ghost magic, and had nothing to do with the terror overpowering her common sense. Now that she realized this, it'd be the perfect time to run. Just turn and run. Grab one of those old chairs and hurl it through a window and not stop running until she saw the National Guard.

Smoke-Filled Jack smiled wider, splitting more of the skin in his face and causing more blackness to seep out of the tears in his flesh. "Don't do it," he said, his voice sounding almost like Jack's but with another one just below the surface.

She shuffled her feet towards the doorway closest to her.

"I said," Jack's corpse said, reaching out with his free hand, palm down. "Don't." David's gun floated up into his hand, the barrel now aimed squarely at her.

"Come here," he said.

She shook her head, inching again towards the doorway.

"Christine. Come. Here." There was a click as he pulled back the hammer with his thumb.

"You're going to kill me anyway," she said.

"Maybe," he said. "Or maybe I'll kill him," pointing the pistol down at Detective Prescott. "And maybe, when I'm done, I'll go back down to the basement and finish what I started on Mark while you run around up here trying to find a way out."

She shifted her feet again.

"And when I'm done with that, I will come and I will find you, and I will make the rest of our time together very . . . unpleasant."

"And if I come with you?"

"Then we can end this much quicker. For you, that would be preferable."

She took a couple of steps towards him, but couldn't bring herself any nearer. He raised the cane and placed it on her shoulder, turning it so that the slightly curved dragon head pulled her in so that the gun rested against her chest. His smile grew wider, and she was close enough to see the almost dried blood seep out of his wounds.

"Silly girl."

He pulled the trigger, and the sudden snap of metal made her jump.

"It's empty," he said, dropping the gun and taking her arm with his free hand. "Let's go get re-acquainted."

He marched her down the steps, a hand on her arm and the cane resting on her shoulder. When they got to the bottom of the stairs she saw Mark lying face down in front of the furnace and just outside the pool of Steve's blood. Jack walked her forward until she was standing only a few feet away from the open furnace door and Mark's prone form. She waited for a sign that Mark was still alive and that she hadn't been tricked again, and after a few seconds he drew in a short, shallow breath.

"Arms up," he said. She complied, and she felt her wrists brush against rusted metal. She looked up and saw a length of chain dangling down from one of the metal crossbars. Jack's corpse reached up and wound the chain around her wrists until it was painfully tight.

"Don't even breathe." He slid the blade from the cane and dropped the sheath on the floor. Holding the tip of the blade on her neck, he stepped back and leaned down to fish something out of Mark's jacket pocket. He pulled something out and stood back up, reaching for the chain on her wrists again.

She looked up just in time to see the padlock click into place.

"There we go. Now we can really get some work done."

He turned away from her to look down at Mark. "Time to wake up, little traitor. I want you to get a good look at what you've done."

"He didn't do anything!" she said, tugging at the chain. For all the age it showed, it was strong, not giving at all even with her full weight on it.

"You have no idea," Jack said, turning back to her. "This is all his fault. Everything that I've done has been because of him, and now he's going to suffer for turning his back on us."

"Wake up," he said, turning back to Mark and giving him a kick in the ribs. Mark groaned and turned away from him.

"Oh, no you don't," Jack said, leaning down and turning Mark over to face him. "I want you awake for this. I want you to get a good look at this and see that there is no escape. Not for her, not for the Detective, and certainly not for you."

"Look at this," Mark said, thrusting the sheath of the cane up and into the hole in Jack's head. With a yell Mark pulled, toppling Jack's corpse headfirst into the furnace.

***

Jack gave a surprised howl of anger, his legs sticking out from the furnace chamber and kicking wildly. Mark slapped away at them until he got a good grip and forced them into the fire. The fire roared out from around Jack's squirming and thrashing body that just barely fit into the fuel chamber. He was trying to turn himself around, and Mark ducked out of the way as the sword blade stabbed out from the flames at him.

"The door!" Christine screamed. "Shut the door!"

Mark swung the door shut as hard as he could. It landed on Jack's flaming wrist with a loud snap, the impact forcing him to drop the blade. Jack's body pushed against the door, almost knocking Mark onto his back.

Mark braced his shoulder on the door and planted his feet as much as he could on the blood-slicked cement floor. Blackened fingers peeked around the edge of the door amidst the smoke and fire escaping into the air. Mark pressed his back against the door as hard as he could and forced it shut. He'd managed to find a tiny patch of the floor that wasn't wet, but it was almost too far away to be of any help.

Mark turned to look through the chamber's window and found himself eye to boiling, flaming eye with Jack. The Darren-smoke swirled around the chamber, almost blacking out the flames behind it. Even through the glass he could hear Darren's scream of anger and the hiss of the flames as they burned away not just as Jack's body, but the smoke that had been Jack's form.

Mark reached over to latch the furnace door shut, but there was nothing there. All that was left of the locking mechanism was two loops of metal. Jack's body pushed against the door again, and Mark could see a tiny tendril of black smoke escape from the gap that had been made before Mark forced the door shut again.

"Fuck, it won't latch!" he yelled, looking back at Christine. She was swinging her legs at him and pulling at the chain on her wrists.

"The sword! Use the sword!" she said, and he realized that she had been kicking it towards him with each swing of her legs.

He stretched out, keeping one arm pressed against the door and the other reaching out for the sword handle. Christine swung again, kicking the blade up against the tips of his fingers. He managed to get a fingernail hooked into a bit of the detail work on the dragon head and dragged the thing fully in his grip.

Twisting around, Mark jammed the blade through the metal loops all the way down to the hilt. The door rattled as Mark got up and made sure the blade wouldn't shake loose. The door shook, but not enough to open a crack even big enough for smoke to get through. On his knees in front of the window, catching his breath, Mark watched the flames and the darkness swirling in them. The roars of anger had been replaced with a high pitched squeal, and the furnace was shaking as the power of the flames grew.

It's eating him. Whatever is in there is so blind with hunger it's devouring whatever power it had given him. Not too shabby, kiddo. I'm going to take back some of the things I said about you.

"Is he . . ?" she asked, looking over his shoulder at the tiny window.

"Yeah," Mark said, getting to his feet and wiping his hands. He walked over to the gauge on the furnace and turned all of the dials up as far as they could go. "But let's make sure that bastard cooks." Looking over the various levers and knobs, he had a twinge of memory. It was someone explaining to him how the furnace worked, and reminding him that he had to make sure that the valves on all the pipes leading up into the house were open if the heat was going to come through.

The furnace is very old, Justin, and has a lot of quirks to it. It'll be sure to keep us warm, though. Lord knows it can burn hotter than any other thing I've seen.

Mark reached up, shutting each valve and making sure that whatever was left of Darren was trapped in the furnace until he burned away into nothingness. The furnace rumbled again, vibrating with the intensity of the heat now trapped in its chamber.

"Mark?" Christine said, bringing him back to his senses.

"What?" He said, turning back to face her.

She jangled the chains around her wrists. "A little help?"

"Oh," he said, running over and peering at the twisted knot of chain and lock. "Geez, it's padlocked."

"I know," she said. "He got it from your jacket. Is there a key?"

"No," Mark said, squinting up at it. "Jesus! This is my lock from junior high. Where the hell did he find this?"

"What's the combination?"

"I . . . oh, shit," he mumbled. "36 . . . 24 . . . I dunno, 36, maybe."

"Mark!" she yelled. "That's from a song! Can't you remember?"

"I'm sorry!" he yelled back. "I've taken a couple of blows to the head in case you haven't noticed, and the yelling isn't doing anything for the ringing in my ears!"

"Jesus, I'm sorry, okay? Can you pull it, without tearing off my wrists? I think I might've weakened it."

"I'll try."

He pulled at it until he was almost purple in the face. There was a slight bend in the bar above, but that was it. He tried again, this time pulling himself off his feet and hanging in the air. Again, nothing.

"Ow, ow, ow!" she said, wincing as it tightened the chain around her wrists.

"Sorry," he said. "I'm going to try to fin--" he started, but then furnace exploded.

She shrieked with surprise, and he winced as tiny bits of metal pelted his back. They looked back and saw that one of the pipes had ruptured under the pressure and was now shooting flames upwards and into the ceiling, which was already beginning to catch fire.

"Oh god!" Christine screamed, joined by high-pitched hissing as one of the other pipes began to give. He turned and kept tugging, hoping the explosion had done something to loosen the chain or the crossbar holding it up. The only thing it had done was make it hotter and harder to breathe.

"Mark!" Christine said. "Get out of here! Get help!"

"No, there's no time!" he said, yanking and pulling at the chain also. "I'm not going to leave you here."

"Mark," she took a deep breath. "Don't! Just go before it's too late."

"No. This is my fault, and I'm going to get you out of here."

She opened her mouth to say something, but there was another explosion. Not the furnace this time, but a gunshot. The chain spilled off the bar it had been wrapped around and down onto the floor.

"We're all getting out of here," David said, down on one knee, using his knee to steady his gun arm.

"The gun . . ." Christine said as the three rushed up the steps.

"Spare clip on my belt," David said.

They sprinted through the kitchen and when they got to the front door they found it open. Whatever had been keeping it shut was hopefully too busy being burned out of existence. On the first floor smoke was already pouring up through the floor boards. Regular smoke, Mark noted before he left. Not the black and evil kind.

"Go," David said, waving them on after they left the yard. "Don't stop running until you get down the block."

"What are you--" Mark said, looking back over his shoulder as he ran.

"I need to radio this in, get some fire crews here. Go!"

They did as they were told, stopping and leaning against a tree across the street at what they hoped was a safe distance. David ducked into his car for a few seconds, and then went over to the houses on either side of Corwin's, which was now producing a steady stream of smoke from the basement and ground floor windows.

Christine looked over at Mark, who was watching the scene with a blank face.

"We can go further down the block and wait, if you want," she said.

"No," Mark said, not looking away. "I want to watch it burn. I want to see it burn to the ground."

CHAPTER THIRTY-FOUR

"We need to come up with something," David said softly.

They were in a small, curtained off exam room at the hospital, waiting for a nurse to come back with a doctor to put stitches in David's head. After running to warn the neighbors, he'd almost fallen over from exertion.

"What do you mean?" Christine said, rubbing her wrists where the chains had chaffed them raw.

"We can't exactly tell them the whole truth," David said.

"Why not?" Mark said. "I'll just tell them everything, and they can just do whatever. I don't really care."

"Mark, I know you've had a hard day, but that's the stupidest thing I've ever heard," David said.

"Why?" Mark snapped, and then lowered his voice. "I did it, remember? This whole thing is my fault. I don't need to drag you guys into this any further than I have. I don't care if they--"

"Stop it," Christine said. "If you let them take you away, if you tell them that you did those things then Corwin will win."

"Christine, it wasn't like that. It . . . it wasn't like that."

"What do you mean?" David said. "That's what I thought this thing was about too."

"It was, and it wasn't."

"You better talk fast," David said, "because I can only stall answering questions for so long."

Mark took a deep breath and he told them everything.

He couldn't bring himself to look up when he told them what Darren had revealed to him and how he knew it was true. They didn't question him at all, just stayed quiet.

"Mark," David said, coming close and putting a hand on Mark's shoulder. "This doesn't change anything. This wasn't your fault and you didn't actually do any of those things. He used you, and I'm not going to blame you for something that may have happened in a past life."

"I guess." He looked over at Christine.

"You're right," she finally said, looking up at the two of them. "It doesn't change anything. Not really."

"Okay," David said. "Let me think, and as hard as it is, we need to remember exactly what happened, as quickly as possible. I think I can fix this."

***

It turned out that fixing it was easy, because everyone wanted it fixed. Neat, tidy and packed away so that Cedar Ridge was a nice place to live again. All they needed was a story, and Detective Prescott and Mark were happy to give it to them.

All they had to do was pin it on Jack, and his unhealthy fixation with Mark. It was a fixation that ran so deep that, after reading about Cedar Ridge's one and only serial killer in a book from his father's rather extensive local history collection, he decided to investigate it for himself. In doing so, he found Corwin's murder weapon and what he thought would be the perfect way to terrorize Mark.

Jack targeted Mark's friends and the school guidance counselor who had, on several occasions, called Jack "trouble" and "dangerous." It was also at this time that Jack's friends noticed his increased interest in Mark, and they even believed that Jack had been involved in a traffic incident and assault in the following weeks, perhaps with some other group of boys they didn't know.

On the final day of his life, Jack snapped and killed his father, and then headed for Mark's house. Mark wasn't there, but his Uncle Joe was. He and Jack fought, and Jack pushed the man down the stairs, killing him. When Mark came home he found a note from Jack telling him to call him or more of his friends would die. When he did he demanded that Mark meet him at Justin Corwin's house. Panicked, Mark called Christine to warn her. She called Steve who then called Detective Prescott and all of them made their way to the house.

When Christine and Mark arrived, Jack took them hostage. When Steve and Detective Prescott showed up Jack disarmed him, executed Steve and beat Detective Prescott into unconsciousness. After that, Jack and Mark struggled, Jack was shot, and the three of them escaped before the fire that Jack started in the old furnace got out of control and burned the house down.

The details the three of them cobbled together all checked out. They thought they'd lucked out when they found that Jack's Dad had the same book that Mark had checked out of the library, but the real nail came when they found a sheet stained with Ryan and Mr. Baker's blood. None of Jack's friends were eager to associate themselves with him after what he'd done to his father came to light. After a talk with David they were more than willing to corroborate the group's story. It was thin and far-fetched, but it was all the Cedar Ridge police had and they were more than willing to put a close to the case that had put them in an uncomfortable spotlight.

Mark went over their amended version of events in his head so many times that in the following weeks when he was telling it to police officers, lawyers and child services agents, it felt more real than what had actually happened.

Christine's brother's funeral was the day after their ordeal in Corwin's house, but Mark didn't go. Christine's father woke up the following day and didn't say anything coherent enough to damage the official version of what happened.

Mark didn't go to Jack's funeral, which he was told was very small and organized by relatives from out of state who dealt with the matter with as much speed and little fanfare as they could muster.

He did go to Steve's funeral. David went with him, and Mark insisted that they stay as far away as they could from Steve's parents. That didn't keep Steve's mother, hysterical with grief, from spitting at Mark and cursing at him at the top of her lungs as they were leaving. At least now she has a real reason to hate me, Mark figured.

Joe's funeral service was small and put together by most of his friends down at work. Mark had known so few of them he hadn't stayed at the service long, not wanting to hear them extolling Joe's virtues as a friend and drinker.

After that, Mark decided he had enough of funerals.

"But things are getting better, right?" David said, passing Mark the gravy.

"I guess," Mark said. "I mean, I guess it's not like prison, but . . ."

"It's still a group home. I know. It's not exactly the best place to be." David said.

"What's a group home?" David's son Eric asked.

"It's a place where boys and girls go who don't have a family, sweetie." Monica, David's wife said.

"Oh," Eric said, forgetting all about Mark and digging into his turkey.

"Thanks again, Mrs. Prescott," Mark said around a mouthful of food. "This is really nice. It's been a long time since I had a Christmas dinner like this."

"Well, it's the least we could do Mark, and please, call me Monica. I'm still too young to be called 'Missus' all the time."

David opened his mouth to say something, but the phone rang. "I'll get it. And if it's telemarketers on Christmas Eve, I'm going for my gun."

They all laughed and Mark took another bite of food. David pulled a couple of strings and got Mark a pass to spend the holiday with his family, which definitely beat the alternative of sitting around waiting to be assigned to a foster family. Christmases with his Uncle had always been kind of dour, but even though he was going back to the home later in the afternoon Mark figured this one was going to seem like a picnic in comparison.

"Mark," David said, hand over the mouthpiece of the portable phone. "It's for you. You can take it into the study."

"Oh," Mark said, getting up and taking phone. "Thanks."

"Hello?" he said when he got in the study.

"Hey," Christine said.

"Hey yourself," he said.

"How're things?"

"Good. You?"

"Good. It's kind of weird here, but my Dad is home and it looks like he's going to be getting better."

"That's really good to hear. I was worried about him."

"Yeah, we all were. I can't talk long," she said. "My folks would . . . well, I don't think they'd approve."

"I understand." They paused, and, grasping for something to say, added. "How's the new school?"

"Okay, I guess. Kind of like every other private school I went to. Strict with terrible dress code but other than that it's school."

"Cool, cool."

"Look, Mark," she said. "I just . . . I just wanted to wish you a Merry Christmas and say sorry about things getting weird. Y'know, after."

Mark nodded. Aside from a couple of hearings they hadn't seen each other at all since that day, and every time they'd been close she hadn't so much as glanced in his direction.

"No," he said. "I'm . . . I'm real sorry about everything. I wish you had a chance to not have things be so--"

"It's okay."

"I mean, if you hadn't met me, then--"

"Mark," she interrupted. "Even with everything that happened I'm glad I knew you. Everything that he said, even if it was true, wasn't *really* true. It took me a while to really digest everything but I know it wasn't your fault no matter what your past life might have been."

"I know. I've been thinking about this a lot, and I think you're right."

"Good, I just didn't want you to be, y'know, blaming yourself for stuff you couldn't control. I may have blamed you at first but I was wrong and I'm sorry."

"It's okay, I--"

"Mark I gotta go, my Mom's coming."

"Okay. Well, take care of yourself, okay? Merry Christmas."

"You too," she said, and then hung up. Even though he'd done everything he could to make peace with what had happened he could now feel the final piece of the puzzle click into place and a weight lifting from his shoulders.

Oh sure, everything's fine. All you have to do now is live in a crappy "group home" with people that make Jack look like Sunshine Bear while you wait for some family to decide you're worth having around. Then you get to go out in the world with the small bit of life insurance money Joe left you. It's nowhere near enough to go to college so good luck finding a job in a crappy economy with the albatross of being connected to a mass murder spree around your neck. Yeah, everything's coming up Watson.

"You know what," Mark said. "I don't think I need you anymore."

Mark waited, but there was no response. He went out to the dining room, finally looking forward to the future.

THE SHADOW OF VICTORY

THACHER E. CLEVELAND

FOREWARD

Before we get started, let's take care of the elephant in the room.

Yes, this is the fourth volume in The Winston & Churchill Case Files. The previous three volumes are their own trilogy, and while the effects of it are felt in this installment you don't have to have read those before reading this one (provided that I did my job right). As someone who has spent a lifetime reading comic books, I'm acutely aware of the need for entry or jumping on points for an ongoing series. While this series doesn't have the fifty plus years of stories like a Batman, Spider-Man, or their associated friends (amazing or otherwise) has, I felt like it was a good idea to make this one of those points. If you read this and enjoy Henry & Martin (and/or are curious as to where Lexie is), you're more than encouraged to go back and read the previous collections.

Yes, this is also a sequel to my first novel, "Shadow of the Past." I suppose you don't have to have read that to enjoy this, but be warned there are spoilers aplenty for it in here. So consider yourself warned. I've tried to provide the basics of what happened in a non "info-dump" kind of way so you don't feel lost (or if it's been a while since you read it).

Okay, thanks Mr. Elephant. Moving along.

It took me roughly twenty years to write Shadow of the Past. To be fair, I wasn't writing it the whole time, and I even had to completely start over around the ten year mark as the floppy disk I had it saved on crapped out, but it was a long journey. Once it was done I shifted gears pretty quickly to other assorted projects, and while it was the first physical book I produced I leaned pretty heavily into the Winston & Churchill series.

In my mind, Shadow of the Past and the Winston & Churchill stories always took place in the same "universe." I've always loved that kind of stuff even before it became as ubiquitous as it is now (see the above remarks about reading comic books my whole life). Martin was always from Cedar Ridge, and I knew that age-wise he'd be relatively close to Mark and Christine, so consciously or not I laid the groundwork for the "crossover" from the get go. Knowing that I am the way I am, it really was only a matter of time before it happened. With Covid providing a good stopping point for the Winston & Churchill gang's adventures for a bit, this seemed like as good a time as any for it to happen.

I had heard from some folks who read Shadow of the Past that they hated the ending. Not because it was bad, they assured me, but because it left Mark in a pretty dark place and not-so-great circumstances. Given everything that happened in that book, it felt like the only way things could have been resolved. Hopefully those people will be satisfied at what's become of Mark (and Christine), since then.

Although, let's face it, having your friends and loved ones murdered when you're a teenager is going to have some lasting effects, so don't be surprised if it's not all sunshine and roses.

So with that said, on with the show...

CHAPTER ONE

"Fuck Covid!"

It was at least the fifth time it'd been yelled, but it still drew a large cheer from everyone at the party, temporarily drowning out the heavy bass of the track shaking the foundation of Tim Meyer's house. Martin Green hadn't been close with Tim in high school, but after almost a year of being trapped in his parent's house he was ecstatic to see anyone but them. It turned out "anyone" included the privileged choad he'd had four years of homeroom with, and who was also the kid who crashed the SUV he'd been given for his sixteenth birthday six weeks after he got it. And then the replacement he'd gotten two months later. Then it was just a regular old Mercedes. New, not used, of course.

Martin's need for a parent-free zone overruled his annoyance at Tim being handed a whole-ass house this time. Once the pandemic got into full swing his parents permanently moved to their summer place in Martha's Vineyard and Tim had himself a whole new place. Martin had almost left when he found out Tim worked in some sector of finance and managed to make money in the last year and a half. Meanwhile, Martin had walked the two and a half miles there so he didn't have to pay for an Uber twice in one night.

Human contact was human contact, though. He'd been a little surprised the invite had found its way to him, since he'd been staggeringly unremarkable in high school. He'd been a quiet, anxious, and gangly teen with a pretty small social circle, whose only extra-curriculars were editing the art and literature magazine and being vice-president of the Jewish student union. He hadn't even been invited to many parties back then, but now he was less-quiet, still anxious (but medicated), and had grown into his slender frame he was ready to give this a shot. The warm feelings of inclusion had cooled significantly when he realized practically everyone in their class had been invited, and with reunion the upcoming weekend (after being delayed because of Covid) there were plenty of others from the adjoining classes of Cedar Ridge High as well.

He might have turned back into a shrinking wallflower, but at least there was enough free alcohol to take the edge off.

"Marty!" Tim yelled, emerging from the crowd and throwing an arm around Martin's shoulder. "How the fuck are you, bro?"

"Good, good," Martin said, leaning away from him not out of fear of infection (he'd been double-vaxxed as soon as possible) but to escape the cloud of liquor breath and second-hand weed-smoke he exuded. New Jersey's recent marijuana legalization was also being celebrated, and in an incredibly vigorous fashion.

"But what have you been *doing*? Like, I know it's not our reunion, but we should, like, reconnect and shit. Give me the deets, brother."

Martin downed the rest of the drink in his solo cup, trying to figure out how many deets he should actually share. "Not much. Just an office job."

"Yeah, but in the city, right? Jen Robards said you were working for a cop or something?"

"A detective agency," he corrected. The Robard's friendship with his parents had always been a thorn in his side, especially since Jen was now a resident at Mt. Sinai. "I'm a...," he almost said 'secretary,' the word thrown at him by his parents in their most disappointed tones at least once a day. "I'm an *associate*."

"No shit!" Tim cried, throwing his arms into the air and giving a chance for Martin to duck out from under his grasp. "I'm an associate too, dog!" Martin faked a smile and gave Tim the high-five he was craving.

"That's fuckin' dope, dude. Associate bros! Finance and...wait, you said detective? Like Scooby-Doo or some shit?"

"Remarkably similar," he said, realizing Tim was past the point of being able to retain any long-term information. "Lots of monsters, definitely some ghosts. Not enough old white guys in masks, though."

"Fuckin' wild, bro. Like...how do you get into that shit?"

"I had a bad break-up and used magic," Martin shrugged. "Turned myself into a demon-gorilla thing. Now I'm studying how to do it for a living."

Tim had been staring off into the crowd, nodding along, and then some of what Martin had said must have sunk in. "Wait...what? With like. ..scarves and bunnies?"

"I wish," Martin said, patting him on the shoulder. "Anyway, I gotta go see a guy about my sanity." He headed for the makeshift bar, leaving Tim to bro-out with another of his guests. The ridiculousness of the truth, coupled with the trauma of memory, had left him thirsty. He took another solo cup of what had been labeled "Drank," and parked himself in a corner, memory and alcohol gelling into melancholy as he realized this was absolutely not the human contact he'd been missing. Tim may be the money-making kind of associate and live in a spacious, modern, and basically free home, but at least Martin was able to consider his bosses friends, and felt like they actually respected him.

Well, definitely Henry. Probably Lexie. Maybe.

Both had reached out to Martin on his birthday a few weeks ago, and even though Lexie's move back to upstate New York was supposed to be temporary, it'd been just over a year now. Henry had been working on some small cases on his own for his wife's law firm, but things had slowed down considerably. The other side of the business, the "Scooby-Doo shit", had ground to a halt as well. With things returning to normal he knew it wasn't going to stay that way forever, and handling their unique brand of danger without Lexie's help made him queasy.

He'd tried to push Henry to teach him more casting during their time off so he could do more than just research, answer phones, and digitize a twenty year old file system, but there wasn't much more he could learn over a Zoom call. His own ability to study and practice was hampered by his parent's constant and overwhelming presence, not to mention how freaked out they'd be if they saw him with any supernatural paraphernalia.

Martin had taken a spot at the end of the hallway toward the back of the house, right across from the wide archway leading into the massive living room space dominating the first floor and where the bulk of the party raged. It wasn't what he'd had in mind for his night, but at least the people watching there was good even if the music from the over-powered sound system wasn't. He was about to get another refill when a heavy burning smell hit him full force. There was enough space around him he didn't think it was coming from anyone in particular, but as he looked around he could tell it was coming from behind the closed door he'd been leaning next to.

He opened the door a crack and the smell lashed out at him so hard he stumbled backward and bumped into a guy passing behind him, spilling his drink

"Whoa, man!" the guy said, and then recoiled as he experienced the scent as well. "Dude, rank!" He scurried away, glaring at Martin over his shoulder.

"Sorry," Martin said, flushing in embarrassment. "It wasn't me though!"

Martin opened the door wider, risking further blame. On the other side was a set of stairs going down about half a flight and then turning to the left. Whatever might possibly be on fire was down around that corner for sure. With no Tim or someone Tim-adjascent in sight, he placed his cup on a table and headed downstairs.

"Hey, is everything cool down here?" he said when he reached the landing, trying to make sure he was neither screaming or whispering and somehow failing at both. The light he'd found on the stairs was dim and didn't reach the room below.

There was no response.

"Yer a wizard, Marty," he said to psyche himself up. Lexie had started teasing him by saying it in the months before she left, complete with horrible accent, and remembering it encouraged him to walk the rest of the way down the stairs.

When he turned the lights on, it was clear the well-furnished basement was empty. The space was large and ran under the whole house, and was decorated like a frat house inspired by Scarface. An uncomfortable amount of naked and nearly-naked pictures of women covered the walls. Where there wasn't nudity there was neon signs of various beer brands and slogans that, among other things, reminded him to "Be the Alpha." There was a pool table and bar to his right and a home theater system on the far wall rivaling the one upstairs. If it wasn't for the overwhelming stench of old barbecue and trash he'd have wondered why the party hadn't spread down here. Across the room was the only other door, which stood partially open, and the room beyond it was dark.

He walked towards it and then stopped halfway. The smell was stronger, and most certainly coming from there, but there was no glow of flame or heat coming from it. Martin tried to let his eyes adjust so he could see what was beyond the doorway, but nothing revealed itself. He took another step and a rush of cold spread out from the center of his body, stopping him. He tried to convince himself it was from the alcohol and hits he'd taken making him paranoid, but the familiarity of it made him think it was something else. He waited for it to go away, and when it didn't, he turned around and headed toward the stairs. The feeling faded as fast as it'd come on, and he convinced himself it was nothing to worry about.

Behind him, the door closed.

"Oh, come on," he said. The feeling returned, more insistent than before and strong enough to sober him up some. He looked over his shoulder, and while the door had closed there was still a thin crack to remind him of the darkness beyond.

"This is fine. This is *fine*," he said to himself, walking carefully back toward the door.

"I'm sure you're just some folks having a good time," he said loudly as he approached. "But please don't be fucking or about to do a jump scare. I don't consent to either thing."

There was no reply, and the smell had either begun to fade or he was somehow getting used to it. He pushed the door open with the barest touch of his fingertips, body tensed to run at the slightest surprise. When there was none, he reached around and felt for a light switch. Turning it on revealed the room beyond was barely five feet square, with a stacked washer and dryer, small wash sink and cabinets on one side, and a laundry chute on the other.

"Alright then," he said, taking a few steps inside and then nodding to the laundry chute. "That's tight, though. You don't see a good chute nowadays." The smell got stronger but it didn't have the physical force behind it like it had before. If anything, Tim had probably tossed filet mignon not to his liking down into the laundry room. Looking at the overflowing piles it was clear they'd been left alone for a while. "Motherfuckers haven't even *earned* a chute," he grumbled.

There was a heavy thud above him and the overhead light went out.

"Shit!" he jumped back, clawing for where the switch was. He flicked it a few times but the light didn't turn on. The room shuddered with another impact, this one coming from all around him, and then something lit up behind him.

He turned and saw the inside of the dryer in flames.

"Oh, come on!" he cried, the heat overwhelming him and making him stumble backward. The dryer door was closed and the window was browning and warping, the plastic edges already starting to melt.

He opened his mouth to yell but the flames sputtered out, leaving behind a massive cloud of smoke and the the lung-burning return of the burned meat odor. His eyes were burning and he waved away the smoke, trying to assess the damage. Despite everything, there was a panic at his core at how this was his fault for messing with the lights. Most likely, Tim would want him to replace them with the fanciest and most expensive ones in existence. The inside of the dryer was still thick with smoke, and he reached out tentatively for the deformed handle in case it was still hot.

A hand slammed against the window from the inside.

"Dude, what the fuck!"

Martin shrieked, tripped, and fell on his ass. The hand pushed door open, letting out waves of smoke and stench. The hand, and the arm it was attached to, flopped down against the front of the washer with a wet slap. The entire thing was horribly burned, the skin blackened and cracked all over, and in some places scorched down to the bone. The smell was charred flesh, he realized, and it was now so fresh and powerful a primitive part of his brain remembered he hadn't eaten earlier.

The burned hand twitched, the exposed bone of fingertips clicking on plastic until they found purchase and began to pull itself out. A head, shoulders, and second arm emerged from a space they shouldn't have been able to fit in to, and all of it was just as burned. The head, which looked like a peeling lump of over-cooked shawarma meat, lifted up and there was a hole where his right eye should be, tunneling all the way through the skull to an even larger hole in the back.

There was a shift of meat and the bloodshot, but otherwise undamaged, remaining eye appeared. More sliding meat sounds and teeth, cooked like steak bones, were exposed in the worst and meanest smile imaginable.

"Great party, huh Marty?" it gurgled, the voice rough and male.

The thing pulled itself forward more, exposed ribs rattling like a xylophone against the bottom of the dryer's opening until it flopped down at the waist, palms resting on the ground. With most of it out of the way, Martin could see the inside of the dryer stretched back impossibly far, with dancing flames in the distance like a warp-pipe to hell.

"Do you see it, Marty?" the thing said. "Can you see Him?"

Even with its ruined, impossible voice, Martin could hear the reverence in "Him." Martin crawled backwards as the human turducken pulled himself fully out of the dryer and started to crawl forward.

"He can see you," it continued. "He can see you and you're just what he needs."

The burned hand reached for Martin's shoe, only a couple inches away but close enough to bring him to his senses. His attempt to spring up to his feet ended up as a half-crabwalk, half-cartwheel, and he had to flail his arms wildly to stay upright. Despite being a burned corpse, the thing got to its feet with less of a struggle.

"He's going to love you, dude." It made a noise that could have been a laugh. "I bet you're fucking delicious."

The extreme terror did a great job of clearing his head of drugs and drank, and he took a deep breath and held out his hand, palm facing out.

"Yer a wizard, Marty," he remembered.

He closed his eyes, focused his intention, and under his breath he recited the words to the most powerful ward he could channel. He felt a push against his outstretched arm and he planted his back foot, leaning into it.

"I *am* delicious, motherfucker."

There was another push and then the resistance was gone, fast enough to almost make him fall forward. He opened his eyes and the thing was gone, the only smells now an overabundance of Febreeze and dirty laundry. Across from him, the dryer was flame free and undamaged. Martin's body ached and his appetite had returned and brought friends. He backed out of the laundry room and towards the steps, not taking his eyes off the dryer. When he felt his foot hit the bottom stair he reached for the switch while he flipped off the whole room.

"Yeah, you better run," he called, turning off the light with a flourish and hurrying up the stairs. He found Tim and his brother right away, holding court for a group of guys that were definitely still in high school and completely enraptured by them. "Hey," he said, putting a hand on Tim's shoulder and interrupting. "Can I talk with you two a second?"

"Kind of in the middle of something here, bro," Tim's brother Eric groaned.

"You'll survive," Martin said, not looking at him. "Tim, it's kind of important. There's something going on in the basement."

"Oh shit," Eric laughed. "Did you see a ghost?"

That got Martin to look at him. "What are you talking about? What ghost?"

Tim shrugged Martin's hand off his shoulder and rolled his eyes. "It's bullshit. A couple of our housekeepers said they heard something down there, or smelled something, or whatever, but we never find anything."

"Just excuses," Eric said, looking over at his assembled pupils. "We had to get rid of two of them in a row. No one wants to work any more. They got handouts over the pandemic and now that they got a taste they want to live off our tax dollars." The student body nodded in solemn understanding.

"Do not listen to this corporate trash," Martin said, pointing at Eric and turning back to Tim. "Did they say anything else? Anything specific?"

"The fuck should I know?" Tim said. "You think I chat with the help? It's gotten so weird and funky I don't even go down there anymore."

"Try to remember," Martin said, beginning to lose his composure. "It's important."

"They wouldn't be able to see it," one of the teenagers at the back of the group said in a familiar voice. He was tall, white, and sandy haired, standing so Martin could only see his left side. "And you were right. You're *scrumptious.*"

He turned his head, and Martin recognized the fist-sized hole through the right side of his head.

"Fuck," Martin whispered.

"Fuck what, bro," Eric said, turning to look right through where the as-of-yet unburned teen stood.

"He's going to have so much fun with you." The teen smiled in a way somehow worse than before. Martin started backing away and the teen saluted him with his solo cup, then took a drink. As he did, the skin around his head-tunnel caught fire. It spread quickly, up to his hair and down onto his clothes.

Martin raised both arms and drew in what energy he had left, but it was immediately apparent what was left didn't amount to much of anything. The now fully immolated teen walked toward Martin, and the heat was withering and the smoke so cloying he almost fell over.

No one else could see or feel it, making Martin's stumbling retreat look insane. A tide of "Dude"s and "What the fuck"s rose up as he pushed toward the front door. The crowd was the only thing keeping him from sprinting, and he risked turning away from the thing so he could go faster.

"Sorry," Martin said, shoving through them and feeling the hair on the back of his neck beginning to singe. "I need some air."

When he got to the front door Martin looked back. The flaming teen had effortlessly moved through the crowd without anyone noticing him, although a few people he passed looked around for where the faint burning smell was coming from. Martin yanked the door open and stumbled onto the lawn, gasping for clean air, and he didn't turn around until he was on the sidewalk.

When he did, he saw the thing standing in the doorway, waving at him. "See you soon, Marty!" it called out. "He'll see you real soon!"

Martin pulled out his phone and went to his contacts. The line rang for a few moments, and then Henry picked up, despite it being just after midnight.

"I really hope this is important," he said, obviously having just been woken. Martin looked back up at the house and there was no sign of the burning teenager, although he could still smell the smoke all around him.

"Yeah," Martin said, taking a breath. "You could say that."

CHAPTER TWO

Henry Churchill checked himself in the mirror one more time. He was still Black, short, and more overweight than he'd like but, unlike the most of the past year, wearing one of his suits and dress shirts. He adjusted the glasses he was still getting used to wearing, the unfortunate by-product of closing in on his forty-eighth birthday. Being properly dressed and not in his regular "stuck at home" uniform of sweatpants and a t-shirt, did wonders for his disposition.

"I've got to head into Jersey today," Henry announced, emerging from the bedroom.

His wife Monica, sitting in the breakfast nook of their apartment on Manhattan's Upper East Side, looked up from her tablet, eyebrow raised.

"I take it this has something to do with the call you got last night?"

"Sorry," he said, giving her a kiss on her forehead. "I didn't think I woke you."

"I know," she said, turning back to her reading. "I'm just glad you didn't take off right away. Martin?"

"Yeah," he said. "He was pretty freaked out."

"I should hope so if he's going to call that late," she said with a mix of fake and real annoyance.

Henry laughed, but just over twenty years of marriage gave him a pretty good idea of what was bothering her. His partner Lexie's absence, coupled with the shut down, had left him with painfully little to do over the past several months. Monica's law firm had still been open and managed to have some jobs for him, but it was all low effort computer-based stuff, netting little pay and having nothing to do with the private investigation agency's more "specialized" work.

The agency hadn't been in great financial shape before, thanks to them losing some lucrative yet unethical work his previous partner had kept from him, but now things were so tight he was worried about keeping the office in Washington Heights. He'd tried to keep giving Martin some nominal pay as he worked through their backlog of digitizing things while at his parents', but there was only so much he could work on without coming into the city, and to Henry's embarrassment he had to stop. Martin had been more than understanding, which made it worse, but Henry had made it up to him by continuing his training while Monica was at work and the kids were at virtual school.

In some ways, the break from the supernatural was a blessing, as the agency had been featured on a conspiracy website, alleging they'd instigated a riot in an affluent Jersey suburb. They'd been partially right, but Henry had gone to great lengths over the years to keep them under the radar. It was a relief the publication had happened just before lockdown and the site, "New Borderlands News," had moved on to medical disinformation and anti-vax nonsense. Not great for their subscribers, but it also moved the spotlight away from the fact the majority of their information had come from a reporter who died under what they called "mysterious circumstances." It wasn't explicitly stating Lexie or Henry were involved in it, but they had been and their failure to intervene and save him weighed heavily on Henry.

New York City, especially Manhattan, was a dangerous place to be asking questions about the supernatural, and Henry knew first hand the lengths those in that world would go to keep things from the public eye.

Not having to deal with it all had been a relief at first, but now left him feeling aimless and unprepared for when the other shoe would drop. He'd been able to focus on keeping their teenagers on task and from killing each other, but with Monica going back to the office and the kids out of school he felt like he was in a holding pattern waiting for Lexie to return. Her texts had gotten more infrequent than usual, and he was worried the longer she stayed in her northern New York hometown the less likely she was to return. They'd only been working together for a year and a half before she left and, despite a few rough patches, they'd begun to work well together. Martin hadn't been with them for very long, and Henry didn't have the heart to tell him he may not be ready for regular field-work for a long time, if ever.

"Whoa, Dad's actually wearing real clothes!" Their son John strode out of the hallway, grinning at Henry. "You going to the office again?"

"No, just have some work in New Jersey with Martin."

"'Bout time," John said, heading into the kitchen. "I thought you were giving up the monster hunting."

Henry could see Monica tense in his peripheral vision. They'd kept the kids from the nature of his work for as long as they could, and their discovery of it over a year ago had been violent and traumatic. Monica didn't want them to ever have anything to do with it, but with it out in the open and the initial shock worn off, John's curiosity and laissez faire attitude about it had become a constant source of stress for her.

"You know that's not what it is," Henry said.

"I know, I know," John said, coming out of the kitchen with a cup of coffee and a nearly overflowing bowl of cereal. "But it's good, though. I was beginning to think you'd be staying in those sweatpants."

"Not a chance. You know I've got too much style."

John choked on his coffee when he laughed. "Okay, keep telling yourself that."

"And what have *I* been telling you?" Monica said, the tone stopping him before he retreated back to his room to do whatever he did back there.

He groaned, but Monica's raised eyebrow straightened him out. "College applications."

"Yes, please," she said. "We're already behind and I don't want you to miss anything."

"I know," John said. "And I'm on it. Promise."

"Good," she said as John headed back down the hallway. "And wake your sister! I don't care how late she was up on the computer last night." John disappeared around the corner as he gave them a thumbs up.

"As for you," Monica said, standing up and giving Henry a once over. "I want you to be careful out there, okay?"

"I'm always careful," Henry said, giving her a kiss on the cheek.

"We both know that's not true. When are you going to be back?"

"This afternoon. I'll text you," he said, heading out the door

It was a quick walk to the parking garage where he kept the "company car," a school bus yellow '76 Gremlin held together with literal magic. Once at the car, he texted Martin he was on his way, and then put on the 90s hip-hop playlist he'd all but given up on listening to at home thanks to his children's incessant commentary and teasing about it.

Yes Lillian, they should not be using "the gay F-word."

Yes John, "Whomp, there it is" is four words to get busy, not three.

Yes Lillian, Kanye is very problematic.

Yes John, "bump your head and then you wake up in the Dawn of the Dead" sounds like House of Pain is describing The Walking Dead.

Yes Lillian, all women are not bitches.

Yes John, Biz Marquis absolutely was inappropriate to his female employee in "Just A Friend."

He was thankful to have such socially-conscious children, but he'd expected them to turn their gaze to the rest of the world instead of their father, who just wanted to happily enjoy a golden age of music far superior to the one they'd been born into. He turned up the music and then headed for the tunnel, hoping he'd beaten the weekend traffic but resigned to the fact you never could.

***

Martin was waiting for him at a retro looking coffee shop nestled among Cedar Ridge's pricey suburban boutiques that could only exist in a climate of vast disposable income. Martin sat at one of the weirdly shaped plastic booths in the back corner and waved Henry over as soon as he walked in.

"I'm sorry we couldn't meet at my house. My mom is still adjusting to my 'questionable employment choice,' and if she heard us talking shop it would be just...," he just shook his head.

Henry held up his hand. "Believe me, I hear you. You said you got something about that place?"

"Yeah, and let me start by saying if I'd known it was built where it was I wouldn't have gone."

"There's a history?"

"Oh yeah," Martin said, pulling his laptop out of his backpack. "It's the Cedar Ridge Murder House. Where it used to be, I mean."

"Murder House?"

"Not the catchiest name, but neither was 'The Cedar Ridge Slayings,' which is what they called what happened there in the 50s." The laptop opened to a picture of an old front page of the Star-Ledger dominated by a picture of a scrawny and terrified White man looking to be in his late twenties. He was wearing shackles and a prison uniform while being roughly dragged away from a screaming mob of people. The headline read "Justin Corwin Arrested for Cedar Ridge Slayings!" Below, a bit smaller, it read "Community Demands the Death Penalty."

"So Justin here," Martin said, "kidnapped five kids, locked them in his basement, and then tortured and eventually killed all but one of them. Oh, and he offed his parents too."

"Jesus."

"Oh, don't worry, it gets worse. Apparently, he didn't just kill these kids. He dismembered them so he could burn the bodies in his furnace, which was one of those old-timey, coal-fired ones."

"Hence the outrage," Henry said.

"Oh yeah, they wanted him dead real bad. But he didn't even make it to trial before hanging himself in his cell. But here's the potentially interesting part. He said the furnace was instructing him to kill."

"That is interesting."

Martin switched to another tab. "The whole thing kind of got swept under the rug on account of, well...the suburbs. Fast-forward to ten years ago, when disgruntled teen Jackson Cole does a Cedar Ridge Slayings remix to terrorize some other kid. He kills six people, kidnaps that other kid, and they end up at said Murder House. Cops come find them, Cole gets killed, and the house ends up being burned to the ground to no one's dismay."

Henry nodded. "And your friend's family bought the lot it was on and built their own house."

"Acquaintance at best," Martin said. "Murder House 2.0 went up about six years ago, after the whole thing blew over. Surprise, surprise, the original buyers end up selling after only a couple years. For a loss too, if Zillow is to be believed. Turns out Tim's folks got themselves a real good deal on a haunted house."

"Definitely could be a haunting," Henry said, running a hand against his closely cut beard as he skimmed the report on the screen.

"Could be?" Martin said in exasperation. "I may have been getting crunk but there was definitely something there."

"Crunk?" Henry said, raising an eyebrow.

"You know, drunk a--"

"I know what it means. I just don't know why *you're* saying it."

"Right, sorry. But seriously, if it's not a haunting then what?"

"I'm not saying it is or isn't anything. Haunting is a possibility, but haunting spirits don't usually send people out to do errands. And you said the new kid didn't actually live there?"

"Nope," Martin said, checking some facts in another window. "He lived way up on the hill with his Dad, who he killed in his last spree of murders. They figured Cole was using the house as a place to stash all his gear, but it doesn't look like there's any actual evidence of that. Plus, they didn't really get a chance to sweep it for clues afterward."

"Interesting. Was it local PD or the Sheriff's Department handling the case?"

Martin clicked through a few more screens. "It looks like it was locals."

Henry nodded. "Good. They tend to be a little more receptive than Sheriffs. Let's see if we can find who was in charge of the investigation and if they can give us any specifics on what went down."

"I'm excited," Martin said, packing up his laptop. "My first witness interview. And also first interview with the cops." That slowed him down. "First *conversation* with cops, actually."

"Must be nice," Henry smirked as they headed for the door.

"I get that," Martin blushed. "Total privilege move, for sure."

"I'm playing with you. I've been spending too much time with the kids."

"I bet," Martin laughed. "They told me about catching you doing what passed for dancing in the living room."

Henry stopped short. "When the hell did they tell you that?"

"Oh," Martin said, taken aback. "It was in the group chat."

"Of course there's a group chat," Henry muttered. The whole office, plus his family, seemed to have multiple ones and he'd asked to be kept off as many as possible. Clearly that was a mistake.

"You're just lucky there wasn't video. Lily was totally going to try to get some." Henry stopped and glared. "For educational purposes," Martin added. "It sounded like you need better moves."

"You," Henry snapped, "are the last person I'm taking dance advice from. Now dance yourself into this car and navigate us to the police station."

***

"Detective David Prescott? He hasn't worked here in years," the desk sergeant said, looking back down at the screen in front of her.

"You wouldn't happen to have any contact information for him, would you?" Martin asked.

"What am I, a Google?" she said, not looking back up.

"No, of course not," Martin said, looking over his shoulder at Henry, who was standing a few steps behind him. After Martin's initial excitement had been replaced with anxiety, Henry reminded him that this was what came with field work. Resigned, he said he would give it his best. "I'm a writer and I'm, ah, writing a book about the Jackson Cole case and--"

"Sounds fascinating," she said, glaring up at him. "I can't help you. So unless you have other business, I'm going to need you two to step aside."

Martin looked back at him with impending panic and, with a sigh, Henry stepped forward.

"Sergeant, can I have you take a look at this?"

She looked up at Henry, the expression of irritation falling from her face when she saw the silver dollar being flipped across his knuckles. "Now," Henry said, quieter as he stared into her vacant eyes, "can you point us in the direction of someone who knows about the case?"

Her head tilted and her pupils raced back and forth like she was dreaming. "Ronald Lobrazzo, the Chief of Detectives, was involved in the case," she said in a slow, low voice.

"Wonderful," Henry said, hating his satisfaction at how quickly she fell under the charm. "Can you get him for us?"

She nodded slowly, picked up the phone, and dialed an extension.

Martin sidled up next to him. "You did the mind-trick on her?" Henry nodded, not wanting to lose his focus.

The Sergeant hung up the phone and looked back at Henry. "He's on his way," she said, now sounding like she was on the verge of a quiet breakdown. "How else may I serve you?"

"That's new," Martin whispered.

Henry cleared his throat and deposited the coin back into his pocket. The hold on her was slow to fade, and Henry wondered if he could get her to reveal a secret, give her a command for later, or have her--

Knock it the fuck off, he snapped in his head.

The thought receded, leaving him with a sullen twinge of disappointment.

"We'll be over here," Henry said as the Sergeant's eyes refocused. He turned and headed towards a set of chairs in the waiting area.

"I thought that was for emergencies," Martin asked as they sat.

"Well, best not to waste time."

Martin nodded enthusiastically. "I got you," he said.

"It's still dangerous," Henry added, knowing he was setting a bad example. "And not something that should be done often, but since we're on a little bit of a deadline I figured I should grease the wheels some."

"When are you going to teach me that, anyway? It'd come in real handy when my mother goes on one of her 'wasted potential' rants."

"What did I just say? This is why I haven't taught it to you yet." Henry didn't add that it wasn't really something that could be taught.

"Can I help you?" a heavyset White man in a too-small suit and a too-thick graying mustache asked them from the bullpen door.

"Chief Lobrazzo," Henry said, getting up and extending a hand. "So very nice to meet you. My name is Henry Churchill and this is my associate Martin Green. We were hoping to talk to you about the Jackson Cole case."

"We're writing a book," Martin smiled unsteadily.

"Huh," Lobrazzo said, appraising them with narrowed eyes that seemed even smaller under his large forehead and massively unkempt eyebrows as he took Henry's hand. "Shelly," he called over to the Sergeant, "I got it from here." She nodded, a look of confusion on her face as if she hadn't realized the three of them had been there the whole time.

"I figured it was a matter of time," Lobrazzo said as they followed him back to his office. "That case was weird from the jump, and it only got weirder."

"It does seem that way," Henry said.

"Oh yeah," Lobrazzo said, taking a seat behind his desk and motioning for them to sit as well. "I didn't get assigned to it at first, but once it started going off the rails they called me in to straighten it out." He leaned back, a smug "I told you so" edge coming into his voice.

"David Prescott was the lead on it, right?"

Lobrazzo nodded. "Yup. He was all over it. On it way too close, if you ask me. I was the head of the Investigative Unit then and for some reason the Chief let him run with his bullshit theories."

"You don't say," Henry said, relieved that they wouldn't need more magic to get information out of him. "You had a different take on it?"

"I sure fucking did. I mean, there's physical evidence that tied Cole to the murders, but it was that other kid who never sat right with me."

"Who now?" Martin chimed in.

"The other kid, the one he was going after. He was a twitchy little weirdo and, honestly, I always thought he and Cole had a little something going on and that's what the whole thing was about." Lobrazzo waggled his hand in what Henry assumed was an indicator of gayness. "Kid wouldn't talk, though. Probably because Prescott babied him the whole time, and when I stepped in they wouldn't let me really put the full-court press on him."

"That is a shame," Martin chimed in, his nerves having settled a bit. Lobrazzo looked at him, smart enough to realize it could have been insincere, but Martin covered with a smile.

"You said it was weird?" Henry said to refocus Lobrazzo's attention.

"Oh yeah. We never released this but...," Lobrazzo paused, and Henry couldn't tell if it was for dramatic effect or genuine worry at being overheard. "The first murder, victim's place was set on fire. But her? Not a cinder. She was laying on the floor in an unburned circle. Fire said they'd never seen anything like it."

Henry had, but he wasn't going to tell Lobrazzo where.

"The murder weapon itself was something weird as hell too. Like a sword or some long blade that was old, thin, and really fucking sharp according to the lab. Like, where the hell do you get something like that?"

"Sword store?" Martin said. Henry gave him a look that he hoped conveyed that there was relaxed and then there was *too* relaxed.

"We don't have a lot of those," Lobrazzo said, demeanor stiffening again.

"It wasn't recovered?" Henry asked, trying to draw back his attention.

"Nope. We figured it burned up when the place caught fire."

"How did that happen, anyway?" Martin asked.

"That," Lobrazzo said, pointing his finger at him, "is an excellent question, and one I wish I could answer. The only people there were Prescott and two of the kids Cole 'kidnapped.'" The air-quotes were readily apparent. "They said Cole started the furnace because he wanted to, y'know," he made hacking motions with his hand, "but it exploded somehow and then the place just went up like a matchbook."

"So there were two other kids involved, not just one?" Henry asked.

"Yeah. The weirdo and a girl that was seeing him and whose family, by the way, were attacked by Cole. While she wasn't there. At nearly one in the morning." Lobrazzo's significant eyebrows rose with each sentence.

"That wasn't in any of the reports," Martin said, looking pointedly over at Henry.

"Yeah, you know, juveniles and privacy and all that. The timelines for all of them that day were screwy. Probably some kind of sex thing. Usually is, especially with teenagers. Maybe love triangle gone bad, maybe some Satanist stuff on account of the burning and all. But after six murders people wanted to get the whole thing wrapped, so here we are." Lobrazzo threw his hands up in the air.

"That's wild," Henry said, nodding in sympathy. "What about the weird kid? Any follow-up or anything?"

"Nah. Ended up going into the foster system but must have turned out okay. I keep my eyes peeled in case he gets picked up on something. If he does, I'm gonna open this thing up again and really put the screws to him."

"So who is he?" Martin asked. "Maybe we could, y'know, put the screw-gie on him ourselves." He accompanied this by twisting his fist around in a nearly obscene gesture, which seemed to just confuse and irritate Lobrazzo.

He held up a hand to stop whatever it was that Martin was doing. "I'm good, thanks. Like I said, privileged and sealed information. Nothing I can do."

"Aw nuts," Martin huffed in exaggerated dismay. "You sure about that?"

Lobrazzo's brows eclipsed his eyes. "Yeah. I am."

"Well alright then," Henry said, slapping the arms of his chair and getting to his feet. "Chief, you've been a real help." He extended a hand and Lobrazzo stood and shook it.

"My pleasure. And if, by some chance," he looked over at Martin, "you find anything out I'd appreciate knowing about it."

"Of course," Henry nodded. "Always willing to lend a hand to law enforcement."

They made their way out of the building, taking a wide berth around the desk Sergeant, and when they got outside Martin let out a great sigh. "Okay, that was kind of cool."

"Screw-gie?" Henry chuckled, shaking his head.

"Sorry. Seinfeld has been my comfort show."

"I'll give you that. So, Mr. Investigator, what's our next step?"

"Oh, the sister for sure!" Martin was practically skipping. "Nothing said she was there and if she was involved with the other kid she probably knows a lot more. Especially given that this thing is most certainly spooky."

"Got it in one," Henry said, giving him a congratulatory pat on the shoulder.

***

They headed back towards the coffee shop and by the time they got there Martin had found Christine Baker, sister of murder victim number three and daughter of the only attack survivor. She was living in New Mexico, was a sales rep for something that was either an insurance or pharmaceutical company, rented a condo, was in just a bit more debt than the average Millennial, and had no arrests or court cases. Her social media was pretty basic, with a bit of a Southwest-witchy vibe, and was, as Martin put it, "not unattractive."

"I'm going to handle this, if you don't mind." Henry said, putting the phone in the dash holder and putting it on speaker.

"For sure," Martin nodded. "This is definitely not my forte."

It rang twice and then went to voicemail. Martin opened his mouth to say something but Henry held up a hand. "Ms. Baker, my name is Henry Churchill, a detective with the Cedar Ridge Police Department. I wanted to talk to you about some new developments and information regarding the attack on your family a few years back. If you could give me a call back at this number, that'd be great," he said, and then ended the call.

"And now we wait?" Martin asked dubiously.

"I'm willing to bet she'd be interested in hearing about 'new developments,' especially if the story they gave was a cover."

"Or she could be too traumatized and just wants to forget," Martin said. Henry looked over at him. "Okay," he added, "she can be two things."

Henry was about to respond when the phone buzzed, displaying her number.

"Never doubt me, son," Henry said, giving him a wink.

"Is this Ms. Baker?" he asked when he picked up.

"Yeah," came the tentative female voice. "Is this Detective Churchill?"

"Just Henry, please," he said, projecting as much warmth in his voice as he could. "And I've got you on speaker with my associate, Martin."

"Hi," Martin piped up, giving a little wave and then rolling his eyes at himself.

"Hi," she said, her tone clipped and defensive. "You said you had information?"

"We do, but we were hoping we could review your statement with you if you have a moment."

"Fuck's sake, do you think I'm going to remember anything more than I did ten years ago? Just tell me what you've got, I need to get on a meeting in a few minutes."

"There's been another incident," Henry said. "At the Briarcliff house."

"That's not possible," she snapped. "It burned to the ground."

"You saw that first hand, correct?"

There was a pause. "Yeah. And?"

"There's a new house on the property and we have reason to believe that the occupants may be in danger in a way that's related to your case."

"I really doubt that, *Henry*," she said sarcastically. "The person responsible is dead, so whatever it is it has nothing to do with what happened to my family."

"He's dead like, shot through the eye and leaving a big hole in his face dead?" Martin chimed in. That landed an even longer pause.

"Who told you that? Was it Detective Prescott? Was it...Look, it doesn't matter how you know because--"

"Because I saw him," Martin continued. "Saw right through what looked like his very douchey head. It, and he, were deeply unpleasant. Also on fire."

Another pause.

"Ms. Baker," Henry continued slowly, "we know there was a supernatural element to the crimes centered around the Briarcliff house, and I have reason to believe that now it's, for lack of a better term, waking up. We could really use your help to make sure no one else gets hurt like you and your family did."

"Jesus Christ," she whispered. "Jesus fucking Christ." There was another pause. "You aren't actually with the cops, are you Henry?"

"You did catch me in a lie, yes," he said. "But my associate and I handle things like this regularly and this...re-emergence came to our attention. No one has been hurt yet, but in my experience with things like this it's only a matter of time."

There was a long exhale and from the noise on the line it sounded like she'd started walking. "Shit, shit, shit!" Another long breath. "Have you talked to Mark? Mark Watson, I mean."

"I take it he's the boy Cole was stalking," Henry said. "They kept his name, and yours, under wraps since you were minors."

"Thank God for small favors. Okay, I can send you the info I have and you can probably find him. He's still in Jersey."

"That's helpful," Martin muttered.

"I have to go into a meeting, like, now so I don't have the time to get into it, but he knows all about this. In the...supernatural sense, I mean."

"Got it," Henry said. "Send us what you have and we'll take it from there."

***

What she had was just a neglected Facebook page, but it plus what Lobrazzo had told them was enough to run a search. He was renting a condo in West Orange and worked at Clairidge Collision & Auto, also in West Orange. His credit was decent, he owned a '79 Jeep, and like Lobrazzo had said, kept himself on the right side of the law (aside from a few speeding tickets). Henry decided in this case, and because West Orange was so close, they should try him in person and headed to his job.

The garage was a very polished non-chain or dealer-owned one, and looked to service mostly high-end luxury and classic cars. When they asked after Mark the receptionist nodded and paged him over the intercom. After a few moments he emerged from the swinging doors across the lobby.

"Can I help you guys?" he said. He was of average height and in good shape, just-barely shaved, and his hair was close-cropped on the sides with the length on top slicked back. He rubbed his dirty hands on his equally dirty overalls as he looked them over, trying to place where he might know the two of them from.

"I'm Henry Churchill, Mr. Watson. I'm a private investigator and--"

"Shit," he muttered, immediately dropping his customer service mask. "Is this about Ashley? Because I told her plenty of times it was over and I'm not going to couples counseling with a girl I dated for two months."

"Oh yeah, don't do that," Martin said, shocked. "But this isn't about that, thank god. I'm Martin, by the way."

"Okay," Mark said warily, appraising them cautiously. "So what can I do for you guys? We're kind of slammed today."

"Is there somewhere we can talk privately?" Henry asked.

"Not until I know what this is about," he said, smiling in a most unfriendly way.

"It's...," Henry shifted, turning away from the receptionist and lowering his voice so he couldn't be heard from across the room, "about the house on Briarcliff Avenue."

Everything in Mark's body seemed to shut down for a second, and then rebooted as a block of steel. "What the fuck is this?" he said through a clenched jaw. "Is this some kind of *Investigate the Unknown* bullshit?"

"No, not at all," Henry said in a well-practiced, 'talking calmly to an upset white man' voice. "I handle cases of this nature and I got your name from Christine Baker."

"Huh," he said, his tension easing for a moment but returning just as fast. "Look, I'm not talking about that shit, so you guys are just wasting your time. Tell Christine I said hey, and good luck with whatever."

"It's back," Martin said, a little too loudly as Mark turned away.

Mark snapped around and gave Martin a death glare. "Keep your fucking voice down," Mark hissed, and then registered what Martin said. "And that's bullshit. I saw him...it, whatever the fuck it was, burn and die. Or however that works. If there's something else then it has nothing to do with me."

"It's not that easy, Mr. Watson," Henry said. "We just want to talk about what you experienced so we know what we're dealing with and can protect the people who live there now."

"People *live* there? Of course they fucking do, it's the suburbs." Mark closed his eyes and took a few deep breaths and a fraction of the tension in his body faded. "That sucks for them, but I'm not going to be a part of this. It wasn't my fault, and that shit is in the past. The way past."

"I understand that what happened to you was traumatic," Henry said. "But the more I know the more we can--"

"If you think I have any insight into what happened then you're mistaken." Mark let out another breath and Henry could feel the adrenaline pouring off of him. Mark took a step back and then said, loud enough for the receptionist to hear, "I'm sorry, I can't help you guys. Best of luck to you."

Before Henry could say anything the man spun on his heel and disappeared behind the doors he came from.

"Well alrighty then," Martin said as they walked back to the car. "What now? We're not going to have to, like, pester him or something, are we? Because he seemed...intense."

"We'll give him some time to cool off," Henry said. "We did just drop in to casually talk about the worst thing that's ever happened to him."

"Good point," Martin said. "But how long do we give it?"

"Until we've exhausted the rest of our options."

CHAPTER THREE

Options were exhausted in a little over a week, although for a couple of days Henry took a break for paying (thank god) PI work. They'd reconnected with Christine a couple of days later and she'd given them a pretty brief overview of what Mark had told her after the Briarcliff house burned down. The official story was, as Henry had known, mostly bullshit. It'd been Mark, not Jack (as Jackson was known) who committed the murders, but while being controlled by what she helpfully called "a darkness ghost of some kind." Mark said he'd dreamed about what happened at the house in the fifties, seeing it through the eyes of one of Corwin's victims, but also the murders being committed in the present (the mystery murder weapon being a sword-cane, of all things). The "darkness ghost" was tied to the furnace of the house and ended up reanimating Jack's corpse after he'd been killed.

It was clear why they came up with something else, but what was irritatingly not clear was what the entity in the house really was. It could be a "cursed land" situation, but if that had been the case it'd have made its presence known before the Corwins lived there. A house haunting was also unlikely, as those tend to end when the structure is destroyed. Even if it was a haunting, it would have been unheard of for it to reach across town and latch itself onto a random teenager that'd never noticed the place before.

There had to be some kind of connection between Mark and the house, but she told him that the only thing Mark came up with was that he'd been connected somehow to the kid he'd been dreaming about. Henry's bullshit detector had pinged a little bit on that, so he and Martin started looking through birth records and family histories both in the fifties and when Mark was born, but there was no connection. The boy Mark had been dreaming of was Corwin's final victim, Darren Cox, who was also the only survivor of the kidnappings. Cox had an unremarkable life after that, never married or had children, and ended up purchasing the Briarcliff house and ultimately killing himself there shortly after. Tragic, and a definite suspect for a haunting presence, but that would have been after Corwin's supernatural encounter.

There was a piece they were missing, and it was the one that would tell them what kind of magic or ritual was needed to put whatever it was down for good. Martin had walked by the house daily over the course of the week, and he said that now that he was looking for it he could feel the same undercurrent of malevolence he'd experienced before. On the pass he'd made earlier that day he said he smelled smoke outside, and when he paused to look closer he'd seen Jack's burned and one-eyed presence waving at him from a window.

It hadn't just woken up. It was getting stronger.

Henry told him to hold off on any more walk-bys in case it was feeding off of Martin's presence and magical acumen. They'd called and left messages for Mark until they both were blocked, so he called Christine again. He'd been avoiding doing so as she'd requested, but she couldn't remember anything specific Mark had said about the rituals Corwin was performing. Her response was emphasized with the sharpest of "fuck off" tones, and when he asked if it was possible for her to reach out and talk to Mark she hung up on him.

He could just let the whole thing go, but the mystery of it was something his brain needed to pick at, not to mention what could potentially happen if things got worse there. If the rituals Corwin had been performing had cracked open some kind of gate or managed to summon something, then things were going to get a lot worse a lot faster.

"Hey Dad."

Henry looked up from the book he hadn't really been reading as John dropped onto the sofa. In a lot of ways, John was the kind of teenager Henry had wished he'd been: confident, athletic, tall, and with a clear idea of his future. Even better, he'd gone to diverse and private schools, giving him an opportunity to be around other kids of color, something the Westchester suburb Henry had grown up in had been sorely lacking.

"What's up, my dude," he said, immediately cringing at his attempt at being "with it."

He could tell John wanted to get on his case about it, but instead he looked around the room and started to fidget.

"Uh, you know when Mom's getting home?"

Henry closed the copy of *Ancient Infernal Summoning Rites* in his lap and straightened up his recliner. John's tone suggested this was about a different kind of horror, one deeper and more existential. "She's working late. What's up?"

"Lily's gaming so I just was hoping we could talk without them around."

"Okay," he said, trying not to start fidgeting himself. "Speak your mind."

"It's about...you know..." He gestured to the book on Henry's lap, as well as the other ones stacked on the table next to him. Henry held back a sigh of relief at this not being a more personal and life-changing teenage boy emergency, but chided himself for getting too comfortable and thinking he could do research in the living room and not have it be an issue.

"Oh," Henry said. "What about it?"

"I know Mom doesn't really like it, so I get why we don't talk about it any more but..." John trailed off. When the secret was out and they'd answered the kids' questions, it was made clear that it was never to be discussed anywhere but home, but as more questions continued to come up it was made readily apparent that talk even at home put Monica on edge, so conversation ceased. John's comment when Henry had gone out to Jersey had been the first one in nearly a year.

They hadn't told the kids she hadn't found out about this until after they were married, or that it was part of the darkest part of their marriage and had almost split them up. After things had worked out as best they could, she accepted Henry was making it part of his work life, but made it clear she wanted nothing to do with it. When she was pregnant with John she told him she didn't ever want their kids involved either, something he was more than happy to agree with.

"I'm happy to answer anything, but for a lot of reasons the less you know the better. I told you how dangerous it is."

"I get that," John said with exasperation. "I just..."

Before Henry could interject he started up again. "Why are you teaching Martin to do more magic if that's the case?"

That was unexpected, and Henry leaned back as he gathered his thoughts.

"When did he tell you that?" he asked, buying himself some time to come up with an answer.

"We text and junk," John said a little sheepishly.

"Mmm-hmm." That goddamn group chat again. "And what did he tell you?"

"Just that he was learning new stuff while he was out there. But he also said I should talk to you if I had more questions."

"That's good," he said, relieved that Martin had enough common sense for that at least. "The thing is, Martin had already used magic when Lexie and I met him, and he experienced the consequences of messing with it. He's well aware of the risks, and doesn't want anything like that to happen again. Plus, teaching him some stuff is helpful when we need a few more hands on deck on a case."

"Because not everyone can actually do it."

"Exactly. Like Lexie, who is one of the least talented I've ever seen. Just absolutely terrible, and not just with her pronunciation," he laughed, but failed to lighten the mood.

"So why teach him more, especially if it puts him in danger?"

Henry hesitated. "It was his choice. He was having a hard time after what happened and it's helped him feel more in control and secure." John raised an eyebrow at that. "Okay, slightly more secure."

"But having someone else around who can do magic is helpful."

"Right."

"So, by that logic, you should have as many people who can do magic helping you as possible, right?"

Boy, did it suck to have a kid that's smarter than you, and especially one that was on the debate team. "I see what you're doing, and I'm going to stop you right there," Henry said, sitting back up and pointing at him for emphasis. "This is not up for discussion. You are never--"

"Really?" John snapped. "*Never*? Is it that obvious that I can't do it?"

Henry took a breath.

"It's not about that. I don't know if you've got the talent or not and I don't want to know. You shouldn't either. Like I said, it's *dangerous*."

"I know, I know. But Martin says that it runs in families, so it's a possibility, right?"

Henry shook his head. "That's never been proven. No one else in my family can do it, so there's no proof you'd to be able to."

"How do you know? You said you figured out by accident, and so did Martin. Maybe everyone else just never had a chance to find out. Can't you at least do some kind of test or whatever on me? Or did you already do one and you don't want to tell me about it?"

Henry ran a hand across the top of his head, hoping it'd help him formulate some kind of strategy. "Here's the thing," Henry said, leaning closer for emphasis. "Magic has a cost. Sometimes it's obvious, sometimes it's not. What I'm teaching Martin is basic, mostly harmless stuff or things to keep him safe that don't take as much of a toll on you. Anything more, you get into taking years off your life, permanently damaging your health, and even your soul. I've explained this to him so he can figure out what he wants to stay away from. Not to mention the fact he's an adult."

John rolled his eyes. "So in like, two years, I can try? That doesn't make any sense!"

"In *no* amount of years can you try," Henry said. "This is not for you."

John exhaled sharply, looking down at his feet. "I just don't get why you're willing to teach...some guy and not me. What if you need someone else to get your back?"

Henry got up from the recliner and sat on the couch next to him so he could put a hand on John's shoulder. "I am never, ever, going to put you in harms way. So the magic stuff is never going to happen, okay?" John slumped, hearing the finality in Henry's voice.

"But what if...what if Mom or Lillian need it and you're not around? If I've got to protect them...what can I do?" Henry pulled him into an awkward, one armed embrace. The kids had been spared the worst of the attack that let the magical cat out of the bag, and Henry had tried not to think about the lasting and non-magical toll it had taken on them.

"Hey, it is not your job to protect this family. That's on me, and I'm sorry I couldn't do a better job of it, but nothing like that is going to happen again."

John looked at him skeptically. "You don't know that for sure."

"Okay, you're right, but I can tell you that the more involved you get in this, the more likely something *is* going to happen." John looked dubious at that, and Henry continued before he could interrupt. "Knowing about this has made things very difficult over the years. If I'd have left it alone, these kinds of things would never happen at all. And over the past twenty-five years I've seen things that people should not see, and done things and made choices that I'm not proud of. I couldn't live with myself if you had to experience anything like that."

"Is that why you didn't tell us how it all got started?"

"Yeah," Henry said. "It was horrible and not something you need to worry about." John looked like he was going to argue but then stopped himself.

"And you don't have to worry about backing me up. I back *you* up, okay? Your Dad's the big dog, remember? He can take care of himself. Sometimes you just need an extra set of hands for stuff, and that's where Martin comes in. You're still my favorite son, after all."

"Yeah, yeah," John rolled his eyes, having heard that corny joke ever since Lillian was born, and slid his way out of the embrace with a chuckle that could have been genuine.

"You've got too much going on for you to carry this weight. Let it go, focus on school and the college search. By the way, ha—"

"No, I haven't finished with that pile Mom gave me."

"Please get to it, she doesn't need to be stressing either."

"I know, I know." Shoulders slumped, John turned back to the hall.

"Hey," Henry called after him. "We good?"

John gave him a weak smile over his shoulder and said "We good" just before he disappeared around the corner.

Henry leaned back and let out a deep sigh. He'd known something had been off with him these past few months, but Henry had stupidly attributed it to the horrors of the real world taking its toll. He'd been too focused on those things as well, but he knew he'd have to do a better job of making sure they were okay. The upside was that while his son may be smarter than him, but he couldn't spot a lie like his old man could.

***

The next day, feeling like he had no other option, Henry followed Mark home from work. He knew where he lived, but the casual suburban pursuit was also a good way to see if the charm he'd placed on the Gremlin would, in fact, keep him from being consciously noticed. Given that he'd been able to pull into the spot next to Mark's without him giving Henry more than a glance was definitely a good sign. Henry followed Mark through the maze of upscale condos from a good distance and rounded the corner as Mark was stepping through his door.

"Mr. Watson," Henry called, closing the distance between them in a quick stride. "I need to talk to you."

Mark's confusion lasted a second, and it was enough for Henry to put his foot against the door.

"What the fuck, man?" Mark said, tossing the keys and handful of mail onto a table. "I told you I don't want anything to do with this shit."

"I know, but this is important. Lives are at stake."

"I don't *care*," Mark said, leaning against the door to get it to close but unable to budge Henry's foot. "Look, I don't like the optics of it, but I *will* call the cops, okay?"

"Mr. Watson, whatever made you kill those people is waking back up, and I need to stop it." He didn't want to swing the biggest club he had, but Mark looked frustrated enough to follow up on the threat.

Mark took a step back, gasping. "Fuck," he muttered, his voice sounding like it would've in high school. "Fuck you, that's not..." His face went red, and Henry raised his hand to calm him down.

"I know you didn't. Christine told us everything, okay, and it's not your fault. I'm not blaming you."

Mark's expression rolled back a click from "impending meltdown" to "confused fury" and he shook his head. "Fucking Christine. Great, so you know everything, that should be more than enough for you to fix it, right?"

"No, not right," Henry said. "There are too many variables, and if I try the wrong thing it could make it a whole lot worse."

"Then that's a real big problem for someone else," Mark said.

The coin was out of his pocket before he could reasonably claim he'd thought about it. He danced it along his fingers and it caught Mark's eyes immediately, slipping him into a trance state at the same faster than normal speed the desk Sergeant had before. He didn't want it to come to this, but it was clear this was the only way Henry was going to be able to find out what Mark knew, and the growing danger outweighed the right to privacy.

Yes, keep telling yourself that.

Henry refocused on Mark's mind, but before he could get a command out there was a push from somewhere inside Mark's head that broke the connection. Mark snapped back to reality, looked confused for a few seconds, and then remembered Henry's presence.

"Look. Enough is fucking enough, okay? Please don't make me physically get you off my doorstep," he said, looking Henry up and down.

"You don't look like you're in great shape and I really don't want to hurt anybody."

Henry backed up. There were other ways to proceed but they were much more invasive, and Henry knew he'd been through enough and didn't deserve that. Even with the looming danger hanging over them. "I got it. I'm going, Mr. Watson."

"Stop fucking calling me that," he said, following Henry as he backed out of the doorway. "Mr. Watson is my dead dad."

The door slammed.

Henry walked back to the car, dropping the coin he was still clutching into his pocket. It hadn't felt like Mark had pushed him out of his mind consciously, but something was in there that didn't want Henry poking around, most likely part of his previous encounter. It created a new wrinkle to the problem as well, since it might affect him like it had before. Without knowing what caused it in the first place, Henry wouldn't be able to protect him even if Mark wanted to cooperate. Henry thought again about how he could force the issue and what he could do to mitigate whatever side effects there might be, but he shook those thoughts off.

"That's a last resort," he said to himself.

Henry drove off and pulled into the next gas station he saw. There were no good options left, so even though he told Christine he wouldn't call again he figured he'd bend the promise by texting her. An idea came to him as he was wondering what to send to her, and even though he didn't really like it, he typed out the message, muttered to himself, and then hit send.

CHAPTER FOUR

"Come on-a my house, my house-a come on..."

That fucking song was stuck in Mark's head the rest of that day, even after he smoked himself halfway to oblivion that night. He hadn't thought about it, Briarcliff, or anything Cedar Ridge in years and entirely by design. He'd been able to hold them at bay for a decade that guy and his nerdy sidekick had been pestering him, but the surprise visit must have been the last straw for his formidable powers of denial. He spent most of his mental energy working on tricks various therapists had given him when he was triggered, but none of them helped.

He wasn't just triggered, he was detonated.

The only remote positive was the mention of Christine. It was hard to shove her into the box with the rest of that shit, but it felt stupidly nostalgic and comforting to think about their brief relationship. He remembered being told by Therapist Number Three he shouldn't be so fixated on the past, and tried to push those thoughts and the memories of Cedar Ridge as deep as possible.

It's not your problem anymore.

He was on the afternoon shift that day, and after he clocked in Bethany stuck her head in the break room to call him over. "There's someone waiting for you," she said.

"Why wouldn't there be?" he smirked, covering for the sudden panic. If it was Churchill again he knew he was going to wind up on the internet as another crazy guy yelling at a Black dude, which would probably lead to people finding out why Churchill was there, and then everything would be opened up for everyone to know and to stare at him and everyone else would find out who he really was and then--

"Shut up," he growled under his breath as he headed to the front. This was catastrophising and spiraling out over nothing, he told himself. In the words of his Therapist Number Two, that was "negative self-talk" and he should "say it isn't welcome here." Take a breath. Clear your head. He stopped at the door leading out to the waiting area, did just that, and then stepped out.

See, you were crazy thinking this had anything to do with all that stuff! Anyway, look who's here!

It wasn't Churchill, so that was great, but when he saw the shoulder-length, light red hair of the slender woman sitting in the customer lounge scrolling through her phone with Starbucks cups on the table next to her, he recognized her immediately. Even after ten years.

Christine *fucking* Baker. Not 48 hours after he'd been ambushed in his own home, here she was for the first time in a decade from all the way across the country.

Wasn't this what you were hoping would happen when you were scrolling through her Instagram the other night?

He tried to remember the reasons he should be mad at her, even though they were ancient history, but then she looked up at him and smiled. She looked mostly the same, nearly his height and dressed in a relaxed-yet-expensive way. The only obvious change he could see was a black-and-white tattoo of twisting ivy descending from under her short right sleeve and ending just above her elbow. On her wrist he could see a smaller one that seemed to be a pair of dates with an infinity symbol underneath.

"What the hell," was all he could come up with to say by the time he reached her. Some things never changed.

"Hello to you too," she said, giving him a hug. His breath hitched for a moment and then he returned the embrace. He held the hug longer than he should've, but not as long as he wanted.

"What are you doing here?" he asked.

She tilted her head a little at that. "I think you know why I'm here. But I'm also fighting jet-lag from the late flight and I'm still two hours behind. Can we talk somewhere?"

At least someone understands privacy.

Mark shrugged. "Yeah, sure...but I just got in. Can it wait?"

She raised an eyebrow. "Really?"

"It's busy today," he said, not adding that it was busy every day. "But I'm only here for a few hours. Can it wait that long?"

"Sure," she said, despite the fact she obviously didn't think so.

"There's wi-fi," he said, pointing at the ceiling for some reason. "And I can get them to change the TV to whatever you want."

"Look at you," she snickered. "Wielding so much power."

"I'm very good at what I do," he said, cheeks blushing.

"Then do it quickly," she said, pointing at the service bay doors behind him.

"I'll do my best, I promise," he said, backing up and not looking away from her until he absolutely had to.

***

It was amazing how fast work could get done given the right incentive. After closing his tickets a half hour faster than he'd expected, he spent the rest of the time in the restroom, scrubbing hands like he was a surgeon and being thankful he kept extra pomade and deodorant in his locker. He stopped at the door to the lounge, did some of his breathing exercises, and then headed in.

"I went as fast as I could," he said, arms raised in apology.

"It's fine," she said, nodding towards the two late middle aged women with impeccably coiffed hairdos behind the reception counter. "Tracy and Jeanette kept me entertained."

"Those two," Mark smiled, jabbing a finger at them as they walked past, "are not to be trusted. Especially Jeanette!" The two women giggled and waved at them as they left and headed around to the parking lot.

"They were very interested to hear what you were like in high school, by the way," Christine said, giving him a knowing glance.

"Oh Jesus," he said, rolling his eyes. "I can only imagine the shit they'll give me over it, so thanks for that. Do I even want to know what you said?"

"Well, they were very interested in the idea of you with long hair and, for some reason, they seemed very surprised that you weren't...how did Jeanette put it? Oh yeah, a 'smooth-talking Casanova back then.'"

"Fucking hell," he said, unable to keep from smiling. He paused and then added, "You didn't tell them why you were here, right?"

"Of course not," she said. "I said I was here on a work trip and surprising you. Just being impulsive since the world was closed for so long."

"For sure," he said. "I'm guessing you made it through okay?"

"As well as anyone, I guess," she shrugged. "I started working from home and still am, so that was something." She stopped when Mark did, eyeing his car suspiciously. "This is you?"

"Indeed," he said, giving the cherry red Jeep a pat. "1979 Jeep Cherokee Chief, fully restored."

"I know," she said, pointing at the door. "It says it right there. Is that in case you forget?"

"Very funny," he said, unlocking her door and then going around to the driver's side.

"They also have a thing where you can unlock it remotely, too."

"I'll have you know," he said, once inside, "this is a classic. But that is on the list of things to add."

"I should've figured that you'd end up being a car guy," she said, side-eyeing him with a smile.

"I do pretty okay as a car-guy," he said.

They both paused, the weird giddiness of reconnecting fading and the impending doom of the real reason for her visit looming large.

"Do you want to get something to eat? I know there's not much in the vending machines."

"No shit," she said. "And I don't want to talk about stuff on an empty stomach."

"I know a good place right around here," he said, pulling out of the lot.

"I bet you do," she smirked.

***

He drove them to Panucci's for a late dinner, and after being seated they ordered drinks (white wine for her, Coke Zero for him), and did his best to look like he was actually reading the menu so the conversation hanging over their heads was delayed as much as possible.

"They have a great Alfredo here," he said, putting his menu down.

"Oh, I'm sure you'd know," she winked at him over hers.

"What's that supposed to mean?"

She put her menu down as well. "You're telling me this isn't where you bring all the ladies you're try to woo?"

"Not at all," he said, not volunteering that this was a go-to second-date spot for the pre-wooed. "And who said this was a date?"

"Touche," she said. "I guess I'm still surprised that Mark Watson grew up to be such a player."

"I think you mean 'smooth-talking Casanova,'" he said. "And I'm not. I'll have you know that according to my therapist I have attachment and abandonment issues, so if I were such a thing it wouldn't be my fault."

"A man who goes to therapy," she said in a playfully shocked tone. "Definitely not the kind of thing one expects from a car guy."

"Jesus, why the fuck wouldn't I be in therapy?" he laughed.

"Fair point," she said. "My longest relationship has been with my therapist."

"I somehow feel both happy and sad for you."

"Same, honestly." She took a drink. "So do you want to talk about why I'm here?"

"Abso-fucking-lutely not," he said with a smile. "I'd like to have a good time tonight, not re-live that nightmare. You can't possibly be eager to do so yourself."

"Most of the time. And that's fine, we don't have to do it now, but we need to talk about it at some point, okay? It's important." She stared at him intently.

"Sure," he said. "But for now, tell me about your life."

***

As they waited for their food, she gave him the short version. She finished high school in Connecticut, where they'd moved after Briarcliff so her Aunt could help them recover, and after years of physical therapy her father could walk again. Slowly, and not for long periods of time, but it was something he was still getting better at. Her mother had thrown herself into taking care of him, and once he was mobile again she latched on to local and on-line communities for mothers who'd lost a child "to violence." Christine provided the quotes herself.

"I get it, I guess," she said. "But it feels like she wears what happened like a badge of honor. If I had a nickel for every time she referred to herself as 'a mother who lost a son,' we'd be rich again." The medical and therapy bills, coupled with her father's inability to work, had made a sizable dent in their finances. After college (Northwestern) she moved to Albuquerque for work, which was in "business intelligence" for a company that "provided insurance solutions in the light industrial and benefits field." Mark didn't know what any of that meant but was too afraid to ask.

"So what about you," she asked, finishing her second glass of wine. "I'll confess that I've looked but you're a hard man to Google."

"By design," he said. "But it was okay. Y'know, after. I was only in the system for a couple of years, and the family I ended up with, Rashawn and Amy, are great." He left out how not great the first few were, or how even less great life in a Newark group home had been. "Until they moved away, I would see David, y'know, Detective Prescott, and his family pretty regularly." It was a generous use of "regularly", and he left out how after the move they'd messaged several times and he'd essentially ghosted them.

"Another Coke, hon?" the waitress asked, appearing at his elbow.

"Sure," he said.

"You sure you don't want anything stronger," Christine said after she left. "Given our impending conversation?"

"I have other vices," Mark winked. "Besides, when you grow up with someone who abused alcohol you tend not to have good associations with it."

"Oh," she said, putting down her glass. "That makes sense. I'm sorry, I wasn't thinking. I could get something else if you--"

"It's fine," Mark interrupted. "I'm past being bothered by other people drinking."

"Good," she said, watching the waitress come back with his drink. "Because I'm going to need at least one more."

***

One more turned into two, which she said was just enough to make things fun.

Mark held his tongue as a flurry of sly responses rushed through his brain.

After dessert, they headed out to his car. "Where to?" he asked. "I'm assuming you got a hotel somewhere?"

"Yeah," she said. "And it sucks. Do you live around here?"

"I do indeed," he said, keeping his tone neutral.

"Then let's go there and get on with it."

Once again, Mark made a supreme effort in keeping his mouth shut.

She can't just keep teeing you up like this without an ulterior motive, right?

He drove them to his "surprisingly spacious" condo, as Christine put it. He was relieved he'd left the place almost clean, but made a mental note to not let her go in the kitchen on account of the dishes in the sink.

"Just you then?" she asked.

"Oh yeah," he said. "After growing up in close quarters and in small spaces, I can't live that roommate life." He waited a moment and then asked "What about you?"

"No, thank god, but my place is much smaller," she said, taking in the living room and its plain white walls sparingly decorated with framed monster and kung-fu movie posters, a scarcity of actual furniture, and his impressive wall of fancy electronics.

"I do some custom restoration work on the side," he said as she moved from the living room to the dining area that Mark used as a library and display area for various statues, models, and toys.

"You weren't kidding about the other vices," she said, waving at the nerdy miscellany and ending at the shelves that held bongs and dab rigs.

"I'll remind you that I have PTSD and those are purely for medical use."

"Smart," she said. "I should look into that. And also becoming a mechanic, apparently."

"It has its perks," he said, feeling the rush of pride and confidence he got when thinking about the stability and security it'd finally brought into his life. "We kept busy during lockdown too, so that was something."

"I'm glad you're doing something that you enjoy," she said, a bit of wistful envy in her voice.

"That's a bonus," he said, steering them back to the living room. "A lot of the time working on stuff is the only way life makes sense. Plus, I'm decent enough with computers to handle all the electronic shit they keep putting in cars now. And I got to do it without having student loans hanging over my head, so I've got that going for me."

"Fuck you and your happy life," she sneered, and then took a deep breath. "So are we going to get to it or what?"

"I mean, I still have a lot of cool shit going on in my life we can talk about."

"Whatever," she said, walking back to the living room "Get me something to drink, if you have any booze. Judging by the smell, I don't want to go rooting around in your kitchen."

"I think I might have something," he said, blushing.

He went to the fridge and, remembering her choice at dinner, poured her a glass of white wine from one of the two boxes he kept in his fridge for company. As he passed through the library, he grabbed his humidor but decided not to bring any glassware. Christine was meandering around the living room and looking through her phone. "Here you go," he said. "And if you'd like to partake, I'm happy to provide for you," nodding down at the humidor.

"What a gentleman," she said. "If that's what it's going to take for us to talk then sure. In the meantime, give me your WiFi so we can have some ambiance." He gave her the info and rolled them a joint while she looked through her music app for something "suitable."

"Oh, this is perfect for reliving the past," she snickered after a few moments. As Mark sealed the joint his sound system came to life, blaring auto-tuned guitar riffs through the room before Timbaland asked what somebody like them was doing in a place like this.

"Jesus Christ," Mark said, taking a hit. "I forgot about this song, and for good reason."

"I can't tell you how many parties I heard this at," she said, tossing her phone onto the couch and taking the proffered joint. She inhaled deep and coughed immediately. "Speaking of high school parties," she said. "It's been forever since I smoked." She handed it back to him and started swaying in place. By the time Katy Perry started singing in the background and the tempo picked up, she was dancing with abandon.

"Come on," she said, beckoning him to join her. "Let's have some fun while we can."

"We can have fun for as long as you want," he said, leaning back, "Right now, I'm just going to enjoy the show."

She rolled her eyes, grabbed his hand and pulled him onto his feet, barely giving him a chance to put the joint down. "Don't be a creep." She drew him in close and took hold of his other hand to get him moving.

"I am not great at this," he said, trying to keep up.

"You're fine," she said. The song slowed and she moved closer, mouthing along as Katy took over the vocals. "*Baby tell me, what's your story, I ain't shy, don't you worry,*" she sang along, holding him with her gaze. He raised an eyebrow at the next line where Katy confessed to flirting (with her eye, no less), and that she wanted to leave with him tonight.

"You already did," he said, discovering that dancing and trying to be witty at the same time was beyond him. She looked away, hopping up and down as the chorus resumed. He joined in and they both started scream-singing along to the chorus .

"*I'll nev-er be the saaaaa-aame, if we ever meet again. Wooooo-n't let you get awaaaaa-ay, if we ever meet again.*"

The tempo slowed again and she let go of his hands, putting her arms around his neck and pulling herself close. As they swayed in place, Katy and Timbaland asked to be kissed all night and never let go, and they figured they'd give it a try.

***

'All night' turned out to be 'a solid 45 minutes.' "Respectfully," he said, "That was a horrible time."

"Excuse me?" she said, raising her head off of his chest to glare at him.

"For music," he laughed, taking another hit from the joint that he'd retrieved from the living room, where he'd also turned off the "Hit Songs of 2010" playlist that had been in the background the entire time they'd been otherwise occupied. Not the best ambiance, but at least he could now say that he'd gotten head while listening to 'All I Do Is Win,' which he figured was on someone somewhere's sexual Bingo card.

"Sorry, the first part of that train of thought was in my head."

"Fucking stoner," she said, taking the joint for herself. "Who would of thought the incredibly delicate young man I dated in high school would turn out to be a pothead car guy. Who also fucks pretty good, turns out."

"I contain multitudes," he deadpanned. "But also...'pretty good?' I give a five-star experience, miss. You clearly haven't read my reviews."

"It was more like two, two and a half," she winked, reaching over him to put the joint in the overflowing ashtray on his bedside table. "Maybe if you'd been able to hang on for a *little* bit longer it would've been three."

"Challenge accepted," he said, rolling her onto her back.

"Mark," she said, a hand up to stop him. "I promise I didn't fuck you so we could talk about what's going on, but we absolutely have to."

"And now is the perfect time, sure," he said sourly, extricating himself from her.

"Mark, come on," she said. "You can't just ignore this."

"I have Avoidant Personality Disorder, so I assure you I can." He stood up and looked for some underwear, deciding that if he was going to talk about when a bunch of people they were close to got murdered he wasn't going to do it with his dick out.

"The only reason that I'm here is that the PI guy told me you could be in danger. Just like last time," she said, sitting up.

"How in the hell would he know that?" It suddenly felt like a fist was squeezing his heart.

"They deal with this stuff for a living, and while that may be totally insane I'm going to assume that he knows what he's talking about. Not to mention how they described how Jack died, something no one else knows about."

Just think, you could have another type of reunion as well.

"All the more reason to stay the fuck away. Even if it is true." He had to concentrate on keeping his hands steady so he could zip and button his pants.

"What about the people that live there now? And what if that thing finds a way to get out? Do you think you, or anyone else, will be safe?"

"We will spread His fire across this town, across the world, and nothing will be able to stop us."

"Fuck's sake," he said, trying to get the memory of what the thing had told him out of his head. "If anything, I should stay the hell away from there. He...or it, whatever the fuck, was trying to get me, specifically, and I'm not going to just hand myself over and let it use me again."

"Then just talk to them! Tell him what I don't know so this thing can actually be over. It's just a conversation! Then at least they can get off my ass." She moved to the edge of the bed, looking for her own underwear.

"I'm so sorry you were inconvenienced," he sneered. "By all means, let me open about the worst thing that happened to me and the horrible things I did so you can be more comfortable. Also, I wouldn't even be in this position if you hadn't given them my fucking name. So thanks for that!"

"This is hard for me too, Mark. You're not the only person who went through it."

"Yeah, but I'm the only person who...no fuck this" he snapped, throwing on a t-shirt. "This was great and all, but I have work in the morning and I'm not going to stay up all night arguing." He picked her bra up and tossed it on the bed.

"Wow," she said, drawing the word out to be as reproachful as possible. "You really *are* good at this. I haven't heard 'I have to get up early' in years. Is that part of the five-star experience? Do I get a little gift bag too?"

"Go fuck yourself," he said, leaving the room so she could get dressed.

He was tidying up his humidor when she came back to the living room. "That's what I like about you, Mark," she said. "You're always *almost* a nice guy. I should've picked up on your total fuckboy vibes from the start."

Not the first time you've heard that, is it champ?

"Don't forget your phone," he said, picking it up.

The screen woke as he touched it and he glanced down at her notifications. Something jumped out at him and he jerked the phone away before she could take it. It was a quick read, and when he was done he tossed the phone at her with a derisive laugh.

"Some people really don't change. You forgot to check in with Travis, by the way. He loves and misses you."

Her fair complexion made her blush even more pronounced. "Fuck you," she said, shoving the phone into her purse. "You're not the only one with attachment issues, you know."

"Well, I guess your problem, as usual, is too many attachments," he said, self-righteousness permitting him to look at her now.

She scowled, and he knew she was embarrassed she'd lost the precious moral high ground. "Talk to those guys, don't talk to them, who gives a shit? I figured, given the chance, you'd want to be a grown up about it. Then again, you were always happy to let other people die as long as it meant you didn't have to take responsibility for anything."

He looked down at the large joint he was rolling so he didn't have to watch her storm out and slam the door.

But is she wrong, though? Is she?

CHAPTER FIVE

"You said it didn't go great?" the Kid asked.

Christine sloshed the ice in her Starbucks and took another sip. Thanks to last night's onslaught of booze, weed, and terrible decisions she couldn't remember either of their names. She wasn't sure why she thought of the younger one as Kid, as they looked close in age, but the "kid in class who was too excited for the field trip" vibes weren't doing him any favors. She'd woken up in the very late morning to his texts asking if she and Mark had talked yet in the weirdest ways possible, the last one being "Hey just checking in to see if you're getting these," followed by an unhinged amount of emojis.

There were no messages from Mark, and even though she hadn't really expected anything she'd held out hope for some kind of apology. She'd have even taken some wild rant about what a bitch she was just so she wouldn't have to be the first one to re-open the conversation.

When she'd stormed out of Mark's last night, she'd come real close to packing her bags and heading to the airport. When Henry sent the text about Mark possibly being in danger she couldn't stop thinking about it, and how the other people who lived there were in danger as well. By the next morning, she was texting Travis to ask if he could spot her the cash to buy a last-minute ticket. And the hotel, if it wasn't too much trouble. As always, she swore she'd pay him back, but also knew he'd never let her follow through on it (as if she realistically could). She hated how easy he made it, but what she hated more was the look he'd give her after she got home and asked about her trip. It'd be genuine, but with the undercurrent of "you couldn't have done it without me" he liked way too much. Especially since he knew she'd repay him in other ways, as was the theme of their situationship. She'd texted him back last night from the Uber, saying she was sorry and she missed him too.

She'd never said "I love you" before and she wasn't going to start now.

When she finally woke up she texted the Kid back that things hadn't gone well, and of course he wrote back right away, saying they were on the way to her hotel to talk. She'd barely had time to throw on leggings and a t-shirt and get a coffee from next door before they arrived. Wanting to avoid feeling like they were negotiating a seedy hotel threesome, she waited for them in the unnervingly sparse and empty lounge in the lobby.

"That's a kind way of putting it," she said.

She'd forgotten how chaotically emotional Mark was, although part of her was impressed how he made it look like he was fine and just the kind of sensitive, in touch with his feelings but kind of vulnerable guy who made you feel safe. She'd initially chalked the hook-up up to trauma wrapped in nostalgia, but in the Uber she remembered his well-practiced deep questions about her life and his unbelievably rapt attention to her answers. He'd been running a full-court press on her, and it was clearly not his first time at bat (or however sports went).

The Black Guy, clearly the teacher on this little field trip, leaned forward. Not teacher, she realized, as the lived-in looking suit, thick-rimmed glasses, close cut hair/beard combo and the patiently stern manner he had was total college professor vibes.

"Have you been able to remember anything from just being back here?" the Professor asked. "Any kind of rituals or strange language that was used? Anything that seemed out of place? Even something mundane could point to a supernatural element we're missing."

"Like I said a thousand times before, no. I was too busy being traumatized while threatened with a gun and a sword. That was out of place enough." She paused, took a drink, and added "I'm still trying to get over how fucked up it is and that this stuff is actually real."

She'd known it'd been heavily assisted by denial, but a big part of her recovery had been telling herself the whole "ghostiness" of it all was something she'd projected on to her memories. She'd gone through an embarrassing Wicca phase in college, the idea being if she knew "magic" she could keep herself safe from other "spirits." When she realized none of what she was doing was having any kind of tangible effect, she'd pivoted to a "I was wrong and confused, that stuff isn't real" stance, leading quickly to the realization of "Oh shit, I need to get into therapy."

The first call from these two had shaken the deliberate fiction that'd been keeping her from constant terror and it only seemed to be getting worse as it was confirmed things like ghosts, haunted houses, and past lives (and whatever the fuck else) were real. So real, even, there were people who dealt with it for a living.

"They are," the Professor said in a tone suggesting this wasn't the first time he'd had to ease someone into this reality. "It's just that there are too many variables at play to narrow it down, and anything could really help us out."

"Fucking crazy," she muttered. "But that sucks, and I'm sorry I don't remember anything else." It was a lie, but after how upset Mark had gotten last night she decided it was best not to volunteer anything else. "But please don't start telling me about other stuff that's real also. This took long enough to forget."

"Generally speaking, the less you know the better," the Professor said, giving her a smile. She nodded in appreciation, but then realized how intent his gaze was on her. He was sincerely concerned, she was sure it, but now she could feel his gaze on her like a physical force. This was a guy who not only deals with supernatural shit, but also PI shit and could probably spot a lie a thousand miles away. While he'd been nothing but cordial while picking her up from the airport and driving her to the hotel, she didn't want to feel that invisible pressure on her for much longer.

"Good to know," she said, standing up. "I wish I could do more, but I guess that's it."

The Kid and Henry (the gaze had shaken her into remembering) looked at each other before getting to their feet as well. Henry's right hand dropped down into his pocket and there was a clink of metal, like keys hitting loose change. The Kid glanced over at him, somehow radiating even more nervous energy. It was clear they weren't done with this, and she realized she was stuck in their orbit until her flight later that evening.

Henry sighed, taking his hand out of his pocket and extending it for a handshake. "Thank you for your time, Ms. Baker. I appreciate you coming out here for this."

"Sure thing," she said, taking his hand delicately and for just a quick shake before stepping back. "Good luck, I guess? I hope this gets taken care of and people don't get hurt."

"I hope so too," he nodded solemnly. The Kid's nerves seemed back under control now and the two of them headed for the exit. She turned back to the elevator and then she felt her phone buzz in her pocket.

It was Mark, texting to ask if they could talk.

She stopped and looked over her shoulder and saw Henry and the Kid were in deep discussion and hadn't made it to the door yet. She knew she could just get on the elevator, not write Mark back, watch a shitty movie on cable, and just get on the plane later.

Henry looked over at her, like he'd sensed her wavering. They locked eyes and he gave her that intense stare again.

"You are so fucking stupid," she said to herself. "Hey," she called, holding up her phone. "He wants to talk."

***

"Are you fucking kidding me?"

It was the welcome she'd expected from him once he realized she wasn't alone. They'd headed right over to Mark's place after she changed clothes, figuring if she was going to confront a boy about demons she should at least look cute.

"I wish," she said. "Can we just do this, please?"

With a defeated look, Mark opened the door to let them all in. "This is harassment, dude," Mark said as Henry walked by.

"Oh my god, settle down. You said you wanted to talk, and I'm going to tell them everything you'd say to me so I don't have to deal with it anymore either." She narrowed her eyes pointedly at him. "Unless you were lying and just wanted me to come over for another reason?" That reeled in his indignation.

"Look, I...," he started to tell the detectives, but he kept glancing over at her. "I'm sorry, can you give us a moment?" he said to them, nodding towards her. "If that's okay?" She gave him a nod, a little pleased with herself he was so rattled.

"Whatever you need to do," Henry said, sitting down on the sofa. The Kid was immediately enamored with what he could see of Mark's "library" and made his way over there. Mark nodded to the patio doors off the kitchen and she followed. She leaned against the railing as he closed the sliding glass door and looked back with guilt smeared all over his face.

"I'm sorry things got so...out of hand last night," he said.

"In what way? The sex or assuming I'm some kind of cheating bitch?"

"I never said you were a bitch."

"It was implied. So which is it?"

"Well, not the sex for sure," he gave her a little smile, which retreated as soon as he saw how unamused she was. "The snapping at you thing. And making assumptions about what I saw on your phone, which I probably shouldn't have looked at in the first place."

"A good start."

"Oh, come on. It's perfectly reasonable to not want to talk about horrible shit from my past with strangers."

"I'm not a stranger. I am, in fact, one of the only people still alive who also went through it. Instead of wanting to face that, you put all of your efforts into fucking me and then getting rid of me as fast as possible."

He slumped. "Okay, that's fair. But I wasn't *just* trying to fuck you. I'm sorry if I made you feel that way. I'm genuinely happy to see you and I wanted to know about your life."

"It's whatever," she said, clocking the conditionality of the 'apology.' "I'm just mad I fell for your whole...thing," she said, gesturing at him. "Just tell me, are you going to be straight with these guys or not? They clearly need a lot more than I can offer them."

"Sounded like you told them plenty," he grumbled. "What did you leave out?"

"I didn't tell them about the whole...past lives aspect and how it related to everything."

He groaned, running a hand through his hair. "Fuck, so just the worst part then."

The worst part for you, she wanted to say, but shrugged instead. "It may not even come up. It could be something else that gets them to leave us alone. I wouldn't try bullshitting them, though, because I'm pretty sure Henry will know if you're lying."

"What, through magic?" Mark said.

"Probably. Maybe. Either way he seems like the real deal"

"I was just hoping more people wouldn't find out that I'm...y'know?"

"I get it," she said, trying to push away how angry she was so he'd feel safe enough to open up. "But...I don't know, maybe they can fix it somehow?"

"I doubt it." He slumped against the railing, looking into the condo with a wave of anxiety cresting over his face.

"No use waiting," she said, taking him by the arm and leading him inside like the petulant child he was emulating.

"Those are some cool ass Gundams, dude," the Kid said, scurrying after them. "Do you have a favorite series, because--"

"I don't know, man," Mark said, waving him off. "I just think robots are cool."

"Right. Sorry," he said, following them back to the living room where Henry waited.

"So what do you want to know?" Mark asked as they sat down. "I think Christine, and probably the internet, told you all the high points."

"We covered a lot of ground, but I'd rather just hear it directly from you. Just start from the beginning, and try include as many details as possible," Henry said, and then added "I know a charm that can help you relax and sharpen your memory, if it helps."

"Are you for really-real with this stuff?" Mark said, squirming in his chair. "I get there's got to be something legit going on, given what we saw, but actual spells and stuff just seems..." he trailed off.

"I get that, Mr. Wa...Mark. Just an offer, although we may have to do some casting later. With your permission, of course." Henry's patient veneer seemed to crack a little, most likely from finally being this close to answers and Mark still avoiding them.

Mark shrugged, and then threw his arms up in the air with a laugh. "Shit, why not? Let's see some magic."

"It's not going to look like much," Henry said. "We're just going to be talking." His voice took on a kind of low echo, and Christine couldn't tell if it was real or imagined. "Just look at my eyes and hear the sound of my voice as you think about what happened." The echo rolled through the whole next sentence, and for a second her vision tunneled as she watched Henry's mouth move inaudibly. It took a little effort to look away, but it was clear this swas all too real.

She looked at Mark instead and watched his face go slack, his mouth trying to match what Henry was whispering but failing miserably. "It's fine," Henry said, his voice thankfully returning to normal in every sense of the word. "It takes a second for it to really take hold."

Mark slumped back in his chair, rubbing his face with both hands. "Okay," he said. "That was...impressive." He put his hands down and looked around the room. "And clearly something is happening to me now, because--" the calm expression on his face skipped a beat, and then halfheartedly returned. "--yeah, I remember a lot now."

"Let's get to it, then," Henry said, laying his phone out with a recording app open as the Kid took a notebook out of his bag.

***

He told them everything, including stuff Christine had never fully known. He didn't give many specifics about the murders themselves, which was good as she wasn't sure she could take a vivid retelling of her family being attacked. When Mark was finished he let out a long exhale and wiped away the tears that started flowing almost as soon as he began. He looked over and gave her a shrug and a smile that said 'What a surprise, Mark Watson is crying again.'

"Oof," he chuckled, voice now full of the emotion he'd been suppressing. "That was not fun."

Henry looked over at the notes the Kid had taken and nodded in satisfaction. "First of all, I know talking about all that was very hard, for both of you, so thank you." He nodded at her. "Give me just a second to confer with Martin, if you don't mind."

"Confer away," Mark said in a close to normal tone of voice.

The two detectives nodded and then scurried out of the room like excited school boys. After they were out of sight, Christine leaned forward and put a hand on Mark's knee. "There's no way that kid is a colleague, right?" She whispered, hoping it'd calm him down.

Mark gave a sharp laugh as he finished wiping his eyes. "Right? He's an intern, at best." He smiled, his emotional storm letting up a bit. "I hope this didn't freak you out too much."

"Just the expected amount, but I guess it'll help in the long run. You know what they say, doing the right thing is never easy."

"I'm sure that will help me get to sleep tonight," he grumbled.

"For real," she nodded. "I feel like I haven't cared about 'the right thing' this much in my entire life."

They sat in silence for a few moments, and then Mark sat up and tried to get a look around the corner where Henry and Martin disappeared. "It does not seem great they're taking so long," he said.

"It could mean they've got answers," she said, unconvinced.

A couple of minutes later the two detectives came back into view. Their expressions were those of having answers but not really liking them.

"So," Henry said, sitting down. "What you've said, especially about the past life connection, has definitely narrowed down our options."

"I believe," Henry said, being obviously cautious in his wording, "what we're dealing with is demonic in nature."

"Fantastic," Mark said, nodding sarcastically. "It's just demonic possession. That's all, huh?"

"Not possession, per se" Henry said. "I believe what was, and still is, in the house is a demonic entity of some kind. The way Corwin was compelled to make his victims look into the flames to see something, the worshiping nature of his speech, and the ability to extend its...attentions while still being bound to a spot are part of a pretty clear pattern."

"Well I'm glad I could be so helpful," Mark said, getting to his feet. "So if we're done here...?"

Henry grimaced and waved Mark back down. "It's not that simple."

"Why would it be?" Mark rolled his eyes and dropped back onto the couch.

"There's not a lot of consensus about past lives in my line of work," Henry said. "They can be remembered, and at times affect the current one when there's unfinished business or a supernatural encounter. Clearly Corwin had one, and that's how you've ended up with this connection."

"Connection is a way to put it," Mark said, looking away.

"I know, but I'll just say you two are different people by every possible measurement and leave it at that. It does, however, leave us with a fairly significant problem. In some ways, demons are like radiation. They leave traces wherever they go, and it can have lasting effects. Everything Corwin did, and especially the sacrifices he did in its name, exposed him quite a bit. And that's without knowing how long this entity had been affecting him before the killings started."

"So I have cancer," Mark said. "Demon cancer, no less."

"In a sense," Henry said. "When I put the charm on you I could sense demonic energy still with you." Out of the corner of her eye, Christine saw Martin look in confusion instead of just nodding intently as he had been. "It's how it was able to control you. And, if it gets more of its strength back, be able to do it again."

Mark shot out of his chair. "No. No fucking way. Cut it out, whatever it takes. I'm not going through that again." He paced through the room in sudden and total mania. "Get rid of it, and if you can't I'll throw myself in front of a train or something."

"Whoa," Martin said. "Suicide's never the answer."

"Shut up, intern!" Mark snarled, lunging at him. "You may've heard all my disgusting shit but you have no *idea* what it was like!" Martin leapt back, almost losing his balance.

Mark turned and started to pace frantically, rubbing his hands together like he was trying to get them clean. "It used me to kill all those people, and made sure I remembered all of it! I'm not going to let it take me again. No way. I'd rather die than be a killer for it again."

"It's okay," Henry said, moving between Mark and the rest of them with his arms wide to signal he wasn't a threat. "We can fix this."

Mark turned away, fingers clawing through his hair. "Shit. Shit, shit, shit. It's going to be bad, isn't it?" He looked back at Henry, his voice now soft and childlike. "I'm going to have to go back there, aren't I?"

Henry nodded in confirmation and apology. "I'm afraid so."

Mark dropped to his knees and screamed at the top of his lungs, sending Christine out of her seat and back a few steps before she realized she'd moved. The scream petered out into a low howl, and Mark rubbed his face with both palms, smearing fresh tears and snot away.

"Okay," he said, getting to his feet. "Let's get this thing out of me."

CHAPTER SIX

Henry explained it wasn't that simple, but assured them this was one of their specialties, leaving out his own equally horrific entanglements with demonic forces.

"Some demons," he explained once everyone had re-settled, "grow in power through various forms of worship, and human sacrifice is an incredibly potent one. Corwin's acts and eventual conversion of the other boy, Darren, gave it massive amounts of power. Darren's suicide in the house later was an even more powerful sacrifice, and it was probably commanded by the demon so it could sustain itself over the years. It also gave Darren the ability to take control of you."

"Because Corwin's soul, my soul, was full of demon cancer," Mark said matter-of-factly. His outbursts had worn him out, and now he held his head in his hands and stared off into space.

"Exactly," Henry said, not wanting to quibble with the terminology.

"Not all the murders happened in the house," Christine said. She'd gone and refilled her Starbucks cup with wine during their break, and when she returned she sat on the couch as far away from Mark as possible. "What about their souls or whatever? Are they..."

"They aren't tied to the demon, no," Henry said, sparing her from directly asking about her brother. "The people killed outside of the house were done in its name, though. Still a sacrifice, but not as potent. More than likely just enough to wake it up and let it start building up power again."

"And it made me bring all of them," Mark waved weakly toward Christine, "to the house. So it could get itself a real meal."

Henry nodded. "That's what it still wants. If it gets powerful enough, it'll be able to use the sacrificed souls to do its bidding."

"Jesus," Christine said, and she and Mark looked at each other for the first time since his outburst. "That's how many?"

"Six," Mark said without a pause.

"Eventually," Henry continued, "it'll be strong enough to send them off the property to start gathering more, not to mention affect Mark again."

"And that'll happen when, precisely?"

"I don't know, so it's best to get started right away. Everything being concentrated at spot does make things easier, as I can banish it and break those spirits free all at once."

"And I'd have to be there too, of course," Mark said.

"We could try banishing it here, but there's no guarantee it'll be drawn back to the house. It could just as easily find a way to attach itself to something, or someone, else. It's your call, though."

Mark shook his head. "I'm not taking any chances. I can't go through this again."

"Okay then." Henry ran a hand over his beard before he moved on to the other bad news. "Before we do that, we need to figure out where this presence came from. It'd have to be some kind of prolonged contact or major incident."

"It's not just an evil house or whatever?" Christine asked.

"If that were the case, this would have been over when the house burned down. That's what's been throwing me." He didn't like to project anything but confidence in front of a client, but he knew how much he'd need to impress the importance of the next step so Mark didn't freak out again.

"I don't remember anything else," Mark said with exasperation. "Just what Darren showed me and the flashes of Corwin's life at the end."

"I figured as much. You weren't going to be shown anything you could use against it. To find out I'll have to go deeper into your mind this time, all the way back into Corwin's memories."

"Oh," Martin piped up. "I've done that before. It's...fun. Well, fine. You'll be fine." Henry looked over his shoulder pointedly at him and he quickly went back to typing.

"Don't oversell it," Mark grumbled.

"There's no danger," Henry said, forcing a smile. "I've done it numerous times and Martin's was a unique circumstance. In fact, we have everything we need for it in the car." He stood up. "If you'll excuse me. Martin?" He looked up. "Can you give me a hand?" Henry said through clenched teeth.

"Uh, sure." Martin said in obvious discomfort as he got to his feet.

"I'm going to need more wine," Christine said, heading into the kitchen as Henry and Martin went to the car.

Halfway there, Henry stopped Martin with a hand on his arm. "We need to work on your people skills," he said, which was the kindest way he could think to put it.

Martin winced. "That bad, huh? I'm sorry, you know I babble when I get nervous."

"You need to be less nervous, then. If you can't project confidence to the client then they can get skittish. And Mark's as skittish as it gets." Henry kept walking, hoping his tone wasn't too harsh.

"For sure, for sure," Martin said, trailing after him. When he caught up with Henry at the trunk of the Gremlin, he continued. "So I was wondering...you said you could sense the presence in Mark from doing the charm, but I thought you could only do something like that with a more intense connection, so--"

"Look," Henry said, pulling out one of the several bags tucked into the hidden compartment in the trunk and thrusting it at him. "I may have taught you everything you know about magic, but I haven't taught you everything *I* know, got it?"

Martin audibly gulped. "Oh. Okay. I'm so--"

"Save it," Henry said, the irritation he had with him since his conversation with John boiling over. "And while we're at it, do *not* talk to my kids about magic again. They are to be as far away from this as possible. Clear?" He walked back towards the condo without waiting for a response. After a long pause he heard Martin hurry to catch up.

"Yes, sir," he said in a quavering voice making Henry feel like he'd stepped on a puppy's tail. "I'm sorry. Really. It won't happen again."

"I know," Henry said, guilt now far outweighing the thrill of laying into someone you thought deserved it. "Just be better, okay?"

"For sure," Martin said, relief creeping into his voice. "Will do."

When they came back inside he saw Christine had filled her cup to nearly overflowing and Mark was rolling himself a joint. He looked up at Henry just as he was about to lick it shut and said, "Is this okay?"

"I mean, I'd prefer my family not smell it on me when I get home," Henry said, taking off his jacket and laying it on the back of a chair. "My kids would never let me hear the end of it."

"For later, then." Mark licked and sealed the joint before putting it back in the humidor.

Henry rolled up his sleeves and motioned towards the table in the kitchen. "We need to set up a circle, just to make sure nothing gets loose."

"I'm so glad that's a possibility," Mark said, walking into the kitchen and pulling out a chair. He nodded at Christine and said in a low voice. "Does she need to be here? Especially if there's a chance something could happen."

"They're my ride," Christine called from the living room. "And I'd kind of feel like shit Ubering back to my hotel after talking you into this."

"Fair enough," Mark said, and he and Martin began moving furniture out of the way while Henry sifted through the vials in his bag for the one with the most potency. Once they got Mark into the center seat, Henry took out the large wet-erase marker and began to plot out the circle while adding various glyphs and warding symbols. "Don't worry," he said, catching Mark's concerned look. "A little Windex and it comes right off." He started writing and then added, "You do have a vacuum, right? That'll help with the salt-mixture cleanup."

"Despite appearances, yes," Mark said, agitation growing. Henry considered letting him smoke up anyway, but figured it'd be best not to chance anything. Once the circle was prepared, Henry got to his feet with a groan and a flare of pain from his bum knee. Martin signaled from outside the circle he was ready, and Henry moved behind Mark's chair and laid his hands gently on his shoulders.

"If all goes well," Henry said, patting Mark on the shoulder, "you'll feel like you woke up from a dream."

"Did you hear the part where I dreamed about my body being used for murder?" Mark said, taking a deep breath. "Am I supposed to relax or something?"

"That'd help," Henry said, closing his eyes and reciting the spell to himself from memory.

"Well, I don't think there's much of a c--"

"--ome on, Corwin! Keep up, or I'm going to think you don't care about getting your pecker wet," DiBenzo called back to him over the chaos in the street. Justin pushed his way through them, still not used to the crowded and hectic Calcutta streets, even after six months of being stationed here.

They'd been told helping the British keep their hold on India and keeping the Japs from getting further into China was vital, especially since the fall of Burma, but they hadn't seen any action at all. Not that he was eager to, but he'd expected he'd be "doing his part" on the front lines, not helping the Brits keep their hold over a people who clearly didn't want them there. He thought the occasional trip into Manhattan with his folks when he was a kid would have prepared him for anything, but this was like nothing he'd ever imagined. Children and adults lined the streets begging for food, while the flow of factory workers employed by the Brits (mostly Burmese refugees) both ignored and surrounded them.

He'd started hanging out with DiBenzo because he was the only one in the unit also from Jersey, but that was where their similarities ended. DiBenzo was allegedly a Catholic, but the way he drank and whored around made Justin think he had a different definition than his. Burly and loud, DiBenzo seemed to enjoy Justin's nervous and proper demeanor, dragging him to bars, brothels, and other raucous joints on nearly every one of their weekend passes. This time was no different, and now he was dragging him deeper into the city, claiming he knew of the perfect "professional" who could help Justin with what DiBenzo called "a terminal case of virgin-itis." Justin had known confiding in him had been a bad idea, but he couldn't hold his liquor as well as Benzo could. This often led to tearful confessions of fears and insecurities being used to "playfully" tease Justin later.

"I'm coming, I'm coming," he said, mumbling an apology to the women in Benzo's wake he'd roughly shoved past.

"You will be, Corwin," Benzo said, reaching back and pulling him up along side him with a thick arm. "These Indian chicks are expertly trained, y'see? They got this thing, a karma-suit-a-ra, and they get all bendy and flexible. I was able to bend this one around like a damn pretzel last time. I'll show you how its done."

"Great," Justin said, terror creeping up his spine. It was bad enough he was being dragged to what was probably a disgusting brothel, but apparently Benzo was going to be supervising the whole affair. Here he was *thinking his first time was going to be on his wedding night, not being watched over by the guy who regularly farted into his pillow.*

Benzo yanked him off to the side and into an alley that seemed to appear out of nowhere. They stumbled down it for a few paces, and then Benzo stopped to look around as he emptied the bottle he'd been carrying in his other hand.

"Are we lost?" Justin asked, praying in his head as hard as he could. "Because I'm sure we'll get another pass some time, and they're playing--"

"Nah, shut up," Benzo said, tossing the bottle away. "I just needed to get my bearings." He lurched forward again, dragging Justin through a maze of narrow alleys where suspicious and frightened eyes watched them from behind curtains and corners.

"I don't think we're supposed to be here," Justin said, discomfort multiplying. "The guidebook said we should avoid--"

"Screw the guidebook," Benzo said, coming to a stop and looking back and forth between two doors on opposite sides of the alley. "Here we go," he said, deciding on one and proceeding to pound on it with his fist.

"This, ah, doesn't look like a...well, you know."

"Because it ain't a 'y'know,'" Benzo winked. "I never said she was a professional. Just a really talented amateur. I followed her home after I scooped her up last time because I knew I'd want seconds." Somehow, Justin realized, this had gotten worse. Before he could say anything, the door opened a crack and the sliver of a face peered at them. The eye went wide with surprise upon seeing Benzo, who just grinned and shouldered his way into the house. The middle aged Indian man who had opened the door tumbled to the ground, and there was a shriek from further in the apartment sounding like a young woman's.

"Benzo!" Justin called after him as the bigger man staggered down the hallway towards it. Justin knelt down to try to help the man up, but he was screaming at him in whatever language they spoke and flailing his arms trying to get Justin away. "I'm sorry!" he said, hoping the clasped hands and bowing conveyed the right message. Did they even bow here? He asked himself as he hurried in the direction DiBenzo had lumbered.

The place was nicer than Justin would have imagined from the outside, and larger too. He ducked his head into the rooms off the hallway until he came to the end and rounded the corner. The room looked like a mixture of a bedroom and living room, with banners and other decorations on the walls. Benzo stood in the middle, hand gripping the upper arm of a girl who couldn't be older than twenty. She yelled again, pelting Benzo with kicks and punches he was laughing off.

"She's a real spitfire," Benzo said, a feral glaze filling his eyes. "Let me loosen her up for you and then you can have your turn."

"No," Justin said, waving his hands so emphatically he surprised himself. "Let's just go, okay? Let's g--"

"Go!" the man, the girl's father or guardian or whatever, yelled in heavily accented English as he pushed past Justin. "You go now! Get out!" It wasn't the smaller man's yells drawing Benzo's focus but the large butcher knife he'd picked up on his way.

"Look," Benzo said, letting her go and turning his attention to the older man. "Just shut up and--"

The man slashed at Benzo's out stretched hand. Benzo tried to grab it but the knife cut deep into the side of his palm.

"Motherfucker!" Benzo snapped, jerking his hand back and flinging droplets of blood across the room. The man advanced but Benzo, who loved to "mix it up," slid forward and landed a crushing jab into the smaller man's face. He gave a surprised gurgle, barely audible over the girl's screaming. "You fucking cut me," Benzo said, smacking the knife out of the man's loose grip before grabbing the front of his shirt and decking him again.

Justin saw the girl start to lunge forward but he beat her to it, shoving Benzo from behind with the effect of a gnat trying to move a rhino. "DiBenzo!" Justin yelled, in as close a tone to their Sergeant as he could muster. "Let's go!"

Without even looking, Benzo shoved Justin back, sending him stumbling into the far wall. Justin lost his footing in a tangle of rugs and fell on his ass. The impact on the wall shook the trinkets and shelves on it, and then the contents of one fell on his head. Tiny statues and other knickknacks pelted him, and then a long, thin object bounced off his skull and landed in his lap. It was a cane, Justin realized, wrapped in beads and other decorative papers like it was a museum piece of some sort.

Justin went to toss it aside, but as soon as he wrapped his hand around it he felt a jolt like he'd put his hand on a hot stove. It clattered to the ground next to him, and Justin realized despite the chaos and screaming he couldn't keep his eyes off it.

He picked it up, ready to toss it away if it was somehow still hot, but it had subsided to a dull heat spreading up Justin's arm and settling right behind his eyes. He stood up, hand gripping the cane tighter, and the silver top of the cane, an elegant, curving sculpture of fire, caught the light and flashed into his eye. Benzo shoved the girl to the ground and then slammed the man into the wall again, even though he already looked like he was unconscious.

Justin shoved Benzo again, the cane still in his hand. He should probably drop it but he didn't really want to.

"What the hell are you doing, Corwin? I'm trying to help you out here," Benzo said, poking Justin in the chest so hard it pushed him back against the wall again.

"Let's just go," Justin said, a panicked whine creeping into his voice.

"You take your little souvenir and go. I'm not done yet," Benzo grinned like an animal, turning back to the bleeding and unconscious man. The girl cowered in the corner, her path to the only door blocked by the crowd of men. She'd stopped screaming and now was looking at Justin in abject terror, as if this was his fault. His hand squeezed the cane hard, the heat from it rising again.

"Hey!" Justin snapped, his voice louder. "I said let's go!"

Benzo turned back to him again, all traces of amusement gone. "The fuck you say?"

As Benzo took a step forward, Justin adjusted his grip on the cane. His thumb had moved up against the base of the silver top and he could feel a little button there. Not thinking about it, Justin flicked it and then reached over with his other hand, grabbed the top, and pulled it free from the cane. There was another gleaming flash of light, and then Justin swung the piece of metal from the inside of the cane upward with a nervous yell.

Benzo stopped.

They both looked down as the bottom half of Benzo's tie fell to the ground. Before it touched the floor a gush of red sprung forth from the line across his lower chest.

"What?" Benzo said, dropping down on one knee, hands moving to keep as much of the viscera starting to ooze out of him in place. Justin backed up, hitting the wall. He scooted sideways along the wall, his feet trying to move him further from the blood gushing from DiBenzo's chest and stomach. The girl started shrieking again, and the man began to stir. When he raised his head and opened his eyes as much as the swelling would allow he let out a scream of his own.

"Shut up!" Justin yelled, and as he did Benzo began to let out a slow, worried moan.

"I said shut up!" Justin screamed again. He swung the thing in his right hand again and it slashed across Benzo's face, taking his nose and several teeth off this time.

A sword, Justin realized. It's a sword hidden in a cane.

Benzo's moan had turned into wet flapping as his jaw opened wider than it should, now held in place by just the meat of one of his cheeks. His tongue lolled out aimlessly and then he fell forward. The girl was still wailing and the man stood up, holding out his hands to Justin as he got up on his knees. "No!" he shouted. "You give! Bad thing, very bad!"

Justin clenched the sheath and the hilt of the blade tighter as it felt like a blaze was erupting from inside them. No, Justin thought, Not give.

Mine.

He backed toward the door and the man crawled towards him, hands still reaching out for it. Justin swung the sheath at him, smacking away his greedy, grabbing little hands.

"No!" Justin roared again, stumbling into the hallway. He turned and ran toward the door, absentmindedly flicking what blood he could off the blade before sliding it home without even having to think about it.

He barreled out into the alley, weakly trying to pull the door shut behind him. When that failed he took off running and turned the first corner he came to. He slowed, trying to look nonchalant as he walked with the cane. The bottom of it tapped against the street, and Justin felt himself leaning into it like it had always been a part of him.

***

"Fuck you," Mark called from the bathroom in between bouts of vomiting and dry heaving. "Waking up from a dream my ass, dude!" He retched again and Henry headed back into the kitchen, where Christine was leaning against the wall and twirling hair around her fingers at an alarming pace.

"I feel like my confidence in your abilities goes down a little every time we see each other," she said, turning her attention to him.

"I'm sorry," he said, trying to keep his tone neutral. "This keeps becoming more and more complex, but I'm confident we know everything we need to."

"See, I just didn't think it'd take this long for us to get there though," she said, walking towards the kitchen. She stopped right before crossing the barrier of the circle still drawn on the tile. She sighed and turned around. "I don't need another drink that badly," she said.

"No shit," Mark said, coming out of the bathroom and wiping his mouth and chin with a towel. "Let me guess: my demon cancer is terminal."

"We can still exorcise this from you," Henry said, remembering to use his calming tones. "All this means is we're dealing with a presence a little more powerful than I thought. It's challenging, but not insurmountable."

"I do so love a challenge," Mark snapped, walking past Henry and into the living room. "I'm absolutely smoking that joint now, by the way."

"That's fair," Henry nodded.

Martin came back inside the condo and headed for the sink. "For the record," he said to Mark, "your dumpster is very hard to find." Mark had yelled for them to "get that shit out of here" while he was running to the bathroom after waking up. Once they'd quickly swept up the salt mixture from the edges of the circle, Martin had volunteered to take it outside.

"Sorry it was so *challenging*," Mark said, passing the joint to Christine next to him.

Martin looked about to snap back but Henry waved him off. "It's alright. You've got to remember most people aren't used to this," Henry said, bringing Martin back into the kitchen with him and talking low enough so Mark and Christine couldn't hear. "Even if they've had an encounter."

Before Martin could respond, Mark hollered "You're scrubbing that off my floor, right?"

Martin nodded to Henry in annoyed understanding.

"Now," Henry said. "I've been down on my hands and knees enough today, so I'll spray while you wipe. Deal?"

With many hands making less work, the two of them had all traces of the supernatural off the floor by the time Mark and Christine had stopped smoking. "Are we good to talk?" Henry asked, walking into the now-hazy room.

"I thought you didn't want your clothes to get smelly," Mark said. The anger had left his voice, but there was still an edge to it.

"I'll manage," Henry said, a little grateful for the second-hand smoke so his own irritation wouldn't start showing.

"So what's the prognosis, doc?" Mark said when Henry sat down.

"Like I said, we're still on track, and I'm sorry the memory was so jarring. It takes a very strong presence to project like that, even with you still being connected to it." Henry said. "So this demon was bound to the blade at some point, and powerful enough it could latch on to Justin that fast. You said shortly after he got home he killed his parents, and disposing of their bodies in the furnace freed it from the blade and let it take up residence there. Despite the fuel from the murders ten years ago, it still didn't have the strength to escape when the house was destroyed. That means not only did it take residency in the ground, but it's more powerful than your average demon."

Mark smiled "I've always been a fan of being above average. So what does that mean for us now?"

"It means I'm going to have to head back to the office and get some more powerful gear. Do you know where the cane ended up after everything?"

Mark shrugged. "Last I saw it I was using it to lock my high school bully's demon-possessed corpse in a murder furnace. Which is not a sentence I ever expected to say."

"It's a sentence no one should say," Christine added. "Half those things shouldn't even exist."

"And yet here we are," Mark said, throwing his hands up in amused exasperation.

"Okay," Henry said, trying to regain their attention. "With the house burned down around it--"

"Plus it exploded," Christine interjected.

"The furnace, not the house," Mark added.

"Guys," Henry said, having to dip into his angry Dad tone.

"Okay, okay," Mark said. "So when are we doing this?"

"As soon as possible, so once we get back from the city with supplies. Are you good with that?"

"I absolutely am not," Mark said. "But at the same time, knowing the full extent of this fucked-up-edness, plus the fact I might be used as a murder-puppet again, is quite motivating. So tonight it is."

"Good," Henry nodded, getting to his feet. "Ms. Baker, we can drop you by your hotel on the way?"

"He's so formal," Christine said to Mark.

"It's what you like to see in a magic, demon-hunting exorcist," he replied with a solemn nod.

"Christine," Henry said with a pointed look.

"Right," she said, looking over at Mark. "I'm gonna hang out for a bit, if that's okay?"

"Hundred percent," Mark nodded.

"I'll text you when we're on our way back," Henry said, picking up his bag and heading for the door with Martin close at his heels. He was more than happy to leave those two do what was needed to process everything that'd been dumped in their laps.

Trauma bonds were a hell of a thing after all.

CHAPTER SEVEN

"So who is he?" Mark asked after they'd finished. "Travis, I mean."

It was hard to remember who initiated, but he was sure they'd started making out before Professor and the Kid (as Christine called them) had left the parking lot. He stopped before their clothes came off to ask if she was still mad at him, and she rolled her eyes and told him to shut up. This time they hadn't made it to the bedroom, just stayed on the couch and fucked so intensely Mark forgot the impending horror looming over him for a while.

"He's just a guy," Christine said. She was laying her head on Mark's chest, and he had his arm around her to keep her from rolling off the inconveniently narrow couch.

Mark made skeptical noise.

"What does that mean?" she asked.

"I mean, if he's not family or a close friend, then why is he saying 'I love you?' Just a little curious, that's all." He was more than just curious but he hoped it didn't show.

She glared at him, and Mark was worried he'd kicked off another fight.

The annoyed look faded and she shrugged. "He's just a guy. He's very interested in me and I'm..."

"Not?" Mark added after the pause.

"Cautious. He's a nice guy, nothing really wrong with him, but it's just...whatever. We spend time together, go places and stuff. It's nice, I guess."

"And do you, y'know?" He raised his eyebrows in a not so subtle manner.

She paused for long enough a 'No' would be unbelievable.

"Sometimes. Not often. But don't worry, you're *much* better than he is." She said in a deeply condescending tone, as she patted him on the chest.

He narrowed his eyes. "That's not what this is about. I just don't want to get in the middle of something. I've done that plenty." He'd lost track of the number of times he was told by women he was looking to "reconnect" with that they had new boyfriends who didn't want her to talk to him.

"I bet."

There was a pause and then he said, "I'm going to go out on a limb here, and stop me if I'm wrong, but would there be an age-gap element to this non-romance romance you have?"

"Not really," she said, blushing and somehow making her look even prettier.

"Not a no. What are we talking, twenty years? Fifteen?"

"No!" she snapped, and then mumbled something indistinct.

"What was that?" He held his free hand up to his ear.

She glared at him and said. "Ten years is not a big deal."

"Ha!" he barked, raising his hand and pointing his forefinger in the air.

"Like you haven't chased younger women before," she said, sitting up.

"That's fair," he said, again worried he'd fucked things up again. "But," he couldn't resist adding, "Ten years younger would be a crime. But I'm just teasing. We both have our issues, no judgment."

"Good," she said. She bent down to pick up her bra and then thought better of it. "Y'know what? I'm going to take a shower, sober up a little bit, and then you can take me back to my hotel."

"I said I was sorry," he said.

Way to fuck things up again, Romeo.

"I'm not mad," she said, shimmying the rest of the way out of her skirt. "I just need to pack, change clothes, and check out. Then we can head over to Briarcliff."

"What do you mean 'we?'" he asked as he followed her to the bathroom.

"My flight doesn't leave until this evening. I'm not going to just sit around in the airport waiting for some text saying 'Devil killed, thumbs-up emoji'."

"He said it's going to be dangerous." Mark grabbed her arm lightly and turned her to face him. "You don't have to do this."

She took his face in her hands and looked at him intently. "I don't *have* to do anything, but I have the incredibly stupid urge to make sure this thing is actually finished. I don't want another text in ten years about all this. Besides, this thing killed my brother and crippled my Dad, so I'd really like to see it get destroyed." She pulled his head down and gave him a quick kiss. "I'll leave some hot water for you."

"We coul--" he started, but her head immediately shook.

"No, the logistics never work. Plus, it's my last chance to talk myself out of this." She let him go and then closed the bathroom door in his face.

"This could be my last night on Earth," he called out. "*Our* last night on Earth, even."

"I'll take my chances," she yelled back as the shower started running.

***

After she packed, changed, and checked out they had time for a late lunch at one of the chain places always lurking around hotels, malls, and airports. She'd been quiet the whole time, and their eatin' good was fraught with uncomfortable silences in the neighborhood.

"Are we okay?" he said when they got back in the Jeep. "I hope you're not regretting...y'know."

She looked at him askance and then smiled. "Yeah, it's fine. And I'm not having regrets or anything." She paused, and then said. "That's a lie. I have lots of regrets, but they're mostly about how I act when things get crazy. Sex isn't really the cure-all you think it's going to be in the moment."

"Ah," he said, starting the car. "I just hope I didn't make it worse."

No more than you already have, you mean.

"You didn't, so don't worry about it, okay?" She smiled at him and he smiled back, knowing he'd absolutely worry about it.

The rest of the drive was quiet, and when they crossed into Cedar Ridge he gripped the steering wheel tighter, not realizing he was doing it until she asked if he was okay.

"Not even a little bit," he said. "I haven't been back here since I collected my stuff from my Uncle's house." She gave him a comforting pat on the thigh and he almost told her how much it meant she was still here. Her phone buzzed before he could embarrass himself, and it was Henry and Martin letting them know they were on their way back. Plenty of time, he realized, to sit in a parked car and continue to be overwhelmed by memories of the time they'd been together.

When they reached Briarcliff he parked at the first available spot he saw, about a block and a half from the source of his life's misery. It was early in the evening, the summer sun already behind the hill where the affluent Cedar Ridge residents lived in the gigantic houses he always both hated and coveted. They sat in silence, Christine scrolling through her phone and Mark trying to replace thoughts of how horrible this was going to be with the pleasant memories he had of Christine. There weren't a lot, honestly, but enough to make him question if it'd been the best relationship he'd ever been in (once you removed the fear and murder from the equation).

"Can I ask you something?" he said, unable to restrain his curiosity.

Now it was her turn to give him the side-eye. "I guess?"

"It's nothing bad, I just...I was just wondering what you saw in me. In high school, I mean. I was such a mess, but you really made me feel special. And that's why I got so...well, you know."

"I don't know," she said. "It was just..."

She trailed off and the pause was interminable.

"Forget it." he said, forcing a smile. "That spell or whatever just has me in my feelings." He wasn't lying, but the fact they were just hanging and he wasn't trying to impress and then fuck her put him in unfamiliar territory.

"You just took me off guard, relax," she said. "I just...I needed a friend. And you were nice. And it probably didn't hurt I could tell you thought I was pretty."

"That obvious, huh?" he laughed, somehow feeling even more foolish. "Well, I'm glad I could help you out."

"Mark," she said, putting a hand on his arm. "I was getting used to another new school in another new state, and that's just how I survived. I drifted until someone noticed and picked me up."

He nodded, hoping he looked dispassionate about it. "Makes sense. I just feel bad you had such shitty luck in who did the picking."

"It's not like you knew all *this*," she waved up the street, "was going to happen. I don't blame you. Anymore." The last bit was quiet, but it was confirmation of what he'd worried about for years, and the reason why he never reached out to her.

"That makes one of us," he said, looking back out the window. He'd spent his whole childhood wondering what he'd done wrong to deserve having his parents and then his Aunt die, leaving him with an Uncle who didn't want him and the overwhelming urge to panic if someone looked at him the wrong way. When he found out about his past life and what he (no, *Justin*) had done it made everything make sense. Therapists had told him things don't happen to people because they deserve it, but he wondered what they'd think if he'd shared his memories of child murder and dismemberment.

After a couple years, when things began to turn around for him, he started to think being made to kill the people who cared the most about him had balanced the scales, but now he realized he should have known better. Those were just more deaths he was responsible for, and he hadn't paid the real price for them yet.

Looks like you're going to pay now, huh? For Clara, and Steve, and Christine's brother, and Ms. Kennedy. Even Uncle Joe, although that one hasn't really keep you up at night.

He shook his head, trying to shut off that side of him again. If the kids in school had known how much his own brain bullied him they'd have saved themselves the trouble.

"So what about Steve?" he said, grasping for the last big question that'd loomed over him for years.

"Ah," she said. "Yeah, unfortunately that was also part of the pattern. Shoring up my self worth by making sure I was noticed and pursued, which was pretty fucked up. But it seemed easier than letting people get to know me, especially since there was a chance we could move away at a moment's notice."

"I get that," he said, not getting it at all, but realizing bringing up his dead best friend she'd made out with was not as distracting as he'd thought. Especially given how Mark had murdered him just up the street. "Fucking high school, right?"

"The worst," she said with a weak smile.

He stopped asking questions, and eventually she went back to looking at her phone. Mark stared out the window, trying not to think about anything and failing miserably.

***

By the time Henry and Martin arrived the last bits of sunlight had just disappeared. They parked their faded yellow Gremlin across the street, and even from a distance made Mark wonder how it could still be running.

"Are you ready for this?" Mark asked before they got out.

"I don't think that's possible," she said.

"Fair enough."

They walked over to the car, where Martin and Henry were rooting around in the trunk. Henry had changed into a light jacket, dark turtleneck, and jeans and Martin was dressed in the junior version. Mark wasn't sure what he expected for their "work clothes," but a pointy hat and robes hadn't been out of the question. Henry took a well-worn leather satchel from the trunk, and when he turned around and saw Christine his calm demeanor seemed to crack for a moment.

"You don't have to be here, Christine," he said. "There's a good chance it's going to be dangerous."

Mark shrugged. "I tried to tell her."

"I'm a big girl," Christine said, an edge in her voice. "I'm not going to just sit around in the airport and wait for this to be over."

Henry obviously wasn't pleased but still nodded in acquiescence. "Fair enough, but you don't have to come inside"

She smiled at him. "I came all this way, so why not? Even if it's completely insane."

"Anyway," Mark said. "What's the plan?"

"I've been texting Tim," Martin said, gesturing up the street, "but he stopped responding the other day. I let him know earlier I was stopping by with friends to take a look at what's wrong with his basement, so theoretically he knows we're coming. I was hoping he'd gone out of town or something but his car is in the driveway."

"We're going to walk up nice and normal," Henry said, "and then get him to leave before we go to work."

"Just casually kick him out of his house?" Christine asked.

"I can be very persuasive," Henry said. Both seemed to be appropriate. "Once he's gone, we head to the basement and I drive the presence out of Mark. If the demon doesn't react to us, that'll definitely wake it up. At that point, Martin is going to cover you while you both get out, and once you're all clear I'll banish the demon."

"I'm guessing it's going to be more difficult than it sounds," Mark said.

"Most likely," Henry said. "But not something I haven't handled before."

"No offense," Christine said, nodding at Martin, "but you're sure he'll be able to keep us from getting murdered or possessed or whatever?"

"Martin's been studying with me for a few years and he's been an excellent student. Plus, he was able to push back the specters it generated before, so I'm confident he'll be able to keep you safe."

Christine looked over at Mark and smiled. "I told you he was an intern."

Mark couldn't help but chuckle at the hurt expression on Martin's face. "I'm not an intern. I'm an apprentice, and I get paid."

"They pay interns sometimes," Christine said.

"Okay, true but...," Martin looked over at Henry for help.

"He's not an intern," Henry said, giving Martin a reassuring pat on the shoulder. "He has plenty of experience with this, and I trust him with my life. You should too." That chased the hurt expression off Martin's face, and he actually blushed in an "Aw shucks" kind of way.

"In terms of possession," Henry continued, reaching into the satchel. "I've got these." He handed Mark a pair of beaded bracelets with gold and silver charms dangling from them. "They'll keep the demon from accessing your mind. You may still feel it trying, but it won't be able to control you."

"You're sure about that?" Mark asked, looking at them skeptically. "This isn't some 'the power was in you all along' shit?"

"I've used them plenty of times," Henry said. "On myself as well. This thing may be old and powerful but it still has weaknesses."

"You're the expert," Mark said, looping them tightly around each wrist, making sure they couldn't slip off.

"Alright," Henry said. "Let's get to work."

***

When the house came into view Mark chuckled at what had become of the infamous Cedar Ridge Murder House which had caused him misery across two lifetimes. The original had been set far back from the street, obscured by jungle-esque lawn and unkempt hedges so tall you could only catch a glimpse of the dark and crumbling roof from the sidewalk. If you pushed your way through the bushes where there'd once been an opening to the stone path, the smaller than expected house waited, sagging in on itself like it was drawing back to pounce. It was mostly wood, with some simple brick columns supporting the overhang on the treacherously decaying porch. Whatever color it had been faded to diseased gray, and the front door had turned an ominous black.

This house, however, was built to show itself off. It was closer to the sidewalk, with a perfectly maintained lawn and vibrant flower beds nestled against the house. Tiny lights illuminated the path to the front door, which was a bright red and lit in a soft and inviting manner. The house was taller than the previous structure and wide enough to be obnoxiously close to its neighbor on one side, with a long driveway on the other where a black Porsche was parked. The place was somehow both boxy and angular, with plenty of windows placed around the front seemingly at random, and even a small row at the bottom hinting there was a cozy basement underneath which absolutely had not been used for murder.

"Well that's a glow-up," Christine said as they walked up the path. Even so, it still made Mark uneasy. He couldn't tell if it was because of the obnoxious modern excess of it or because he knew there was a demon lurking underneath.

The lights inside were on but they couldn't see anyone. Once at the door, Henry waved Mark and Christine to the side of the doorbell camera while Martin rang it. They waited a couple of seconds and then he rang again. This time they could hear running footsteps from the other side, and then the door opened enough for a guy Martin's age to peer out.

"What the hell, bro?" he asked. As he looked past Martin to the rest of them his expression hardened.

"Tim, hey buddy," Martin said with a wide, fake smile. "I texted but you must not have gotten it. I remembered what you said about the problems you were having with your basement, so I brought my plumber friends over to take a look. This is the one night they're free before they head back home so I figured I'd bring them over real quick."

Tim looked at them in confusion, opening the door a little wider. "Thanks, I guess? But it's not a good time. I'm, y'know, entertaining and it's not like there's an emergency."

"You'd be surprised," Henry said. "These kinds of things get worse the longer you put them off and can really affect the property value."

"I'm willing to risk it," Tim said, closing the door. Mark stepped forward, stopping it with his foot.

Tim looked down at it and then up at Mark with what he assumed was the smaller man's "tough guy" face. "My guy," Tim said, "this is not okay."

"Neither is a plumbing emergency," Mark said, putting his hand on the door and pushing it open. Tim tried to resist it, but Mark outweighed him by about twenty-five pounds, most of it being muscle.

"Dude, what the fuck? Get out of here," Tim snapped as the rest of the group followed Mark inside. He took up position threateningly close to Tim, arms crossed and feet planted. It'd been a while since he'd had to fight someone (thanks foster system), but this guy was definitely making Mark want to give it a go.

"The thing is," Martin continued with an "aw shucks what can you do" smile and shrug, "the work is going to be really noisy and smelly and unpleasant, so maybe you guys should just head out for a little bit, huh? Hit a bar, catch a movie, y'know?"

Tim looked from Mark to Martin in irritation, and then noticed Henry and Christine making their way further into the expansive front room, complete impressive stone fireplace, that dominated most of the first floor. He was about to say something when a younger woman who may or may not have been out of high school emerged from the archway at the opposite side of the room.

"Tim? Is everything okay?" she said, confused in a way which could very well have been her natural state.

"Absolutely not," Christine said, walking over to her. "I cannot believe Tim would do this to me, especially with our baby on the way."

"Bitch, what the fuck!" Tim said, turning to follow her.

Mark reached out and placed a firm hand on Tim's chest before he could get very far. "Yeah, we're not doing that," he said, moving in front of him.

"Look buddy--" Tim started, but Mark cut him off.

"I'm not your buddy, guy. And you don't talk to her like that."

Behind him he could hear Christine saying something to the girl, who then let out an incredulous gasp. She hurried through the room, grabbed her purse off the sectional, and headed for the door. As she passed Tim she gave him a disgusted look and said "I can't believe you said you weren't married!" Tim grabbed for her, professing his innocence, but Mark held him by the collar of his ostentatiously pattered shirt and held him back until she was out the door.

"This is bullshit," he sputtered, and Mark just shrugged and tightened his grip. Tim flailed his arms arms as he tried to pull free but then Henry sidled up next to Mark, hand up and flipping a coin around his fingers as if he was also the other kind of magician.

"It's okay, Tim," Henry said, and his voice made Mark shudder. "You're okay. Why don't you calm down?"

Tim's thrashing subsided and he looked at Henry with a dazed and wondrous expression. "Yeah, okay. That's tight."

"Very tight," Henry nodded in agreement. He glanced over at Mark and he relaxed his grip on the little douchebag's shirt. "Now that your date's over, why don't you go see a movie or two? We'll have this place all squared away by the time you come back."

"For sure," Tim nodded, and Mark was convinced he could let go without him throwing a tantrum. Tim wavered unsteadily on his feet and started to move toward the front door, but then stopped and shook his head a little. "I should clean up," he said, looking back at Henry. "That steak was mad expensive."

"Sure thing," Henry said, pocketing his coin. Tim shuffled down the short hallway to their left, which led to the back of the house and, presumably, the kitchen and dining room.

"Must come in handy," Mark said as they followed Tim from a distance.

"Once or twice," Henry said.

Martin stopped them at a barely noticeable door halfway down the hall. "This is it," he said, pointing at it but keeping his distance. As he got near, Mark felt a sudden and oppressive heat close around him like a fist, nearly baking the air in his lungs.

"You okay?" Christine said, putting a hand on his arm.

"You don't feel that?" Mark said.

"What is it?" Henry asked.

"It's hot," Mark said, licking his desiccated lips. "Real hot."

Henry nodded and said "Get ready. It's probably going to get worse before it gets better."

"Story of my life," Mark said, steadying himself against the wall. Henry put his hand on the doorknob, and Mark expected him to draw back in pain from the heat. Henry gave him a look and Mark nodded, bracing himself. Henry opened the door and a thick burning smell and blast of dry heat hit him in the face. The others recoiled, clearly smelling it now. Mark gagged but kept himself under control, despite knowing what the rancid meat smell was.

"Oh my God," Christine said, covering her nose.

"That's definitely gotten worse," Martin said, fanning himself. "It wasn't this bad, or this hot, before."

"It's getting worse," Tim said, appearing behind them and still wearing his eerily chilled-out expression. "I think something died down there."

"No shit," Mark mumbled.

Henry patted Tim on the shoulder and gave him a slight push toward the front door. "It's okay, we'll take it from here."

"Tight," Tim said, walking past them. "Oh wait," he said, stopping as he passed behind Mark. "There was something else."

Mark looked over his shoulder and he saw the knife in Tim's hand a second before he stabbed it into Mark's side.

"How do you like the new place, Justin?" he growled in Mark's ear.

CHAPTER EIGHT

Martin and Christine screamed in unison.

Tim yanked the three inch steak knife, which must have been tucked up his sleeve, out of Mark's side, sending blood arcing across Christine. She recoiled, her lower back slamming painfully into the narrow table behind her and sending some of the assorted knickknacks and family pictures to the floor. Tim shoved Mark into Henry and the two of them stumbled, trying to keep their balance.

Martin lunged at Tim with a strained battle-cry, hooking an arm around Tim's before he could stab Mark again. Tim pulled free and elbowed Martin in the face, who made a different kind of cry as he fell back. Mark looked up from his now very red side just in time to raise an arm and stop the knife as it swung down at him. The surprising amount of force behind the slice was enough to push Mark back even more and leave a long gash across his forearm as he and Henry fell to the floor.

Tim turned his attention to her with a familiar feral grin.

"Well look wh--"

Christine reached behind her, blindly grabbed something off the table, and smashed it against the side of Tim's head.

The something was a heavy picture frame and the glass shattered, leaving tiny cuts across the side of Tim's face and sending him staggering into the wall. As whatever was in his mind tried to process what was happening, she grabbed for the knife. Tim came to his senses and tried to push her away, but she was clamped down on his wrist. She slammed it, and her own hands, against the wall and the knife fell from Tim's grasp. She kicked it away, but turning away from Tim allowed him to grab a handful of her hair and yank her head back around to face him.

He snarled at her, and he had the same rabid look in his eye Mark did when he'd had her in a similar position. "You--"

She kneed him in the stomach and whatever misogynistic bullshit he was going to say was replaced by all the air rushing out of him. He let go of her hair and she swung an elbow into the injured side of his face, giving her enough room to raise a leg and kick him onto the floor.

Before he could get to his feet, Christine dropped down, pinning his right arm with her knee and then punching him in the head as much and as fast as she could with both fists.

"Whoa, whoa!" Martin said, waving his hands in front of her face around the ninth or tenth hit. "There's still a guy in there!"

Christine stopped, catching her breath. Tim's head fell to the side, and his face was already beginning to swell. He let out a weak groan and his eyelids fluttered then shut. Her knuckles were on fire, but she was thankful she remembered how to throw a punch without hurting her wrist. "Final girl rules," she said, catching her breath as she got off of Tim's chest. "Never stop attacking."

"I need some help!" Henry yelled from behind them.

He was kneeling next to Mark, glasses knocked off and pressing his wadded up jacket against Mark's side. Christine and Martin ran over, but stopped when they both realized panic was keeping them from knowing what to do.

"Towels," Henry said, trying to keep Mark from away from him in pain. "And belts or ties for straps."

"On it," Martin said, running to the stairs she'd glimpsed at the end of the hall. Christine followed but continued into the kitchen. Hand towels were in short supply but she grabbed as many as she could find, and then checked the freezer. She'd assumed correctly there'd be a bottle of vodka chilling there and brought it back with her too.

"Ah, shit," Mark said, realizing what the vodka was for.

"Good call," Henry nodded, taking the towels from her and pressing them against Mark's side. She knelt down, opened the bottle, and then poured some on the six-inch incision in his arm. She traded the bottle for one of the towels Henry was holding and wrapped it tightly around the wound.

"So unpleasant," Mark said, and then howled a string of obscenities through a clenched jaw as Henry poured vodka on his side. He'd been stabbed an inch or two below his rib cage, and it was pouring so much dark red blood it was either look away or start throwing up.

"I've got stuff!" Martin yelled, bounding down the stairs. He was clutching a bunch of belts in his hands and carrying an armload of bath towels. He dropped them at Henry's side and backed away. She was glad she wasn't the only freaked out by seeing so much blood.

Henry looked over at her and tilted his head down toward Mark. "Can you?" She swallowed hard and then nodded, taking over putting pressure on the wound as Henry and Martin laced together the belts.

"I told you this could be my last night on Earth," Mark chuckled weakly at her.

"Shut up," she said, pressing a little harder.

"I don't think it will be," Henry said from behind her. "It's deep but I don't think he hit anything vital."

"Oh good," Mark winced. "It only *feels* like I'm dying."

"Remember when I said it was going to get worse before it got better?" Henry said, coming back to Mark's side with a string of three belts tied together.

"I hate you," Mark said, and Henry nodded sympathetically.

They eased Mark onto folded bath towels and then wrapped the belts around them, cinching them so tightly Mark yelled until he was red in the face. Christine was both unnerved and thankful it seemed like Henry and Martin had done something like this before.

"I'll be right back," Henry said, heading over to Tim. Before Christine could ask, Henry knelt down and placed a hand on Tim's head. Henry closed his eyes and at first nothing happened, but then Tim began to twitch and let out little groans. When they faded, Henry stayed by him for a few moments before standing back up with a middle-aged grunt of exertion.

"That should both drive the presence out of him and make sure he stays asleep for a while."

"Great," Mark said, trying to sit up. "Now let's get this over with."

"The hell are you doing?" Christine said, pushing him back down, "You need to go to a hospital right now!"

"I'm not waiting to get this thing out of me. If it can get that guy then it can definitely get me, and I'm not going to wear charm bracelets for the rest of my life."

"Dude, come on," Martin said incredulously, and then looked to Henry for support.

He remained quiet.

"This guy gets it," Mark said, nodding in his direction. "We'll have to come up with a lot more bullshit to explain everything that's already happened, and if we leave coming back to try again will be even harder. And all while it's going to get stronger."

Christine looked at Henry, desperate for him to disagree. The look on Henry's face made it clear he wasn't going to.

"He's not wrong," Henry said. "We can still cover for this, although it won't exactly be easy."

"You heard the man," Mark said, struggling to get to his feet. "Uppy-ups."

She let go of Mark's hand and the guys pulled him to his feet, each supporting him under his arms. With Mark off the ground, the pool of his congealing blood looked huge. Slow rivers of it crawled along the wood floor, and when she stepped away from them her body started trembling. She hunched over, hands on her knees, trying to keep from vomiting everywhere. She wanted to believe it was the fight adrenaline wearing off, but she knew it had more to do with seeing another lake of blood in this deathtrap.

When she successfully defeated the urge, she looked back up at the other three who stared in concern.

"I'm fine," she lied, "but I...," she started, but couldn't bring herself to say it. This was too much, and whatever urge had driven her to make sure she saw this through was now a distant memory.

"It's okay," Henry said, watching her closely. "I can get him downstairs myself. You and Martin get Tim out of here, and then he'll come back for Mark."

"I'm fine," Mark said, face pale and beginning to shiver a bit. "Don't worry about me." She didn't have the heart to say not only did she not need his approval, but his safety wasn't foremost on her mind.

"Okay," she said, nodding in relief.

Martin helped them with the basement door while she moved away and back towards Tim. Another wave of meat-stench struck her, so strong she wanted to just bolt out the front door and not stop running until she was home. Mark looked back at her before they disappeared down the stairs and all she could think to do was give a weak wave and say "Good luck."

"Right, let's do this," Martin said, hurrying over to Tim. They bent down, each grabbing him under an armpit, and then lifted. Christine moved toward the front door but Martin stopped her.

"Backyard. Someone is absolutely going to call the cops if they see a passed out White guy on the front lawn."

"Fair enough," she said. "Is he going to be safe out there?"

"Yes?" Martin said through a forced smile. "At least, safer than he would be in here."

"Good enough for me."

Tim's knees dragged across the floor as they carried him to the sliding doors in the back, which led to a mostly concrete patio. They dragged Tim across it, along the stone path running through the plants and flowers and into the lush and expansive back yard.

"I can't believe you're friends with this guy," she said when they'd stopped to take a brief rest.

"I mean, not really?" Martin said, catching his breath. "But I was so starved for human contact I couldn't wait to come to his stupid party. I wondered why he'd invited me, but I guess this is why."

"What are you talking about?" she said as they picked Tim up again.

"A lot of the time magic things can get drawn together. People, places-_"

"Things?"

He chuckled. "Yup. All the magic nouns can get drawn to each other in weird ways, and it's not until after the fact you realize you're just getting put where you're needed to be. Here's good." They lowered Tim down, having just enough strength left to make sure he didn't get dropped on his face.

"Are you saying it's God?" she said as they headed back.

"Who knows if it's *Hashem,* but I think there's got to be something on our side giving us a nudge now and then."

Christine was quiet, lost in thought as she worried about being pulled into more of this bullshit and not realizing until it was too late. Martin jogged to the patio, looking back as they reached the wooden fence separating yard from driveway.

"Go on," he said, waving toward the door in the fence. "I'll be right out."

She slowed a little, wondering if Martin would actually be able to drag Mark up the steps and out of the house on his own given how much trouble Tim's limp body had given them. She stamped down the urge to help, remembering the pool of blood on the ground, the past trauma, and the confirmed presence of demons, and hurried toward the fence.

Just after she reached the stone path leading to the fence door her foot hit something and she tripped. She fell forward, but her foot was stuck, so she just teetered off-balance on one leg. Looking back she saw her shoe was caught on something in the mulch between the stones.

Before she could pull away, whatever held on to her foot pulled so hard her other leg skidded out from under her and she fell on her side. There was another tug on her leg and she scooted back with her free leg and elbows. There was an eruption of soft earth as she retreated, dragging whatever held her out of the ground.

It was a half burned, half skeletal kid clutching her ankle with its tiny, rotted hands. His body was cut in half at the waist and it pulled itself closer with its free hand.

She screamed and tried to shake it off. Soil tumbled away, revealing more gray and rotted skin, empty eye sockets, and lipless mouth.

"Welcome back, lady," it said in a voice sounding like something from Little Rascals. "I never got to play with girls before," it said. "But I'm going to have so much fu--"

"Not today!" Martin said, landing with both feet on the tiny back and then stomping on its head and giving her a chance to pull free. "Go!" he yelled at her over the crunch of tiny bones and the thing's screeching. She didn't need to be told twice.

She only made it a couple more steps toward the fence before something else burrowed up from the ground in front of her. It was another dirt-covered child's body, equally rotted and burned, but with limbs broken in multiple places, strings of flesh just barely keeping them together.

"Eric's a creep," the girl-thing hissed. "I just want to make you one of my dollies." Christine backed up.

"Hold on!" Martin yelled, giving Eric a final stomp before rushing over to her. He drew his leg back to kick the girl-thing out of Christine's path, but as he swung she folded in on herself, the multiple joints dropping her flat to the ground in an instant. Martin's kick went right over it, and as he tried to recover its limbs uncoiled and it was standing again. It jumped up, grabbed Martin's shirt, and tugged him to the ground.

The thing swung its floppy arms down on Martin, battering at his head while he tried to protect himself. Christine grabbed one of the metal patio chairs and swung it into the thing, knocking it off Martin's chest. As he stood up a fist-sized rock struck him in the small of the back and he shouted in surprise and pain.

"We ain't done playin' yet, lady!" The thing called 'Eric' rolled toward them, dried and broken bones clicking together like a sack of marbles. On the next rotation of its torso it threw another rock, this one coming within an inch of Christine's face.

"Strike!" Another rotten boy child called out from their right. This one was decayed but not burnt, with a cut through its neck so deep its head was held on by just a few strands of flesh. It had a shovel gripped in both hands and stalked toward them faster than the other two seemed capable of. "My turn at bat!" it yelled, swinging the shovel at them in a sweeping arc. Christine pulled Martin back and it just barely missed him.

Once he regained his balance, Martin pushed Christine behind him. "Hold on," he said, holding his arms out in front of him. He took a deep breath, but before he could do anything another rock struck him in the side and he yelled in pain.

Shovel Boy scurried forward and swung again, pushing them back to the house. To their left Broken Girl shuffled toward them, and in front of them Eric the Half Kid picked up another rock and hurled it at them.

"Inside!" Martin said, ducking it. She slid the glass door open and closed just as the shovel smacked into it, spreading a network of cracks through the glass. The two of them backed away, waiting for another swing, but the nearly-headless Shovel Boy just stared at them and smiled, tapping the glass.

"Out the front it is," Martin said, gesturing behind him while keeping his eyes on the glass door. "Go, I'll keep an eye on them."

Christine turned back to the hallway and caught sight again of the lake of blood filling the hallway. She turned and headed through the dining room and into the living room. It may be the longer route, but she wasn't about to try to tip toe through or jump over it. If she got any more blood on her she wasn't sure she'd be able to function.

Halfway through the living room a deafening burst of static erupted from the speakers surrounding her, and she jumped and covered her ears. Martin yelled something from the back of the house, but the static was so loud it felt like a physical thing shaking her body. The massive television on the wall came to life, the screen filling with digital noise and distortion, and then the fireplace roared to life, flames spitting at her from across the room.

She made it a few more steps before sparks shot out the speaker right above her head, making her jump back. The static was abruptly replaced by over-powering electric guitar riffs and a bone-rattling beat.

"Fuck's sake," Christine said, registering what song it was. Martin hurried into the room, a look of confusion on his face as he tried to figure out what was happening.

"Is that--" he started, but as the words to the song started they were joined by a mocking voice echoing down from the chimney.

"What's somebody like you doing in a place like this?"

A pair of heavily burned hands reached out from the inside the chimney at the top of the fireplace, curling around to grab the mantle.

"Did you come alone or did you bring all your friends?"

An equally cooked head dropped into view, the flames behind shining through the hole plowed through its skull.

"This fucking guy," Martin said.

"This *fucking* guy," Christine snarled.

Out of the corner of her eye she saw the nearly headless terror come around the corner and make a beeline towards the distracted Martin, shovel clutched in both hands like a baseball bat.

"Look out!" she hollered over the music. It was loud enough, and Martin jumped into the living room just as Shovel Boy caved in part of the wall where his head had been.

Christine ran for the front door, but Shovel Boy's distraction gave Jack enough time to pull himself from the chimney and tumble into her path. He leisurely rose to his full height, shaking his arms and legs in time with the music as if to stretch whatever muscles were left on him.

"What's somebody like you doing in a place like this?" he sang again, a mean smile spreading across what was left of his face. The tempo of the song picked up, and Jack lunged toward her, grabbing a thin metal floor lamp along the way.

"Oh, Christiney," he yelled, swinging the lamp at her. "I've waited so long for this!"

Behind her she heard the impact of shovel against wall, and she glanced back just in time to avoid running right into Martin. They both retreated, Jack and Shovel Boy each blocking one of the exits at the far ends of the large room. With the heat of the fireplace bearing down on them, all they could do was move closer to the giant sectional in the middle of the room.

The two monsters came at them from opposite sides, swinging their makeshift weapons almost in time with the beat. Christine vaulted over the back of the couch just before Jack could cave her skull in with the heavy base of the lamp. Martin made it most of the way over as well, but his foot dipped into the space between cushions and Shovel Boy hit him in the side. Martin fell awkwardly to the floor, gasping in pain, and Shovel Boy leapt down at him.

Jack vaulted on to the back of the sofa, swinging the lamp back and forth to block either direction she could run in. "Fitting soundtrack, hmm?" His head moved as if he was winking at her with his missing eye. "Darren always sang that stupid old song, so maybe this'll be my jam." He grabbed the lamp in both hands, raised it above his head, and jumped at her.

She ran, unable to get to the front door but able to put a recliner between them. Jack cackled in laughter as he jumped first on, then over it, driving her further back to the billowing flames of the fireplace.

Something popped up from behind the couch and where she'd last seen Martin. It arced high, almost hitting the ceiling fan, and then bounced off the coffee table and onto the floor. Jack turned to look and she jumped forward, grabbing the end of the lamp and tried to pull it from his grasp. He kept his grip and she found herself in a tug-of-war with it until Jack let go and let her fall on her ass.

"Wooooooooon't let you get awaaaaaaayyyyyyyy," he sang along, stepping on his end of the lamp so she couldn't pick it up.

"Hey!" Martin yelled. "Leave Katy Perry out of this." He charged forward, shovel out in front of him like a spear. Jack turned just enough for Martin to stab it in the chest, the momentum pushing it into the wall and pinning him there.

"Motherfucker!" Jack screeched, reaching out and swiping at Martin but unable to reach him. Holding the end of the shovel with one hand, Martin raised the other and closed his eyes. The atmosphere around Christine changed to something akin to a storm about to sweep in. Jack, instead of clawing at Martin, grabbed the shovel and pulled itself forward. It slid up the handle a couple of inches and reached out for Martin's hand. Just before they touched, blue sparks arced between Martin's fingers and Jack was pushed back hard against the wall, the arm it had been reaching out with crushed against its chest.

Jack made muffled gurgling sounds and Martin moved closer to him, the invisible force from his hand crushing the thing against the wall like a trash compactor. Martin's face was red with exertion but he pressed forward until what was left of Jack's skull imploded and the rest of him crumbled into dust on the floor. As he did, there was another quick burst of static and the music mercifully stopped.

Martin straightened up and wiped the sweat from his brow. "How'd that taste, asshole?" he said between gasps of breath.

Martin dropped to one knee, gasping for breath. Before Christine could try to help him up, she heard the pattering of running feet coming towards her. She turned and saw the now completely headless boy's body tottering toward them unsteadily. Christine yanked the shovel out of the wall, spun around, and smacked the thng into the roaring fireplace. It twitched and hissed, and from across the room she could hear the high pitched squeals coming from its head.

The headless and now flaming body tried to crawl out of the fireplace but Christine pinned it in there with the tip of the shovel. "Taste what?" she said, glancing in Martin's direction.

"You had to be there," he said, walking across the room. "But also, what the hell was up with that song?"

"You don't want to know," she said. The flames had died down from supernatural inferno levels and were now coming almost entirely from the still twitching flaming child's body. Across the room, Martin bent down and carefully picked up Shovel Boy's head by one of its remaining tufts of hair.

Martin walked over, head shrieking high-pitched obscenities. "Fair enough. Besides," he tossed the head into the fire, where it immediately burst into flame. "'Teenage Dream' is her best work anyway."

When she was sure the child-thing had stopped moving she let the shovel drop to the ground. "Is that it?" she asked, looking around for the next nightmare to come leaping out at her.

"Should be," Martin said, guiding her toward the front door. "I gave Jack the old 'Get thee behind me douchebag,' so he won't be giving us any more troubles. Now let's get you--"

He was interrupted by a bellowing scream from beneath them.

CHAPTER NINE

Mark swore with every stair they stepped down. His arm was around Henry's shoulders, although Henry was a little too short for it to be comfortable. With every step the hole in his side moved and introduced him to a new kind of pain. When they reached the bottom, Henry lowered Mark on to his back as gently as he could, which still felt like he was being ripped open. The basement was vastly different now, and everything Mark had envied as a kid. There was a huge home theater set-up, arcade cabinet, and even a pool table. The unlit neon beer and pot-leaf signs, as well as the excessive amounts of "tastefully nude" photography, did wonders for curbing his envy. Mark craned his neck up to look at the far wall where the furnace used to be, but the area was blocked by a new wood-paneled wall with a single door in the middle.

He let his head fall back to the floor, trying to let the makeover fool him into thinking he wasn't bleeding out on the same ground so many others had before. With effort, Henry sat cross-legged next to him, rolled up the sleeves of his dress shirt, and then studied the room.

"This is bad," Henry said.

"Yeah," Mark said. "Who uses wood paneling nowadays?"

Henry gave him a wry smile. "You know that's not what I meant, but you're not wrong." He took a deep breath and reached into his bag. "This place is radiating a lot more demonic energy than I was expecting."

"God forbid anything be easy."

"In this line of work, you learn to be adaptable," Henry said. He took a small, golden statue out of the bag, held it out in front of him with both hands, closed his eyes for a few seconds, and then placed it in front of him. Mark was going to ask what it was, but he was hit with the overwhelming but familiar smell of smoke and charred meat.

Human meat, you mean. How many people can say they can recognize the difference?

Mark gritted his teeth and tried his deep breathing exercises, but with every inhale he could taste the burning air tinged with cooked blood.

"I think you're making it mad," Mark said.

"Good." Henry placed a hand on Mark's chest. "You ready?"

"As I'll ever be, Doc." Henry closed his eyes and Mark did likewise.

A heat rushed through his body, and Mark thought the furnace flames had caught up to him, but these were soothing and peaceful, like being wrapped in a warm blanket. He had the sensation of floating, and when he opened his eyes he realized he was standing up and the pain in his side was gone.

The refurbished basement was gone too, having returned to the decayed and bare state of ten years ago, complete with cracked cement floor, wooden beams overhead with dangling chains, and an oppressive dry heat snuffing out any sense of comfort. The furnace was back as well, in all its black-iron glory, with pipes snaking out from the top like an upside-down spider. In the front was the two-foot square door to the fuel chamber, and through the dirty glass window in the middle he could see the flames roiling and hungry.

"It's okay," Henry said from behind him, putting a hand on Mark's shoulder.

"Not even remotely," Mark said, turning around to face him. Over Henry's shoulder he could see the rickety wooden stairs in the same place as the ones they'd descended minutes before. Underneath them was the makeshift metal cage where the children had been kept before being tortured and made to see the furnace's demonic resident.

The one you built. The one you kept them in.

Mark jumped and spun around. That wasn't just "negative self-talk," it was whispered in his ear in a rush of hot, smoke-filled air.

"It's okay," Henry said, turning Mark to face him and placing his other hand on Mark's shoulder. "It's not going to go without a fight, but I'm here with you."

Mark nodded, and smoke began to seep out of Henry's eyes like tears. Before Mark could say anything, he felt something moving against his shoulders as if something was squirming under the skin of Henry's palms. "What is--" Mark started, but Henry closed his eyes and shook his head.

"Don't worry about it," Henry said, his voice deeper and with a slight echo to it. "This is...perfectly normal."

"You have a fucked up version of normal," Mark said, and then Henry turned him back around to face the furnace.

"You have no idea," Henry said. "But that'll get us through this. Hang on, this is going to be uncomfortable."

You're used to that, aren't you?

He swatted at the air next to his ear.

"Fuck off," Mark whispered. The heat exuding from the furnace was making him drip sweat, and his chest clenched when he realized this was what Corwin's victims felt before their gruesome ends.

Your victims, buddy. Let's not forget that, hmm?

Mark started to say something but the clenching pain in his chest magnified, sucking all the air out of his lungs and making him drop to his knees. Henry's hands didn't leave his shoulders, and whatever was under his palms wriggled around even more. Just when he thought he was going to pass out, the pain relented and he was able to breathe again.

"It's okay," Henry said from behind with his double-voice. "This is what we want."

There was a screech of metal and the door on the furnace swung open. Flames poured out into the room, and Mark winced at the unnaturally bright fire inside.

Ah, come on, Justin. That was your whole thing, wasn't it? Make them see what was in the fire and all? Don't pussy out of it.

"Get out of my head," Mark snarled, shutting his eyes and focusing on where the damn voice was coming from.

I can't get out! I'm YOU, remember? The psychopath child-murderer who took the pussy way out! It's not going to be so easy now, kiddo, that's for damn sure!

"I know you're not me," Mark said. "You're just evil stuck to Justin's soul."

And how do you figure that?

"Because you never called yourself 'I' before."

The pain in his chest rose again, but this time he was ready for it. He could now feel the thing inside clenching against his heart. Mark grabbed at his chest as if he could tear it open and pull the poisoning thing right out.

"There you go," Henry said. "You got th--"

Henry's voice cut off and his hands disappeared from Mark's shoulders. He swayed, almost falling forward, and the pain in his chest shifted to his stab wound. Mark opened his eyes, confirming he was back in the frat basement. The only change was the heavy pounding of bass shaking the lights hanging from the ceiling. Next to him Henry lay on his side, glasses knocked off and eyes closed. Someone stepped over him and stood over Mark, a pool cue held casually in his hand. The light on the ceiling behind him blocked his features, but he could see light coming through a hole in his head.

Not his head, he realized, but his neck.

"Hey buddy," the wheezing but familiar voice said. "Look at you, all grown up."

He knelt down, sitting on Mark's chest with his knees on either side of him. He leaned forward, the remnants of long hair hanging in front of its burned face, and pressed the pool cue down across Mark's throat.

"We've got a lot to catch up on, huh?" Steve, his high school best friend, said.

The same best friend he'd killed in this basement.

***

Henry knew hurrying was a rookie mistake, but he thought he'd be quick enough to exorcise Mark before going on the offensive.

"It's been nearly a year since you've been out on a case. A real one," Monica had told him before he left. "Not since Lexie got hurt, so I want you to promise to take it easy and be careful, okay? You may be a little out of practice." He brushed it off, mostly so she wouldn't worry, but as it was with most things she was right. The pain in the back of his head was bad, but the realization he'd broken a promise and was going to have to explain another head wound to his wife stung more.

He pushed himself up onto an elbow and saw Mark next to him, a burnt teenager sitting on his chest and crushing his throat with a pool cue. Mark's legs kicked as he tried to push it off, but he wasn't having much luck.

Henry reached out, but something grabbed his wrist and yanked him back. It pulled him up off the ground for a second and then he crashed down on his back. A young man loomed over him, but unlike Mark's attacker he wasn't burned. His was shirt unbuttoned, revealing a long scar from lower hip up to the opposite shoulder.

"Not so fast," it said. "Those two have a score to settle."

Henry tried to pull his arm free, but his head was still swimming and his limbs weren't doing what they were told. This was Darren, he realized, the one who'd controlled Mark's body a decade ago and had willingly sacrificed himself for the demon. Darren grabbed the scar at the center of its chest with the free hand, dug the fingers deep into the flesh, and pulled. The scar ripped open like a zipper and a cloud of thick black smoke descended down over Henry's face.

He tried to wave it away, but the smoke thickened and then held his arm in tentacle-like strands. He could feel the solidifying smoke gather around his head, and even though he kept his eyes and mouth shut it pushed against them and tried to force its way inside.

"In the meantime," it said. "I'm going to add a few more souls to the roster."

***

Mark could barely keep the cue up long enough to catch his breath, and every time he got it up Steve dug his heel into the stab wound on Mark's side.

"Hurts, huh?" Steve said, mouth moving but the sound coming from the off-center hole in his neck. "I hope it's as much as it did when I was bleeding out on the floor over there. Do you know how long it took me to die, Mark? Five minutes, at least. Five minutes of drowning in my own blood while you just watched me. I died looking at your stupid fucking face, you little pansy." He finished the sentence by jabbing his heel into him with every word.

"You're not Steve," Mark said, straining so hard to breathe he couldn't tell if he was audible.

"You wish," Steve snarled. "I remember wiping away your tears and comforting you every time you got too 'stressed' or 'freaked out,' which seemed to be every other goddamn day. How much of my very short life did I waste on your bullshit? Too goddamn much, that's for sure."

"He was my friend," Mark said, anger helping him find a reserve of strength. "I may have been a crybaby...but Steve was at least funny about it."

"Oh, you want funny Steve?" it said, smiling wider than he'd have been able to without the burns and rot. "This one's a riot." Steve gestured upward with his head.

"The third in our love triangle is upstairs right now, and Jack is having a good time with her. She's going to be hurt a lot, and then I get to take a turn." Steve leaned forward, pressing more weight against Mark's throat and lowering its face right above his.

"I can't wait to absolutely impale 'ol Christine. And I mean that in *every* way." It laughed, and Mark winced at the puffs of fetid air blowing from the ragged hole in its throat. "And there's nothing you or the diversity-hire over there can do about it."

Mark looked and saw Darren standing over Henry, dark smoke oozing out of his chest and crushing Henry like a squirming mass of pythons.

"And when we're done with all of them, we're gonna to take turns crawling up inside you and make you do the most heinous shit imaginable. And this time, you're going to be awake for all of it."

CHAPTER TEN

Henry shook his head back and forth, trying to keep the smoky tendrils from forcing their way into his unprotected nostrils and ears.

"You really thought you could just walk in here and face our God? That He hasn't harvested enough souls to defend Himself? Who do you think you are?"

"Not the one to test, that's for damn sure," Henry growled through clenched teeth. He balled his hands into fists and he could feel his insides building up heat and power. "I've got my own furnace."

Darren looked confused for a second, and then its eyes opened wide in surprise as the clouds around Henry's arm and face began to burn away. Darren let go of Henry's arm, but now it was Henry's turn to hold on.

"I don't think so," Henry said. Darren had backed up enough for Henry to plant a foot against its lower stomach. Bearing down, he pushed with his foot while pulling with his arm. Darren tried to shake free but Henry's grip was so tight he could feel what passed for bones begin to crack under the pressure. Henry felt the thing's torso snap and tear with the opposing pressure, and Darren's sustained scream of agony echoed off the walls around them. The last of whatever was holding it together snapped and tor in half along the path of the scar. The lower half of its body was kicked across the room and the top half swung over Henry's head and hit the ground behind him with a solid, wet thump.

Henry struggled to his feet, keeping his grip as Darren tried to pull itself away with its other hand. Henry stepped on what was left of its chest, and then fire roared down the thing's captured arm. Darren screeched and writhed as the flames quickly spread to its torso. Unbothered by the heat, Henry raised his foot and stomped down on the flaming skull, shattering it. The screaming ceased, and the rest of its body twisted and burned until all that was left were crispy piles of ash. Henry let go of the arm and it crumbled onto the ground.

"Holy shit," said Martin from the stairs behind him.

Henry turned and saw Martin and Christine were almost to the bottom of the stairs, looking from him to the struggling Mark with equal amount of shock. Henry could feel the power he'd let loose swirling around him, and judging by the way Martin was transfixed he could see it to. Not ideal, but not the immediate problem.

The thing on Mark's chest looked over its shoulder at Christine and let out as good of a wolf-whistle as it could with a hole through the neck. "Aren't you a sight for sore eyes," it said. "Let me finish here and we can pick up where we left off."

"Enough," Henry snapped.

The thing turned to look just in time for Henry to palm its rotting face. It dropped the pool cue and grabbed Henry's wrist with both hands, but Henry's fingers dug deep into the ruined skin and scorched bone. There was a hiss of flesh sizzling, and then white flame burst out of its eyes and neck hole. Henry pushed forward and slammed the back of its head against the floor, where it exploded in a flash of fire and ash. The rest of it twitched and then dissolved into smoke.

Mark sucked in massive gulps of air, and Martin and Christine rushed to his side. Henry reigned in the magical energy rippling through his body and knelt next to Mark's head.

Mark glared up at him. "This plan is really going great. I'm excited I'm a part of it."

"It's going about as good as they usually do," Martin muttered. Henry shot him a look but Martin didn't make eye contact.

"We can still do this," Henry said, placing a hand on Mark's forehead and diving back into his mind.

***

"Jesus," Mark said between coughs. "Why does my throat still hurt in here?"

They were back in the original murder basement, and Mark was doubled over and Henry next to him with a hand on his shoulder.

"It's a projection," Henry said. "Metaphysical stuff we don't have time for. You ready to try again?"

"Go for it," Mark hacked, straightening up. The coughing had taken his mind off of Steve's ghost or whatever trying to kill him, and he knew he should've mentally prepared for the possibility. Steve's death here, while an accident, was still Mark's fault no matter how hard he tried not to think about it.

You did it to yourself, man. Have you tried not *killing your loved ones?*

Henry's hand gripped Mark's shoulder harder and he felt the thing in his chest squirming again. Mark bore down and he could feel it being forced up into his throat.

"I'm so goddamn sick of you," he said, right before his airway was painfully blocked. He heaved, trying to force whatever it was up and out. It buzzed and shook like an angry beehive, and then tiny, sharp things grabbed on to his back teeth and dug into his soft palate. Mark opened wide and reached deep into his mouth to grab it. It was hard and cold, and tried to pull itself away, but Mark grabbed onto one of the protrusions with his thumb and forefinger and started to pull.

It came out of his mouth, scraping against his tongue and teeth as it thrashed. Mark grabbed what already emerged with both hands and pulled. Feelers kicked and scratched against his nose and chin as it fought him. For a moment he thought it was going to be like some evil, never-ending magician's scarves, but when his arms were fully extended it popped out of his mouth.

Nearly three feet long and pitch black, it shifted from feeling soft and dough-like to hard and chitinous, like insect's shell. As it tried to free itself, little multi-jointed legs formed and then were drawn back in at a frantic pace.

"There you go," Henry said from behind him.

Mark cocked his arm back, turned, and hurled the thing at the furnace. It hit about a foot above the fuel chamber door, but the thick metal crumbled like he'd thrown a boulder. Flame spouted from the cracks, and the maze of pipes overhead burst open with black steam.

Mark flinched away and closed his eyes for a second, and when he opened them he was back in reality. The others had their hands on his arms and shoulders, trying to keep him still as he tried to sit up and expel the phantom object from his throat. He waved them away and was reminded of the knife would in his side.

"Back up, back up," he said, trying to speak as loud as he could.

"No time," Henry said. "You guys need to go."

Christine and Martin got on either side of Mark and helped him to his feet. They were taller than Henry so it was easier to step along with them as they climbed the stairs, but it was twice as painful as the descent had been. He could feel blood dripping down his side, the straps holding the towels in place having been loosened with all the attempted murder. There was a rumbling from underneath them, and Mark looked over his shoulder just before his line of sight was blocked at the first landing. A crack had appeared on the floor, right where Mark had been laying, and an angry red glow was shining from it.

"I don't recommend looking back," Martin said.

"I'm pretending this isn't even happening," Christine said.

Mark hoped he'd get there one day, but he severely doubted it.

***

"Show yourself," Henry commanded, voice reverberating around the room with magical authority.

The ground shook again and another crack appeared in the floor. Henry backed up, loosening his hold on the power within him and readying to strike. Dark smoke like what had poured forth from Darren began to seep up from the cracks, and as the cloud obscured the ground there was another small quake. Henry held out his hand, ready to burn away whatever emerged, but something dropped from the ceiling and on to his arm.

It was the top half of a burned child, clawing and biting at his arm. He shook it to get the thing off, but then something duing skittered at him from the side and crashed into his bad knee. He buckled, but was able to remain upright as the multi-jointed corpse of an equally young girl wrapped itself around his leg, trying to pull him even more off balance.

"How dare you come to our neighborhood? Into my house!" a man's voice growled from behind, and two sets of arms reached around him, grabbing his torso and trying to wrap around his neck. The angles of the arms were all wrong and glancing back he could see it was a man and woman's body parts mashed together into a single abomination. The man's head was at Henry's shoulder, but the woman's was down by his side and just under his arm.

"My son! You killed my son!" it shrieked before biting into Henry's side. They were Corwin's parents, Henry realized, clearly unaware of who actually dismembered them. The weight drove Henry down onto his bad knee as they continued to pummel, scratch, and bite him. The black smoke swirled around his ankles, and he could make out clicking and scraping sounds inside over the racial epithets the corpses hissed at him.

"Enough," Henry snapped. A torrent of magic burst through him as he stood. Flesh popped and burned behind him as wings of flame burst from his back and right through what had become of Mr. and Mrs. Corwin. They fell to the ground, reduced to cinders. He grabbed the half a boy clinging to his arm, raised it in the air, and then smashed it into the girl clinging to his leg over and over again until it tumbled to the ground in a heap. Henry raised the torso in the air again and smashed the two together again, this time with a burst of flame.

"Is that the best you can do?" Henry screamed, his voice only half his. The wings on his back rose and then swept down, blowing the smoke around his feet back to where it had emerged. As it retreated, multiple insect-like legs and crustacean-esque claws scurried back to where they could hide again.

There was another rumble from the ground, and the clacking of claws and legs grew in volume as solid black clouds rose from the cracks like ink floating in water.

You dare, it snapped in Henry's mind. *I will devour your entire existence! I will shred your soul into--*

"You're not doing shit," Henry said. He strode forward and plunged both arms elbow deep into the swirling column of darkness. It squealed in surprise as Henry grabbed the first solid thing he could find and started to squeeze. The fire that erupting from his hands burned away the darkness, reaveling the outline of the maggot-shaped thing covered in legs, claws, and feelers. The top of it plunged down around Henry's upper body and circled him, lashing out with its multitude of appendages.

I will bury myself in you and make you my instrument, it cried out in Henry's mind, full of desperation.

A rumbling rose up from Henry's core. *This one is claimed*, a voice deep inside Henry roared. *And you are nothing before me, you weak little insect.*

It wailed in agony as Henry's hands began to rend and twist the center of its form. The remaining darkness was pulled down into his grip, and what was wrapped around him drew back as well. Henry gathered it in his hands like he was violently crumbling paper into a ball, and when he had its essence compacted down to a single handful the room shuddered and pulsed around him. Even as just an irregular wad of darkness about the size of a golf ball it still tried to slip between his fingers and escape.

I think not.

Before he realized what was happening, Henry's head tilted back and he dropped the thing into his open mouth. It fell through Henry's essence with a painful flash of cold and then it vanished. He doubled over and coughed for a few seconds, hoping something would come out, but there was nothing coming back up. He stood and pulled back the fire he'd let loose, slamming doors shut in his mind.

"That was disgusting," Henry said, wiping his mouth with the back of his hand. "Don't ever pull that crap again."

The room was silent, and then his stomach grumbled loudly.

CHAPTER ELEVEN

The waiting room in the nicer of the two hospitals in Cedar Ridge had been remodeled, so that was nice. Christine was grateful she didn't have to stare at the same ugly paint she had the last time she'd been here, waiting to find out if her father was going to die and processing that her brother already had. The paint was still ugly, and Mark was going to live, but there was plenty of other stuff to ponder and worry about.

Henry had emerged from the house after a nerve-wracking amount of time. She'd wanted to take Mark to get checked out immediately but he'd insisted they wait until Henry came out.

When he did and said it was over, she felt a rush of relief unlike anything she'd felt before, although Henry warned them "now comes the hard part." They retrieved Tim from the backyard, woke him, and Henry "explained" what had happened. It was a simple case of an old friend bringing people by to take care of weird plumbing issues in the basement, but then a bunch of them took an unfortunate tumble down the stairs while holding tools carelessly. Whatever Henry did was effective, and they loaded Tim and Mark into the Jeep. Christine asked how they were going to account for all the damage, but Henry told her they would take care of it while she took the other two to the hospital.

The bored resident who stitched Mark up seemed to buy the story, as Tim was quite expressive about it, but the nurse working with him clearly did not. She gave Christine a look and when she nodded in an "I'm fine and not in danger" manner, the nurse replied with a "guess it's none of my business if two idiots get in a fight and one of them stabs the other" shrug. While upset over the whole thing, whatever Henry had done to Tim kept him from wanting to press any charges or get the police involved.

Mark was admitted for observation, wanting to make sure he didn't take a turn for the worse in the night and require a splenectomy. She grudgingly decided to cancel her flight and try to get another one once she knew Mark was going to be okay, and she opted for some alone time while he lay in the hallway waiting for a room. She'd reached peak doom-scrolling when Henry walked over with a couple of cans of soda and two bags of suspiciously generic "party mix."

"That seemed a little fast for home repair," she said, taking the offered snacks.

"It may surprise you," he said, "but we have ways to make it go faster."

"I bet. Where's your sidekick? I need to thank him for saving my ass."

Henry chuckled. "He insisted he was fine, so I dropped him at home. I wanted him to come get looked at, but he's still on his parent's insurance and he didn't want them to find out he'd gotten hurt."

She shook her head. "Kids these days."

He smiled, and then asked how she was doing.

"Seriously questioning my sanity, and not just from fending off a dead teenager while dance music was playing. Or seeing Steve...like that."

"Those kinds of things are never easy," Henry nodded. "The thing to remember, especially in circumstances like this, is that it wasn't really those people. Just warped echoes of what they once were."

"Well that clears it up, " she snickered.

"I know, easier said than done for sure. And believe me, I've had to be reminded on a few occasions."

There was a lull as they both crunched away at their dinners, and then Henry spoke up again.

"You said that wasn't why you're questioning your sanity. May I ask what is?"

"Such a gentleman." She thought about it and then said, "I'd reached a point in my life where I really thought I'd put all this stuff to rest. I'd packed it away, cried about it, journaled about it, and was done. But I still came all the way out here, hooked up with the guy from the worst relationship I've ever had, and *voluntarily* went into a place I knew was literally filled with ghosts. It's so stupid."

Henry nodded solemnly. "I'm sorry about that, I really am. I was worried calling you was too much pressure, and I should've known better than to be so...persistent." He was either using magical acting tricks or legitimately holding back tears. "I honestly think you were what got Mark to help us, and if he hadn't this would have ended up a lot worse."

"I wish I could say I was glad I did my part."

"I shouldn't have let you come inside. I could've...I *should've* pushed back harder, and it almost got you really hurt."

She nodded, not wanting to think about how many brushes with death she'd had in the past twenty-four hours. "It was my own stupid fault. One last crazy push so I could go home and really know it's done." She looked over at him. "And you're *sure* it's done, right?"

"As done as it can be," Henry said. "It's not trapped in something like before, it's been banished back to whatever hell it came from."

"Good," she said, not wanting to address the concept of multiple hells. "And the people it...ate, or whatever, they're free? In heaven or something?"

"Or something," Henry said. "There's not a definitive answer, but they're wherever they need to be."

"Good for them," she said. She took a drink and added, "Earlier Martin said magic stuff is attracted to people who've already experienced it. Is that true?"

Henry nodded. "In a sense. Those people tend to find themselves in these kinds of situations more often."

"Is there some sort of whammy or magic rock you can give me to keep them as far away as possible? Twice in almost thirty years is enough."

He smiled a little. "You should be okay."

"I want more than 'should,'" she said. "I don't want to just cross my fingers and hope I don't buy a haunted car or discover my next Tinder match is a vampire."

"Be careful on there anyway, but I'll tell you what I've told my kids about avoiding this stuff, and that's to trust your gut."

The look she gave him made him nod apologetically. "I know," he said. "It sounds dumb, but it's true. Those hunches and feelings people get don't just come from nowhere. On some level, people can sense things that don't belong here. Sometimes it's nothing that can be seen or harm them, but other times it's a lot more. Knowing what those things feel like will make you more aware of them. When you feel them, pay attention. If you're not sure you are, listen anyway."

"So I'm just waiting for the vibes to be off?"

He nodded cautiously. "I wouldn't put it like that, but I guess so."

"I'm never leaving my house again," she said, putting her head in her hands. "This is so insane."

"Just be careful. Does a place make you uneasy? The driver seem a little bit off? Just get out of there. It's not going to happen often, unless you're actively looking for it."

"I would never," she said. "I didn't even want to know about it at all."

"Honestly, me either. I just kind of...lucked into it."

"And then you were just like 'Hey, let me go hunt ghosts and learn magic'?"

"Not in the least," he said. "How do you think I know it works? I didn't take it and now..." He waved his hands in the air to indicate situations like these, but stopped when he saw a hefty man who definitely did not look like a doctor walk by. Henry's gaze followed him intently until he disappeared around the corner.

"Now you follow your gut, but in the opposite way," she said, nodding in the direction the man had gone.

"That's the job, like it or not," he said, standing up. "Besides, there's a lot more to follow nowadays." He smiled and patted his stomach. "In more ways than one." He turned to go and then looked back at her. The smile was gone and his expression was soft and apologetic. "I really am sorry about all this, but you really made a difference."

She didn't agree but nodded in what she hoped passed for appreciation. Henry followed after the man he'd noticed and she went back to her phone to check on flights.

***

They'd just finished setting Mark up in his hospital room when the thick and sour-faced guy strode in and studied Mark with the aura of someone who's used to being in charge. He was familiar, but before Mark could place him, he identified himself as Chief of Detectives Lobrazzo of the Cedar Ridge Police.

"I'm pretty sure Tim didn't want to press charges," Mark said, the pain in his body taking a backseat to the sudden rush of anxiety. A regular cop wouldn't have been a big deal, but someone with a fancy title showing up felt like the worst case scenario.

"That's what he said, Mr. Watson," Lobrazzo said, moving uncomfortably close to the side of Mark's bed. "But I have to tell you, I'm really having a hard time understanding exactly what happened."

"I'm not sure I follow," Mark said, hoping he was making himself look just the right amount of confused.

"Well, my understanding is you're a mechanic and not a plumber," he said, checking a handheld notebook. "That correct?"

"Yeah, but I dabble...in the plumbing. I've...plumbed." The pain killers had begun to do their job at the worst possible time.

"Sure," Lobrazzo nodded. "Who hasn't?" He went back to the notebook. "I'll hold off on asking how someone gets stabbed in the side while falling down stairs, but I'm very curious as to why you'd decide to...." he looked up a Mark with an arched eyebrow, "'plumb' at the house built on the spot where you'd nearly been killed. Allegedly."

Pain killers be damned, that jogged his memory. This was the cop who grilled him the hardest when he'd come close to being arrested for the murders back in the day. Detective Prescott had used every ounce of his pull to get Mark off the hook, but this guy had been stewing in the corner of every conversation and watching him far too closely.

"Was it?" Mark said. "I try not to think about that stuff."

"I bet." Lobrazzos eyes narrowed to tiny little pits under his eyebrows. "Is there a reason why Christine Baker, of all people, was at the scene as well? Especially since she currently resides in New Mexico?"

"Just here for a visit," Mark smiled. "Old friends and all."

"Did she also forget what happened there?"

"I...," Mark trailed off, hoping something would come to him.

"Chief Lobrazzo," Henry said, walking into the room with a disingenuous smile. "So nice to see you again."

Lobrazzo glared at him. "Mr. Churchill. What a surprise. I guess you found a way to connect with Mr. Watson after all."

"I did, and he's been very helpful. Although I'm sorry he got hurt while showing us what he's been up to nowadays."

"Doing more research for your book?" Lobrazzo said.

"I'm thinking I might put a pin in it for now. The publishing marketplace has really changed after the pandemic."

"I'm sure it has." Lobrazzo said, turning to give Henry the full weight of his gaze. "I was surprised to find out you're a private investigator and not a writer. Trying something new?"

"Everyone has to have a hobby," Henry said, smiling wider.

"I found a fascinating article about you and your lady-partner on the *New Borderlands* site. A lot of talk about ghosts, monsters, and so on."

Henry's hands were clasped behind his back and he did an exaggerated nod of embarrassed acknowledgment. "I know, and I've been trying to get them to take it down for a while. A lot of allegations and assertions without any evidence, which I think is what's called 'fake news.'"

"I bet. I was just asking Mr. Watson here--"

Henry raised a finger to stop him. "I hate to interrupt, but it's been a hell of an evening for us, and I'm pretty sure they told Mark he needed to get some rest."

Mark nodded. "Yeah, I'm pretty beat. Can we do this later or something?"

"It'll only take a moment," Lobrazzo said, not taking his eyes off of Henry. "If you don't mind?" He gestured toward the door.

"Actually," Henry said, moving around between Lobrazzo and Mark. "It's probably best Mark gets that rest, and he'll be happy to talk to you in the morning." He turned to Mark. "Right?"

"I'd really appreciate it." Mark sank down lower in the bed, like a kid trying to stay home from school. "These drugs are just...knocking me right out."

Lobrazzo narrowed his eyes. "Like I said, it'll just take a--"

"I hate to be a stickler," Henry said, taking a step forward and forcing the larger man to move back. "But I'm fairly certain that if you want to *make* him answer more questions, you're going to have to charge him with something. Honestly, I can't think of what that would be. Clumsiness, maybe?"

The detective looked down at Henry, glaring more intently. "Okay," he said. "I'll come back tomorrow morning. Hopefully you'll be more well-rested then."

"Fingers crossed," Mark said, forcing a giant yawn.

Lobrazzo left, and Henry closed the door behind him.

"Thanks," Mark said. "So much for the cops not getting wind of this."

"It was always a possibility. When we'd talked before the Chief made it clear he wasn't satisfied with how things ended before."

"Wonderful. There's no way this bullshit is going to fly if he's already suspicious. I'm fucked."

"Not necessarily," Henry said. "I'll talk to him and smooth things over."

"I'm sure that'll go over well."

"Remember," Henry winked. "I can be very persuasive. Just worry about getting better and I'll handle him."

"I can definitely multitask my worrying," Mark said. There was a soft knock at the door and Christine poked her head in. "Everything okay? That guy seemed pissed."

"It's fine," Henry said. "I just wanted to check in and say that if anything like this comes up and you need help, please don't hesitate to text me." He smiled at Christine. "I'll even fly to New Mexico. Promise."

CHAPTER TWELVE

When Chief Detective Lobrazzo pulled into his driveway a few hours later, Henry was waiting for him.

"What the hell are you doing here?" Lobrazzo said. As soon as he saw Henry, he'd stopped in the middle of the driveway and got out, walking toward the tree Henry was leaning on.

"Hoping none of your neighbors are going to call the cops on a Black guy 'lurking in the shadows.'"

"There's an easy way to avoid that," Lobrazzo said, utilizing his "standing too close to you" tactic. Given his size Henry was sure it usually worked for him, but knowing the intent significantly lessened its effectiveness.

"Very true," Henry said. "But I wanted to talk to you about Mark Watson before you got anything in motion."

"Now you want to talk? You have some information I should know about?"

Henry shrugged. "In a sense. Just know the responsible party for those murders has been dealt with, and Mark Watson isn't involved and should be left alone."

Lobrazzo chuckled and feigned giving it some thought. "Sure, sure. You want anything else? A pony, maybe? Rocket ship?"

"I assure you I'm being serious."

"Look," Lobrazzo said, stepping even closer. "I'm sure you're very clever, but I'm telling you to let me know whatever you have or I'll charge you as an accessory after the fact."

Henry sighed. "If anything it'd be obstruction of justice. I'm really disappointed in your lack of legal knowledge, especially for a man of your station."

"You may think I can't touch you in New York, but I've got friends there. I know people who can make things *very* difficult. Given your reputation, I don't think it'd be hard." He jabbed a finger in Henry's face. "Tell me what you know."

"Here we go," Henry muttered. Before Lobrazzo could question, Henry raised his hand in front of the man's face and said "Watch this." The coin caught the light from the headlights and twinkled, catching his attention perfectly. Henry concentrated, giving just the slightest push into Lobrazzo's distracted mind. Lobrazzos's head cocked to the side and his right eye blinked rapidly, and then he slumped backward, giving Henry some space.

"You ar--"

Lobrazzo stood up straight and held up a hand to block the light reflecting into his eye.

"Knock it off," he snapped, moving up on Henry again. "Talk to me, or you're in deep shit."

Henry flipped the coin into his palm and dropped it back in his pocket. This wasn't something pushing Henry out, just an annoyingly strong will shaking off his usual light touch. That, or he'd been relying on it too much and had let himself get sloppy.

Either way, it meant he was going to have to do this the hard way.

"Okay Chief, let's calm down." Henry raised his hands, trying to make some space between them. Lobrazzo stepped forward and pushed Henry back into the tree with a meaty finger.

"You don't come to my house, threaten me, and *then* tell me to calm down. Let's see if you'll give me what I want after you've spent a night in jail." Lobrazzo reached behind his back, but then must've realized he wasn't wearing handcuffs.

"Get in the car," he said, grabbing Henry's arm.

"Stop," Henry snarled. There wasn't any build up this time, and waves of magical energy coursed through his voice.

Lobrazzo's arm fell limp at his side, and then he dropped to his knees. He made a little whimper, and then his face began to get red as he ceased breathing.

More rookie mistakes.

"Stop what he's doing, not his body."

Lobrazzo gasped for air. He reached up at Henry but his arms only moved an inch before they were held in place. The confusion on his face turned to fury.

"No talking." Lobrazzo's mouth snapped shut.

"You're going to leave Mark Watson alone. Just let it go, okay? This whole thing is over. You're going to tuck this back into the closed cases and forget all about it. I'm sure your lovely town has more important things for you to be doing."

Lobrazzo glared, terrified but defiant.

"You're not the only one with friends," Henry said, putting his face a couple of inches from Lobrazzo's. This close anyone could feel the energy coming off of him. "And mine can reach out and touch you wherever you are, understand?"

The Chief winced in pain for a moment and then the defiance was gone.

"We have a deal? Nod for yes."

Lobrazzo nodded.

Henry thought about it and then said "What does he really think?"

He winced and then roughly shook his head.

"Goddammit," Henry snapped. "Do you think I'm playing with you?"

Lobrazzo stared, wide eyed.

"You're already figuring out how to get back at me, aren't you? This just makes you more interested in the whole thing, right?" He peered over his glasses and deeper into the man's eyes. He pondered him for a few moments and then straightened up, running a hand across his scalp.

"There's just no convincing you Mark is innocent, is there? You might let it go for a bit, but one day down the road you're going to remember this and start poking around at both him and me, despite all this." Laid bare like this, Henry could feel Lobrazzo's will blocking him.

"You did this to yourself," Henry said. "Open up his mind."

Henry placed two fingers on Lobrazzo's forehead and the man's body went rigid again, this time eyes rolling back in his head. Henry plunged into the mental depths, which were immediately unpleasant. There were lies and abuse and cheating and anger, and Henry knew how easy it'd be to crush them all in his fists. He could rip and shred and make the man a halfway decent person, although not a very functional one. What was left of him would probably still be able to walk and talk, but at least he'd have empathy.

Henry refocused and looked for Mark and the Briarcliff murders. Once found, he made sure his pushing and rearranging was enough for Lobrazzo to consider everything resolved and nothing he had to think about again. He lingered, even though he knew Lobrazzo was in agony, but he told himself it was just because he was making sure he didn't miss anything.

With the mental I's dotted and T's crossed, Henry broke the connection. Lobrazzo's head slumped forward, face red and covered in sweat.

"Stand up."

Lobrazzo obliged, although quite poorly.

"Calm down. Move past the pain."

His breathing, which had been rapid and shallow, returned to normal.

"He won't remember this. He stayed in his car listening to something about sports on the radio." A simple command not requiring the strip-mining he'd just finished.

There was a small nod.

"He--," Henry caught himself before he said *--will feel that pain for the first ninety seconds after he wakes up for the rest of his life*. He pushed it back, pissed off at yet another sloppy mistake.

"Go sit in the car."

Henry followed him, and when Lobrazzo got in his car Henry said, "Released in three and a half minutes after you lose sight of me."

Lobrazzo closed the door, and Henry walked around the corner where the Gremlin was parked. Once inside, he texted Monica he was on his way, and then he navigated back to the garage.

"Watch it," he said to himself in the rear view mirror. "Don't forget who's in charge here."

CHAPTER THIRTEEN

When Henry left, Mark and Christine just stared at each other.

"At least we didn't die," Mark said, shrugging as much as he could.

She smiled a little. "I could've lived without all the trying."

"Couldn't we all." He yawned, the drugs pulling him down into sleep. "But also I think I'm going to crash. I'm sorry. For everything, not just the crashing."

"I get it," she said, walking over and taking a seat in the chair. "I'm feeling that too."

"Right on." He closed his eyes before he could invite her to "hop on in," which was probably for the best.

When he woke, he could feel how late it was. The noise of running water from the bathroom stopped and Christine came out. She'd changed clothes and put her hair up, and when she saw he was awake there was a flash of disappointment on her face.

"Hey, you're up," she said after fixing her face.

"You taking off already?"

"Yeah," she said, looking at her bag by the door. "A seat opened up on the early morning flight, and I didn't want to wake you."

"Ah," Mark said, a pit growing inside him. "I...shit, I was hoping we'd have a chance to decompress and talk about stuff."

"I get it." She took a seat on the edge of the bed. "But I really don't want to. Ever. I'm putting it behind me."

"Okay, that's fair." He gave a weak smile. "But we could still talk for a bit. Maybe you could do that remote job of yours from here for a while and nurse me back to health. It'd be fun." Hearing it out loud made him want to die a little.

"Mark," she said, putting a hand on his leg. "Coming here was a huge mistake. Yeah, we fixed shit and had some fun, but this is not a thing. And I'm not going to try to build a relationship with a guy I've known for a combined total of what, two months? Ninety percent of which was decade ago."

Mark never felt smaller. "Okay. Yeah. Message received." He could feel himself turning sour and mean, but he closed his eyes, took a breath, and pushed it away.

"It's not that I don't like you, I just--"

"No, it's silly. I shouldnt've said anything. I just...I've always wanted to see you again. When this happened, I hoped I would and it'd go...well, and I just didn't want that part to end."

She sighed and then stood up. "I think you built me up as some kind of perfect girl, and that's just not who I am. This happened because of the horrible things we went through, and now that it's out of your system or whatever you need to find a way to move on. And also get your shit together, because you're kind of a mess."

Sour and mean was starting to sound better, and it must have showed on his face.

"I know, so should I," she continued. "I've been trying my entire life, and maybe now I can actually do that." She leaned down and gave him a kiss on the top of his head. "I was wrong," she said. "You *are* a nice guy, you were just dealt a really shitty hand. Think of this a chance to start over, because that's what I'm going to do."

"Sure," he said, and true to form he could feel tears coming on. If she noticed, she didn't say anything.

She walked over to her bag, picked it up, and then turned back to say, "Take care of yourself, okay?"

"You too." He waved back, dropping it when the door closed behind her. It sucked, but she was right. There'd always been a part of him desperate to see her again and give it another shot. He'd known it was childish, but it'd been lurking under the surface for a decade. Now dredged up and laid bare before him, it was clear he'd wasted a lot of time focusing on it.

Starting over wasn't something new to him, but he realized now he could at least do it better without the what if's hanging over his head.

"Okay," he said. "Let's give it another go."

***

It took Henry a few months to relax.

He was pretty confident he kept from Monica how much things had gone wrong, so that was a relief. It wasn't like he hadn't made mistakes before, but these seemed to have piled up on each other like an accident on the highway. Next time he had to make sure he was better prepared and, most importantly, in better control.

The first feeling of relaxation dawned on him late at night as he sat in his chair in the living room, headphones on, eyes closed, and listening to his music. The summer was coming to an end, and meaning children back in school and the hope things were finally getting back to normal.

Are they though?

Henry opened his eyes. He wasn't in his living room anymore.

"I'm still mad at you," he said, glancing around at the void. "I told you, no games."

I play no games. I was just...what is it? Lending you a hand.

"You're bound to my will. Don't forget it."

There was an animalistic growl from behind him. Henry turned and saw the wall was still where it'd been for the past twenty-odd years, stretching in every direction. Not as he'd built it then, as the section across from him wasn't solid but had thick bars like a cage at the zoo.

The thing on the other side made what passed for an expression of disdain. *Don't patronize me, jailer. This was the bargain, these were the rules.*

"And the rules say I'm in control."

They do. There was a clacking along the bars as it paced in front of him. *For now. And despite how much you loathe me, you have enjoyed making use of me again. It's...exhilarating.*

"It was necessary," Henry said. "I only let you out when you're needed. And I can lock you up again if I have to."

But why would you? You wouldn't have been able to crush that insect without me, and your mind still reeks of panic when you think about why you loosed me in the first place.

"It was what I had to do. Not the best way, but the only way."

But I AM the best way. The fastest, the easiest way. Which is why you sought me out in the first place, so that I could fix what you were unable to.

"Those days are over," he said. "I've got more ways to solve problems now."

Like enchanting that girl? Is sending one of your new little charms through the phone device to push her to comply one of those new ways?

Henry gritted his teeth. "It was what I needed to do. It was the only way."

Of course, of course. Its form rippled as it made a low chuckle. *Which is why I made sure it had enough power to last. I knew how...important it was to you.*

"Don't you *ever* do that again," he snapped, slapping the bars between them.

It shrunk back in disingenuous fear. *Whatever you desire. I exist to serve.*

"And don't forget it," Henry said, turning and walking away. Henry was relieved he hadn't botched the charm he'd sent Christine, especially since it was an untested and recent addition to his repertoire. However, the fact that his prisoner could affect the intensity of his magic without Henry realizing did a great job of stifling said relief.

Don't you forget, jailer. I'm here because of you, and I know what you desire. You wanted to force open the mind of that insect's pawn to find out what you needed to know, and would've if you could. And you were oh so happy to torment an enforcer of laws again. I know how it's your favorite.

Henry woke up. The playlist was over and it was hours later, and he had to concentrate on releasing his grip from the arms of the chair. When his heart stopped pounding he closed his eyes, shaping what had been bars into a solid wall again. He'd been so stupid, and he'd forgotten how devious it was. It twisted desires, feigned servitude, and had always claimed to be on his side. The only side it was on was its own, and the only thing it truly desired was freedom.

And probably a lot of revenge.

Henry stood and stretched before walking back to the bedroom. He was halfway down the hall when he remembered what it was like to have the demon from Briarcliff and its minions clawing and tearing at him. When he'd fallen to his knee there was a moment when he thought it was all over, but his prisoner was able to save him. Not because it cared, but because Henry was its foothold here. As long as he lived, it got to play and torment and hurt as much as Henry would allow.

Would he be able to forgive himself if he didn't use every option available and the worst happened? Especially since he was the one who'd brought all of this into their lives. It wasn't a matter of if something that dangerous could happen, but when.

He thought about the wall, but before he did anything his phone buzzed several times in his hand. They were texts from Lexie, and reading them answered why she was sending them uncharacteristically late at night.

What's best/easiest way to kill werewolves?

Like, a whole lot of them.

Kind of an emergency.

"Goddammit," he huffed. "Why does it have to werewolves?"

THE END OF

"THE SHADOW OF VICTORY"

BUT LEXIE WINSTON & HENRY CHURCHILL
WILL RETURN IN

"A DISEASE OF THE WILL"

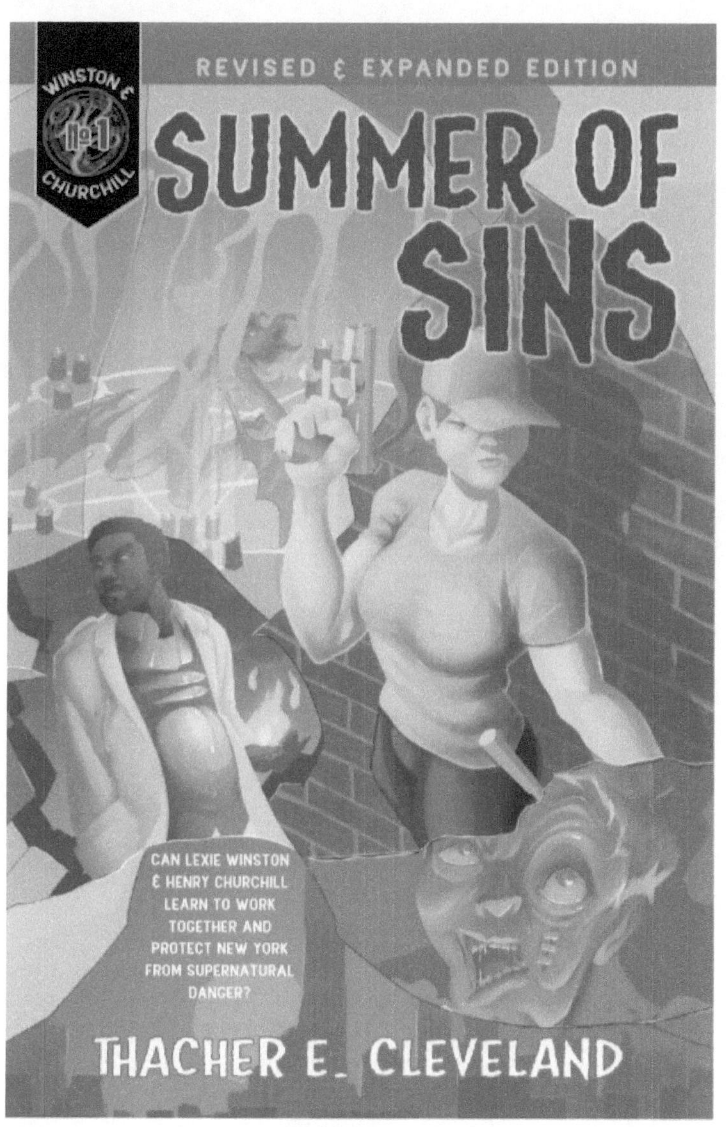

READ LEXIE AND HENRY'S ADVENTURES FROM THE BEGINNING IN THE NEW AND REVISED EDITION OF

"SUMMER OF SINS."

ABOUT THE AUTHOR

Thacher E. Cleveland grew up in New Jersey and upstate New York and has lived in Ohio and Tennessee. He's been a bookstore manager, murder mystery actor, pen salesman, and game show host.

Currently, he lives in Chicago (for the second time) with his dumb orange cat, a spoiled whippet, an anxious greyhound, and an amazing partner. In addition to his comic and prose writing appearing in anthologies, he also publishes his books and comics through his Demonweasel Studios label. In addition to writing, acting, and hosting, he letters comic books, is a graphic designer, and (kind of) an artist.

You can find his books, like the Winston & Churchill Case Files, and comics (GRIM REEFER, MYTHPOCALYPSE, and the upcoming FORBIDDEN KNOWLEDGE) at www.demonweaselstudios.com. He's active on Instagram, BlueSky (@demonweasel), and TikTok (@demonweaselstudios). You can also find his dumb art on merch on Etsy (@demonweasel)

For the most recent news & events, scan below.